THE CRACKS IN THE
LIFE OF MIKE ANAMI

THE CRACKS IN THE LIFE OF MIKE ANAMI

TED SHIGEMATSU

KONSTELLATION PRESS

Published by Konstellation Press, San Diego, www.konstellationpress.com

ISBN: 978-0-9991989-7-1

Cover design by Scarlet Willette and Lily Mihalik

Copyeditor: Lisa Wolff

To my parents

PROLOGUE

1990

It rained last night and the sea must have raged, for green kelp and seashells—broad-ribbed cockles, yellow-orange scallops, cornucopias, mother-of-pearls—lie scattered on the sand. They blush as an azure opening in a sky crowded with thunderheads lets the sun through. This winter afternoon the air carries only the pure essence of the sea and the beach is all mine. The boarded-up equipment rental shacks fill me with peace, and I'd like to lose myself in the sensation of sand sinking under my feet, in the sea breeze caressing my face, in the seagulls' calls. But today I must attend to the promise I made my son to write about my war years, when I fought for my country, the country that threw me in an internment camp because of the shape of my eyes and the sound of my last name. Before I can write I must remember, and so I need to reach for another time, relive the experiences of long ago that brought me here. I walk near the water where the sand is easier to tread, hands in my jacket's pockets, breathe deeply and gaze at the horizon. Through fifty years, another sea comes into view.

1

1941

I broke through the waves and hungrily filled my lungs. With a few strokes I reached my inner tube, threw the abalone in the gunny sack tied around it, and held on. The afternoon sun finally burned through the clouds and reached my skin. With eyes closed, I rested my head on the black, patched tube. The smell of rubber triggered a succession of images: my father's beat-up Ford, the dusty bus I would soon take back to Los Angeles, the university, Professor Kesselman standing in front of the class weaving philosophical arguments in brilliant, aesthetic designs. Between cool water and sun's warmth, far from land, in a torpor, I watched the parade of my thoughts float by when suddenly, my brother's piercing voice startled me.

"A shark, a shark!" he yelled out. He waved his arms as he bobbed up and down, thirty yards away. "Shark!" he repeated as he began to swim toward shore. I lowered the goggles over my eyes, plunged my head underwater, and scanned the rocky bottom—a white torpedo shape, at least ten feet long, glided below me. My heart pounded as a chill took hold of me. I almost left the inner tube behind, but as I dashed toward shore, grabbed it. I glanced toward land—a yellow stucco house perched on a green hill sparkled in the sun, like a beacon; the cove lay to the right of that house, so I swam toward the golden light. I scanned the bottom but the water had become torpid, and I could only spot undulating branches of brown kelp. What brushed against my feet? Were massive jaws lined with razor-sharp teeth going to clamp on my legs and tear them off? I kicked my feet and cut the water with my arms, trying not to splash too much. *Now. It's going to happen now.*

Why am I here? Summer vacation, my love for the sea, diving for abalone—it's all crap. I don't belong here. I'm helpless, just a piece of meat. I want to live, but it could happen now. Now. These thoughts squirmed like snakes throughout my body as I mechanically, rhythmically, pushed through the water, water that suddenly had become thick and sticky. Finally, the familiar cove came into view and soon after, near the narrow stretch of beach, I heard my sisters' laughter intermingling with the surf. Steve had almost caught up with me. *A few more strokes, just a few more strokes*, I kept telling myself, until my feet touched sand and rocks. I waded through the surf, stumbling, and as the retreating waves pulled the ground from underneath me with a hiss, I fell on my knees. I closed my eyes for a moment and then tried again, dragging the inner tube behind me, not looking down. I walked unsteadily toward Umeko and Myoko lying on their backs, soaking up the sun.

"Are you all right?" Umeko asked, propping herself up on her forearms to look at me. "There's a shark out there," I replied almost in a whisper as I dried my head with a towel. "You see them every year," said Myoko without opening her eyes. "Yeah, but this summer's different—that wasn't a leopard shark. You guys better not go in the water." I knelt on the sand and opened the sack to look at the abalone; there must have been at least twenty, bigger than my hand, brown shells that hid iridescent blue-green interiors and delicious meat. We'd have a great dinner with some of these, and the people back home would be thrilled. Steve had staggered onto the beach with his inner tube, his slim and muscular frame shivering in the breeze. "You okay?" I asked.

"Thought I was a goner," he replied as he untied the sack from the tube. "I only had eight when I saw the shark— could've have gotten more, damn it." He plopped down on his back, closed his eyes, and said nothing more. His dripping body shimmered under the sun, and his chest heaved up and down. "I better go tell them about the shark," he said after a couple of minutes, and got up to go warn the other bathers.

I sat on a towel and dug my toes into the cool sand, taking deep breaths. The sandstone wall behind us, the sky, the breezy air glowed as the joy within me overflowed and spilled all around. *I'm alive, I'm alive.* I faced an ocean of sparkling jade framed at the sides by cliffs. A pelican, its wingspan at least eight feet, glided low and gracefully, then suddenly dived into the water in a burst of spray, only to fly back up and away.

I lay down, resting on my forearms, and gazed into the distance. The sun pressed on my head, penetrating my shoulders, legs, and feet, the heat sweeping thoughts and images from my mind, until I felt like one of those lizards that lie on hot roads in summer and don't get out of the way of cars.

Then I felt a hole deep inside, something that wanted to suck my guts out, and I started thinking again. *What if there's no difference at all between a shark and me? Am I not much more important than a shark in the scheme of things, I who have reason and language?* According to Plato and Aristotle, reason made me almost divine, but I couldn't forget the cosmic indifference to my fate I had sensed in the water.

Earlier we had gathered fist-sized rocks into a pile, and now Umeko and Myoko added twigs to start a fire. As Steve went to help my sisters cook the abalone, I grabbed *Newsweek* from Umeko's straw hat and flipped through it: the Sea

Conference was considering a fight to the finish against the Axis; the Navy must stand ready to fight Japan; the Germans made their first major gains of the war in the Ukraine. A tightness in my guts made me go over the international news quickly until I found the movie review. Spencer Tracy and Ingrid Bergman gave fine performances in *Dr. Jekyll and Mr. Hyde*, even though some critics wondered if there was a need to remake it in 1941 when Fredric March did a great job in the 1931 film. I must see it as soon as I had a chance. I didn't care much for Tracy, but I had a weakness for Ingrid Bergman. When I saw her in *Intermezzo* I had been struck by her ethereal beauty and elegance, and for days I couldn't stop thinking about her.

"Ready for next week?" Myoko asked as she sat next to me. She drew her knees to her chest and hugged her plump legs, stubby toes playing with the sand. Twenty years old, the youngest of us, she emanated exuberance as if it were perfume, and in her red swimming suit she looked like a little girl at a beach party.

"Professor Kesselman is teaching a seminar on Heidegger," I said as I glanced at her, squinting against the glare.

"You always get excited over that stuff. And next year onward to the PhD?"

"The way things are going . . ." I replied as I threw the magazine in Umeko's straw hat.

"What things?"

"Hitler, Mussolini, Japan, all the talk of war."

"Don't worry about that faraway stuff," she replied as she tenderly squeezed my arm. She studied my hair. "You need a cut—drop by the shop tomorrow."

We sat in silence watching the sandpipers run away from the splashing waves on their spindly legs, and then return to stick their long, pointed bills in the wet sand, searching for tiny crabs. As the waves retreated, the dark sand glistened under the sunlight and the cliffs exuded an otherworldly brilliance. I inhaled deeply, my heart slowed down, my neck and shoulders relaxed.

"Come on!" Steve yelled at us. "It's ready." We joined the others by the fire. Abalone meat cooked on the hot rocks, and the smell made me hungry. We ate the tender fillets with balls of cold rice covered with sesame seeds, quenched our thirst with cold beer. I didn't like beer much, but Steve did, and he always made sure we had plenty of it at the beach. He sat cross-legged, taking huge bites, chewing so avidly that rice and sesame seeds hung from his droopy mustache, and with his mane of hair puffed up in the breeze he looked like a starving savage.

"Too bad Okasan and Otosan couldn't come with us this summer. They would have loved this abalone," said Umeko. The whole family usually came on vacation every year, but this summer my mother hadn't felt well, so she stayed home with my father.

"Must be at least 110 degrees down there; they're probably huddled inside," said Steve. I pictured them in the living room, my father reading the Japanese-language newspaper and my mother knitting, while the water cooler spewed humidity all around.

"Guys, let's not forget to go to Put's before we take off, okay?" asked Myoko, reminding us that this year, too, the ritual must not be forgotten: on the last day of vacation, before leaving La Jolla, we had to have a shake at Put's Drug Store.

"Sounds good to me," I said, "a big chocolate one—what do you think, Umeko?" She just nodded, lost in her own world. I thought of Umeko, almost thirty, as an old woman, but as she knelt in front of the fire to toss more sticks into it, the breeze freed her long hair, exposing her still youthful beauty. After feeding the flames she sat back down and began to talk, but her words didn't reach me as I lost myself in thoughts.

The dream is going to blow, the writing on the wall is clear, it spells war between the U.S. and Japan. What's not so clear is what will happen to us of Japanese descent. Umeko seemed to sense it, but my brother and younger sister were too wrapped up in the routines of their daily lives, as were my parents. And then for some reason I thought of Carmelita.

"Confia en Dios," trust in God, she'd say, but how can a philosopher trust in God? I see myself as a child, kneeling on a wooden chair in her small kitchen, watching her stir the beans. The smell comforting me, making me wet my lips. She stands in front of the potbellied stove just as Padre Juan Velasquez stood in front of the altar of the church where she'd take me on Saturday evenings. Her back straight, she moves her hands in sacred ritual. Skinny and tall, her brown skin all wrinkles, white hair in a bun, she turns her head toward me and smiles serenely, as if she were standing in the center of the world, stirring her pot the most important task in the universe. *"Hijo,* God knows what he is doing!" She moves to the narrow counter, peeks out the window at the salt cedars, then her ancient, wise fingers quickly roll little balls of dough. She flattens them with a stick, throws them on the stovetop to cook, scoops beans from the pot, wraps them in a hot tortilla and hands it to me. *"Muy bueno, Carmelita, muy bueno."*

Ha, Carmelita! I always felt so safe and at peace in your kitchen. Cold water reached my feet and I jumped. The tide rose, forcing us to move closer to the rocky wall behind us, and the sun edged closer to the horizon. We sat quietly, admiring the clouds, a red coat draped on the shoulders of the dying day, until the sun fell and melted to the seagulls' dirge.

We packed our things in the car, including a beer cooler full of abalone packed in ice. *Goodbye, La Jolla, for another year. Goodbye to your rolling green hills, the bungalows, the cove, the ocean.* We took Prospect Street to get to Put's, drove by the swamps and then on to El Cajon Boulevard, with its diners lit up. We stopped at Irma's for coffee and then drove through the mountains. I sat in the back next to Myoko, who had fallen asleep with her head next to the side window. My right leg moved nervously up and down as I shifted around, trying to get comfortable. Next summer, around this time, would we be coming back from La Jolla?

"Slow down, Steve! Do you have to go to the bathroom or what?" asked Umeko, in alarm, as the Dodge started to careen toward the edge of Mountain Springs Grade. A narrow indentation cut into the sides of the mountains between San Diego and the Imperial Valley, the grade exacted its sacrifices frequently on truck drivers who lost their brakes, motorists who fell asleep, and speeders like my brother. "Maybe all the abalone you ate gave you diarrhea," she suggested as she glared at Steve.

"Okay, okay, calm down. You make it sound like I'm going a hundred miles an hour. Relax!" Steve glanced at the rearview mirror and frowned. I met his eyes and made a face, as if to say, "What can you do? You know how she is." He twirled the right side of his mustache and lit a cigarette. I looked through the window at the waxing moon above the bare hills, then I stared at Myoko. In the relaxation of deep sleep, the child she'd so recently been seemed to reaffirm itself.

I smiled remembering our childhoods as I turned my head toward the car window and acknowledged the sea of stars above me. I wanted to lose myself in that brightness, to devote my life to forging some sense out of it, trying by a sort of squinting of the mind to glimpse the threads connecting me to all those stars. I could see my life's vocation involving the quiet study of philosophical works by Plato, Kant, and Hegel. I could see myself in my study late at night reading books—could feel their solidity, smell the pungent scent of paper, ink, and cloth. I saw myself writing articles and essays, pictured myself in front of a classroom, my mind a bridge between ideas and students. The warmer, humid air rushing in through the partly opened windows announced our plunge into the desert. The stars, fat, pregnant, ripe, hung heavy over the darkness below, a blackness that pushed the scattered yellow lights of the Imperial Valley and Mexicali close to the ground in the far distance. As Umeko and Steve talked about football, I closed my eyes and drifted into sleep.

2

1941

In Southern California, about one hundred miles east of San Diego, lies what the Indians called "the palm of God," a desert floor where irrigation canals fed by the Colorado River turned dry, dusty ground into a fertile valley. Lured by this fertility, my parents, like other immigrants from many parts of the world, found their way there.

After ten years of work on other people's land, my father finally managed to lease eighty acres and became a successful farmer. His cantaloupes, lettuce, and tomatoes were highly prized by the buyers. My brother enjoyed working the land—right after high school he threw himself into farming full time—but I always felt out of place. As a child I would stand in front of our fields, heat and humidity rising from rows of cantaloupes, and wonder what was beyond them. I felt pulled by the horizon, as if by gigantic invisible hands. In school I became aware of a whole world beyond the rim of this desert, a world not only of people and places, but of ideas that excited me as farming never had.

After high school graduation, on a scholarship, I began to study philosophy at UCLA. My dream of escape came true. Still, during summers I returned to help on the farm. Before our two weeks' vacation at the beach we had plowed the land, and now, before I left for LA, we had to clean the ditches that supplied water to the fields.

I woke up with a shudder. For a moment I didn't know where I was. A familiar aroma of coffee reached me through the balmy air of my room, a sign that Steve must be up already. Every morning, without fail, he made a strong pot.

"Get up, professor!" Steve called out as he turned on the light.

I squinted as I sat up. "Are you crazy? It's the middle of the night," I said, even though I knew the routine.

"It's four already. How soon we forget," he replied as I slipped into my jeans. The wooden planks felt good under my bare feet as I stumbled toward the kitchen. I loved the coffee fragrance released by the percolator on the stovetop. My brother bought whole beans, and every morning he would grind them fresh. I filled a mug to the brim, then, holding the old, chipped cup, I sat at the table, enjoying the warmth seeping into my hand. I stared at the dark spot on the red Formica top through the haze of sleep, the burn I accidentally made with a cigarette when as a child, I tried to smoke one of my father's fragrant Chesterfields.

"Where's Otosan?" I asked Steve, who stood by the sink, smoking a cigarette. He wore his uniform: faded jeans with pant legs rolled up a couple of inches, denim shirt, and brown work boots.

"In his bed, sleeping like a baby, what do you think?" He took a deep drag and exhaled slowly; the white smoke swirled around the lamp hanging from the ceiling and turned yellow in the bulb's glow. From a pan on the stovetop he scooped some rice on a plate, grabbed a container full of broiled abalone from the icebox, and put them in front of me.

"Better eat something—we'll be out there a while."

I ate the warm rice with the cold abalone, had another cup of coffee, then went to get ready.

Crickets' chirping rose as we approached the fields with our shovels, the sky sprinkled with thousands of stars. Back in Los Angeles I would miss these dark skies crawling with Van Gogh stars. The ditches, narrow trenches connected to a main canal, in the course of the year became covered with weeds and grass that kept water from flowing freely. They were dry now, so we could work in them. As I dug away, the shark I saw at La Jolla Cove began to swim through my thoughts. Primordial mechanism driven by mindless will, it began to tear at my certainties. Didn't reason, the life of the mind, culture, have objective, "cosmic" value? Of what importance is a dumb beast compared to Plato, Michelangelo, Beethoven? And yet, if I had been devoured, my consciousness, with its thoughts and memories, its life of history and culture, would have gone out like the light from a broken light bulb. I would have been just meat, my bones regurgitated. The shark glided through my mind, then went deeper into my guts.

We had been hard at work for almost two hours when dawn broke; soon the sun would be unleashed upon us. We cut the thick grass with shovels and threw it in piles behind us. I wore gloves, but my palms burned. I glanced at Steve: he kept on going in an unbroken rhythm, thrusting the shovel in the side of the ditch, forcing it down with his right foot, scooping grass out. His shirt drenched in sweat, absorbed in the task, he kept on going as if at his favorite pastime, and watching him made me realize that I didn't belong here. *Soon it'll be 100 degrees and I'll be covered in sweat and dirt.* I wanted to be in a cool room far away from here, sitting in an easy chair, reading Hegel. This mechanical digging, this repetition, filled me with emptiness. I stopped and rested for a few minutes, my right foot on the shovel's shoulder, my forearms on the handle top, and watched the sun rise rapidly like a giant balloon. Purple and yellow patches opened up around it, and a pale light began to touch the top of faraway cottonwoods. A flock of seagulls flew past a line of eucalyptus, black silhouettes against translucent reddish gold. My father, at the other end of the field, worked his way toward us. I stopped for a minute and watched my brother's furious pace.

"How's Rosa?" I asked, hoping to slow him down. He glanced at me as he said, "Still working at the restaurant, more beautiful than ever." The lines in his face relaxed as I reminded him of the girl he loved.

"When are you guys tying the knot?" I asked him, and as I did so I realized the cruelty of my words, since such a marriage would have been considered unacceptable by my parents and Rosa's family.

"I'm already married," he announced, continuing to thrust the shovel into the thick layer of grass.

"You're full of shit," I blurted out. He grinned.

"I'm married to this land and my car; I thought you knew that."

"Talk to Otosan—after all, this isn't Japan."

Steve replied by thrusting the shovel's head deep into the earth as if it were a lance pushed into flesh. Thick veins squirmed under his neck as he stabbed at the weeds. I knew deep down that my father would not have consented to Steve marrying a non-Japanese, so why did I even suggest it?

We worked until eleven o'clock, stabbing and cutting, until, spent, we headed back for lunch. My father, short, not an ounce of fat on his body, with his thick glasses hanging over his nose, led the way.

"Mike, when are you leaving?" he asked, turning around.

"Monday."

He nodded, his face impassive, then he continued to walk, stooped, his eyes toward the ground, the shovel's handle resting on his shoulder, and for an instant I saw only a tired old peasant walking home. My father seldom spoke of his youth in Fukuoka Prefecture, but I could imagine the forests, the ocean, his parents' postage-stamp-sized plot of land that didn't produce much, and in that instant I saw him in a timeless moment, a man working the ground, his material pleasures a warm bowl of rice with some vegetables and fish, tobacco, sound sleep. And yet my father wasn't exactly an ignorant peasant. He liked to read the Japanese-language newspaper and enjoyed listening to music on the radio.

My sisters worked in El Centro, Umeko as a secretary for an insurance company, Myoko as a hairdresser. They commuted in Umeko's old clunker, but today, after work, Umeko had to go to her Japanese class, so Steve and I drove into town to pick up our little sister. It was almost five in the afternoon. The desert sun burned fiercely, turning the sky into ivory. A blast of hot air blew in from the car windows, mussing up our hair as sweat dripped down our faces. I slouched in the passenger seat and gazed toward Mount Signal, not very imposing, but the only mountain around here. More than two thousand feet tall, with many peaks, it looked completely different depending on your angle of observation. On the other side of it, Mexico. Steve's lead foot pushed on the accelerator pedal and the car lurched forward on the dirt road.

"Why so fast all the time?" I asked, as the back end began to go its own way. Steve stroked his Fu Manchu mustache and said nothing. Fields, fallow or covered with alfalfa, spread as far as I could see, a flatness broken up here and there by eucalyptus trees and cottonwoods. We turned left on La Brucherie Road and soon rode down Main. We passed by the courthouse, with its classical facade, turned on Broadway, and stopped in front of the hairdresser shop. We walked in the small room kept cool but damp by a groaning water cooler. An old woman with glasses sat on a barber's chair reading a magazine as Myoko, standing behind her, worked on her hair. "You Are My Sunshine" played on the radio I had given my little sister for her birthday.

"Hi guys, be done in a jiffy," she said with a smile as she combed the old woman's coarse hair.

"Sis, we'll be at Mel's," said Steve, nodding at me to go.

"Order one for me too—I'm almost done," she said.

Mel had the best root beers in El Centro. When you ordered one, he took a glass mug from an icebox, poured root beer from a big wooden barrel, and then he'd hand you the frosted mug full of sweet, dark, ice-cold liquid. Ah, what could be more refreshing than that, on a blistering August afternoon in El Centro?

You sat on a stool at the counter, under a ceiling fan, the water cooler giving you respite from the heat outside, and maybe you ordered one of his famous cheeseburgers. Mel was a quiet man who looked like the Bob's Big Boy mascot, but older and with less hair. We walked toward Main, thirsty and hot, eager to sit down with a root beer, when suddenly a stocky man barged out of a shop and bumped into Steve. The guy took the cigarette that hung between his thin lips, said, "Watch where the fuck you're going, stinking Jap!" and continued to walk.

"Hey, you!" Steve yelled out. The man stopped and turned around. Steve walked up and stood right in front of him. He said nothing for a moment, then slammed a fist into the side of the man's face. The stranger fell on his side onto the street and Steve kicked him.

"Steve, Steve, stop it!" I pleaded as I grabbed him and tried to pull him away.

"I'm going to kill this bastard—leave me alone, goddamn it!"

Someone was calling us. I turned and saw Myoko, running toward us. At the sound of her shaky voice, Steve stopped and I knelt down to check on the man. He bled from the mouth and the eyebrow.

"Let's get out of here," I said. Myoko's face turned white, her eyes widened.

"What happened?" she asked, her childlike face hard and pale.

"We didn't want a root beer after all," I replied. We got into the car and Steve sped off. "You want to ruin your life over an insult?" I said.

"Nobody's going to call me a stinking Jap," he replied and pushed on the gas. Nothing more was said about the incident.

That night, after dinner, instead of sitting in the living room with the family listening to a jazz concert by Duke Ellington on the radio, I went in my room to pack. A narrow cubicle, this had been my "sacred" space for most of my life: a bunk bed next to a tree stump I used as a stand, a desk my father had made for me when I graduated from grammar school, a dresser, a print of the Camp of Miracles with the Leaning Tower of Pisa on the wall. The latter had been part of a calendar that Mr. Fasso gave me the first time I went to eat in his restaurant.

I had been curious about Italian food since Mrs. McCracken, my Latin teacher, told the class about her vacation in Italy, so one afternoon, after a movie, I took Yoshiko to Fasso's, the only Italian restaurant in the Valley. It had wood-paneled walls covered with prints of the Colosseum, the Leaning Tower of Pisa, and a kitschy fresco of the Bay of Naples with Mount Vesuvius framed by grape leaves and fat, naked youths holding wine-filled goblets. Mr. Fasso, hurrying to welcome us, escorted us to a table. It was a Tuesday evening, so there were just a few people there. Yoshiko ordered eggplant parmigiana, I had spaghetti al ragù; we talked, joked, and laughed, especially at my attempt to eat spaghetti, and later my white shirt, splashed with red sauce, looked as if I had been repeatedly stabbed in the chest.

It seemed so long ago now. I could hear Duke's music through the thin walls, but the limpid, upbeat notes made me sad. I finished packing my suitcases and got into bed but couldn't sleep. I stared at the track trophy, my old high school texts and other books piled on the desk. The day after tomorrow I would be in Los Angeles, beginning a new academic year; I would buy books, attend lectures, read and study. Tomorrow I must go visit Carmelita, and finally, in the evening, I'd get to see Yoshiko.

~

I strolled alongside the canal toward Carmelita's house; the dry, alkaline soil radiated heat, the scattered tamarisk and eucalyptus trees, the dry clumps of weeds witnesses to the true nature of this place. The sun, straight above, burned on the back of my head. The canal, a ten-foot-wide band of bluish-gray water, flowed by, reminding me of mountain streams and cool creeks. Since childhood I often went to see Carmelita, who would feed me beans, tortillas, albondigas soup, and other things we never ate at home. She and her husband, Ramón, had worked as farm laborers for my father until Ramón began working as a *zanjero*, or "ditch rider," for the Irrigation District. Hundreds of miles of ditches and canals fed prescribed amounts of water to the farmers, and it was the *zanjeros'* job to open and close the gates. One morning, trying to open a canal gate he slipped, fell in the churning water, and drowned. Now she received a little pension and lived in a hut a mile away from our farm.

She put a plate on the table in front of me and sat down. The smell of hot beans and tortillas filled the tiny kitchen.

"*Hijo*," she said, "I had a dream this morning as I walked in the fields. I had a dream, but was awake. I saw an empty city in the desert, then people came from many places and the city changed into a flower I had never seen before, and then it was gone."

"What do you think it means, Carmelita?" I asked with my mouth full of food.

"Ah, *hijo, yo no se.* I was afraid, but the flower was *muy lindo.*" She got up again, poured sun tea in a glass and handed it to me. "What do you learn in school, *hijo?*" she asked. Her question caught me by surprise, and I tried to find words that she would understand.

"I read books, learn what important people have thought about life." She looked at me with a frown.

"What is important about life is in your heart," she said as she put her open palm on her chest.

"But it is good to also study what others have thought; the world is a big mystery," I replied as I picked up the glass ball from her credenza and shook it. A blizzard began to rage around the small village enclosed in it, and snow swirled around the church campanile and fell on the houses' red roofs. As a child I used to make believe I lived in that village, and tried to see myself someplace there, maybe on top of the campanile, looking up.

"It is good for the world to be a big mystery, and yes, it is good to study; just don't forget that to be a mystery, a mystery has to remain a mystery—see what things you make me say!"

I put the glass ball down, got up, and drained the glass.

"And how's *tu novia?*" she asked me as she stood up, pushing on the table with her right hand for leverage.

"Her mother had a flare-up of TB, had to go to the hospital in Phoenix. Yoshiko has been there for the past couple of weeks, had to miss work and couldn't teach her Japanese class. She came back today, so I'll see her tonight."

"I'll say a rosary for her."

I thanked her for everything and she gave me a hug, saying, "*Andale, vaya con Dios, hijo.*" She stood in front of her little house, waving goodbye, as she watched me go.

I walked under the white sun along a line of eucalyptus. From here our home seemed a toy house forgotten by a child. I grew up in the Valley, but part of me always felt a stranger. *I can't wait to be back on campus, away from here. Why, then, is gloom taking a hold of me at the thought of leaving?* The cicadas chanted insistently as a powerful stench made me recoil. In front of me lay a dead cat, food for ants that covered its whole body. I held my breath as I hurried by.

As I approached the house, my mother rushed toward me. Her wrinkled face looked older than her forty-four years, as she stood there in her pair of old shoes, hands clasped together, staring at me with uncomprehending eyes. She told me that they took Steve away, and then my father, who had come out of the house, explained that two sheriff's deputies came to take Steve to jail for having assaulted somebody.

I grabbed the spare keys to Steve's Dodge and drove into town. Steve had always had a hot temper, but I had never seen him go off like he did yesterday. Of course, no one had ever called him a stinking Jap before, either. I parked in front of the pink stucco building and walked in. Behind a heavy metal desk sat a deputy, his face hidden behind a copy of *Life*. He glanced at me and went on reading.

"I've come to post bail for my brother, Steve Anami."

The deputy, who looked like Spencer Tracy with a big nose, put down the magazine, flipped through some papers, and said, "Assault and battery, bail is fifty dollars." He lit a Lucky Strike, took a drag, and picked up the magazine again. I put five ten-dollar bills on the desk. He dropped the magazine with annoyance, took a form out of the drawer, slammed it shut, threw the piece of paper on the counter in front of me, and told me to fill it out. As I stood at the counter writing I began to feel like an object, something alien, a thing that wasn't supposed to be there. I gave him the form, and smirking, he said, "It'll take a while—make yourself comfortable."

I sat on a wooden chair in front of the coffee table covered with old issues of *Desert Magazine*. Five other chairs lined the pea-green walls. A fading President Roosevelt stared from a portrait hanging on the wall facing me. I gazed for a long time out the window at a palm tree across the street, green against blue sky. Then I began to flip through magazines, glancing at pictures of sand dunes near Yuma, wildflowers in Anza-Borrego, local cactus varieties. I calmly turned the pages, but a wave of foreboding threatened to sweep me away. The walls, Roosevelt's face, the *tip-tip* of the typewriter, the drone of the cooler, and the deputy's dour expression became visible manifestations of something dark, subterranean, that threatened to push through the reasonable surface of things. I felt light-headed; beads of sweat began to run down my forehead. I closed my eyes. *Steady, steady*, I told myself as I put the magazine down. I rested my elbows on my knees and held my head, as I began to breathe deeply and slowly until I heard the deputy say, "Okay, go 'round to the prison door—he's ready to come out."

I drove home as Steve stared out the passenger window. He kept rolling the right side of his mustache with his thumb and index finger, and then said, "All I wanna do is live my goddamn life." We drove west on Ross, the sun blinding us; even with sunglasses on and the visor down it was hard to see. We left a trail of dirt behind us as we passed fields and farms.

That evening, after a meal of steamed rice, catfish that my father had caught in a canal, salad, and pickled vegetables, I borrowed the Dodge. I stepped on the gas, the tires screeching on the winding road to Westmorland, the nearby town where Yoshiko lived. Hiroshi Nishida, Yoshiko's father, had come to the United States with his sister in 1912. He had gotten in trouble with the authorities due to his communist politics and hadn't had much choice but to emigrate. His sister, Etsuko, decided to accompany her young brother to America. A friend of the family who worked on the New Mexico railroad sponsored them, and so one rainy morning they left Nagasaki. A smart, educated, and English-speaking woman five years older than Hiroshi, Etsuko soon found work as an accounting clerk while her brother began working for the railroad. Hiroshi and my father became friends, and three years later they traveled to San Francisco to pick up their mail-order brides. In 1921 Yoshiko was born in Dayton, and the family moved to the Imperial Valley, where Hiroshi began to farm tomatoes in Westmorland. Haruko Maki, Yoshiko's mother, was sickly and melancholy; it took her many years to finally give birth to a child. She didn't like the Valley and longed to go back to Japan. At times she would say, "I wish I could die! I wish I could die!" over and over. She grew lethargic, stopped eating, and at the Brawley Hospital they told Hiroshi that his wife had TB. Then one day Hiroshi died in a truck accident, and Haruko and Yoshiko moved in with her aunt, Etsuko. Yoshiko worked at Etsuko's notary office and taught a Japanese class on Saturdays.

The humid smells of irrigated fields rushed in the open windows as the heat still rose from the ground and white butterflies, like snowflakes, splattered on the windshield and the hood. I turned on the radio and Gene Autry's singing filled the car. A Johnny owl perched on a post, startled by the car's high beams, flew toward the eucalyptus lining the road. After a few curves, I turned into a dirt byway and slowed down as the car began to buck over the uneven ground. I had reached the house, parked right in front, jumped out, ran to the porch, and knocked. "Yoshiko!" I was going to call out, but she had already opened the door. She wore a white sleeveless blouse and a blue soft cotton skirt, her leonine black hair framing her ceramic doll's face. Her slender body felt so good in my arms, and after a long kiss, we stepped inside.

"I'll get some tea," she said as I sat on the sofa and closed my eyes. I felt empty, and yet so heavy that I doubted my ability to get up again; my head sank into the back of the sofa, as sparks of electricity seemed to shoot down my legs and arms. My mind flittered, thoughts and feelings scattering in the penumbra, so I opened my eyes again and latched my attention to things in the room: a rocking chair, the floral-themed wallpaper, the teledial of the Grunow console radio, the tall case grandfather clock, a moth circling the floor lamp. Yoshiko came back with two tall glasses, ice cubes clinking, handed me one, and sat next to me. I told her about all the abalone we brought home, and how happy her aunt had been when I brought her some.

"How was Phoenix?" I asked. I could see in her eyes long days spent with her mother in the hospital, staying at the house of one of her family's friends, cooking rice, fish, and vegetables for her mother, washing her clothes.

"It's not only her lungs, she cries a lot. Hopefully, she'll get better." She took a sip of tea, then stayed quiet for a while. "I had to miss my class."

"You love teaching those brats, but I'll bet they jumped up and down with joy, chanting, 'Yay! Miss Nishida is gone, no class today!'"

"They're sweet kids," she protested with half a smile. "We'll just have to make up the work next Saturday. You leave tomorrow?"

"On the first bus," I replied, and I sensed again the hint of a crack, a fissure, somewhere inside. Yoshiko had been a star swimmer at Central High, but tonight she looked fragile; her face paler than usual, she had barely enough breath to bring the words out. I knew tomorrow morning she was going to go back to work at her aunt's notary office. I put my arm around her shoulders and drew her close to me. She smelled of Skylark perfume, oranges, sunny days, and long moonlit nights. I kissed her gently on the neck and she sighed. I closed my eyes and felt at peace. If only time froze, this moment would be paradise. But the grandfather clock went on ticking, and the cooler struggled to keep the room cool, so to escape the heat we went outside. A balmy breeze lazily stirred the eucalyptus trees by the side of the house. We held hands and walked along the nearby canal. A bright half-moon floated gently on the dark water and crickets serenaded us.

"What are you thinking about?" Yoshiko asked softly as she turned her head toward me.

"Oh, about how often Steve and I played cowboys and Indians around this canal, making believe it was the Rio Grande. And you?"

She gently touched my hair and said, "That I'll miss you, especially when the moon is out like tonight, and the breeze plays with the trees."

I turned to face her and looked into her eyes: reddish brown, like the mountainsides near the town of Julian, when splits made by the rain exposed the deeper flesh of the earth, a rich brown earth that still nourished the roots naked under the sun; I looked in those eyes and fell into them, and I hugged her tight and kissed her as we sank under the trees; and I lost myself in the earth, in the warmth, in the caresses, in the crickets' music.

3

1941-1942

Steve gave me a ride to the depot. The bus left at six to get a head start on the sun. I sat by a window, behind the entrance door, the taste of Yoshiko still on my lips, the anxious expectation of what lay ahead snaking inside me. The driver, a young man with short blond hair and a mustache, smoked a cigarette and talked to a brunette sitting behind him. A few sailors in the back smoked and talked, and an older Mexican couple behind me drank coffee the woman had poured into terra-cotta cups from a thermos. Judging by the fragrance it must have been freshly roasted, dark Mexican coffee, and I wished I could've had a cup.

El Centro gave way to alfalfa fields and then to the desert, the Coyote Mountains in the distance. Soon after the town of Ocotillo began the long, slow climb up Mountain Springs Grade, a narrow road etched in the side of the Jacumba and In-Ko-Pah Mountains. Peaks and ridges showed only rocks and slabs tanned by the sun, barrel cactus and century plants the only living things I could see. The smells of coffee and tobacco mingled with the stink of burned oil that came from the front of the bus as the motor whined, struggling to pull us up and around the steep bends. Up ahead on the road, two huge crows picked at the carcass of a cottontail. As we reached the top of the grade the sun erupted behind us, infusing boulders and plants with yellowish and pink hues. To the left, thousands of feet below, the Valley lay hidden in a rosy mist. Soon we would stop at Jacumba, renowned for its hot springs, then continue through the foothills and mountain slopes of East San Diego County.

I took a deep breath, relieved to be out of that desolate basin, and felt like a diver who has finally reached the surface, the air and the light. I glanced at the brown leather satchel I had placed on the seat next to mine. My family had given it to me as a Christmas present three years ago; everyone had pitched in, a tangible sign of their support for my dream. It had probably been Myoko's idea, since my father couldn't understand why I wanted to go to the university, and only later, begrudgingly, had supported my decision. I took the schedule of classes out and flipped through it. I couldn't wait to register for courses, talk to Professor Kesselman, see my buddy Tom Nakama. It's strange that my best friend would turn out to be an engineering student and not one of my fellow philosophy classmates. We met at a coffee shop near the campus while eating breakfast at the counter a couple of years ago. He noticed I was reading Plato's Symposium and he started talking to me about how he tried to read it while taking an Introduction to Philosophy class. As Japanese Americans, we shared a common ethnic background that strengthened our bond. We became good friends and even rented rooms in the same old Victorian house.

After more than five hours and a changeover in San Diego, I finally arrived in Los Angeles. I hailed a cab and fell asleep in the backseat only to wake up when the driver shook my shoulder and told me we had arrived. He had already unloaded my suitcases.

As the taxi sped off, I stood in front of Mrs. McClurg's front yard and dried the sweat from my face with a handkerchief. The back of my shirt stuck uncomfortably to my skin, but a cool breeze began to refresh me. The house had a wide front porch supporting an ornate balcony. Staggered gabled roofs crowned tall, narrow windows on the second story, and the faded brown siding, terra-cotta friezes with no longer recognizable figures in bas-relief, gave the house a sense of mystery. Surrounded by rosebushes and trees, this had been my home for the past three years, except for summers and holidays, and it felt good to be back. I picked up the suitcases and walked toward the front door. Mrs. McClurg, a thin lady in her seventies with short black hair and thick eyeglasses, was stooped over a bush, pruning shears in her gloved hand.

"Well, here's the philosopher! Had a good vacation?" she asked in her squeaky voice.

"You know how hot it gets in El Centro during the summer, but San Diego was cool breezes and nice days at the beach," I replied. A playful expression appeared for an instant in her eyes.

"San Diego . . . my poor late husband and I went on our honeymoon there. We rented a cottage in Point Loma, fished, spent long days on the beach—well, go ahead, get situated, young man, must've been torture on the bus." She turned toward the roses, and in her blue dress and black flats, she looked ready for a dance.

I opened the screen door and climbed up the creaky stairs, dragged the suitcases on the landing, and managed to get in my room. I found the single bed made, the black cast-iron potbelly stove cleaned, my books all in place in the bookcase. Next to the art deco stuffed blue chair, the Underwood waited on the middle of the desk by the window. It gave me a depressing feeling to see the desk so bare, but I would remedy that soon enough. I placed the two suitcases on the bed and as I started to put my clothes away, Tom came in with a smile on his face.

"I didn't know you were here already," I said, surprised.

"Got back yesterday," he said and sat on the edge of the bed. He looked dapper in pressed khaki pants and a light blue shirt. He studied me for a few seconds with a mischievous glimmer in his eyes. "This is going to be a great year."

"I don't know . . ."

"What's wrong?"

"Don't you read the papers? War in Europe, the Japanese bombings in China."

"But it is a great year. I met a girl this summer, heaven on earth, Mike."

"You're always in love with some girl, but there's no such thing as love, poor deluded mortal," I said with a laugh as I put my clothes in the drawers.

"Yeah, just instincts and social conventions; the intellect is everything. To a philosopher maybe. But you don't believe that—you love Yoshiko."

"I have feelings of affection for her, she's attractive; I tell her I love her because it's expected of me to say that," I said jokingly as I put my socks away. Tom shook his head, a puzzled look on his face.

"That sounds cold, man, even for a philosopher," he said as he took a cigarette from the pack he carried in his shirt pocket and lit it.

One of the things I liked about him was his logical, scientific bent, but he also had a shallow romantic side. He would fall madly in love, though usually only during vacations, since when classes started, he let nothing interfere with his studies.

Tom, almost six feet tall, had played basketball in high school and excelled at math. He regarded philosophy as a fun game, but only took seriously what he could measure, calculate, and prove with precision. So he had fallen in love again, just like last year, when he went home for Christmas vacation and met a girl while working at his father's hardware store. At the beginning of the semester he wouldn't stop talking about her, but by Easter he had already forgotten her.

"You don't realize it, but you're a romantic. I know you'll deny it because you see yourself as a down-to-earth engineer, but you're always falling in love. Come on now, don't shake your head—you might as well face it: you're aspiring to become a Casanova," I said in a playful tone as I placed the last pair of socks away and closed the drawer.

"You're jealous of my abilities to charm the ladies." He took a pair of rolled-up socks from my suitcase and threw them at me. It was going to be a great semester.

In the evening we went out to get something to eat. After sitting in the bus for so long I looked forward to a long walk. Even before we reached Westwood I could see the white tower of the Fox Theatre, its blue-and-gold neon sign pulsating on its three-sided spire; an urban lighthouse of the imagination, it seemed to announce, "Come, embark on exciting journeys of fantasy and feeling—here you will find the latest Hollywood films, here you can laugh and cry in the dark and be safe." As we passed the theater I read the marquee: *Blossoms in the Dust* with Greer Larson and Walter Pidgeon.

"What's it about?" wondered Tom, who knew I avidly read the reviews of new movies.

"It's the latest tearjerker in bright Technicolor," I replied. "I've been thinking about the use of color in films about sad stories. According to Hegel, everything contains its own negation. A living organism its own death, a blossom its own overcoming in the fruit. A tragic or sad story filmed in cheerful color seems to negate itself. You feel sad but at the same time, the soothing warm colors negate or blunt the painful feelings." Tom lit a cigarette and threw the match in the gutter.

"Hegel . . . isn't he the old German idealist no one understands?"

"I plan to take a course on him next year. Last semester I read a few selections from his works in a History of Philosophy course. It's torture to read him, but if you're persistent, after much digging, gems can be found." Muffled jazz music spilled out from a nightclub as we walked by, only to recede behind us.

"I prefer black-and-white films; to me they're more real than the ones in Technicolor. Strange, since real life isn't in black-and-white."

"I'm with you," I replied. "Black-and-white films sift the distractive surface elements of things, so you're left with the essence."

"I just asked you if you knew what the movie was about, and here we are talking about Hegel," he replied, shaking his head.

We were now in the heart of Westwood Village, not far from Mrs. McClurg's house, the university on a hill nearby. Twenty years ago this had been a three-thousand-acre ranch with fields and cows. Rich department store owners bought it and came up with the idea of transforming it into a mecca for wealthy shoppers, and so Westwood Village was conjured from the countryside.

It came alive at night with bright neon signs, crowded bars and restaurants, and packed movie houses. Down Broxton Avenue we found a diner, where we had a couple of beers and chicken enchiladas. Afterward, we walked to the "Tropical Ice Gardens." All lit up, with dozens of people gliding over the gleaming surface, the laughter and cries of skaters who fell, the swoosh of blades cutting the ice, the scents of cotton candy and popcorn in the air, the rink seemed a surreal dream. We stood by the fence for a while, then walked back to the boardinghouse and talked until the early morning hours, so sure of ourselves, so aware of our eloquence, inebriated by the knowledge that we were young and smart with our whole lives ahead of us and the whole world to explore.

Early the following morning I registered painlessly for my courses and eager to see Dr. Kesselman, strode across campus to his office. When I first saw this place I knew I had followed the right path. Built in Italian Renaissance style, Royce Hall and the library looked like basilicas, and Kerckhoff Hall with its Gothic spires gave me the impression of being in Italy during the Middle Ages. Even the air and the light reflecting from the red and mauve bricks brought forth the presence of a hallowed purpose: transmission of knowledge, search for truth, love of learning. I remembered how on that first day, as I walked by Royce Hall, I thought of my father's fields and was struck by the contrast. The library and the classroom halls spoke of the life of the mind, of scholarship; the fields of the Imperial Valley of toil and dependence on the whims of nature.

I belonged in this university as rice belongs to Japanese cuisine. The sun bathed the jacaranda and amber trees in crepuscular light, and two white butterflies chased each other on the green lawn. *Hopefully Dr. Kesselman will be in his office.* My favorite professor, he made philosophy a terribly important matter, and his enthusiasm inspired me greatly. He surprised me at times with books I'd never heard of, books that opened up new ways of seeing.

"Come in." I opened the heavy wooden door and entered.

"Mike, you look great. Lots of sun, I see. Sit down, sit down. Have you registered for classes? Good. The summer is over; it's time to get to work. Germany is going to hell, but Herr Heidegger's philosophy—ah *mein Freund*, earthshaking. A revolution, my dear Mike. A revelation, a . . . never mind. We'll have the whole semester to savor its aesthetic ramifications, its sublime intricacies, its symmetrical designs—here it is, *Sein und Zeit*, or *Being and Time*. I brought a copy especially for you; yes, I know you can get through it, besides, I'll go over the technical language; as for the ones who don't know German, I'll translate essential sections and with my lectures … Mike, go home and read this book. Between these covers you will find something that will change your life. Just read it, as fast as you can, then come see me with all your questions …" Professor Kesselman sat, or, rather, tried to remain seated behind his desk. He smoked a Camel and the smoke hovered in front of him. Short and chubby, with a balding head, dressed in loose pants and a denim shirt, he looked like a truck driver; but in his office, surrounded by his books and the buddhas he had picked up in his travels through China and India, behind his clouds of smoke rising like wafts of incense or the gaseous emanations seeping from the floor of the temple of the Oracle at Delphi, he seemed a god possessed.

"Thank you for the book, Professor . . ." I picked it up and it felt good; it was a solid tome. "Professor, I heard that Heidegger's political views—that they are close to the National Socialist Movement's . . ."

"Heidegger's political views are controversial, and there are those who would reject his philosophical work because of them, but that's unwarranted. The text must be evaluated on its own. Once the author has written it, it becomes an independent entity, and it must be judged on its merits. We are not psychologists or even worse, moralists. When we try to understand a philosophical text, we need to evaluate the claims and the line of reasoning supporting them. The author's personality and behavior do not enter into that critical evaluative process."

"I agree. Before critically evaluating a text we must make sure we understand it, which requires reading it with an open mind."

"And only then can we ascertain whether there is something in the work that would, of necessity, lead to certain political views. I don't think so, but that's for you to determine after you read it carefully with an open mind. See you Monday morning. In my first lecture I'll explain the background and go over the technical terms. And take good notes."

I thanked Professor Kesselman again and left. As I walked home, I opened the book to the table of contents and realized it was no ordinary text. It seemed mysterious and urgently important, as if the meaning of life might be revealed in its pages. A shiver ran down my back as I ran my fingers over the cloth cover, smelled the pages. That texture simultaneously rough and smooth, the scent of ink deep and dark, were the physical manifestations of philosophy, of truth. Go home and read this book, Kesselman had said.

My grasp of German was elementary; it took me weeks to plod through it, but with the help of lectures and discussions, I began to penetrate through the lines of print and found a cathedral of bright light, where at times existence became transparent like the Laguna Mountain brooks in spring, when on camping trips with my brother we waded in the cool, crystalline streams and spied crawdads and minnows trying to hide under rocks.

Professor Kesselman translated key sections of *Being and Time* and every week handed us mimeographed copies. Ours was a special topics course for philosophy majors, so most of the fifteen registered students had been my classmates in previous courses. We often talked about philosophy during breaks or after classes, and six of us had formed a study group. Gordon Wallace, wiry, always elegantly dressed, majored in biology as well as philosophy. Arthur White, a Los Angeles native, had an affinity for analytical philosophy and was especially fond of Bertrand Russell. Gladys Valla, who liked William James and Charles Pierce, was the class pragmatist. Her father was an officer in the Navy, and she had lived in several places around the world. Robert Brock, originally from Texas, had moved to Glendale with his family as a child. His declared major had been chemistry, but after taking an intro course he switched to philosophy. And then there was Natalie Young, an attractive brunette who was probably the smartest of us. She had a special interest in Plato and ancient philosophy. We usually tried to sit in the front rows, and before tests we met at Crumplar's Restaurant to study, drink malts, and eat French fries.

My favorite classroom was in Royce Hall. Its white walls, high ceiling, marble floor, and arched windows vaguely reminded me of a temple. Thirty student desks faced a podium, a heavy mahogany teacher's table, and a blackboard. The windows were open, since for the past two days it had been sweltering; even in the third week of October, summer had no intention of leaving. Did the Imperial Valley's scorching heat follow me? This morning bright sunlight and the scent of freshly cut grass filled the room, and I looked forward to the lecture.

Professor Kesselman came in, put his thermos on the table, and walked to the podium. He laid his notes down and flipped through them. He wore charcoal-gray slacks, a white shirt, and black oxfords. He looked at each of us for a few seconds as he stroked his chin. Was he wondering how best to begin, or was he struck by the brute fact of our just being there, in front of him, questioning entities waiting for him to become our Plato?

"Good morning," he finally said, in a tone that made it so. "Good morning," we all answered in chorus. Then he continued. "We have now covered the introduction and the first three chapters. Before going any further, I want to make sure you understand what Heidegger is attempting to do. Western civilization is dualistic. Human beings are considered subjects, and the world a multiplicity of objects to be analyzed and categorized. This way of thinking has given us science and technology, but it has also obscured the fundamental unity of human beings and the world. It is this 'primordial' unity Heidegger proposes to uncover. Are there any questions?"

Arthur, who sat to my right, glanced at his notebook and raised his hand.

"He could've used clearer language. Take the word *Dasein*, for instance. It's a common German word he employs to refer to human existence, but it's vague, confusing."

"Familiar words like *human being, rational animal*, and *body and soul* are already burdened with pre-established determinations. He invites us to ponder human existence before it comes, preformed, out of anthropological, psychological, or theological molds. That's why in the book he uses words and expressions new to us. Granted, we might be unable to completely escape those molds, but to be aware of how they shaped us can help us become freer. But more on this later— remember, we barely finished the third chapter."

Arthur began to write in the notebook as Kesselman unscrewed the red cup from his Coleman thermos and poured coffee into it. The earthy aroma seemed to enrich the discussion. Gordon Wallace scratched his blond crew-cut hair. He wore a long-sleeved shirt and tie, and he loosened the knot as he straightened up.

"Yes, Gordon?"

"It seems to me that Heidegger mystifies 'being.' He makes a big deal out of it, but maybe it's just a word that has a function in the way our language is structured, that's all."

"We are here, we exist. If we were not, if we did not exist, we would be dead, and I don't know about you, but I'd rather be than not. So this question of being opens up an existential ground. You're right, in grammar 'being' has a specific use, but it also refers to existence, and Heidegger is saying that whatever 'to be' means is of concern to us—"

"That's why he begins by questioning the questioner, namely human beings," interjected Natalie as she stopped writing. She sat next to me, usually wore Tabu perfume, and the lingering scents of patchouli and vanilla distracted me. She had a Servall fountain pen with a gorgeous celluloid barrel, burgundy with mother-of-pearl, and she now balanced it between her index and middle fingers. She always took copious notes and would occasionally stretch her hand, and when she did, her pale, slender fingers with long red nails and the pen moved in a hypnotic dance. Last year, at the campus bookstore, I bought myself a black Sheaffer and had become intrigued with fountain pens. I especially liked Natalie's.

"Right," boomed Kesselman, bringing me back to the moment. "That's why in the first chapter he embarks on an analysis of the questioner. What does it mean to be a human being? Remember, for Plato, our essence is in the realm of ideas, for Aristotle it's in the faculty of reason, for Descartes it's in our consciousness. Heidegger says, no! Our essence is in our being, we exist and we ask questions, but who are we who are doing the asking?"

Natalie leaned forward, her fingers now in full control of the pen. She wore a white blouse and a gray skirt, and as I glanced at her crossed ankles and white-and-brown saddle shoes, I began to lose the thread of the discussion. I moved my eyes toward Professor Kesselman, who walked back and forth holding his coffee cup as if it were a sacred relic to be laid on an altar.

"I think I understand what he's getting at, but it's rather abstract. When you finally cash the chips in, what do you get?" asked Gladys, who sat behind me. The way she looked —petite, with long curly brown hair in a half-upswept style and heavy makeup—betrayed her down-to-earth, analytical mind. Kesselman took a sip of coffee, set the cup on the table, and continued walking to and fro, gesticulating.

"His terminology might seem abstract, but he's actually more concrete than many philosophers past and contemporary. What could be more concrete than starting with my being here? I find myself in a world. *In-der-Welt-sein!* It's a unity we have broken apart and forgotten to put back together, and if that is the case, then psychology and the other sciences cannot adequately explain our selves."

"Why not?" asked Robert, a baffled look on his face. Kesselman walked closer to our side of the room, and I could see a sparkle in his eyes. His face seemed younger; his stocky frame emanated energy.

"Because the sciences study human beings as if they were just other entities in the world, but we 'create the world' in a manner of speaking, then question it through the sciences. So, to get back to what Natalie pointed out earlier, we must question the questioner. To truly know ourselves we have to embark on an existential, ontological analysis of what it means to be a human being. That's what Heidegger is doing, but we just started the book. Let's give him a chance to develop his analysis."

Kesselman then looked at Gladys and continued, "What you get when you cash the chips in is the possibility of understanding the world and yourself in a new light, and of creating a life based on your own choices and values, instead of on the expectations of others, on social conventions. But Heidegger is going to unfold this in the chapters to come."

As I sat at the desk writing in my notebook with the Sheaffer pen, gold nib gliding over white paper, listening to the Professor and my fellow students, feeling the warm breeze on my cheeks as the tower bell rang the hours, I became aware of a palpable presence. The middle-aged man in front of us had received a doctorate from Columbia, had studied in Europe, had written books and articles. As he stood at the podium, as he paced back and forth asking questions, explaining, he strove to help us reach beyond our surface understanding of things. A magician of sorts, a necromancer of the mind, he hoped to bring forth wonder, insight, a passion for truth, to give it shape, to make it live. I could touch the contours of this presence, and told myself, "Yes, I want to dedicate my life to the love of wisdom."

I sat at my desk and tried to read a chapter of *Being and Time* as a sonata by Beethoven played on the radio. My desk was right in front of the window, so I found myself staring at the grayish-white sky, at the jacaranda tree's blue flowers, at the Mexican palms' branches swaying back and forth in the wind, at Mrs. McClurg's rosebushes splashed with crimson, pink, and white. I usually didn't study with the radio on, but I'd wanted to listen to this piece. The elegance, brilliance, and mysterious longing in the music seeped into the roses, trees, and white sky and took me away from the book, the chair, from myself, and for a moment I experienced a sense of perfection, of timelessness. Surely this is what they call paradise, the Kingdom of God, eternal life; but then I began to think about the seminar, about Yoshiko, about the future, and the moment popped like a soap bubble, and I returned to my chair, to my loneliness, to my average everydayness.

Besides the Heidegger seminar I also took medieval philosophy, metaphysics, and epistemology. I liked all the professors in the department, but Kesselman came across as someone for whom philosophy became a way of life, a job to be done in rolled-up shirtsleeves.

As the heat gave way to cold weather, the leaves on the liquid ambers on campus turned vividly red and yellow, the days became shorter, and the rain began to wash the summer from dry, dusty roofs and streets.

In the mornings, on the way to my classes, I would stop at Crumplar's Restaurant for breakfast. I liked to sit at a small table by the window, drink coffee, and read the paper. Tom also had a class that started early this semester, so we usually walked to campus together and stopped for a bowl of oatmeal or eggs and toast.

It was Friday and we looked forward to the weekend. Soon after we sat down, Hazel came by with a smile. She was a tall woman in her early forties, with blond hair up in a bun, broad shoulders, and a thick neck. Very friendly, she seemed always cheerful, and today was no different.

"Good morning, sweethearts," she greeted us. She poured coffee in our mugs and the steam enveloped my face.

"I really need this cup of joe, Hazel," I said as I blew in the mug to cool it down a bit.

"What'd you do, sweetheart, study all night?"

"Until two," I replied. We ordered eggs, hash browns, and toast and sipped our coffee. I took the *Los Angeles Times* out of my jacket pocket.

With trepidation I looked at the front page, since every day the headlines spoke of war. Yesterday, American ships had engaged Nazi warships in a big battle off the coast of Iceland, fresh German troops were getting ready to launch attacks on Moscow and Rostov, and Japanese warships and troop transports were moving fast toward the coast of northern Indo-China. I rapidly went to page 16, to the "Drama" page, since I liked to read movie reviews and sample Hedda Hopper's "Hollywood" column. My eyes were caught by a photo of Simone Simon, who sat on a chair and looked at the camera with a sultry expression. The caption explained that Simone was going to be in the new movie *All That Money Can Buy*. After staring at the photo for a while, I began to read Hopper, and a couple of paragraphs in, I began to laugh.

"What's so funny?" asked Tom.

"Listen to this tidbit by Hedda Hopper. 'I loved Jean Gabin's reply when asked if he felt comfortable speaking

English. He said, 'Oh yes, very. But I can't speak without thinking first.' Wouldn't it be wonderful if Hollywood cultivated that habit?"

"Hell, it'd be wonderful if *everyone* cultivated that habit, not just people in Hollywood. Anyway, what new movies are out this weekend?"

"Let's see . . . *The Maltese Falcon* with Humphrey Bogart, Peter Lorre, and Mary Astor is playing downtown, *Citizen Kane* with Orson Welles is at the Hawaii, and *Sergeant York* with Gary Cooper is at the Balboa."

He put the coffee cup down. "Mmmm, *The Maltese Falcon* sounds intriguing. Bogart was swell in *High Sierra*. Maybe we could see that?"

"Let's go next week. I have to write a paper and have lots of reading to do." I flipped through the pages until I found the radio schedule and saw that the Crosby Orchestra was on KHJ at eleven thirty. I'd listen to it for a while to wind down after working on my class assignments, I thought.

"You always have your nose in a damn book or are writing papers—you have to take your mind off that stuff and relax sometimes."

"Tom, you try studying Heidegger, then you'll see. And I have three other courses besides, not to count the fifteen hours a week I work at the library."

"Here's your eggs and toast, sweethearts," said Hazel as she placed our dishes on the table. "I'll be back with more joe." She shuffled toward the counter, rubbing her side. When dust storms ravaged her family's farm in Texas, they came to California. Last year I had given her a copy of *The Grapes of Wrath* as a Christmas present, and she told me she cried when she finished it.

Tom thought of my philosophy work as boring drudgery, but to sit at my desk embraced by stacks of books, pounding at the typewriter, each click giving birth to a letter soon followed by others, forming words in patterns that brought forth meaning, created thoughts, dared to touch the unknown, I would not have traded for anything.

I did find the time to go to the movies and to read the papers, though. The news was all bad. Packs of U-boats kept sinking Allied ships in the Atlantic, the Nazis had executed 100,000 people in Axis-occupied countries, and Japan threatened to enter the war. Last year I saw a dead man lying on the street. There had been a car accident; the police at the scene waited for the coroner's van to arrive. I kept thinking about him for days, wondering if he had a family. Maybe he was on his way home; maybe his children were waiting for their daddy who was never going to return. But I couldn't even visualize 100,000 dead people. I only felt a dark foreboding, feared the escape of the beasts we keep locked up in the dark chambers of our psyches.

I pushed the chair back and got up from my desk. I had been reading the assigned chapter in my medieval philosophy text for an hour and needed a break. I stood in front of the window and watched the sun sink behind the trees. The jacaranda and the rosebushes had lost most of their colors as the day came to an end. It was getting cold and I started to pace. The open book on the desk waited for me, but I went to see Tom.

His room, like mine in size and layout, was sparse: a desk and chair, bookcase, stove. He sat on the bed, his head propped up by pillows, reading from a notebook.

"I'm dying reading Thomas Aquinas—let's get out for a while," I said as I sat on the chair by the bedside.

"The philosopher is tired of reading? You must be sick," he said, looking up from the book. "But hydrology isn't much fun either on Saturday evenings." And so we went for a long walk in twilight; our jacket collars up, hands in pockets, we passed by neatly trimmed lawns, bungalows, and Spanish-style homes as the bark of dogs greeted us now and then. Tom noticed my distraction.

"What the hell are you thinking about?"

"I can't get the news out of my mind."

"Hell, the news is always bad. Stop reading the paper for a while." We walked for another thirty minutes, then spotted a diner on the other side of the street. It was crowded, so we sat at the counter and ordered a cheeseburger and fries. After a long wait the burgers arrived, and they paled compared to Mel's. We ate quickly and decided to go to the movies. The "Supercinema" was not far, and luckily we made it in time for the last showing.

Dr. Jekyll's innocent face filled the screen.

"After all, that's the problem of civilized man's soul, that the good and the evil in it are constantly fighting one another," he said as he sat at the dinner table, trying to defend his views from the criticism of scandalized, respectable friends. *Poor Dr. Jekyll*, I thought, *so troubled by his desires and so disappointed in the world that he wants to improve on God's botched job.* In images dissolving into one another he appeared in his laboratory, amid beakers, white rabbits, and rats, feverishly experimenting with the potion that would dispense with free will and the courage to make decisions and accept responsibility for them. A Victorian armed with medicine, he wanted to excise, as if it were a tumor, the troubling part of man. The potion was ready at last, a dark liquid with white bubbling foam; the music rose to a melodramatic crescendo as he lifted the graduated beaker to the light and gulped it down.

Ah, poor Mr. Hyde, incarnated in Spencer Tracy in need of a haircut, wide eyes shifting left and right, reduced by Hollywood to tripping people up and starting barroom fights. Gorgeous and seductive Ingrid Bergman became his battered girlfriend, then the plot ground so predictably on its Hollywood tracks. It was pathetic how Mr. Hyde, supposedly an evil mastermind, could only be a petty criminal, a common murderer.

It began to drizzle as we left the theater and hurried home. What trash the movie seemed, compared to the book! And yet, I couldn't stop thinking about the movie, and as Tom and I took great strides under the rain, a fear hatched within me, a fear that the whole world had consumed Dr. Jekyll's potion and soon Mr. Hyde would burst upon the scene, incarnated not into one man, but into millions.

Back in my room, I started a fire in the potbellied stove and fixed a cup of tea. I sat by the stove and opened my copy of *Sein und Zeit*. I moved the lamp closer and began to read. The warm yellow light bathed the grainy white pages. The black words, mostly German, but at times Latin and Greek, became mysterious and vast, so that for an instant I felt dizzy and afraid to fall into them, as if they were cracks in reality, and the world, for a second, seemed a thin veil. What did it mean to exist?

Certainly this had always been my big question, even as a child, when I lay in bed just before getting up in the mornings and marveled at my being there. I could remember walking around in my father's lettuce fields, the buzzing of insects in my ears. The heads of lettuce like strange flowers had pushed themselves out of the earth. The humid trembling air caressed my cheeks, I could hear the seagulls' cries overhead, and I, fairly new to the world, could barely stand it. "I'm alive! I am! I am!" I would yell in my head, but how did it happen? Why was I there? Why was anything there? Yes, to uncover the meaning of being, of what it means to be, one must investigate the questioner, and so Heidegger plunges into an analysis of what it means to be human.

To be human is to find oneself in a world with others, to emerge into a time, a culture, a language, a family, limited by one's genes and environment. Believing what others believe, doing what they do, desiring what they desire, but ultimately to have the possibility to create a life informed by one's own values and projects.

I sat in the stuffed chair sipping tea as the light shined on the book, leaving the rest of the room in shadows, and the pine logs hissed and spattered. I had been lucky to have found such a large room so close to the university. The walnut bookcase by the door bulged with books and my desk stood buried under papers and stacks of more books. The warmth given off by the stove had the effect of a tranquilizer, and I put the book down on my lap and closed my eyes.

What the hell am I doing here? Where am I? It's a large living room but the walls and the ceiling are made of glass, and beyond the glass, there is water. Thump! Thump! *Something is hitting the glass behind me, making an animal sound like a dog makes when he chases a gopher into a hole and can't get to it. I turn my head; a black shark with something human in its head bumps its snout against the glass, its wild and cold eyes fixed on me, its body and tail moving frantically. I hide behind a sofa, but I still hear it, swimming around the walls, thumping against the glass, making those strange squeals.*

Thump! Thump! Thump!

I opened my eyes, and Sunday's bright light coming in from the window made me close them again.

"Mike!" I recognized the shrill voice as Tom's. I got up from the chair, trying to straighten up.

"What's going on?" I asked as I unlocked the door. Tom rushed in, wearing only his boxer shorts.

"They bombed Pearl Harbor, Mike. The Japanese bombed Pearl Harbor. Do you know what that means?" He sat on the edge of the bed and looked at me for a few seconds in silence, then he slowly got up and walked toward the door. "I'm going to call my parents," he said.

As the door closed, I glanced at my books and felt far away from them. I got up and paced back and forth. The reptilian brain, crawling so close to the surface of reason, will be stirred even in the land of the free and the brave. I could see its shiny, cold head breaking through and its fangs sinking into whoever might be near. What is philosophy, art, religion, whatever makes humans really human, but a delicate veil on a lump of mindless, throbbing, hungry flesh?

In the following days as I walked down streets or sat in restaurants, I noticed I had become more conspicuous. People's eyes lingered, at times for just a moment, on me. On December thirteenth the winter recess began, so I went home.

During the three weeks I spent in El Centro, I realized Mr. Hyde had already begun to do his work. What a way for the year to end and for 1942 to begin! On New Year's Eve several Japanese were shot by Filipinos, and since all Japanese were ordered to leave Baja California by the Mexican government, Imperial County became inundated by refugees.

The Japanese American community began to stagger under the Pearl Harbor blow. We were now looked at with suspicion or disdain even by those we had considered friends. Many of us tried to go about our daily lives as if nothing had happened; some hid in their homes and refused to venture outside, others postponed weddings or major purchases. My parents presented a stoic front, while my sisters and brother kept busy and hoped life would get back to normal. Yoshiko and I got together a few times, but something broke between us. Maybe it began as a hairline crack when I moved to Los Angeles. Maybe Yoshiko unconsciously resented my going to UCLA, even if she said she was happy for me. After all, she had always wanted to be a teacher, but after her father's death she felt duty bound to care for her mother. Perhaps at some level she resented having to put her life goal on the back burner. And now the Valley was in turmoil. It was dangerous to even venture out of the house, so I spent most of the vacation indoors, reading.

Back in Los Angeles the first week in January, I resumed my classes, which were almost over. I was going to miss Kesselman's lectures on Heidegger, but the thought that I owned the book consoled me. Final exams at the end of the month kept me busy, and on February ninth I registered for four courses. I tried to throw myself into the scholarly life, but the headlines in the paper and people's attitudes became thorns daily pushed into my skin. An editorial that had appeared in the paper on the second of February became particularly painful. Japanese Americans could not be trusted, it proclaimed, because even if they were born in America, they were still Japs. "A viper is nonetheless a viper whenever the egg is hatched." As I laid in bed at night I tossed and turned, haunted by the image of a viper hatching eggs, until I fell in uneasy sleep.

Stopping at the newsstand to buy the newspaper had become one of my favorite morning rituals. I looked forward to the crisp early morning air, the traffic noise, the hurried steps of passersby, and then as I approached it, seeing the splashes of color on racks outside the little shop that coalesced into the covers of magazines like *Life*, *Newsweek*, and *Time*. I'd say good morning to Willie and hand him a nickel. "Morning, Mike," he would say as he handed me a fresh copy of the *Los Angeles Times*.

This semester Tom and I had different schedules, so we didn't see much of each other in the mornings, but in late afternoon or early evening we'd go out for coffee and dinner. One Monday we decided to check out a diner near Ralphs in Westwood. We sat at a booth sipping coffee while waiting for our meat loaf plate. It was late afternoon and the sun had already gone down. From the window we could see people bundled up in overcoats, hats, and gloves hurry by as behind them, Mexican fan palms silhouetted in twilight seemed like small balloons attached to fat strings. We tried to avoid talking about our situation, but foremost on our minds, it forced itself on us.

"Have you noticed a certain coldness from the landlady? Whenever she sees me she hurries away," said Tom as he put the mug down.

"I've noticed that in many people. Even the guy at the newsstand doesn't look at me anymore. What do you expect? Politicians want us rounded up and locked away. And the press isn't helping at all. Did you read today's paper?" I took it out of my overcoat pocket and unfolded it. "Look at the banner headline: 'Singapore Falls to Japs,' and right below, another story, 'Young Captain Kills 116 Japs on Baatan.' Now look, two columns to the left, another headline reads, 'Japs Prepare to Evacuate Barred Areas.' In that story they're talking about Japanese Americans. They call us 'Japs,' just like they call the enemy. But we are not Japs; we are Americans of Japanese descent. They do it all the time, so when people see us they see the enemy. It won't be long before we'll have to leave."

"Leave? Where to?"

"There's talk of concentration camps."

"You're out of your mind. I was born and grew up here!" A young woman wearing a blue checkered dress and white apron, with soft curly brown hair, approached with our steaming plates. She laid them on the table and left without saying a word. Waiting for the food to cool down a bit, I took another look at the Drama page. In the photo above her piece, Hedda Hopper smiled at me. Her column, full of gossipy Hollywood news, had been my sugary guilty pleasure since I began reading her. I didn't have time or the inclination to read her whole column; a few gumdrops from the bag was enough. "Buddy DeSylva wants Ernest Hemingway to read the screenplay for *For Whom the Bell Tolls*, George Mont-gomery's pet name for Hedy Lamarr is Penny, Gene Autry leaves his rodeo show next week, George Raft's sinus trouble is holding up Broadway . . ." I had naively taken for granted that Hedda Hopper smiled at me too, and her column was also for me to savor, to make me feel a bond with the culture I had assumed was also mine, but it became increasingly evident that I didn't belong. Like a toxic foreign body, I had to be expelled.

On February nineteenth, President Roosevelt signed Executive Order 9066, which authorized the Army to remove persons considered to be a threat to national security. Local congressmen urged a speedy removal of all Japanese Americans, and a *Los Angeles Times* editorial on the twenty-first welcomed the order and said that Japanese Americans' "best patriotic contribution will be a willing participation."

A few days later all hell broke loose when according to news reports, a Japanese submarine shelled an oil field north of Santa Barbara. The apparent attack did little damage and resulted in no casualties, but it increased public demand for Japanese Americans to be removed.

On March fifth, I gave Willie a nickel and with downcast eyes, he handed me a copy of the paper. As I walked toward campus I glanced at the front page. The banner headline read, "Jap Hordes Advance in Java," and right below, on the left side, a smaller headline intimated that "Japs May Be Interned in Owens Valley."

I found it increasingly hard to concentrate on my studies. Hegel's writing style drove me to despair, and often I lost the struggle to keep my mind from wandering. I felt as if waiting for the results of a biopsy.

The day before, at the post office, waiting in line to send my mother a foldable fan for her birthday, people's expressions made me want to run out. I forced myself to write to Yoshiko, but felt distant and cold. I went to Crumplar's for breakfast. As I sat at a table I waved at Hazel, who stood behind the counter pouring coffee in someone's mug. She acted as if she didn't see me, and after a while another waitress came to take my order. I went through the motions of eating the fried egg and toast as I read. *A nightmare, this is a nightmare and soon I'll wake up.*

I grew up on a farm in a small desert town in California, and had been taught that I was an American, but General DeWitt said, "A Jap is a Jap," and therefore no Japs could be trusted. The "Asiatic Exclusion League," the "Anti-Jap Laundry League," and public opinion in general told me I was a "Mongolian," a sneaky yellow traitor intent on stealing a white American's job and plotting to rape and kill his wife and kids.

It was almost eight o' clock; I'd have to hurry or I'd be late for the seminar. I paid the bill and as I opened the door, a whisper reached me from a booth: "Dirty Jap." I turned and looked into the face of a middle-aged woman, well dressed, hair neatly combed, who sat next to a little boy. She glared at me as she fed the boy a spoonful of cereal. I stepped out and began to walk in the cold morning air. The whisper, soft and furry, burrowed deep inside. For several days those two words squirmed in my chest.

The evacuation started in late March. Tom and I hoped to finish the semester, but that was not to be. Just a few weeks before final exams, we had no choice but to leave.

I wanted to pay attention to the lecture on Hegel, but I fidgeted as my mind untethered, wandered around the classroom. Professor Kesselman's voice sounded like water flowing in a mountain stream; only intermittently was I aware of words, ". . . for Hegel it is possible to have absolute knowledge, but always of particular spheres which necessarily brings to consciousness the limitation of such knowledge . . ." More water seemed to flow as I stared at the crown moldings on the walls, then words again, " . . . the supersensible world is the inverted world, it is consciousness of being the inverted form of itself in a single unity, as such it is infinity . . ." Finally he gave us the reading assignment for the next session and dismissed the class. Students got up and left in a flurry of rustling papers and loud voices, and I, too, put notebook and textbook in my bag and walked out.

"You weren't paying much attention today—that's unusual," I heard Natalie say behind me. I turned around and smiled.

"It doesn't matter really—I have to withdraw from the university tomorrow," I said, trying to sound calm and detached.

"Can't you finish the semester at least? We have just a few weeks left before graduation."

"They won't allow it," I replied, and she looked down for a moment.

We were standing in the middle of the hallway, two islands in a stream of students going to or coming out of classes. She clutched her shoulder bag as if trying to hold onto something, and standing there surrounded by students and classrooms I began to feel like an intruder. For almost four years Royce Hall, the library, this university had been home to me; now I was being exiled.

"Would you like to go for a cup of coffee?"

"Hey, I'd never turn down coffee," I replied. It was ten in the morning as we walked to Crumplar's under a sky like the striated belly of a sheep. Fan palms soldiered on in the middle of Westwood Boulevard, and the sweet smell of baked goods wafted in the air. We sat, facing each other, in a booth by the window. Hazel busied herself behind the counter, acting as if she didn't see me. After a while another waitress came to take our order—the younger one, with the expressionless face.

"How's the study group going?" I asked Natalie as the waitress left.

"After Gladys didn't want to have you in the group, things got awkward, and it just disbanded."

"You could've kept going without me."

"It wouldn't have been the same," she said softly. "What are you going to do?"

"I'll come back tomorrow to sign some papers and talk to Kesselman, then I have to go back to El Centro. We've been relocated to a camp in Arizona . . . maybe I'll be able to do a lot of reading there." The waitress arrived with coffee and two maple-glazed doughnuts, laid them on the table, and left.

"I love this synthesis of opposites," I said jokingly as I took a bite of the sweet doughnut and a sip of the bitter coffee.

"Mike, I'm really sorry you have to leave. Seeing you in classes with your leather satchel, writing in your notebook, eagerly listening to lectures, asking questions, making comments . . . you made it all seem vital, extremely important. You inspired me and validated my interest in philosophy." Her pale green eyes emanated warmth and a tinge of sadness, and a mixture of feelings swelled up in me.

"Maybe I can find some solace in Epictetus. Remember when we had to read him in Warren's History of Philosophy class?" I said, and her eyes brightened as she began to speak.

"And when we got together to study for the test, Robert said, 'According to Epictetus if we wish to be good, first we must believe we are bad, so I'm going to get drunk.'"

"It was a great study session—he drank seven beers and then threw up on his shoes. But what about you, how are you doing?" I asked as I took another bite. She put the coffee mug down and thought for a few seconds.

"I spend most of my time reading books and writing research papers, but still can't escape from the nightmare. What's happening to the world, Mike? Millions of people dying, so much suffering and pain. As a doctor my father has dedicated his whole life to helping people; my mother, a teacher, to educate new generations; and I hoped as a philosophy professor to help people think for themselves, but what can a few do in a world gone mad? It seems hopeless." The place was getting busy. More people were coming in and sitting down, the clinking of utensils and the cacophony of voices became more insistent, and someone behind the counter dropped a dish, which shattered loudly. *Way to go, Hazel.*

"I often get close to the edge of a bottomless pit, and then I remind myself Socrates and Plato didn't give up when things were falling apart," I said.

"But reason is weak when confronted by powerful emotions. I can't do anything to stop the madness, and don't remind me of stoicism, 'we only have the power to choose how to react to external events' and blah blah—it doesn't help."

"You're sitting here having coffee and a doughnut with me; that's something. Hazel won't even look at me. She used to call me 'sweetheart'—granted, that's what she calls everyone, but she was friendly. Since Pearl Harbor she avoids me as if I were a leper. I have the face of a Japanese man but I'm an American. You understand that. You're a light in the darkness, Natalie, and you need to keep burning bright." She sat straighter as I finished speaking, and her eyes lit up again.

"One day when I was in fifth grade a teacher accused me of having written something dirty on a wall in the restroom. 'Don't deny it, because I can read your mind and I know you did it,' she told me, and they suspended me for three days. My parents grounded me for a month. No radio, no going to visit friends, no movies. I had looked up to adults as authority figures not to be questioned, but I hadn't written anything on the wall. The teacher was either lying or delusional. Either way, adults couldn't be trusted, could be mistaken. I began to question what people told me, what I read. And I'm still doing it. I'm going to become a philosophy professor and help people to think critically, to become more open minded." As Natalie finished speaking the waitress came to refill our mugs. *That's also my goal,* I wanted to tell her, but I didn't say it.

"Mike, I'd like to give you something so you'll remember me and all the philosophy courses we took." She reached in her purse and handed me her fountain pen. I couldn't say anything for a few moments. I thanked her as I turned over the Servall in my hands, admiring how mother-of-pearl appeared and disappeared from underneath the burgundy finish. Then I took the Sheaffer from my jacket pocket and handed it to her.

"It's not as beautiful as yours, but I hope it'll serve you well. I'm looking forward to seeing you in my mind's eye taking lots of notes with it." She thanked me, and we talked for a while longer before leaving. Outside it had warmed up a little. Patches of blue had broken up the gray woolen clouds. We said goodbye and just before going our separate ways, she gave me a hug. I closed my eyes as my cheek rested on her hair. Through the soft woolen sweater, the substantiality of her body came through with warmth, tenderness, and the scent of Tabu.

When the alarm went off I had been awake for an hour, staring at the bookcase. Almost seven feet tall and forty inches wide, walnut with a crown molding adorned with curlicue designs in gold, it was my favorite piece of furniture in the room. I didn't have many books, maybe a couple of hundred, a mix of general education texts, fiction, and of course philosophy, which occupied the top shelves. *The Works of Plato,* a thick volume translated by Jowett, had first place.

I remembered how I bought it two years ago for Dr. Warren's course. Once in my room I took it out of the bag, ran my fingers along the red cloth binding, and admired the gold lettering on the spine. I had opened the heavy volume and held it close to my face hoping to capture, through the scent, something of the life of the great philosopher.

The course on Plato had been one of my favorites, a whole semester spent with Socrates, whom I admired for his courage, his dedication to living a life grounded in reason, and the love of truth.

Professor Warren also taught the course on Aristotle, whose collected writings stood next to Plato's. Working through the *Logic*, *De Anima*, and his *Nichomachean Ethics* made me understand the foundations of Western thought. Next in line, Descartes' *Meditations*.

My eyes rested on the blue cloth spine of the book and I couldn't help but think of the French philosopher's image of the malignant being deceiving us by creating all our sensations and perceptions. Descartes' claim that if we value truth we cannot accept beliefs based on authority made sense to me. We must rely on our intelligence and on evidence. The search for truth requires method, reason. But then my eyes moved on to the gray spine of Kant's *Critique of Pure Reason*, which had given me so much trouble last year. We can only experience the world through our senses, which give us data that is then structured by our minds. Reason can only think about these phenomena; the world as it is in itself is an unknowable realm, which he, however, proceeds to populate with God, freedom, and morality. A questionable move, but while I disagreed with Kant, I found reading him important and thought provoking. Next to Kant stood anthologies of readings by other philosophers, like Spinoza, Schopenhauer, and Nietzsche. In those books I loved the methodical unfolding of arguments, the elucidation of ideas, the reasoned construction of worldviews or the critiques of them.

Warm and safe under the blankets, lost in thought, I didn't want to get up, but I had to. The day began to assert itself through the peach-colored drapes. I dressed quickly, picked up my book bag, and left. "Good morning," I said to Mrs. McClurg, who searched for the newspaper in the rosebushes, but she didn't turn around and hurried back inside.

I had to go to the university to withdraw from my classes and go see Professor Kesselman. On the sidewalk I passed elegant women wearing fedoras and turban hats, men in suits and sport jackets, students toting bookbags. I couldn't meet their glances. What did they see when they looked at me? A snake slithering on the ground? I felt blood surge to my face and I looked down as I walked faster.

"Mike, sit down. I'm sorry you have to go; you have always been one of my best students." Kesselman sat behind his desk, pulled a cigarette from the pack he always carried in his shirt pocket, lit it with his Zippo, and took a long drag. "Life is philosophy, you and I know that; it's not just abstract bullshit or word games. Don't forget what you elucidated so well for me last semester in the Heidegger paper: existence can only be one's own, and reality is based on concern and solicitude. Your life may not seem hopeful to you now, but it is *your* life; stare it in the face, however painful it might be; that is the beginning of authentic existence. And Hegel, Mike, remember Hegel. Life is not a straight line, but a dialectical process; it is through pain that we reach joy, it is through poverty that we become rich, it is through suffering and loneliness that we find love." His eyes moved and found refuge on the buddhas sitting impassively on his desk and bookshelves. Then he rose from his chair and moved toward me.

"Professor, I just wanted to tell you I'll miss you and your lectures. You've been a great inspiration to me." As I uttered these words I felt strangely detached, as if the words had been spoken by someone else. I got up and stood in front of my teacher and mentor.

"Good luck, Mike! This craziness won't last forever; you'll come back and I'll be here. Besides, books and seminars are not philosophy; philosophy is a way of life." He gave me a hug, and the smell of cigarettes and aftershave reminded me of the scent of old philosophy books I used to pick up from the library's shelves, take to a table, and peruse. In that brief hug I felt the presence of the quest for truth, the life of the mind, solicitude, and as I left I knew it would not leave me.

However, as I walked across campus, another thought entered my mind. Heidegger, Hegel, philosophy: just words. When the ground crumbles under you, what good are words? I walked back to the boardinghouse in the pale light breaking through a bank of bluish clouds and watched cars driving by, people on sidewalks, listened to the roar of traffic, to children crying and birds chirping. *What do words have to do with all this? Nothing. Words: black marks on dead trees transfigured into veils of paper. And yet we live in them like Christ in hosts, we kill ourselves within them like lost children in the forest. Without words, what is there? Nothing? But even* nothing *is a word. And if words or the possibility of words preceded human existence? Stop it! I must stop this or I'll go crazy. Relax. Don't think anymore.* I bought a hot dog and a Coke, sat on a bench, and just watched the traffic.

The following morning I woke up to the sound of rain, but by the time I started packing my suitcases, it had stopped. I glanced out the window at the jacaranda tree, at the four boxes of books by the door. I couldn't take them with me, but Tom said his father knew someone who had agreed to store some of his family's possessions, and he would keep some of mine as well. I only took *Being and Time* with me.

As I folded shirts and stacked them in the cheap cardboard cases, I thought that maybe I had been fooling myself into thinking I could have gone to the university and become a professor. After all, wasn't I a Jap, the son of peasants? The scholarship I had won wasn't really enough to cover all my expenses, and even with my part-time job at the library my ability to continue my studies had been precarious.

Tom stood by the door with hands in his pockets.

"When are you leaving for Manzanar?" I asked.

"My father is picking me up tomorrow." He remained silent for a while, then said as if to himself, "I was born and grew up here; I've never even been to Japan."

"Haven't you looked in the mirror lately? Didn't you notice you're a bug-eyed Jap?" I said calmly, as I closed the suitcase. Tom looked at me startled as a car pulled up and a horn sounded.

"That's your taxi," Tom said as he grabbed one of the suitcases. He helped me put the baggage in the trunk and then we shook hands.

"Don't let the sharks bite," I said and got in the cab. As the car sped off in a screech I turned my head toward Tom, who stood in front of Mrs. McClurg's rosebushes, and waved goodbye.

At the bus depot I bought a ticket for San Diego. The sun shone dimly through thick bands of gray and white. I sat toward the back of the bus next to the window and stared at the changing scenery through my own reflection. I hated my black hair, my almond eyes, my high cheekbones. Why wasn't I born with blond hair and blue eyes, with a last name like West, or Wayne? A void inside me made me feel like crumpling, but as the bus moved south on Highway 1, buildings, streets, and traffic gave way to the ocean. That perpetually rolling blue-green vastness framed by billowing white clouds and patches of blue entered into that void and lifted me up.

4

1942

Whenever I returned to the Imperial Valley I had the impression I'd left the real world and entered a dreamy, ephemeral land in a glass bubble, but this time was different. This time the decisions and actions of men thousands of miles away had roiled these sleepy desert towns on the Mexican border. We were losing our homes, getting beaten and killed. The last time I called home Steve told me that a group of Filipinos had stabbed to death Teruo Iashi, a high school friend of mine. He had dreamed of becoming an airline pilot, and I had written in his school annual, "To Teruo, the greatest pilot Pan Am will ever have." Japan had invaded the Philippines, but what did we have to do with what Japan did? We Nisei, born in the United States, had never even been to Japan. The sun hovered on the horizon as we approached El Centro. The bus drove down Broadway, pulled into the little station, and came to a stop. I got out with my luggage and stood in front of the depot, glad to be on the ground.

I stretched, trying to shake the stiffness out of my back, and inhaled deeply. Some guys talked and smoked cigarettes in George's Pool Hall across the street. I couldn't hear them, but through the wide window I could see their lips move as they hit balls with their sticks. The sweet smell of masa and pork cooked in chili made me turn my head toward the sidewalk. A barefoot Mexican boy in a faded tee shirt and jeans approached and asked me if I wanted to buy tamales. He must have been about twelve years old. "*Dos,*" I told him, and he took two from the basket he carried and handed them to me, just as Steve arrived in his car. He stopped at the curb, got out, and helped me put the suitcases in the trunk.

"I don't know why the hell you take the bus to San Diego and then another one to El Centro when you could go straight from LA to here. You would've saved hours." He always said this when he came to pick me up at the depot.

"Because I hate that boring drive through the desert. I like the scenic route, damn it," I replied, as I always did. We drove home in twilight, munching on the tamales, passing alfalfa fields in front of a darkening sky torn by yellow and red gashes. A warm and humid wave of familiarity washed over me.

"We sold almost everything for peanuts—hell, they know we ain't got no choice. They'll come tomorrow to pick up the stuff," Steve said without taking his eyes off the road.

"What about the farm, the truck, your car?"

"We lost the lease, we'll have to leave the harvest in the fields, Otosan sold the truck for practically nothing, and my car, shit, they wanted to buy it for a hundred dollars. I'll burn it first," he whispered as he pressed down on the gas pedal. The car lurched forward trailing a cloud of dirt, and the back end began to fishtail. I said nothing; if we crashed, so be it.

The car screeched to a stop in front of the farmhouse. As I got out, I noticed some furniture and household things on the porch, tags attached to them identifying to whom they had been sold.

Inside, I greeted my mother and sisters, who were busy

fixing dinner. "Where's Otosan?" I asked, glancing around. Nobody said anything.

"Where is he?"

Steve sat on the sofa and lit a cigarette.

"FBI men came two weeks ago and took him away," he said.

I stood in the middle of the living room but felt sick, as if I were on a small boat in rough seas. My mother sat down at the dining room table and began to slice eggplants as Myoko and Umeko went into the kitchen.

"Two men dressed in suits said they were from the FBI. They showed us their badges and told us they had to take Otosan away because he's a security risk," said Steve.

I had a feeling of unreality, as if I found myself trapped in some B spy movie.

"Otosan a security risk? He's just a farmer." I sat on the sofa next to Steve and grabbed a cigarette from the pack that he threw on the coffee table. "Why didn't you call me?"

"We didn't want to worry you. Besides, they told us he'll join us in the camp once he's cleared. We'll see him soon. You couldn't have done anything anyway."

We ate quietly; then I went to my room, the wooden floor squeaking under my feet. I closed the door behind me and sat on the bed, glancing at my high school track trophy on the chest of drawers. A piece of paper tied to a drawer's handle by a string said, "Sold to Simpson." Who the hell was he?

On the desk, the *History of Rome* that Mrs. McCracken had given me as a prize for being the best student in Latin one year stood next to the lamp. Suddenly, these objects appeared alien, as if I had never seen them before.

I got up and opened the window. Cool, dry air rushed in. Eucalyptus trees still stood next to the shed as they always had, and stars, throbbing yellow points, still hung above. I took deep breaths and stood there for a while, then got into bed.

This small room had been my inner sanctum for many years. It was here that I read *Twenty Thousand Leagues Under the Sea*. I understood Captain Nemo now, and didn't see him as a madman anymore; no, I wanted to be with him in the *Nautilus*, gliding in the depths of the oceans, battling the oppressive, arrogant national powers, sinking their ships. He could only be judged mad by the conventional, self-serving morality of the groups in power. Captain Nemo was a Nietzschean superman, a rare individual who lived on the firm ground of his own standards. I could see this now and admired him, and wished I could read the book again, but in a couple of days we'd be in the Arizona desert in a camp surrounded by barbed wire. No matter; I'd take it with me, together with *Being and Time*.

I shut off the light and closed my eyes. I wanted desperately to sleep, to fall into unconsciousness, but feelings of unreality and anxiety hummed in me like electricity. I lay there for a long time, staring at the wall, until I turned toward the window and spied a flickering light through the curtains. I jumped out of bed and looked out, but only saw a reddish glow down the road. I put on my jeans and walked down the dirt road until I saw Steve's car. My brother sat farther back on the edge of the road, staring at his Dodge, now enveloped in flames.

"Steve, what the hell?"

He looked at me and said calmly, "I'm not selling my car."

"You could have given it to someone to keep until we come back."

"Who? For how long? No! To hell with them."

"Let's get out of here— it could blow up."

"The gas tank's empty," my brother said, taking a drink from a bottle of beer.

"The fumes could still blow up the gas tank." He didn't reply, so I went to sit by his left side, on the lip of hard, dried soil that flanked the dirt road, and watched the flames leap out of the windows, dance on the tires. Luckily the breeze blew all the dark, stinking smoke away from us. So many memories attached to that car, like the rides to San Diego and the trips to the Laguna Mountains and the town of Julian, where we bought apples, ate pie, and drank cider.

I listened to pops and hisses, the moans and groans coming from the burning Dodge, and I hurt deep inside because I knew what the car meant to my brother.

My father had a piece of land that he didn't use one season, and Steve planted watermelons on it. After working the whole day with my father he'd work hours on that plot of land, irrigating, weeding, covering the plants on very cold nights, and then with the money he made he bought the car. Now he sat next to me and watched it burn. I looked in his eyes but only saw the reflection of the flames.

"Come on, Steve, let's go in," I said.

"Go—I'll come later," he replied.

I retreated to the house in a daze and found myself back in my room. I got into bed and lay there until I lost consciousness.

Dogs barking and the smell of coffee forced my eyes open. I stared at the ceiling, searching for the familiar dark knot of wood. As a child, I'd made believe that dark spot was a hole connecting my room to a mysterious, magical world. I lay there for a while, then got up. Everyone was already seated at the table as I walked into the kitchen. Steve's face looked puffy as he sipped from his mug in silence. We ate scrambled eggs with rice, my mother and sisters drank tea, Steve and I had coffee. No one said a word about the car or anything else. Soon people arrived with pickup trucks to take the furniture and tools they'd bought. Henry Simpson, a skinny balding farmer, left with my dresser and the kitchen table, while

Danny Rouch bought most of my father's tools and equipment. Whatever we couldn't sell we gave away or left behind.

After a lunch of bologna sandwiches, we carried our things outside and waited for the bus. About two thousand Americans of Japanese descent lived in the Valley and we all had to leave by May twenty-first, so we weren't the only ones going through this. It was only the middle of May, but it must've been in the 90s. My mother and sisters sat quietly on their suitcases under a cloudless sky; my mother, in a blue flowery dress, sat with her back straight, holding a black purse on her lap with both hands. Her hair neatly combed in a bun, she stared ahead through her glasses, betraying no emotions. She sat as if in church, or in a courtroom waiting for a judgment she was ready for. Steve and I stood next to them, smoking cigarettes.

"What a crop! Did you see the cantaloupes? All ready for them to pick," said Steve as he gazed at the sea of melons spreading out to the horizon.

"At least Otosan didn't have to go through this," I replied.

A dusty gray bus approached from the left and stopped in front of us. We struggled on with our suitcases and bags, and sat down. The bus was almost full; I recognized many of the families and nodded to them. As we sped off, I looked back at the house until it slowly disappeared in a cloud of dust.

Once in Arizona, I peered out the bus window—an ocean of white-gray desert filled the view, the flatness broken here and there by saguaros and chollas. Babies cried, people talked; I tried to get comfortable but couldn't. Yoshiko and her family didn't leave with us, but they should be in Poston in a couple of days. I slouched down on the seat and finally fell asleep.

I stand, naked, on the transparent roof of a glass building. I shiver and try to find a way down when I hear a buzzing overhead, like a giant mosquito, and as I look up into the darkness I see a small airplane slowly fall to the ground. As it passes by me I notice that it is made of glass, and the pilot sitting in the cockpit is naked except for a brown leather helmet and goggles. The plane shatters in a white cloud of glass fragments as it hits the pavement below, and the pilot explodes like a ripe watermelon.

I woke up with a shudder and saw Steve, who sat next to me, staring.

"What the hell were you dreaming about?" he asked, lighting a cigarette.

"Nothing," I said, turning around. My mother and sisters slept on the seats behind us. I glanced at my Timex; it was almost noon.

"Hey, is that where we're going?" said Steve, and while it sounded like a question, it wasn't. I looked outside. Way in the distance, surrounded by a tall barbed-wired fence stood a skeletal city of wooden barracks. *It's a movie set, it can't be real,* I thought, *nothing of this can be real,* but the sweltering bus, the children's cries, the pungent smells of dirty diapers and cigarette smoke told me otherwise.

5

1942-1943

The bus slowed as it approached the gate, and I was jerked back by the sudden gear shift made by the driver. Armed sentries waved us through and once inside, we came to a stop next to other buses. The doors swung open as soldiers brandishing rifles barked at us to come down. A black stenciled sign on white cardboard nailed to a barrack's door read "Registration Center." Men, women, and children of all ages snaked from the door, mothers holding infants in their arms, old people with stooped shoulders and backs, children trying to sit on the ground only to jump back up, since the dry, alkaline soil burned.

"Leave your suitcases over there, the latrine is behind the building, hurry up if you have to go," said a soldier without looking at anyone, and soon we joined the line in front of the latrine.

"Soldiers with guns?" I heard Steve utter in disbelief. Or was it sorrow? A deep disappointment in fellow human beings, maybe the kind of pain Jesus felt as he asked his father to forgive his torturers for they knew not what they did? But my brother was no Jesus; if you did him an injustice it was inscribed in reality forever. As a child I took his penknife, and when he asked me if I had seen it I had lied and said no. Upon more persistent questioning by my mother, I finally confessed and took the knife out of my pocket. I told my brother I was sorry, but he didn't talk to me for days, and then even when it seemed he had forgiven me, he would bring it up. So it must be disbelief I detected in my brother's voice, and seeing those rifles pointed at us was a slap in the face that made me realize the truth at a gut level.

After an hour we joined the line in front of the registration barrack, and it moved slowly, because we had to be finger-printed, interrogated, and forced to fill out and sign countless forms. In front of me an old chubby woman in a flowery dress and a white feathered hat propped herself on a wooden cane, and our progress in the line once inside was marked by the *thuck!* the cane made on the barrack's floor whenever she moved forward.

It felt hotter than 90 degrees inside. The electric fans in front of the tables gave only minor relief to our tormentors. Six women and two men sat behind tables, each clerk armed with a typewriter. The air smelled of sweat and cigarette smoke, just like in the bus, but worse. My mother and sisters were farther back in the line; my mother fanned herself with the hand-painted cherry-blossoms-and-bamboo paper fan I gave her for her birthday last year. The insistent tapping of the typewriters, the voices, the crying of children, the *thuck, thuck* of the cane, our being here, exhausted, covered in sweat and sand, when only a few days ago I sat in philosophy classes, made me feel like a character in a Kafka story.

It was almost six in the evening by the time we left the registration center. Each of us picked up what looked like a big burlap bag, which we were told to fill with straw to make mattresses. We trudged across the camp, dragging our bulging suitcases, toward Barrack 60. The sun gave a grim starkness to the rectangular boxes, some still unfinished, their skeletons visible, like huge, alien animals decomposing on the barren soil.

After more than a mile, toward the end of the camp, we found our new home: a black tar-papered shack. Steve climbed the three wooden steps and opened the rickety door. We walked in, drenched in sweat and dust, dropped our suitcases, and looked around. The room had no furniture except for army cots covered with green blankets. It was just a box of uneven pine planks nailed to studs, and the sun broke through cracks in the floor and the walls. Exhausted, we sat on the cots in silence. The windows were open but no breeze came in, only hot, dusty air.

Steve and I left with the burlap bags, and when we returned, each of us carrying three flimsy mattresses on our back, we found a young couple with two little girls who had arrived in our absence, the Hoshimis. We put up a curtain of sheets to separate us from them, and later further divided our side in three parts with screens of cardboard. Steve and I shared one part, my sisters the second, my mother the third.

I went through the days in a daze, and I found that it was better not to feel, to be an automaton and simply go through predetermined mechanical movements. Routine activities previously taken for granted became traumatic. To go to the bathroom we had to walk to a barrack converted into communal latrines one for men, the other for women, where a row of toilet bowls without screens lined one side and a row of sinks the other. At one end were a couple of showers, where once a week we were allowed to wash in cold water. There was also a communal laundry room, where we could take our bundles of dirty clothes and use the washboards.

Yoshiko arrived three days later with her mother and aunt, but I didn't even go see her for two days, and then only out of a feeling of duty. The concern for things and solicitude for others, the care that for Heidegger is our being, had leaked out of me, like water oozing from a punctured canteen left on the desert sand.

Preoccupied with her sick mother, Yoshiko seemed even more distant and cold than I, and it sunk even deeper in my mind that what had been most tender and green within us had been yanked out by "The Relocation Camp at Poston," which is what they called hundreds of flimsy barracks rising like gray scales on the pale skin of the Arizona desert, the home of 18,000 men, women, and children.

After a few days I found out that Poston was actually three separate camps spaced three miles apart. Was it a coincidence or an irony of fate that they built them on the Parker Indian Reservation? A place for the unwanted, distrusted, and despised, in some lost corner of the Arizona desert. What remained of the Mohave, Chemehuevi, Navajo, and Hopi tribes, the once proud people of the sun, ground down by decades of genocidal practices by the conquering settlers—greedy, hungry locusts swarming in their covered wagons—yes, what remained of these people were thrown in an inhospitable patch of land as so much refuse.

And now it was our turn. And so here we were, in a concentration camp for Americans of Japanese descent in a concentration camp for American natives. Every barrack had been divided into four sections called "apartments," bare rooms twenty by twenty-four feet, each shared by two families. Twelve barracks made up a "block," a unit of 250 people with its own mess hall, laundry room, and latrines. And there were other camps, in California, Utah, Idaho, Colorado, Wyoming, and Arkansas.

Three weeks after our arrival, in the late afternoon, we heard a knock on the door. Myoko hurried to open it, and there stood my father, black stubble on his chin, bony frame lost in khaki pants and a dirty white shirt. He must have lost ten pounds. His sunken cheeks exposed the shores of the zygomatic bones; his eyes, magnified into dark pools by the thick lenses of his glasses, revealed nothing.

"Otosan, Otosan!" Myoko yelled out as she greeted our father. We gathered around him as he looked about in silence. As Steve and I bowed in front of him, my mother walked up to him, bowed, and took him by the hand to his cot. He slowly bent his knees, thrusting his left hand down, until he touched the cot and finally dropped his buttocks on the thin, straw-filled mattress. He sat with his shoulders slumped forward and peered from the depths of the dark pools at the cracks and holes in the bare walls, at the sheets that separated us from the Hoshimis, at the cardboard screens, and then he stared at his work boots, white with dust.

Everyone worked in the camp, except for children and the elderly, either in the running of the place or on special projects, such as clearing the Indian land of mesquite trees. The government was supposed to pay us sixteen dollars a month for our labor, but often several months went by before we saw any money. Steve and I joined the brigade assigned to clear the land and our father made adobe bricks. Umeko began working as a secretary for the camp public health department, while Myoko cut hair at the barber shop. My mother helped out at the community center, keeping it clean and posting a weekly schedule of events.

Awakened in the middle of the night by my father's loud snoring, I stared into the darkness. I longed for my room in Los Angeles, for my philosophy books, the desk, the typewriter, the view of the roses and the jacaranda tree. The wind moaned as it forced its way through the thin walls' cracks, a haunting, eerily sustained moan, and then a muffled weeping joined it. It was Myoko.

"It's all right, it's all right, it's all right," Umeko chanted softly as the crying flowed on accompanied by the wind and the snoring.

Three times a day we walked to the mess hall, where more than two hundred people ate in shifts. The food didn't help morale, either. One afternoon, after standing in line for forty minutes outside the mess hall, we sat around one of the long tables as the kitchen helpers brought steaming pots of stew, bread, and butter.

"Not mutton again! Why do they have to serve it all the time?" said Steve.

"How can anyone eat this?" Mr. Hoshimi asked, so loudly that people at other tables turned around. He grabbed the pot by the handles and turning his head away from it, passed it to my father. My father smelled the pieces of gray meat floating in slimy whitish broth and passed it to my mother, who handed it to me. I took a ladleful and passed the pot to Steve.

"You're not going to eat it, are you?" he asked with a surprised look on his face, as he gave the pot to someone else.

"Maybe it's different tonight," I replied. I cut a morsel of meat, put it in my mouth, and began to chew. An overwhelming taste of old animal flesh made me spit out the meat back on the plate.

"Shouldn't even have tried," said Steve as he handed me the dish with the bread.

"The flies seem to like it," I said as I took a handful of bread slices and covered them up with butter. I would have given anything for a bowl of Carmelita's beans and some of her tortillas.

"Why can't we have some rice and vegetables, some fish once in a while?" wondered Myoko as Mr. Hoshimi's moon face darkened.

"Why are they doing this to us? We must let the block manager know that we refuse to be treated like animals; we are human beings. They forced us here, we work, and then they feed us putrid, stinking meat." He got up in anger as he almost spat the words out, and his chair fell on its back on the floor. Suddenly, my father pushed his chair back and stood up.

"I am going to talk to Mr. Hizako, let him tell our guards we are not going to eat this," he said, and walked away with his shoulders back, his chest out. I stopped chewing as I followed my father with my eyes. For the first time, I had seen defiance break through his meekness. As a result of the persisting unrest, management decided to give us bags of seeds and assigned several acres for farming, so my father left the adobe brick-making crew and started farming again. However, the produce was trucked out "for the war effort" and most of our daily fare still consisted of mutton, boiled potatoes, and canned rations.

"You awake?" asked Steve as he lay on his cot.

"How can I sleep with all the snoring around here?" I said as I stretched out on the straw mattress with my hands under my head, gazing at the open window. The balmy air flowed over my skin as a tinge of crimson appeared in the sky. It was going to be another scorching July day. Steve sat on his cot, his arms resting on his knees, a lighted cigarette hanging between the middle and index fingers of his right hand.

A flock of birds flew by in the distance, black against reddish streaks. If only I could have been up there, flying way above this place! Steve stared at me in silence as he scratched his scraggly chin. I waited for him to say something but he just looked at me, so I made a face as if to say, "What?"

"Why the hell are you cutting down trees?" he asked with a perplexed look on his face. "You could've worked in the library, or at the school." He took a drag from the cigarette and I asked him for one. He threw the pack and the lighter on my cot. I lit the Chesterfield and inhaled.

"As some old lady's assistant?"

"It would've been easier than cutting down trees in fucking 120-degree heat, what the hell do you think?" he said as he scratched the mosquito bites on his legs.

"I wouldn't have you to bum cigarettes from in the library," I answered with a grin. He just shook his head. He sat, slouched forward, staring at his feet, comical in red boxer shorts too big for him. I had answered in a flippant way, but his question made me wonder about my decision to join the land-clearing crew.

"And you, why don't you farm? Some people are growing lettuce and tomatoes."

He stared out the window for a while, then turned to look at me.

"I'm not farming in a prison."

I jumped up and slipped my jeans and shirt on. Steve crushed the cigarette butt in the rusty can we used for an ashtray.

"Wish I had some good coffee," he said, then remained quiet. There were times during the day when my brother withdrew into himself in an intense way, as if he were wrestling a powerful opponent and needed the utmost concentration to keep him subdued. I knew that he was thinking about Rosa. It seemed like this was going to be one of those times.

After a breakfast of white bread, jam, and watered-down tea, we hopped in the back of the waiting truck with a bunch of other guys. The Ford, a green 1940 one-ton my brother really liked, took off eagerly, raising a cloud of dust as it bounced up and down the uneven ground, and we had to hold onto the wooden rails not to be thrown off. The sun rose fiercely in the Arizona sky, a god of war. It showed no mercy. Splashes of orange and brilliant gold bled through pale blue. The air, still cool, lapped my face.

The truck stopped three miles south and we jumped out.

A sea of mesquite trees, some more than thirty feet tall, spread out in front of us. Trunks with maroon bark held spreading crowns of crooked branches full of dull green leaves and clusters of yellow flowers. In the beginning the work was hard and repetitive, but cutting down trees relieved the rage that roiled inside me, and after a while I stopped thinking and found peace in the sheer activity. We had been at work for five hours when Yoshi, our supervisor, told us to take a break. We dropped axes and saws and found shade under the taller trees.

"You guys know Takeo Karai, of Barrack 56? He says Japan is winning the war," said Roy, a pimply-faced guy from Indio.

"Japan is winning the war? How does he know that?" I asked.

"He's got a radio—don't ask me how he smuggled it in—anyway, he heard it on a Japanese station."

"On a Japanese station you would expect to hear that," I said.

"It could be true," said a tall, slender guy whom I had never seen before. "You guys are so eager to side with the people that stole our property and threw us in camps. Like dogs, you lick the hand of the master that kicks you."

"What would you have us do? Kill the guards? Escape? Where to?" asked Steve.

"We could resist with dignity. Be skeptical of their propaganda. We're yellow monkeys to them and you still kiss their feet."

"Come on, let's get back to work. One more hour and we're done for the day." It was Yoshi. We walked back to the trees, picked up our axes, and began to deliver blows to the hard, rough bark.

"Who's that guy?" I asked Roy, who worked on the tree next to me.

"Mitsuo Aido, from Barrack 18. He's a Kibei—that's what

we call those guys born in the States who went to Japan for schooling and then came back."

The sun pounded on us as we swung our axes at trees at least twenty feet tall. I had a straw hat on, but an egg could have fried on my skull. The mesquite gave off a sweet smell as the cicadas prayed on and on like chanting monks. As I continued to hack a tree, I began to think about the Kibei and what he had said. He was right about most Caucasian Americans—they thought themselves superior; we were the little "yellow" people who couldn't be trusted.

That night as I lay on my cot unable to sleep, I thought of Mitsuo, the Kibei. He had an oval face crowned by thick black hair, and through large-framed glasses his eyes exuded disappointment and sadness. He looked somewhat like a young Trotsky without the mustache. Later I found out he was from San Diego County. His family farmed celery, and after fifth grade his father sent him to Tokyo to study. He lived there with his uncle and aunt for four years and after graduating from secondary school, returned to San Diego to visit his family. He had planned to return and go to the university there, but now he found himself in Poston.

Japan is winning the war. As the months dragged on I heard it again, mostly from some old-timers who only listened to Japanese stations. Many Issei felt rejected by their adopted country and found a semblance of identity and pride in their country of origin.

Maybe a few even wished Japan would win the war, but according to the reports in newspapers and magazines, America advanced victorious, not Japan. Of course, what we read could have been propaganda, but the Japanese reports could also have been untrue. Whom to believe? Following events and trying to understand them became an important topic of discussion for many of us in the camp as the summer dragged on with a sun burning so bright it turned the sky white. At night it cooled down to 80 to 85 degrees—still uncomfortable, but many of us were used to the heat. Summer lasted until the end of October, when raging storms covered everything inside the barracks with sand.

I stayed out as much as possible, since inside "the apartment" the Hoshimis' little girls seemed to be always jumping around and crying, and everybody's voice attacked my ears like fingernails scraping a chalkboard. One Saturday evening I found myself alone in our barrack. Almost everyone had gone to a block meeting, including my parents and sisters. I sat cross-legged on the floor by the fire as the wind blew and whistled, shaking the thin walls, forcing gusts through the cracks. The coals burned and glowed on the hibachi that Steve had made out of scrap iron. I closed my eyes and emptied my mind, at peace with the whistling wind. After ten or fifteen minutes, I opened my eyes and stared at my brown work boots and the bottom legs of my faded jeans. I wore a denim jacket and a woolen cap but still shivered. I picked up *Being and Time* from the linoleum floor, opened it, and began to read.

The words, in German, had a soothing effect on me. "*Das Sein des Daseins als Sorge. . .*" Fundamentally, the essence of being human is care, solicitude. What does solicitude mean? An anxious, concerned giving of attention to others? It's sad to realize that care is manifested through culture, ideology, and blind emotions, like fear. General John DeWitt and his lackey Karl Bendetsen, President Roosevelt, all the people who threw us in these camps and stole our property, did they act with care? Of course, they would reply, "We care for ourselves, that's why we had to get rid of you; our safety, our national security are at stake, and no, you cannot be included in that 'our' because that is reserved for us." How could I manifest care and solicitude in this camp? They had become ideas unmoored from my life.

Suddenly, the door opened and Steve entered with a gust of wind. He shuffled in and sat on the floor by the fire. The sand pushed its way through the cracks in sibilant moans and the light bulb hanging from the ceiling by a string undulated, casting our shadows dancing across the walls.

Steve's face, a brooding mask scratched by mesquite branches and lack of sleep, took me to an earlier time, a time now lost in the prehistory of childhood. The February rain had turned the desert green and my father had decided to take us to see the wildflowers. I must have been eight years old. Steve kept tickling me as we sat in the back of the Ford and Umeko jabbed us with her elbow. Myoko sat on my mother's lap, trying to stand up and turn around to see what we were up to. My father drove with one hand and with the other pointed to the creosote and sage that covered the desert floor. Ocotillos thrust their green, bony fingers upward, offering red flowers to the sun. As soon as my father stopped the car, Steve and I jumped out and began to chase each other on the hard sand. "Wait for me!" Umeko and Myoko yelled out as they ran after us. We laughed and played until our mother called us. We ran back, and she gave us rice balls covered with sesame seeds as she playfully mussed our hair with her hand. My father, young and handsome, took us to search for beetles under desert dandelions. He showed us the white trumpets of thorn apples, desert lilies, yellow whispering bells, and pepper grass.

"Sometimes part of me wishes that Japan would win the war," I blurted out. "Not because I have any sympathy for Japan's cause—hell, I was born and lived all my life in California—but I wish the racists would be taught a lesson. Those arrogant bastards feeling so superior would be humiliated. Yeah, sometimes to see that, I even wish Japan would win." Steve's blank face changed into a look of interest.

"I'd like to see the expression on their faces," he replied as he sat up straight, a spark in his eyes. "How would they live with such a humiliation, to have been defeated by yellow monkeys? I'd like to see the look on their faces."

"But what would happen to us? We're not considered true Americans, but we aren't Japanese either, even if we look like them. What are we?"

"We're fucked, that's what we are," said Steve softly as he sank back into himself.

"I've got to go see Yoshiko," I said as I got up and left.

In the twilight the wind roared, bursting with sand, stinging my ears as I forced my way through the barracks, my hands in the jacket's pockets and my collar up. Sheltered by a wall, I lit a cigarette, took a deep drag, and as I exhaled I began to calm down. As I walked down the rows of barracks, gritty particles of quartz between my teeth, I welcomed the night.

My aching knuckles banged on the door and Yoshiko let me in. Coals glowed on a hibachi in the middle of the room. A light bulb hanging from a string dimly lit three cots by the walls and a wooden crate. The calendar from the Imperial Valley Drug Company nailed to a wall reminded me of Yoshiko's home in Westmorland, but the suitcases piled up in a corner told a different story. She wore a faded green sweater and an old gray skirt but still looked elegant to me. She hugged me and pressed her warm lips against mine. I tried to find comfort in her arms but couldn't. I was stuffed with straw, not a real human being.

"Where is your mom? Your aunt?" I wondered as I sat on the edge of a cot. The flimsy straw mattress was covered with one of the ubiquitous green army blankets, but by the pillow a white cocker spaniel looked at me with friendly eyes. His long, fluffy ears reached halfway down his legs. So she had brought the stuffed animal I had won for her at the Midwinter Fair last year all the way to Poston.

"My mom's in the camp hospital and Etsuko is visiting her. Her lung problems have gotten worse with the sandstorms," replied Yoshiko as she sat next to me.

"I heard you're teaching at the elementary school. Do you like it?"

"The students test my patience sometimes, but that's good for me," she replied as she picked up a book from a crate that served as a coffee table. She handed it to me and I glanced at the title, *Essays in Zen Buddhism*, by D. T. Suzuki. Yoshiko's eyes lit up as she watched me flip through it.

"Kay Ainara, from Barrack 11, gave me that book yesterday and I haven't been able to put it down. She'll teach me how to meditate. I haven't been so excited since I made the swimming team at Central."

"I hope you find solace in it," I said, as I dropped it down on the crate.

"I thought you'd be interested."

"I'm interested in philosophy, not mysticism."

"But isn't your goal truth?"

"Yes, but the path to truth is through reason."

"The wind blows outside; there's sand on my bed. What do these truths have to do with reason?"

"They can be empirically verified. What would I achieve through meditation? It might make me feel better, but I want knowledge. What does it mean to exist? What the hell are we doing on this planet?"

"Maybe we're just here, that's all." A delicate hand touched my arm as she turned toward me. She gazed into my eyes, and I saw again the reddish-brown mountainsides near the town of Julian, when splits made by the rain expose the deeper flesh of the earth that still nourished the roots naked under the sun. I looked in those eyes and fell into them, and I hugged her tight and kissed her as we sank onto the green Army blanket. The stuffed dog fell to the floor.

~

Two weeks had passed since that night, and I found myself again in the dark, walking outside with Yoshiko on the way to see a movie. I looked up and saw a thick blackness, like the cover of my copy of *Being and Time.* As I walked in silence toward the auditorium, I thought of Yoshiko and it struck me how things had changed. Our fathers had been friends and when our families got together we played hide-and-seek, made poles and fished in the canal, built forts with planks and sticks. In high school classes I sat behind her and teased her long, black hair. We were inseparable. "Here come the twins," people would say when they saw us. Now I was retreating like the ocean at low tide. Even that night, two weeks ago, when we comforted each other wasn't enough to strengthen our bond. Couples fell in love here and married, but for Yoshiko and me, Poston became the acid that dissolved whatever had kept us together.

Yoshiko began to spend more time with Kay, a frail but charming woman in her early thirties who taught English at the camp high school. Yoshiko introduced me to her and her husband, Jimmie, one day outside the post office. Jimmie worked as the camp newspaper editor, a tall, friendly guy who looked very intellectual with his round eyeglasses and gold wire frames. I had a long talk with him, and I could see why he was appointed newspaper editor. He seemed to know a great deal about the politics of the internment. He talked my ears off about the War Relocation Authority having contracted the running of Poston to the Bureau of Indian Affairs. He suspected commercial motives for the choice of the Parker Indian Reservation as the site for the internment of thousands of people who would be forced to work for practically nothing.

The more I thought about what Jimmie told me, the angrier I became. I escaped in fantasizing about being in the *Nautilus* with Captain Nemo. I took the old book with its green cover, read a few pages here and there, and gazed at the pictures, but eventually I found myself at page 359, with the picture of the *Nautilus* being shelled by a man-of-war.

"Chapter XXI, A Hecatomb," read the title. When Professor Pierre Aronnax tried to talk Nemo out of attacking the ship that had been chasing him, the Captain said, "I am the law, and I am the judge! I am the oppressed, and there is the oppressor! Through him I have lost all that I loved, cherished, and venerated—country, wife, children, father, and mother. I saw all perish! All that I hate is there! Say no more!" I read that part over and over. I would picture the bridge, and Nemo behind the pilot, but instead of Aronnax I saw myself there, next to Captain Nemo. "You are right, Captain; allow me the honor of assisting you in any way I can to destroy the oppressors," I would say to him. Yes, to be with Captain Nemo on the *Nautilus*, to roam the oceans of the world and help him to destroy the oppressors of mankind, that was the fantasy that kept me going on many days.

As the weeks passed, I stopped trying to read philosophy. I found the weekly magazines increasingly more entertaining and informative, but maybe because I read them as an outcast, they became open windows toward a surreal landscape.

If you bought war bonds, turned in your scrap, and shared your car, the war would be won. And if you really wanted to help, you'd buy Florsheim shoes, because they are made of the finest leather to last longer, so America would march to victory with the leather you saved. If you couldn't fight, you could keep your eyes and ears open for spies; if you were a woman on a farm, why, you could become a trac-torette, "a woman who wants to help win the battle of the land, to help provide Food for Freedom." The tractorettes, sexy, smiling from behind the steering wheels of tractors, waved at me from the advertisement in *Life* magazine.

According to the news, several Negroes had been murdered in the South in the past few weeks, atrocities overshadowed by stories of a million dead men rotting on the battlefields of southern Russia. Churchill visited Egypt and posed in funny hats for the camera while Marines were killing Japs on the Solomons and Canadians got slaughtered in Europe. If you wanted to escape the war for a while, you could go see the new film *Holiday Inn* with Fred Astaire and Marjorie Reynolds, or you could read John Faulkner's new novel, *Dollar Cotton*. News of apocalyptic world events blended with ads for companies' products that had proven themselves in the war, with reviews of the latest movies and books about the war, so that the war, the economy, and the culture became mirrors of each other.

As I woke up at the cries of the Hoshimis' children or as I walked by the fence, fragments of news and advertisements, distorted images, shards of memories, fears, and regrets would not leave me alone, and I yearned for an escape.

When I lived in El Centro, Saturday evening used to be a special time of the week when I went to the movies or stayed in my room to read. When I went out it was usually with my brother and sisters, and after seeing movies like *The Wizard of Oz*, *Stagecoach*, or *The Grapes of Wrath*, we went to Mel's, settled in a booth, and ordered milk shakes and coffee. We discussed the movie we'd just seen until Mel closed and we had to go home. They began to show movies in the camp, but I hated to go since it reminded me of what now seemed happier times. I wished I could have spent a quiet evening reading, but I couldn't do it in the cramped, communal life in our "apartment."

I had just left the mess hall, where I ate rice, chopped-up fried wieners, and some overcooked broccoli. I actually liked that concoction; it was much better than the mutton or the overcooked macaroni and cheese. As usual, I didn't see my family, so I ate at a table with some guys from the mesquite crew. I missed the family meals we had at home, and I knew that our communal mess hall had upended my mother's world.

My mother, Sachiko Ueno, was born in 1897 in Hakata, a ward of Fukuoka, a harbor city on the island of Kyushu. Hakata had been one of the oldest cities in Japan until it merged with Fukuoka in 1876. Her parents ran a yakitori stall near the Shofuku-ji Temple. She had two older brothers and a sister, and there never was enough money to go around. She managed to go to school for five years; then she had to work cleaning fish by the harbor until just before her eighteenth birthday, when her father arranged for her to be married to a man who had lived on a farm on the outskirts of the city and who had emigrated to America. One morning in early June she woke up early, put on a blue cotton kimono, knelt at the little Buddhist altar, and prayed to the ancestors. Then, after breakfast, her parents and siblings accompanied her to the train station, and as she stepped into one of the wagons with two heavy suitcases, she felt as if she were entering a different world. The locomotive gained speed, and she stood by an open window and watched the people she was closest to get smaller and smaller until they disappeared. She trembled with fear, trepidation, and excitement.

As the steamer she boarded in Nagasaki approached San Francisco, she wondered whether the man who waited for her was true to the photo they had given to her. She had heard that often the photos the men sent of themselves were not accurate representations, but when she saw Dairoku Anami on the dock, dressed in his Sunday best and holding a bouquet of red roses, she wasn't disappointed. He was a little shorter than she expected and his ears stuck out more than they did in the photo, but his timid smile and serious demeanor won her over.

After the quick wedding ceremony on the dock with other couples, including Yoshiko's mother and father, and a long train ride to Dayton, New Mexico, she slowly settled into her new life. She often cried when no one could see her, every-thing was so different; she missed her family, her hometown. But she and Dairoku got along well, and they had two children.

Dairoku worked long hours as a laborer for the Santa Fe Railroad. He heard that there were farming opportunities in the Imperial Valley of Southern California, and as soon as they had saved enough money, they moved. Her life changed drastically again. Yes, they now lived in a house in the coun-try, but what a country it was! Mostly a desert, the few trees dotting the landscape only eucalyptus, cottonwoods, and salt cedars. How she missed the cherry trees she loved so much, especially in spring, when they rained white flowers on her head as she walked to the temple! Whenever she strolled by the canal that brought water to Dairoku's fields, she remem-bered how in Fukuoka, every morning she walked along the Naka River on the way to the harbor and found beauty in the changing countenance of the flowing water. In this desert the summers were almost unbearable. Yes, summers in Fukuoka were hot and humid too, but nothing like those in the Impe-rial Valley. And she had no Hakata Gion Yamakasa Festival to look forward to. She had eagerly awaited the first two weeks of July, each day marked by festivities culminating on July fifteenth, when at dawn, teams of men dressed in white loin-cloths and *happi* coats dragged huge, ornate floats down the streets to the sounds of drums and chants of "Heave-ho! Heave-ho!" Her parents were in an especially good mood then, because the festival was great for their business. But in this dusty desert town, what she could look forward to in July were temperatures of 110 to 120 degrees, when even at night she slept covered in sweat.

Dairoku threw himself into farming; it was as if the powerful yearning to draw from the soil luscious tomatoes, melons, and lettuce had been dormant inside of him all those years he toiled on the railroad, and now erupted. Two more children arrived, and Sachiko was too busy to steep in depression. She cooked rice, made pickled cabbage and grew daikon roots, fried the catfish Dairoku caught in canals or the carp he found in the Salton Sea, and made vegetable tempura and mochi, and at dinner the family gathered at the kitchen table and partook of her ministrations. This sacred time, this intimacy, Poston took away.

While at home my mother ruled over the kitchen as a priestess who through the work of her hands, hands that channeled the customs and traditions of generations, transmuted the offerings of nature into sacramental agents that united the family, at Poston, we often didn't eat together, and sitting at a mess hall with a bunch of strangers and being fed white bread and canned corn, or Spam and wieners on special occasions, she lost her sense of being a mother and wife. The fabric of activities and substances connecting her to the land of her birth, childhood and adolescence, to her family and ancestors, unraveled.

There were nights when she woke up with sand in her mouth, the barrack's walls shaking and wailing as a storm passed through, and she wondered what despicable things she must have done in a previous life to deserve this. Then she remembered the talks she had long ago with the old monk at the temple, who told her that the Buddha said to live is to suffer, but suffering can be overcome. She told herself that since all things are impermanent, even Poston must be transient, one way or another, one day even this suffering would cease.

I was absorbed in these thoughts when I heard someone call me. It was Goro, the older son of the Kotaros, a large family from Holtville, a small town ten miles east of El Centro.

"Hey Mike, you going to the dance?"

"Don't feel like it," I replied with a weak smile as I sneaked away into the darkness. First of all, I didn't know how to dance, and secondly, I couldn't see how anyone could dance here. I enjoyed the cold November weather; it reminded me of Los Angeles, of the evenings when I had the night class in Hegel with Kesselman, before my exile.

"I got a pint of whisky—you wanna help me drink it?" Steve stood in front of me with his hands in his jacket pockets; where the hell did he come from? He scared the crap out of me.

"Yeah, sure," I answered eagerly, and to think that I didn't like to drink even a beer or a glass of wine because I was afraid I couldn't concentrate on my reading. "And where did such bounty come from?" I asked.

"You can get anything you want if you have money: booze, rice, tea, nylons for the ladies, you name it."

We passed rows of barracks as if wading through waves, until Steve pointed toward an abandoned wreck near the fence. Only one side of the barrack still stood. We sat down by it, our backs resting on the wall, and the wooden floor felt slightly warm. Steve took the bottle of Seagram's from his jacket, unscrewed the cap, took a swig, and passed it to me.

"Whisky tides, wash me away," I said, took a swallow, and passed the bottle back as I admired the *Seagram's Five Crown Blended Whisky*'s colorful label. A burning wave rushed down my throat to my stomach and rose to the top of my head. Suddenly, the night seemed welcoming, and I recognized the moon and the stars above the barbed-wire fence as old friends.

"It doesn't look so tall," I said, nodding toward the fence with my head.

"Where would we go?" he wondered as he lit a cigarette. After a few swigs, the edges of things became warmer and the air less sharp.

"What do you miss the most?" I heard myself ask. Steve glanced at me and then stared at the fence.

"I know you can't understand it, but I miss putting seeds

in the ground and watching them grow. I like it all—watering the plants, making sure they have enough fertilizer, getting weeds out, fighting the bugs." I was going to ask him if he missed his car, but I didn't. Steve loved his car, the engine throbbing, flying on the roads by the lettuce fields, the damp air rushing by as Benny Goodman played on the radio. My brother was right; I couldn't understand his love of farming. He made it sound like gardening, but it was nothing of the kind for me, just grueling, backbreaking work. Farming was hard enough, but to do it in the desert, in 110-degree heat, fighting weeds and pests, and then gamble that everything grew well, without a heat wave or frost wiping you out? No thanks, that's not for me.

"And Rosa?" I asked.

"Rosa belongs to a different world—can't you get that into your head?"

"Steve, this won't last forever, and after the war . . ." He looked at me as if I were a stubborn plant that wouldn't grow.

"Do you believe you can turn people off for years and then turn them back on? Life goes on. She's young and beautiful, she'll meet somebody else, get married, and that's what she ought to do. Shit, why should she wait around for me? And for what? You may have lots of school smarts, but when it comes to life, I don't know." He said it matter-of-factly, without animosity. I just sat there smoking the cigarette he'd passed me and staring at the moon. Why did I bring up Rosa so often, when I knew it was a painful subject for Steve? I wished for him to be happy. Maybe my naiveté showed in believing he and Rosa could have escaped the cultural boxes they were in.

"I can't bring myself to believe Poston is the grave where our hopes will be buried," I said.

"What if it's a mass grave, and we're ghosts and just don't know it yet?"

I took the last swig from the bottle and lit another

cigarette. My breath came out in puffs of vapor as the moon shone on the fence and the mesquites. I wanted to put a hand on my brother's arm, squeeze, and tell him, "Steve, we're in it together; let's not forget we have each other. I care about you. Things will be all right." I wanted to, but I just sat there and stared at the moonlight on the fence and the trees.

After the sandstorms of September and October, more and more people began to suffer and die from what they called "desert lung congestion." Winter brought mild weather during the daylight hours, but at night it dropped below freezing, and many people, especially the old and the children, died of pneumonia.

I walked to the mess hall in the late afternoon as a light wind came in. I raised the collar of my jacket and put my hands in my pockets. Captain Nemo, the tractorettes, *Being and Time*, the news about the war—it all swirled around me like dry leaves, sticks, debris caught by a dust devil on the desert floor. Up ahead I saw Mitsuo, the Kibei. I caught up to him, though he walked fast, slightly bent over, his hands in the pockets of his frayed corduroy jacket. "Mitsuo!" I called out and he turned around to look at me, slowing down. "I'm Mike Anami; I'm in the mesquite crew . . ."

"I know who you are," he said, as he kept walking. Now we were side by side.

"I heard you went to school in Tokyo."

"Yeah, I have an aunt and an uncle who live near there; I stayed with them."

"So how was it?"

"Hard at first. Everything was so different, but at the same time I felt at home. It's hard to explain. Why do you ask?"

"I've never really given much thought to Japan until a couple of years ago, but now . . . what does it mean to be

Japanese? I know only a few words of the language; my world is structured through English. I wonder in what kind of a world the Japanese live." A brief look of confusion showed in his eyes, as if caught off guard by the question.

"Well . . ." he said, buying time, thinking. "It's a more cohesive world, full of connections, responsibilities, and duties—that's what I meant really, when I talked about feeling more at home there. I felt as if I fit in and I became more than just myself. I can't explain it, I'm not a philosopher, but I remember riding on a train to Mito, in the Ibaraki Prefecture, looking out the partly open window at the countryside, the green rice fields at dawn covered by a thin layer of fog sparkling with golden light, rolling jade hills, the scents of grass and flowers, the cool wind's fingers moving on my face, the farmhouses and the temples. It gave me a strong sense of beauty, of order, timelessness. That train ride made me love Japan. People here think I'm not loyal to the United States, but that's not true. I was born and grew up in Chula Vista, but there's a lot that's good about Japan. Just because we're at war doesn't mean everything Japanese is evil. People think in simplistic ways."

As we walked toward the mess hall I could see the line outside the door. I noticed a sharp gamey smell; they were serving mutton. I could recognize it anywhere. Mitsuo began to talk again.

"There are still barracks here without windows, medicines are hard to find, often there aren't any. People die every day of pneumonia, TB, dysentery, you name it. I read the government has allocated millions of dollars for the camps, but where's the money? Do you see it being spent here? I'll bet you some people at the War Relocation Authority, or the Bureau of Indian Affairs, or Poston Management are doing very well. It's you Nisei who are running Poston, and you've failed. All you're doing is collaborating with your captors. It's a known fact that management has paid informants in the camp that report any potential troublemakers. Can't you see the suffering, anger, and resentment around you? From what I hear, there's going to be trouble, so you better watch out. Maybe we can talk more another time," he said as he walked away.

As I stood in line, I thought about what Mitsuo said. He was right about conditions at the camp, but what could I do about it? I refused to get involved in the politics of the camp, the constant scheming and infighting among the Issei, Nisei, and Kibei. The Issei were our parents, the immigrants from Japan who came to America in search of a better life. In spite of much discrimination and hardship, and not being allowed to become naturalized citizens, they managed to prosper. They still retained the customs and traditions of their country of origin, which we Nisei mostly rejected. The Kibei, who while born and raised in the US had spent some time in Japan, were more Americanized then the Issei, but less so than the Nisei, so had problems in getting along with everyone. I felt like a laboratory animal forced to live in a confined area with thousands of others under stressful conditions and then have my reactions studied and evaluated as new stressors were injected into the situation. *Let's imprison them in a concentration camp in the desert, force them to live in cramped conditions, and see how they react. Let's make them work and not pay them, let's give them disgusting food and not enough medicine, and see what they do. And then, after having been treated like enemies, let's force them to sign a loyalty pledge and see how they respond.*

What Mitsuo said about the unrest became reality. Two days later a Kibei was beaten almost to death in the middle of the night. At first I feared it might have been Mitsuo; instead it was Isamu, a young man from Camp 3 who was suspected of being a spy for Management. As a result, fifty people were thrown in the camp's jail. In the following days, other people were beaten up and the situation worsened. Out of the fifty, two men were charged with the assault on the Kibei who almost died. Groups of Issei could be seen outside the barracks talking and shouting. "The two men charged with the assault on the Kibei must be released," they demanded. "Strike, we must strike!" they yelled. A crowd gathered in front of the jail, bonfires burned, and Japanese music blared from loudspeakers put up by the Issei.

"We're treated worse than dogs, we're dying for lack of medicines, we work for no pay, are fed rotting food," said my father as he left the barrack to support the demonstrators. Many in the mesquite crew joined the strike, including Steve and me. Why work for nothing? I sat on my cot reading *Being and Time*. My parents were at the community center and my sisters had gone to visit somebody at the hospital. Steve was out taking a walk, and the Hoshimis were gone. Another precious time alone. *According to Heidegger, I am time. Time is not like a river, some external process flowing on. What does this mean for me, for my life?* The creaking door took me away from my thoughts. Steve came in and sat down on the edge of his cot.

"The Army is at the gates with machine guns," he said with a straight face. I put the book down and sat up.

"It's not that funny, Steve," I replied, but even as I spoke, I knew he was telling the truth. Would they really shoot down unarmed men and women trapped behind barbed wire? "Let's go see what the hell's going on," I muttered as I got up and put my jacket on.

Outside, the air smelled of ashes; in the middle of two barracks, flames and smoke rose from a mound of wood planks. Distant-sounding Japanese music provided the surreal soundtrack. Groups of men walked swiftly toward the gate. We followed them in silence. Outside the wooden gate, usually manned by a military policeman who sat inside a small guardhouse, a line of soldiers stood, brandishing rifles. Army jeeps and trucks full of soldiers in combat gear drove back and forth. Acrid smoke, angry shouts, exhaust fumes, threatening voices ordering demonstrators to move back, roaring engines, chanting. Where was my father? Were they going to fire at us? Steve and I stood speechless, fearing the worst, but eventually the dust settled, the Army left, and soon after the fires died down, the Japanese music stopped blaring and the demonstrators went home. In the following days the tension dissipated, and disaster was avoided.

On Thanksgiving Day, after our dinner of leftover mutton stew, as I walked past the white Americans' mess hall, Yoshiko caught up with me.

"Mike, they brought Kay back from the camp hospital yesterday. You want to go see her?" she asked.

"How is she?"

"It doesn't look good." I remembered Yoshiko telling me a while back that Kay came down with pneumonia, but I hadn't heard anything recently about her condition. Maybe I should've asked, should have tried to find out.

"How's Jimmie holding up?"

"He doesn't say much; he's soldiering," she said. It sounded like Jimmie—caring, quiet, stoic. As we walked toward Kay's barrack I turned to look at Yoshiko. She wore a jacket over her green sweater, the gray skirt with wool socks and brown shoes. She walked slightly bent over and suddenly seemed to me frail and lonely. Sparks of tenderness and guilt went off inside me.

"Yoshiko, I don't know what's wrong with me. I feel far away, numb." There was no reply.

As we entered the barrack I saw Kay's and Jimmie's relatives sitting in silence around the bed. We saluted them with slight bows and walked toward Kay. She lay on the bed, her face pale and wasted but still beautiful. Her long black hair shone under the light that blazed through the curtains. When she saw Yoshiko her face lit up and with a hand, she motioned to her to sit on the bedside. Yoshiko moved toward her and squeezed her hand. I moved forward with trepidation, shook Kay's little cold hand, and sat by the window.

"I brought you a flower," said Yoshiko, and Kay took the paper rose and held it on her chest. We sat there, the silence interrupted only by the tick-tock of the alarm clock resting on a cardboard box by the bedside, and the pops of the wood in the stove. The Ainaras were among the few families that were given stoves because of sick family members. Jimmie sat next to his wife, his face blank, his eyes fixed on the window.

"Can you hear the sparrows?" asked Yoshiko. Kay's head turned slowly toward the light shining through the curtain. Her dark eyes seemed to drink in the light, then her breathing changed. She took several deep breaths in rapid succession, then stopped breathing for a while, then took more guttural breaths one after the other.

"Kay? Kay?" Yoshiko stood up and gently shook her closest friend's shoulder. Jimmie got up and bent down over his wife. As Kay's relatives and friends in the back of the room moved closer, I got up and rushed out.

As I walked at a fast pace, the cold air jolting my lungs, I had the impression of standing still, no matter how swiftly I moved my legs. A whisper flew out of the caves and tunnels within me, a soft creature that reached my ears and said, "Dirty Jap! You are not like the rest of us. You don't belong. Look at your eyes. Look at your face. Even your name betrays you. Is Anami an American name? You are guilty, and guilty not just of a crime, but fundamentally, metaphysically, ontologically guilty; your life is stained at the core, hopelessly corrupted by your genes: you are inferior, a bug-eyed Jap, a yellow monkey. Always remember who you are: a dirty Jap." The creature continued, hypnotically, to whisper in my ear; no matter how fast I walked, I could not get away from the barracks. Wasn't that my country's whisper? Kay's murderer?

~

Christmas didn't mean much to us in a religious sense, but every year we'd buy a tree and decorate it. This year the tree was made out of paper and stood in the middle of the table my father had built out of wooden crates. The general store sold Christmas cards and decorations, and I bought the colored paper we used for our tree. I thought of Carmelita. She must have the Nativity scene up in the living room, baby Jesus in the manger, Mary and Joseph around him, the ox looking on. Outside, the shepherds with the sheep, the twinkling stars above. Did she think about me when she set it up? She probably made tamales like she did every Christmas; she would give us a bunch every year. How I wish I could have some now!

Once winter arrived, the hibachi became the point around which the family gathered. My father, smoking a cigarette, sat on his cot as he gazed at the glowing coals. His pale face, made even longer by sunken cheeks and big ears, had become a tombstone. My mother, who sat next to him, said something to him and they began to talk in Japanese. Her deep-set eyes became alive and their conversation filled the room.

I didn't understand much of what they said, even though as a boy I had studied some Japanese. As I sat on the floor next to Steve and watched them, I became aware of how different they were from those of us who were born and raised here. They came from a different world and didn't belong anywhere now; they wouldn't have fit back in Japan and they didn't fit in the United States, but then neither did we Nisei, I guess. I wondered how it was, growing up in Fukuoka Prefecture in the early part of the century. My great-grandfather had been a samurai who fought in the Boshin

War of 1868, according to my father. It had been a hard fall from being a respected samurai warrior attached to the house of a great lord to a *ronin* who wound up trying to squeeze a living out of a miserable patch of soil.

Myoko and Umeko sat cross-legged on a blanket on the floor and played cards.

"After the war I want to open my own beauty parlor," said Myoko as she threw a card down.

"Great," said Umeko, "then you can do my hair." Steve sat next to me bundled up in his jacket and read an old Zane Grey novel. The Hoshimis had gone to some kind of church function, so it was quieter than usual. I got up and went to lie down on my cot. I covered myself with the thin army blanket and closed my eyes. I thought of Natalie and the pen she gave me. I kept it in my leather bag with the two books I had brought with me, and once in a while I held it and admired it. I tried to keep a journal but feared someone might read it. Besides, I didn't want to externalize my thoughts and feelings in the camp. In ink and on paper they would have become more painful. I pictured Natalie in class, taking notes with the Sheaffer I gave her, and fell asleep.

The last few days of the year flew by and 1943 arrived not with champagne and toasts, but with insomnia and the chilly desert night. My mother used to love this time of year; in observance of the New Year she would make two *kadomatsu* out of bamboo and pine branches and place them outside our front door. She believed that the gods came to stay in the pine branches until the fifteenth of January, when we burned them so the gods would be released. She would prepare sweets made with black beans, sweet potato, and candied chestnuts, mochi, tempura, and fried fish.

But in Poston the thought of the New Year opened a door to an uneasy emptiness. What did I have to look forward to? Chopping down more trees, living with my family and the Hoshimis in a cramped box, mutton stews, mutton chops, mutton casseroles, mutton salads, mutton soups? Pneumonia, TB?

And yet, the desert had its beauty, too. Fiery and bright dawns, sunsets steeped in crimson and violet, night skies heavy with stars sinking dangerously close to earth. And the wide-open spaces reflected hopes, longings, and pains like magical mirrors. This beauty in the weeks ahead kept me going day by day, a red long-stemmed rose in the gray barrenness of camp life.

"We all know that our loyalty is in question, they don't trust us; this way we'll prove ourselves. Yes, many of us will die, but that's the price we'll have to pay," someone said.

"Why should we go and fight Germans? We're prisoners in our own country and you want us to join the Army? *Bakatare!*" yelled someone else. Yesterday soldiers came to recruit volunteers for an American Japanese Army regiment. Our block leader had called a meeting to discuss this question, and now gathered in the community center, sitting on wooden chairs around the potbellied stove, we talked, argued, or just listened, like I did. There were about thirty of us in the room, mostly Nisei: the Hidekos, the Hasakis, Jimmie, and some men I didn't know.

"So what the hell do you wanna do? Rot here? We've been here for a year now. People are dropping like flies; my brother is dying of TB. We can prove ourselves in war, we can show those bastards we can die for our country, too!" Roy said. At one time I could only identify him as a pimply-faced guy from Indio. He turned out to be an intelligent, eloquent high school teacher. To join the US Army. I saw myself in a Japanese Army uniform instead, leading thousands of men to slaughter the people who threw us here. But what was the difference? Wasn't death death? I might as well volunteer;

after all, I couldn't stand it anymore in the camp. I had to get out, and Roy was right. Our rotting corpses on the battlefield would have proven our allegiance to our country, and even if we died, our families would benefit.

"You're crazy," said Steve, shaking his head, when I told him I'd enlisted, but my parents and sisters accepted my decision silently.

I sat in the truck sandwiched between Bob Stevens, who drove, and Yoshi Nakamura. Yoshi had asked me if I'd go with him and Mr. Stevens to Yuma to pick up planks of Douglas fir that had arrived from Portland. A new school was being built at Poston, and the planks were for the roof. Eager to get out of camp, I had agreed. We arrived in late afternoon. Driving down Main Street felt like moving into another world; on either side of a wide street, parked Hudsons, Packards, Chrysler Saratogas, and Plymouth convertibles looked sharp in whitewall tires. Well-dressed people walked down the sidewalk colonnades, and signs advertised restaurants, banks, and office supply and general stores, stark reminders that life outside Poston went on as usual. We turned into a side street and stopped at a lumberyard. After loading the planks, Yoshi and I waited in the truck as Mr. Stevens went to get us some coffee, since "No Japs Allowed" signs made it clear we were not wanted.

"Don't take it too badly; I deal with it, too. I'm married to an Indian woman, and many people don't take it too kindly," he told us as he handed us sandwiches and Dixie cups full of steaming coffee. We drove out of town right away, the 1939 Chevrolet truck buffeted by a dusty wind. Almost halfway to the camp, a tire blew. Bob parked the truck on the shoulder and we got out to investigate. The right rear tire was shredded and the spare was flat. Bob placed emergency Miro-

Flare reflectors behind the truck, and then we got back in the cabin to escape the wind and sand.

"Checked that spare last month and it was full of air, god damn it," muttered Bob as he sat back down behind the wheel. He took a Baby Ruth from his shirt pocket and unwrapped it, releasing a fragrance of chocolate and peanuts that raised my spirits. He broke it into three pieces and shared it with us. It was dark now, and while not very cold, gusts periodically shook the truck's doors. Once in a while a car's headlights ignited the rearview mirror and Bob would flash his lights, step out, and wave for help.

Yoshi raised the rim of his newsboy cap higher over his head as if to better face the situation. He sat in the middle, and to get more comfortable he moved his left leg on the other side of the stick shift. He took a recent copy of the camp paper from his jacket's pocket and began to scan the head-lines. Outgoing baggage was to undergo inspections; workers who were recruited to work on the Santa Fe Railroad were to leave for Kansas; two electric motors and fans were stolen from the new garage and service station. Dried fruits were going on sale, the Easter Choir was to rehearse, and the *Washington Post* urged the return of farmers to the West Coast "in order that there might be a 'substantial increase' in food production." In the classified ads, someone was selling a violin and case, a brown zipper billfold was listed as lost, and one hundred women and fifty men were needed to work on a camouflage project. The sports page announced that the Rams trounced the Knights, the Clippers topped the Yaboes, and the Midgets eked out the Dusters.

"If you read the *Poston Chronicle* you get the idea that it's the newspaper of a normal city. There's even a sports page where the exploits of camp teams are listed. We're referred to as 'Postonians,' as if we should be proud to be in Poston," I complained, and Yoshi stopped flipping through the paper.

"It helps folks to carry on if they somehow feel like they're part of a community," he said. "Things are bad enough; many of them, especially the old, give up, get sick and die, or kill themselves. I was born in Takayama, then moved to Kyoto, where I went to secondary school. I learned English and began to read American literature, Poe and Melville, especially. I got the impression belonging to a community didn't play as important a part in America, but it is very important to the Japanese. For you Nisei, who grew up in the States, it may be hard to understand."

"How did you wind up in America?" I asked.

"Reading all those books made me want to come here. I wanted to explore America, I wanted to work and live here, but I had forgotten one thing."

"What?" I wondered.

"That I wasn't white. When I immigrated to Hawaii, even though I knew English, I couldn't get any work except manual labor in sugar plantations, and they treated us like slaves. I saved money and finally made it to California. I began doing odd jobs in Los Angeles, then with a couple of friends went on a road trip across the States. We'd find temporary jobs when we ran out of money, and so I fulfilled my dream of exploring America. But I'll never forget how in many places people stared at us as if we were strange animals they had never seen before. Finally I found a job at a lumberyard in Anaheim, got married, and had three kids."

"What happened to your passion for American literature?"

"It's what keeps me going. When I'm feeling down I pick up a novel, find some good light, and lose myself in another world. Last week I read Raymond Chandler's *Farewell, My Lovely*; this week I'm reading *The Heart Is a Lonely Hunter* by Carson McCullers, and it's a hell of a great story." Yoshi took a sip of water from his canteen and then reached for his pack of cigarettes, but remembering Bob didn't smoke, just gently squeezed the pack as if to make sure it was still there. At the mention of Raymond Chandler, Bob perked up.

"Raymond Chandler—now you're speaking my language," he said. "I can't get enough of that guy. Loved *The Big Sleep*." The rearview mirror lit up and Bob flashed the lights on and off several times, got out and waved after the speeding car, then jumped back in. "Shit, I hope somebody stops soon," he said.

"Bob, you guys did a lousy job building those goddamn barracks we have to try to live in," I said.

"They didn't give us enough time to do it right, Mike. I took wood shop classes in high school, and then began working with my father in his construction business until I became a contractor. Believe me, I know how to build houses, but when I was hired to work on the barracks, they gave us barely any time and not enough materials. Hell, it's a year later and we're still working on it." He scratched the top of his balding head, and then ran his fingers through the remaining blond hair still growing abundantly at the sides. "You guys got a raw deal. There's nothing like fear to inflame prejudice, that's what I think. When Halya and I got married, there was hell to pay. She is a Mohave Indian, and people call me an Indian lover and don't want to have anything to do with me. That's why I accepted the job for the government; it's not easy for me to find work."

We sat in the cramped truck cab, talking and napping, until three in the morning, when a passing trucker finally stopped to help us. He had a tire pump, but once the spare was full and the trucker left, we had to unload most of the planks so we could jack up the truck in order to change the tire. We arrived, sweaty and exhausted at the camp gate, just before dawn. Mr. Hizako, the block manager, waited for us in the humid air, a cigarette hanging from his lips, hands in pockets. He walked up to the driver's window and as Bob rolled it down, he asked what the hell had happened to us.

"A tire blew out on the way and we had a flat spare," replied Bob. Mr. Hizako looked at me.

"Mike, you better run home." Something in the way he said it made me afraid.

"Why?"

"Just go," he said. I jumped out of the cab and hurried home. I strode across the camp, pushing my way against the wind, until I arrived at our barrack. I opened the door and saw Steve lying on his cot, his eyes closed, his face relaxed. My parents stood in front of him in silence as Umeko and Myoko kneeled on the floor, hands on their thighs, heads bent down. Umeko rose and walked up to me.

"They told us Steve got in a fight with a guard and was shot," she said.

I walked up to the cot and lifted the blanket that covered him to his neck. His arms, marble white, lay at his sides, palms facing upward. His chest, muscular and powerful in life, now shrunken and frail, was scarred by a dark, round spot below the left nipple. I dropped the blanket and took a few steps backward, then stumbled out of the barrack and ran in the freezing morning, the sun still hidden behind roofs. Faint patches of red and purple spread behind the barracks. No one was out as I ran, the cold air burning my lungs and white vapor streaming from my mouth. I wanted to become the running, the pounding on the ground, the movement forward; I wanted to be the sharpness of the wind lashing, the coldness of the air scratching, the pale white desert calling. I wanted to be the rising sun.

6

1943-1944

Barracks from World War I: Walls no longer sure of their mission holding up sagging roofs in pale light—if you could call the lard-like stuff oozing from a slab of cement ready to fall and smash them into the ground light. Streets—shallow rivers of mud, pockmarked by steel puddles reflecting tremulous jade pines. Soldiers—shadows in rain, scurrying around seeking shelter. That was Camp Shelby in late April 1943, when I arrived in a rattling bus with other recruits from Poston. It was beginning to warm up in Arizona, but here guys walked around bundled up in Army jackets and gloves.

My stomach complained loudly that it wanted food, my eyes kept closing, and my mind wanted to shut down after countless hours of processing; *yes sir, no sir, right, more forms to fill out, stand in line to get a haircut, stand in line to get clothes and gear,* and this after hours of the same in Phoenix, and the physical examination there. *Yes, Company D, okay, and here I am sitting on the floor in front of a black potbellied stove in a barrack somewhere in Mississippi.* The steady rain falling on the roof is a lullaby interrupted by guys trying to keep warm around the stove.

"I'm George, George Tajima," said a short, wiry recruit next to me. With legs crossed and a blanket wrapped around his shoulders he looked like a monk. "And this handsome guy here is Hideo," he added as he pointed to the cigar-smoking recruit next to him. The handsome guy took the cigar out of his mouth.

"I'm Hideo Nishimura—I came last week from the Minidoka Camp in Idaho," he said. Another recruit bundled up in an Army jacket and a coat sat down and broke into a wide smile.

"Paul Ikehara, but call me Samurai," he offered, as he extended his hand. Rain pounding windows in late afternoon light, faces and voices dream fragments; images and sounds of another world—*Will I wake up soon? But where? In my Los Angeles room in time for the Hegel class? In El Centro? On a bunk at Poston?*

"And I'm Akira Oshima," said a guy who handed me a tin cup full of steaming black liquid.

"Hey, thanks! It's been a while since I had coffee." I took a sip of the strong brew, trying not to burn my tongue.

"It's rationed for civilians, but not here. You're from Poston? I was in Manzanar for more than a year. *Manzanar,* what a strange word—they say it's Spanish for 'apple orchard,' but I swear, there's no apple trees there." He sat down on the warm floor planks next to me and blew into his steaming mug.

"I have a friend who was sent there, Tom Nakama—do you know him?"

"Nakama, the engineer?"

"Well, he was studying to become one."

"That's what we called him because he helped us build the hospital. I talked to him as we waited to go to the recruiting office, then he boarded another bus, must have been assigned to a different company. I'll ask around." The last time I had seen Tom was in front of Mrs. McClurg's house, when I left to go back home. I felt lighter thinking my friend might be here.

Whenever I closed my eyes at night as I tried to sleep, I saw Steve dead on his cot. They said he fought with a guard and was shot with a pistol. Since there were no witnesses there was no way to find out what truly happened, but as far as I was concerned, they murdered my brother.

They wrapped themselves in the flag and uttered words like *national security*, *freedom*, and *democracy* as they called us bug-eyed Japs, stole our property, and threw us in prison camps. It was usually at night, in my bunk, when such thoughts caused my heart to gallop, my muscles to tighten, and I visited Captain Nemo.

In the metal monster, gliding below the surface, I found peace. My cabin consisted of a bunk, a narrow closet, a metal desk, and a couple of shelves. I would lie there and revel in the silence, the stillness interrupted only by a low hum and the fresh air that came from the air duct above. I would get up and walk down the narrow corridor, nod to crew members passing by in the reddish glow of the lights, and once in the library I would admire the mahogany cases full of ancient coins, jewelry, and figurines, marvel at the white stone busts resting on pedestals, then feast my eyes on the books that lined the walls. They were behind what looked like plates of glass, but when I knocked on them they felt like very light material. The glass-like plates could be moved to access the books, and I did so, to pick up a curious greenish pamphlet, *Manifest der Kommunistischen Partei*, and below, in bold black ink, it was signed, "Karl Marx."

"That is one of the most interesting works I have read, Mr. Anami," said Captain Nemo, who was now next to me. "While in Ireland studying astronomy with Lord Rosse I heard that Mr. Marx was in London. I had to go visit him, even though I had sworn never to set foot in that hateful nation. I stayed for a week and we talked every day for hours, taking long walks in Highgate Park and drinking good beer in many a pub. When I left, he gave me that pamphlet."

"What do you think of it?

"I agree with his analysis of capitalism, Mr. Anami, but I doubt that the proletariat will rise and create a classless society—at least not in the near future, but I must confess that for a while I was tempted to join Mr. Marx in his political struggles."

"Why didn't you, Captain?"

"A wave of hatred swept me away into the depths of the sea. But come, let's have a drink." He motioned toward two chairs flanking a small round table, on which lay a crystal decanter full of reddish liquid and two glasses.

"Captain," I said as I sank in the red velvet chair, "there was a time when I believed in the power of reason and thought that ultimately human beings were rational; I agreed with Socrates that men commit evil acts due to ignorance, and if educated, they would choose the good, but I no longer do; human beings are tribal, ruled by fear and hate of the other. I want to join your crew and help your cause."

He handed me a glass and I took a sip of brandy. It was strong and even though it was light it had depth, as did the sea from which it came. Electrical lamps emanated a warm glow making the shelves of books, paintings, and marble busts mysterious, magical; at some unconscious level they were familiar even though I could not identify them and they seemed to be aware of my presence. I closed my eyes and took another sip, telling myself I was drinking ambrosia.

"I want to see their ships sinking, I want the ocean to swallow them."

I heard these words and was surprised at the realization that they came from my mouth. He looked at me in silence, then spoke. "Even though my marriage was arranged, I grew to love my wife and the children we brought into the world— they were my guiding stars. Then they were murdered by the

British—who invaded my country and made it a colony of their empire. When I returned home I could only bury their mangled, bloodied corpses—I swore eternal war against conquerors, colonizers, and arrogant racists who enslaved, oppressed, and exploited others."

"I hope, Captain, to help you sink many of their ships in the future. I am at your service; I would consider it a great honor to be allowed to join your crew."

He raised his glass and clinked mine. "It'll be my pleasure to have you at my side, Mr. Anami. Together we will make them pay dearly for their crimes."

~

We woke up at four thirty in the morning when the Sergeant, Hisao Urada—whom we nicknamed Sarge—barged in the barrack, turned the lights on, and yelled at us to get out of bed. Urada was a twenty-eight-year-old teddy bear with closely cropped hair and a row of white teeth that looked like a piano keyboard. When he smiled, his eyes turned into narrow slits and his cheeks jutted out. No matter how mean he tried to look he never lost his boyish, impish demeanor.

We started the day with push-ups and calisthenics on the field and a run, then we had breakfast, followed by drills and instruction, and so days and weeks passed, and turned into months. Basic training had started in the middle of May, when the cold and the rain gave way to warm, sunny days.

One Sunday afternoon I lay on my bunk with *Being and Time*. I reread the section on "the self," the premise of which is that we blindly accept the attitudes, values, and customs of others, and instead of creating our own self we incorporate the conventional, generic ones.

Were all the other guys who could think of nothing better to do but go play dice or loiter at the PX to pick fights in the fallen condition described by Heidegger? Was I the only one in the barrack who didn't embrace what everyone else was doing? But just because I refused to go out and decided to read instead, did that make me authentic? Not a member of the herd? I didn't think I was somehow superior, but since childhood I'd questioned authority and tradition. That questioning led me to embrace the study of philosophy when my parents expected me to become a farmer. That questioning led me to wonder if God existed when Carmelita would take me to church.

It was warm inside the room but not uncomfortable, and to be alone, what a treat! Birds chirped and dust danced with sunlight as it entered the open window.

"Do you have a light?" I looked up and jumped to my feet, the book falling with a thud on the wooden floor.

"Tom, what the hell, what are you doing here?" I couldn't believe my best friend was in front of me. He punched me in the shoulder and vigorously shook my hand.

"I heard you were in Company D, so I had myself transferred. It wasn't easy, but I really needed to hear some philosophy," he said jokingly. I couldn't find the words to express the joy I felt at seeing Tom after so long.

"You look like you got some muscles," he said, teasing, as he squeezed my arm.

I broke into a smile. "Thanks to all that PT. You've got that same old look as if you knew some secret. How's your family?"

"They're okay, considering." Suddenly the door burst open and in walked George, Hideo, Akira, and Paul, with bottles and boxes.

"Here's the happy couple," said George, and the others laughed. Hideo laid a box on my bunk and I could see rice balls in it.

"I haven't seen rice in a long time! Where did you get it?" I wondered.

"Don't you worry about it," replied Paul. "Never underestimate what the four samurai can do."

"Well, now with Tom, and including Mike, we're the six samurai," said Akira, as he pulled out some plates and chopsticks from another box.

"We're going to have a party," said George. "This reminds me of home. Too bad we couldn't find any sesame seeds for the rice balls, the fish is just broiled catfish, the beer is in short supply, and there's no wasabi, damn it."

"George wouldn't be satisfied unless we also had dancing girls and Hawaiian music!" said Akira, laughing.

"Damn right," replied George, as he handed me a tin cup full of beer. And so we all sat on the bunks and started to devour the rice balls and the catfish.

"Hideo, good job on the chopsticks," said Paul, as he picked a piece of fish with his. I studied mine; it was hard to tell they were handmade.

"Great job, Hideo," I said before sinking my teeth into a rice ball. "Where did you learn to carve wood?"

"In wood shop. My counselor talked me into it—I didn't think I was going to like it, but I found peace in carving decorations in them, in playing around with different varnishes. Of course, these are unfinished." He looked at the chopsticks he was using, decorated with designs that brought to mind the handles of samurai swords, then he turned to Akira and complimented him on the fish. Akira took a swig of beer from his tin cup and smiled.

"I didn't work on a fishing boat for nothing," he said.

"You're a fisherman?" I asked.

"I come from a family of fishermen; we lived on Terminal Island, near San Pedro, had a beautiful boat . . ." His voice trailed off, then he continued. "Tom and I were both at Manzanar but never really talked until that day at the recruiting center, but then we did for hours—isn't that right, Tom?"

"And here we are, having a party in Mississippi," replied Tom. "Hell, it had to be just the state with the name I couldn't spell in school." We laughed, and continued talking, eating, and drinking.

Scott Akers, our platoon leader, at six foot two, towered over us. He was only twenty-five, but his blond hair receded at the sides, so he seemed older. He appeared stern when he looked at us, his green eyes slightly magnified by his glasses seemed like those of a big cat of prey, but when he smiled wrinkles appeared from the sides of his eyes, like chicken feet trying to run away from his face. He was rarely seen without his pipe clenched between his teeth, a pipe of polished dark briar with a long shank, Canadian style. We could tell when he was around even without seeing him, by the lingering aroma of the fine Cavendish blend he smoked. He had just graduated with a degree in English from the University of Portland when he was drafted.

One sunny July morning as we stood, sweating at attention on the field, tired and hungry, ready for lunch, the Lieutenant told us that in the interest of promoting good relations between recruits and the locals, some of us would get the chance to have dinner with a family in Hattiesburg. So the next Saturday afternoon, Akira, Hideo, George, and I, dressed in pressed uniforms, drove to Hattiesburg in a jeep. Akira drove slowly, since the road, unpaved, bore the heavy marks of dried horses' hooves and wagons' wheels. I loosened the tie and felt the back of my shirt stick against the seat; we were all drenched in sweat. It reminded me of the Imperial Valley, so it didn't bother me much, but the other guys started whining.

"Damn, it's hot! Where are we, anyway? Trees, fields, this road from hell," complained Hideo, as he swiped the sweat from his brows.

"Stop complaining," replied Akira. "You think it's going

to get any better when they send us to fight the Nazis? I can't wait to eat some homemade chow."

"Seriously, Akira, are you sure you took the right road? We're not in the eighteen hundreds, so I'm pretty sure there's a paved road—Hattiesburg's not a small country town," replied Hideo.

"Hideo's right," I said. "Look, there's a sign for Hattiesburg ahead—if we turn right we'll be on the paved road." After a few minutes we found the two-lane highway, and as we approached the town I marveled at the buildings. I didn't know what to expect, but not such classical architecture. Main Street, wide and paved, was lined with brick buildings, red, yellow, and white, with signs advertising banks, hardware, furniture, and coffee shops. Cars were parked at the curbs— Plymouths, Dodges, Fords, Chevrolets. I thought of my brother, of how much he loved cars. George, who sat in the back next to Hideo and had said nothing so far, suddenly sat up straight.

"Oh my God, look at her," he said. On the sidewalk, a young woman clutching a handbag under her left arm seemed to glide by. She wore a flowery yellow skirt, a white short- sleeved blouse, black sunglasses, and high-heeled open-toed shoes with ankle straps. Long black hair ran down behind her ears and fell on her shoulders.

"Oh my God, oh my God, oh my God," was the mantra escaping from George's mouth as he stared at the vision.

"Calm down, George," said Hideo, "or you'll have a seizure. Calm down, boy."

She disappeared among the people crowding the sidewalk —young couples, mothers with kids, men and women of all ages. The heat didn't scare those people away. We were supposed to wait at six in front of the post office for James Odell, our host, to show up so we could follow him to his house, which was somewhere in the countryside on the outskirts of the city.

We drove down Main admiring the buildings, on our left one with two classic columns, farther down the Methodist church with its elegant Gothic windows. We stopped in front of the post office, an imposing art deco building with a white stone facade and three large doors. We got out of the jeep and stretched, then climbed up the polished stone steps to the central door. As we walked in, we saw the teller windows were closed. It dawned on us that it was Saturday. We noticed a drinking fountain at one end of the room and rushed there to get some water. Akira started to drink when a voice broke the silence.

"Hey, what are you guys doing? That's for colored only." The man pointed to a drinking fountain at the other end. "Use that one." He was middle-aged, dressed in a white short-sleeved shirt, gray pants, black shoes, and even though it was hot as hell, a tie. His chubby, pink face glistened with sweat. He had just gotten his mail from a box and after he warned us, walked out. We couldn't understand what the guy had told us, but then we noticed the sign next to the fountain that said "Colored." We walked toward the other side and saw another water fountain, bigger and modern, with a sign that said "White." We drank in silence, then went outside to wait for our host.

"What the hell was that, 'colored,' 'white only'?" asked George.

"So he thought we were white?" wondered Akira.

"Maybe they ran out of 'yellow only' drinking fountains," replied Hideo.

After about fifteen minutes, a green 1941 Ford two-door car pulled up and a man in his late thirties got out and climbed up the steps.

"Hello, boys, I'm James Odell, pleased to meet you." He shook our hands firmly as we introduced ourselves. "You been waiting long?"

"Just a few minutes," I replied.

"Good," he said. "You guys must be thirsty. We don't live

too far from here, but it's in the country—just follow me, we'll be at the house in no time." We followed him in the jeep, and soon we were out of the city, driving over a narrow road lined with pines, oaks, and shrubs. It was about six thirty when we pulled up in front of a big bungalow with a sloping roof held up by four brick-and-wood columns. A gable with two windows seemed to look at us, and a chimney jutted out of the roof on the right. As we got out of the jeep, a woman and two kids came out to greet us.

"This is my wife, Aileen," said James, "and these are our two little rascals, Esther and Jerry." We introduced ourselves and then were invited in. My eyes ran over the polished heart-pine floors and the white walls decorated with framed photographs. They seemed like open spaces holding frozen moments of life. Above the reddish brick fireplace hung an ancient shotgun. But what caught my attention was a painting of an Indian woman standing on a patch of grass with a red fox next to her and Irish cliffs in the background.

"Get comfortable, guys—must've been a hard ride in the jeep with the sun blasting over your heads. The bathroom's the last door on the right down the hall."

As we sat down, Aileen brought a tray with tall glasses of lemonade. It was cold, tart, and sweet, but not too sweet, with a slightly flowery taste. I wanted to down it all in one swig but only took a polite sip.

"Are you guys going to fight Hitler?" asked Jerry, as he picked his nose. Nine years old or so, with light brown hair, in shorts and a tee shirt, he stood in front of us, examining our uniforms.

"Now, stop playing with your nose, Jerry," said his mom, "and don't ask such questions." We laughed.

"We're sure going to, as soon as they send us," replied Hideo. James sat on a recliner and lit up a cigarette.

"We're glad you guys are here in Mississippi," he said, and took a drag from the Lucky Strike. "I know some folks don't like you guys being here, but we do. It's a shame what happened to you, the camps and all—there was no call for it, except that it made folks feel safer, I guess; fear brings the worst out of people. Isn't that right, Aileen?"

She sat on the armrest of the chair with her glass of lemonade.

"There's a lot of prejudice here, but there are also fair-minded people who don't hate other folks because of the color of their skin. At the high school, I try to teach them to see prejudice for what it is, a sickness, but I have to be careful." She must have noticed that I kept studying the painting because she said, "I'm not much of an artist I'm afraid, but I took some art classes and that's one of the results."

"Aren't those the famous Irish cliffs in the background? But the woman is American Indian," I wondered.

"That's my grandmother. She was a Choctaw Indian and my grandfather was Irish; they had three boys and a girl, and that girl also married an Irishman."

"And then Aileen married me! I don't know what it is between the Choctaw and the Irish."

"Because of the color of my hair, my grandmother used to call me *chula humma*, which in the Choctaw language means 'red fox.' So the painting represents my grandmother and me, with the land of my grandfather and father in the background. The Choctaw lived in Mississippi long before the Europeans arrived. When I was a child my grandmother used to tell me stories of her people." She brushed aside her long red hair from her eye and got up. "I'd better go check the roast," she said. All this time Esther, who must've been six or seven, stood in front of Akira, looking like a little princess with her reddish-blond hair flowing down her white, frilly dress.

"You have eyes like Mr. Pebbles," she said.

"Mr. Pebbles?" said Akira, surprised.

"Yeah, I'll show you, okay?" she said as she walked into

the kitchen, only to come back a few seconds later holding a big calico cat in her arms. She struggled to put the fat cat on the carpet.

"See? His eyes are just like yours." And indeed, the big cat had such fat cheeks that his eyes looked like narrow slits. We laughed.

"Well, my goodness! I guess you're right! Maybe Mr. Pebbles and I are brothers," Hideo said. She giggled as her father said:

"That's enough, Esther—stop bothering our guests now. Maybe you can go feed Mr. Pebbles, okay?"

"Okay, Daddy," she replied as she walked back into the kitchen with the cat in tow.

"Dinner will be ready in a few minutes; let me refill your glasses and I'll show you the outside," he said as he got up. With our glasses full of cold lemonade we followed James. "Do you know what this is?" he said as he pointed to a huge tree to the left side of the house. "It's a magnolia—look, there are still a few flowers left; usually they're all gone by this time." He pointed to a couple of big white flowers on a branch. "When this tree is in bloom it's a heavenly sight and the flowers are so fragrant they'll make you dizzy. But let's go in the back—I want to show you our victory garden."

We walked by the side of the house and as we passed the kitchen window, the smells of cooking made my mouth water. Aileen waved at us. The backyard had been converted into an impressive vegetable patch. There were tall plants heavy with ripe tomatoes, rows of squash, corn, green beans, peas, and eggplant.

"We love it here. Aileen and I grew up in Starkville, but we met at Mississippi State College. I was in engineering and she in education; we met in a class, fell in love, then I found a job with the city of Hattiesburg and here we are. Aileen began teaching at the high school and then the two rascals arrived. We spend a lot of time in this vegetable garden; we like to stick seeds in the ground and watch them grow into this bounty!" Bees buzzed around, and beyond the planted yard, spruces and oaks extended as far as one could see.

"My parents were farmers; they planted tomatoes, melons, and lettuce. My father would love this, especially the eggplant," I said, admiring the rows of plants.

"Yeah, I love eggplant, too," said Hideo.

"Well hell, let's get some then," said James, as he grabbed some paper bags from a table covered with hoes, pruners, loppers, rakes, trowels, and other stuff. He handed them to us and said, "Here, guys, fill these with tomatoes, corn, green beans, and whatever else you like; I'll fill this one with eggplant."

It must have been almost seven thirty but it was still bright outside, bees lazily buzzing around and mourning doves wandering on the ground, picking seeds. We were busy filling the bags with vegetables when Jerry came to tell us dinner was ready. We left the full bags on the porch by the door, took turns going to the bathroom to wash our hands, then we all sat down at the table. The dining room was full of outdoor light; the wide window overlooking the trees let a warm breeze in, as well as the distant cawing of a crow. On the middle of the white tablecloth, triumphant, rested a platter covered with a big roast surrounded by plates of mashed potatoes, sautéed eggplant, buttered peas, green beans, and sliced tomatoes. James, who sat at the head of the table, took a few slices of roast beef and passed the platter to me.

"Go ahead and eat hearty, guys," he said, "there's plenty more. When Aileen starts cooking, she doesn't stop." We filled our plates with thick slices of beef, mashed potatoes— well drenched with gravy—green beans, and eggplant; at least Hideo, Akira, and I picked the eggplant, while George passed on it. The beef was juicy and tender and with gravy, potatoes, and peas, sublime. Hideo had a worried look as he was passed the mashed potatoes.

"If you're wondering why they look greenish, it's because there's cabbage in them. That's an Irish way of preparing them; it's called colcannon," explained Aileen. Hideo went ahead and took a couple of scoops.

"Well, guys, how's life at Camp Shelby?" asked James as he cut the meat for Esther, who sat next to him.

"We're kept really busy now, sir," said Hideo. "We start the days with PT, then there's drills, marches, instruction periods; usually we just get time off on Sunday."

"Yeah, the weeks go by fast," said Akira. "There are new things to learn every day, and every day we're challenged physically. I like it."

"Have you been given a deployment date?"

"No," replied George, "but we've been told that by the end of the year we should be ready."

As I ate and listened to the conversation I couldn't stop thinking about Aileen's painting, and I decided to ask her about her grandmother before we left. We ate until stuffed, and then Aileen brought out a couple of apple pies, so we each had a slice with coffee, except for the kids, who had milk. James told us about his job as an engineer for the city, then we talked about the latest movies: *The Ox-Bow Incident* with Henry Fonda, *Dixie* with Bing Crosby and Dorothy Lamour, and *Casablanca*, which I hadn't seen yet, and when James said that Humphrey Bogart and Ingrid Bergman were in it, my attention perked up.

"I love Ingrid Bergman," I said. "I can't wait to see it."

He replied that she also starred in *For Whom the Bell Tolls* alongside Gary Cooper. He'd read in *Life* magazine that so far it only played in New York, and that it was supposed to be her first role in a film in color.

I must remember the titles of those movies, I thought. Jerry said that he wanted to listen to *The Busy Mr. Bingle* on the radio.

"Okay, but not too loud," his mother replied, and he ran into the living room with Esther. "Mrs. Odell, you told us earlier your grandmother used to tell you stories about her people; do you remember some of them?" I took a sip of coffee, worried that I might have gone too far, but she put her cup down and began to speak.

"When I was growing up my parents ran a small grocery store, and my grandma, who lived with us, would take me to school and pick me up. As we walked home she would tell me about the time long ago when all of Mississippi was Choctaw land, teeming with villages and farms. The women did most of the farming and the warriors went hunting. The land loved the Choctaw and they loved it in return, and life was good until the Europeans came with their machines and greed, and the people were spat upon, treated worse than dogs, and they had to give up their land or die, so the Choctaw had to leave and take the Trail of Tears, a long trail, covered with the bodies of the dead.

"And as my grandmother spoke I could see the wide, green land full of the villages of the people, crows and eagles flying over the trees, the women harvesting corn, the men hunting bears. And I could see in the evening, when the sun went to sleep and the white moon awoke, the people sitting outside their teepees, smoking pipes, talking and laughing, children playing, the sounds of drums accompanying the distant calls of the coyotes, and I felt happy. But when I saw in my mind the Europeans spit on the people, kick them and steal their land, when I saw them fall on the Trail of Tears, mothers holding their dead babies, warriors now powerless haunted by their stolen pride, the old sitting on rocks and looking at the vultures soon to feast on their flesh, then sadness and anger filled me." She spoke calmly, but her eyes darkened as she took a sip of coffee.

"I didn't mean to upset you by the question," I said as I turned my gaze on the pie crumbs that lay on my plate, at the fork next to the crumbs, and the napkin next to the plate.

"Oh, it's fine," she replied. "I don't mind talking about it. My grandmother was a proud woman who didn't let anything stand in her way. After she married my grandfather, they worked hard and saved until they were able to buy a plot of land and farm it. He died in the influenza pandemic of 1918. I was ten and I still remember my grandmother telling me that he had been taken by the Great Spirit, and if I ever saw a crow nearby, it was him coming to see me. Now whenever I see a crow I feel my grandfather's presence, and I'm happy to see him flying over the trees he loved."

It was dark outside by now. Jerry and Esther had fallen asleep on the sofa in the living room, the radio still on and a lamp casting a warm glow on their faces. It was time to leave. We shook hands with our hosts, thanked them for their hospitality and the wonderful meal, and left.

"Good luck to you all over there," said James.

"We'll pray for you; be safe," added Aileen. We drove off under the waning gibbous moon with our bags full of vegetables in the small cargo area.

"Good people," said George. "I kind of forgot about all the shit and had a good time."

"Yeah. It was weird to be in a home after so long; it reminded me of how life used to be," said Akira, who had traded places with Hideo, who was now at the wheel, a cigar stuck in his mouth. The cool air still carried traces of the long hot day, and whenever the tall pines hid the moon, all we could see was what the two headlight beams revealed.

"Do you remember the directions James gave us?" I asked Hideo, as I lit a cigarette. "Yeah, we follow this road until we come to a crossing, then we turn right and after about fifteen minutes we should see a sign for the camp." I rode in the back now, on the hard little bench seat, and could feel every bump.

An owl, surprised by the headlights, flew from a branch across the road, and I remembered the night I drove to West-morland in my brother's Dodge to see Yoshiko. I felt again the balmy air, heard the butterflies hit the windshield, saw again the owl perched on the post fly off.

"Hey, what's that glow down there?" asked George, pointing down toward the left. In the pale moonlight we could see that the land sloped down toward a meadow, and beyond it in what looked like an oak grove, dim glowing lights seemed to move.

"Yeah, I see it," exclaimed Akira.

"What the hell? Could be witches," said George.

"Let's go down there and take a look," I said.

"Are you crazy? replied George with a fearful look on his face.

"What, are you really afraid of witches?" said Hideo. "Come on, it'll take just a few minutes for us to walk down there. Besides, I got to take a leak!"

He was right—after all the coffee, I had to go too, and so Hideo pulled off the road and turned the engine off, and after we relieved ourselves, we walked down toward the meadow. The air was slightly warmer, and there must have been a stream nearby, as I could hear the clean, cool sound of flowing water. The moon peeked through the clouds, and thankfully illuminated our way.

"Hey, look at those flying lights. What the hell are those?" asked George, as dozens of small, yellowish lights danced over the grass.

"Fireflies," said Akira. "I've never seen them before, but my mother used to tell me about how much she loved to see them, when she lived in Japan. Look, one landed on Hideo's head." We all gathered around Hideo to examine the firefly glowing on top of his hair. Then we heard voices—angry voices, curses and yells—coming from the grove. We walked swiftly to investigate, and deep in the grove, we saw six white men, some armed with shotguns, and a tall black man in torn pants, his hands tied behind his back, struggling against two men who were putting a noose around his head. The thick rope had been swung over the branch of an oak, and two other men held on to it, waiting to raise it up. The black man's muscular chest glistened with sweat in the reddish light, and a look of defiance showed through his swollen and bruised face. When they saw us, they froze, and two of the men raised their shotguns in our direction.

"What the hell you doing here?" one of them asked. "Are you those damn Japs who are supposed to be in the Army?"

"We're on the way to Camp Shelby, saw some lights, came to see what they were," replied Hideo.

"What's going on? What are you guys doing?" asked Akira.

One of the men holding a shotgun pointed at us said, "You better get the hell out of here. This ain't none of your business—go!"

"If you know what's good for you," said another.

Sticks popped in a fire that burned near the tree and sparks and moths danced around it in a frenzy. We stood there unable to move, then the beam of a flashlight hit my eyes and I shielded them with my hand. We backed away, turned around, and put one foot in front of the other. Away from the grove, fireflies still punctuated the night with flashes of yellow-greenish light and the stream continued to flow briskly nearby. We walked toward the car without saying a word.

I stood on the deck platform of the *Nautilus*, trying to scan the horizon with binoculars. As I pumped my feet on the steel platform to keep warm, every exhalation materialized in a cloud of vapor around my heavy jacket, gloves, and knitted cap, so keeping the instrument steady and the lenses clear weren't easy tasks. After about an hour, I spotted what looked like a smoke trail rising from the horizon. After a few minutes I could see it was coming from a ship. I went to the hatch and asked one of the crew members to call the Captain. Nemo appeared a few minutes later, holding his spyglass.

"So you've spotted something of interest, Mr. Anami?"

"Yes sir, you can see the smoke trail, there at eleven o'clock—it looks like a ship steaming west."

"It's a frigate, about five thousand tons, American. Too bad it's not English, then we would have sunk it. I decided some time ago to only sink British ships, unless they threaten the *Nautilus*," said Nemo, still looking through his glass.

"Captain, England's arrogance, imperialism, and belief in the superiority of the white race will be magnified a hundredfold by America in the near future. As Marx wrote in the *Manifesto*, capitalism is a system based on exploitation and profit, and while now England is the ruling empire, it will not be long before America, due to its land mass and resources, will take its place. They will become even worse than the British; justice demands that we also attack American war vessels. When Europeans landed in America they proceeded to exterminate the native peoples and steal their land. They brought hundreds of thousands of Africans to work as slaves. A nation born from such evil beginnings will only bring ruin to the world." Nemo said nothing for a while, then lowered his spyglass and looked into my eyes.

"I must admit my talks with Mr. Marx and my study of the history of America have led me to similar conclusions. Since the slaughter of my family my whole reason for being has been vengeance, hence the reason I have tried to limit my attacks to English war vessels."

"I have read reports of how the Americans—but why call them that? If any people deserve to be called Americans, would they not be the native peoples that have been wiped out by the Europeans?—I have read reports, Captain, of how they hone their shooting skills by killing Indians as they ride their horses, of how they make tobacco pouches out of the breasts of Indian women, after they rape them. My innermost being rebels at these injustices, Captain; millions of human beings spit upon, tortured, exploited, and murdered because of the color of their skin cry out for vengeance."

Nemo stiffened, raised the spyglass to eye level, and searched for the warship.

"Yes, they must pay for their crimes, and tonight a payment becomes due," he said. That day the hours passed slowly, as I awaited our attack in anticipation. The Captain spent some time in the control room, then went into the library. I helped some crew members process the algae and anemones that were used for medical purposes; then, after eating lunch with the crew, I went in my cabin to lie down. I started to think about Nemo's crew. Men and women lost to the world: engineers, workers, poets, artists, philosophers, and scientists, souls singed by the ever-burning fire that went by the name of civilization, sickened by the hate of the other and the stink of greed, like travelers dying of thirst in the desert, they found their way to the healing waters of Captain Nemo. And so a community came into being—more than one hundred strong—a kind of monastic order having abandoned the ant-like existence in the nests called nations, dedicated itself to the struggle against oppressors and to the preservation of whatever ultimately redeems homo sapiens: the quest for knowledge, the love of wisdom, the appreciation of beauty. I understood that vengeance wasn't the only force moving Nemo.

As time passed, and others joined him, he began to discover underneath the thick surface of hate a desire to preserve what he had always valued—the quest for truth, art, and love. I thought about Kanda, Captain Nemo's first officer, a tall African woman even more imposing in the black uniform worn by the crew. She never smiled; her eyes burned with calm determination as she surveyed the deck and gave terse orders. She was a descendent of a royal family from the ancient Kingdom of Kush and in the center of her jacket she wore a gold symbol of the goddess Isis. I wondered about other members of the crew, like Tore, the tall Swede at the helm, who spoke several languages; then I must have fallen asleep, because when I heard a knock on the door and glanced at my watch, it was evening. In the conning tower, Tore, standing between the two huge, round windows, kept the wheel steady, as the Captain stood behind him. Kanda, next to Nemo, pointed at the starboard side; the ship, barely visible, its three masts naked, steamed across the horizon.

"There she is, soon to be no more." Nemo asked Kanda to intercept the ship, and as we picked up speed, my heart began to beat faster and a strange excitement tensed my body. As we approached the starboard side of the frigate, we submerged so that our ram could tear the ship's hull; the *Nautilus*'s engines propelled us at great speed, and the hull vibrated as we braced for impact. Even though I held tight to a steel beam, I almost lost my grip as we rammed the ship. The *Nautilus* shuddered and creaked as we sliced through and kept going.

"We can surface; they won't see us now," said the Captain.

As we surfaced and turned toward the ship, deep, guttural explosions shook the night. Once on the deck platform we could see the frigate on fire, listing to one side. Acrid smoke made me cover my mouth and nose with my jacket sleeve; the piercing screams of the ship's crew filled the darkness.

"My sense of humanity evokes feelings of pity for those men, but they're no doubt certain of their superiority and their God-given right to rule the nations of the world. I need to remind myself of that, to replace regret with satisfaction," said Nemo to the fiery darkness. Deep within myself, I agreed.

~

The rest of the summer passed slowly: training, chiggers torturing us with crazy itching, heat and humidity, the occasional USO dance I never went to, and movies, like *Yankee Doodle Dandy* with James Cagney, *Road to Morocco* with Bing Crosby and Bob Hope, and *The Ghost of Frankenstein* with Lon Chaney. They never showed *Casablanca*. Toward the end of November we finished Unit Training, and after exercises in the field, they told us that sometime in the early months of 1944 we would see combat, at last. Not that I was eager to kill Germans, but I was damn tired of Camp Shelby.

In December, regimental commander Pence finally took us in the field as a unit. It was getting cold, and our thoughts moved toward Christmas and home. But except for many of the Hawaii boys we didn't have a home, so our thoughts moved toward our families still imprisoned in the camps. According to the letters I received from Poston my family and Yoshiko were doing okay, considering the scorching heat that lasted until the end of October, the dust storms, and now the cold nights.

The food situation in the camp had improved, due to the vegetable gardens many of the prisoners started, including my father, who now worked full time raising tomatoes, lettuce, and whatever else the hard soil of Poston allowed. Yoshiko had started teaching English at the high school, which was more to her liking. She still meditated every day and found it a calming, healing practice. Her mother had improved now that some medicines became more available. Everybody eagerly awaited letters from home, and when the Sarge announced mail call, an eerie quiet fell over the barrack. We spent Thanksgiving on maneuvers, eating from cans, but at last for Christmas, back at the camp we had a good dinner. Spring passed in a blur of marches and endless days at the range; it seemed that the training intensified as the time of our deployment approached.

~

Paul, or Samurai, as he liked to be called, eagerly grabbed the bowl of soup Akira handed to him. He shoved a spoonful in his mouth and closed his eyes.

"Ah, the food of the Buddhas, where does it come from?" he asked, and Akira smiled.

"I used to make this in Manzanar. I find whatever vegetables are available, and if possible chicken or some other kind of meat. I traded some plates, knives, and forks for a couple of chickens; you know that woman who works at the bar?" Hideo looked puzzled.

"Plates, knives, and forks? From the mess hall?"

"Yeah, I filled a box with them, gave them to her for two chickens!"

"Well, it was damn worth it," said Samurai.

"What better way to celebrate your birthday?" said George. We were sitting on the floor in the barrack on a warm Sunday afternoon, eager to try Akira's soup. Hideo came in with more bowls and spoons, followed by Tom, who had a case of beer.

"We're going to have us another party now," said Hideo.

The thick soup's steaming goodness filled the place. Birds perched on electrical lines across the street, and their chirping seemed to celebrate Samurai's birthday.

"Samurai, all I know about you is that you're from Hawaii. Tell us about your life there—all I've known is Southern California," said Tom.

"There's not much to say. I was born and grew up in

Kauai, worked in a sugarcane plantation as a steam machine operator, like my father did. That's it."

"But why do you want to be called Samurai, then?" asked Akira before he attacked his soup. Paul put the bowl down on the floor and picked up his beer. He took a long swig, then began to talk.

"My grandfather had been a samurai in the Satsuma Rebellion, and had fought alongside the legendary Saigo Takamori. Before going to bed we'd sit on the porch outside the house and he'd tell me stories about the many battles he'd been in, about the samurai code, and as I gazed at the fiery sky busy with mountains, palm trees, and birds, I could see myself on a horse, galloping across a plain, brandishing a *katana*, one of many warriors protected by black armor and helmets, rushing toward the enemy. Then at Japanese language school a teacher gave me a book on Bushido, and when I read it, images popped in my mind, memories of my life as a samurai warrior long ago." He put the bottle down and began slurping his soup again.

Everyone was quiet for a while, then Hideo raised his bottle and said, "Hell, let's all drink to Samurai on this special day of his life."

We all raised our bottles and drank. As we sat, I looked in the faces of the guys: young, full of life, laughing, eating, and drinking. But any day now we would be on the battlefield, and the thought, like a powerful acid, began to dissolve the materiality of things. How many of us would be alive by the end of the year?

7

1944

I was going to miss *Gaslight*, the new film directed by George Cukor with Ingrid Bergman, and due to my probable death, would never see it. The thought, inconsequential, like a water drop, began to engorge and then spill through the interstices of my mind, weakening its very foundations.

On May 1, 1944, we boarded trains for Hampton Roads, Virginia, and the next day we sailed on a Liberty ship, part of a convoy, on the way to Europe. In the mornings before breakfast we exercised, the usual jumping jacks and push-ups, and then since it was crowded down below—there must have been four hundred GIs squeezed on board—we spent most of our time on deck, sitting around smoking cigarettes and shooting the shit, trying to sleep, or watching dolphins chase each other alongside the ship. Sunny skies, cool breezes, and that ocean smell I loved reminded me of La Jolla Cove and Bird Rock, where Steve and I dove for abalone in the summer. But often the effluvia of grease and oil overwhelmed the scent of the ocean, and squawking loudspeakers silenced the seagulls with information and reminders; they seemed to say to me, *hey, you're on a troop carrier on the way to war, not on a vacation.* I had *Being and Time* in my pack, but it was hard to find a secluded spot where I could read it. At Camp Shelby the Sarge had questioned me about it.

"What the hell are you doing reading a Kraut book?" he wondered, and I replied, "Sarge, before I had to drop out I was studying philosophy—this is a philosophy book!" He picked it up, flipped through the pages, then handed it back. "Hey, far be it for me to be against reading," he said. He asked me to be a translator in the field, but I explained to him that I didn't speak German; I could barely read it.

On the ship, days blended into one another, and we had plenty of time to wonder what we'd face once we arrived. I walked to the stern and stood at the port-side handrail, examining the expanse of ocean, a restless god going nowhere. For Heidegger, time is the horizon for all understanding of being, and as I stared ahead I wondered: *My being here, what does it mean? What purpose does it have? What am I to do?*

All this beauty—waves, dolphins, seagulls, the cool breeze, billowing clouds, the vibrations of the ship as it moves through the water, voices, laughter, the crisp notes of ukuleles—all this is so real; memories, thoughts, hopes, dreams, all this is here on this ship in the Atlantic, and it's taking me to likely oblivion. At the thought of death the horizon shrank, disappeared, it sank like a stone wall below the surface of the waves, down deep into freezing darkness.

"Here he is, wondering why the sky is blue," said Hideo as he approached with the rest of the guys.

"Hell, as soon as he popped out of the womb he looked around and wondered what the meaning of life is," said Tom.

"So what is it? asked Akira.

"I know what the meaning of life is," interjected George just before he lit a cigarette, cupping his hand around the flame to keep the wind from blowing it out. "It's women, Primo beer, and sashimi!" *Ha-ha*, everybody went, *yep, that was George.*

"When I wonder what the meaning of my life is, I have to

think about the future," I said, "and the horizon reminds me of it. When you look out there, at your future, what do you see?"

Hideo gazed in the distance. "I see myself in a technical school learning how to make and repair watches. I see myself working in my shop, coming home in the evening, the smell of a good dinner on the table, the kids coming to greet me, my wife giving me a kiss and asking me how my day was."

"Damn, he sure has it all figured out," said George.

"You know where we're going, right?" Tom asked.

"I can't picture myself dying. I have a powerful feeling I'll get through it, that I'll come home," Hideo said. *Having a strong feeling about something doesn't mean anything. You could still be wrong,* I thought.

"After the war I'll come buy a watch from you, maybe an Elgin like yours," I said. He glanced at his wrist. Hideo had graduated from Broadway High School, in Seattle, where he had been a Boy Scout. He worked at his father's office supplies store, doing odd jobs, keeping the place clean, stocking shelves, and helping customers. On his eighteenth birthday and as a graduation present, his father had given him a Lord Elgin in fourteen-karat gold with seventeen jewels, and since then he had been enamored with watches.

"Mike, if something does happens to me, you keep my watch. I know you'd take good care of it."

"I'd rather come bother you in Seattle and buy one at your shop; then you can invite me to dinner and I can meet your future family."

"I'd really like that," he replied in a soft voice as his eyes, time tunnels, invited me to Seattle, to walk down the street and open the door of his shop as he, behind the counter, sat at a bench, under a lamp, working on a timepiece. He would take his horologist's loupe off and get up with a smile to greet me.

Samurai, his elbows on the rail, his chin resting on his

hands, said, "Why think about the future when you wonder about the meaning of your life? We're here now, it's a sunny day, seagulls are circling above, sea breeze fills our lungs, we're with friends. Can't you find meaning here?" He looked at us and his face was a question mark.

Could I find meaning in this moment? I couldn't. *I'm glad I'm with you guys*, I thought, *but the sun, sky, clouds, breeze, the ocean, they're all imperiled by the lack of a ground*. It was as if they were taunting me, whispering to me, *We're just appearances; there's nothing behind us but death*.

"Hell, when I look out there I see myself on the beach soaking in the sun, two babes dressed in scant bikinis fanning me and feeding me grapes," said George with a grin.

"I see myself on my fishing boat in the late afternoon, coming in with the hold full of tuna. You guys don't know how good that feels!" said Akira.

"I know what would feel better than that, hee-hee!" said George.

"What about you, Samurai, what do you see?" I asked.

"Nothing."

"Come on, Samurai, you can do better than that," said Akira.

"I'm here talking to you guys, that's all. Hell, maybe in a few minutes we'll get hit by a torpedo and become fish food and you ask me about the future? *Bakatare*."

"Yeah, you tell them, Samurai," replied Tom. "There is water and sky, the future is in your head and if a bullet blows it up, there goes the future." Silence, then Hideo began to speak.

"As long as I'm alive, my future exists—my shop, wife, and kids waiting for me when I come home in the evening. I can smell something good cooking, hear music coming from the radio; I can see my children rushing to the door, calling out, 'Daddy, Daddy!'"

Samurai is right, I thought, *why imagine a future whose*

ground could disappear soon? And yet I wanted to project myself forward; something deep inside me screamed to get out, to run toward that field of possibilities waiting on the shore of the future.

~

And so twenty-eight days passed and Mount Vesuvius appeared in view. We stood on starboard in the early morning eying the ancient volcano, more than four thousand feet tall, breathing white smoke. In 79 A.D. it had buried Pompeii and Herculaneum. According to what my high school Latin teacher, Mrs. McCracken, had told us in class, Hercules and Venus often came to pay their respects to the god, but they must not have come of late, for Vesuvius woke up in a rage just a few months before our arrival, spewing lava and ashes on villages and American planes stationed in nearby airfields.

Five miles to the west, Naples looked like a splash of milk on a green blanket. As we approached the harbor littered with sunken ships and bombed-out buildings, war became more than an idea—it looked like an enraged giant had gone on a rampage. We had to navigate through carcasses of vessels partially submerged in the black, oily layer of muck.

On land, bombed-out warehouses and butchered buildings waited for us as our welcoming committee. Once we landed, we found more ruins and barefoot children begging for food. The Sarge put us to work right away, uncrating equipment, de-oiling it, getting it ready. Then we spent several days going on long marches and at ranges practicing marksmanship, until one afternoon the Lieutenant told us that we were going to join the 100th Battalion in Tuscany and get the German Army out of Italy.

~

The 442nd Combat Team was on the move. We rode at night, so we didn't see anything until early morning, when we jumped off trucks in a staging area near the town of Grosseto. We spent a couple of days there to regroup, then moved north, near Gravasanno, in the province of Siena.

The first day of battle: a warm summer day, a clear sky, green hills. Loud, sharp reports of rifle fire, rounds whiz past as we dive for cover. Ears assaulted by angry blasts, heart rate increasing, adrenaline flooding the body, all the senses wide awake, everything more vivid. The first time I aim my M1 at another human being I'm lying down in a golden wheat field, its earthy scent in my nostrils. I see a figure advance slowly, wearing an unmistakable German Army helmet; my heart throbs and my hands start to shake. I'm about to shoot a .30-caliber piece of metal traveling at 2,800 feet per second at another human being, with the goal of ripping into his flesh, smashing his bones, and blotting him out of existence. Even though we trained for a year and it was a question of killing or being killed, the situation appears absurd. I pull the trigger and miss, then other guys open up and get him.

It took me a while to keep my hands from shaking, but I finally managed to do it, or at least to keep the shaking to a minimum. We had trained more than a year for this, and were finally in real combat. There were still moments, after firefights, when I had a strange feeling of unreality. We were dressed specifically for killing each other, and were sent to this place to do it with the best our science and technology had to offer.

Our platoon made camp in a field near a farmhouse. It was a three-story stone structure with stalls for the oxen on ground level, and a stone stairway that led to a terrace and the front door on the second floor. The walls, rusty in color with white and gray patches, held up a slanting roof of faded red tiles. Chickens gathered in front of the stairs as a woman dressed in black descended with a pail. The sun had just gone down and sitting around some oak trees, we ate our rations.

"It's finally cooling down. I sweated like a pig all fucking day!" complained Akira.

"This is nothing; where I grew up it gets up to 120 degrees," I said.

"Hell, you guys are talking about the weather; I'm happy just to be alive," said George.

"You know what I think? If we're careful, with some luck we'll get through this, we'll get back home!" said Hideo.

The Sarge, who had gone to talk to the Lieutenant, approached, holding some chocolate bars.

"Don't ever tell me I don't take care of you guys," he said as he sat down on the grass and handed Samurai the bars. "Share these. There's nothing like chocolate to make things better, my mother used to say." He lit a cigarette and took his helmet off. "Tomorrow we attack enemy positions near Belvedere, about ten kilometers from here. Other companies are moving as well; they'll tell us more when we get closer. Get a good night's sleep—tomorrow will be a busy day." He said it matter-of-factly, leaning back on his outstretched hands, a comforting grin on his teddy-bear face.

We marched for most of the day, and aside from the heat and humidity, it was smooth terrain with gently sloping hills. Solitary farmhouses on hilltops, like white, squat light-houses, overlooked a sea of fields. In late afternoon we approached the town of Belvedere and all hell broke loose. Artillery rounds started biting the ground around us, and the Sarge told us to dig foxholes. Since Akira had already started with his spade, I joined him. It took us three hours to dig a hole about five feet deep and three feet wide, enough for both of us to fit. Luckily, we didn't have to struggle with that many roots and rocks. As long as we remained seated we were well protected. The others were doing the same.

"I could drain this in one gulp," said Akira, as he unscrewed the top of his canteen.

"Better not—we might be stuck here for a while," I replied.

"Yeah, I know," he said as he took a drink and lit a cigarette. We huddled in the hole, and after some time the blasts stopped. The sun had gone down, and it became cooler. A few stars appeared in the sky. We ate biscuits and to pass the time, started to talk.

Reserved and serious, Akira seldom laughed, but when he smiled he made me feel at ease, at peace. He had started to talk more about himself lately, so I decided to see if he would tell me more about his life.

"I bet you can't wait to start fishing again," I said, hoping to get him to open up. He crushed the cigarette stub in the side of the foxhole and after a few seconds looked at me.

"That whole world is gone," he replied. "Fish Harbor, on Terminal Island, between San Pedro and Long Beach, was my world. Tuna boats, canneries, stores, there was even a Shinto shrine where my parents took us every week. Most people lived in cottages leased by the canneries, but we had a small house on a hill, overlooking the harbor. From my bedroom window I could see our boat, a sixty-footer. As a kid, after school, I would go to the Fisherman's Hall to learn kendo. Just before New Year's I loved to walk down the streets and see guys making mochi cakes on sidewalks, in front of their stores. They would put buckets on tall stools and mix sweet rice flour, sugar, and water together, cook it, then pound it with wooden mallets. Watching them make it and smelling the sweet fragrance was even better than eating it."

"All I saw from my bedroom window were the fields we farmed," I said, wondering how it would have been to see fishing boats and the sea instead, to feel the cool breeze instead of hot, humid air.

"My father took me on fishing runs during school vacations. I loved it all—the smell of the ocean, seagulls circling around, catching tuna with bamboo poles, approaching the harbor with the boat heavy with fish, my mother and sister waiting for us at the dock. After high school I began to work full time on the boat, until that Sunday from hell. We had a radio on board and as we sailed home with the hold full, we heard Japan had attacked Pearl Harbor. I didn't understand what it had to do with us, but military policemen waited for us on the dock. They arrested us, and days later threw us in buses and drove us to the Santa Anita racetrack. We used to go there to watch the races, and then found ourselves living there, in a horse stall. You could smell the manure. I can still hear my little sister cry that she wanted to go home. After a month they moved us to Manzanar. Most of the other families were sent to Poston. The government took our boat; our house has been destroyed. Businesses, stores, everything has been either bulldozed or taken over by 'real Americans.' There's nothing to go back to."

My facial muscles contracted and my hands began to shake. "I hate those bastards," I said, "I'd rather kill them instead of Germans!"

"What are we going to do when all this is over?"

"Hell, chances are we won't have to worry about it, Akira." The blasts had stopped, and an eerie silence fell on the bank of trees in front of us. I searched in my pocket for a cigarette with trembling fingers but didn't find one, and Akira had run out too, so I crawled out and went to see if I could find some. The half-moon had come out, and not too far away I found Hideo and Tom sleeping in their foxhole. I asked them if they had any cigarettes to spare, and Tom pushed his helmet back and searched in his jacket. He pulled out a packet of four Chelsea cigarettes and handed it to me. "It's all I got; make it last," he said. As I grabbed the pack, the ground suddenly shook with a loud bang as dirt and pebbles rained on my helmet. I threw myself down as more explosions went off around me. When it was over, I ran back to the foxhole, but could only see a crater. Where the hell did Akira go? I looked around but couldn't spot him.

Then in the dim moonlight, lying on the grass like part of a tree trunk, I saw his mangled body. Tom, Hideo, Samurai, and George were standing by me as the Sarge went to get Akira's dog tags.

Akira's death made real what we had always known: we could die at any moment. But knowing is different from experiencing, and seeing our friend's twisted body lying like a rag doll thrown angrily on the ground brought home not only the reality and finality of death, but the fragility of our bodies and the precariousness of the thoughts, hopes, and dreams that depended on them. We didn't say much about Akira; the void he left in each one of us spoke loud enough. *Maybe before the day is over I'll be lying on the ground lifeless, and the rest of the guys will gather around my body and in some corner of their minds be relieved it wasn't them.*

~

While other companies went to Florence, Pisa, and Leghorn, we fought our way through small, hilly towns from which the enemy controlled vital roads. After Belvedere and Sassetta, we rested for a few days. It was almost the end of June, and the weather was warming up. Swallows flew over the field where we set up our tents.

Lieutenant Akers told us last night we were going to attack the German position at the village of Pastina, so this morning we were on the march. As we approached the hill town they must have spotted us, because a machine gun opened up. Luckily too soon, since we had time to get out of the line of fire. Another machine gun started firing to our right.

I lay down with my face close to the soft soil, and as I looked up I saw clusters of golden grapes. We were in a terraced vineyard. I picked a grape, wiped the dust off, and popped it in my mouth. A burst of sweet liquid hit my palate, and I thought, *hell, if I get killed now I'll go out savoring it.* The sun shone above; a falcon glided up high, indifferent to a bunch of primates killing each other down below. Bees buzzed around and a ladybug landed on my sleeve. The Sarge crawled toward us, huddled next to me, and took a long gulp from his canteen.

"Mike, George, Samurai, go around and silence that bastard; the rest of you, come with me—we need to take care of the other one."

The three of us fell back and crawled carefully toward the left, making sure not to be seen. I looked through my binoculars, up the hill. Behind sandbags, a German fired an MG 42 machine gun. I could see the two bolts of the SS insignia on the side of his helmet. I crawled closer and took aim; my pulse raced, and I kept trying to hold my arm steady by propping my elbow on the ground. I inhaled, then held my breath and pulled the trigger. A loud report, the smell of gunpowder, then the machine gun was silent. I got him. My first kill. The platoon advanced, rifle fire erupted, hand grenades exploded, then everything went quiet, and voices could be heard again. No time to think, only to react.

And that's the way it went, for weeks. Long hours of marching and resting punctuated by the thunder of artillery, thuds of mortar rounds, rifle fire, machine guns, screams of pain.

Other towns on other hills, vineyards, white daisies and red poppies in green fields, swallows crisscrossing evening skies above towns' red roofs. In August we were assigned to the 100th Battalion and on September tenth rode to Piombino to embark on ships bound for Naples.

"I can't believe I'm still alive," said George as he squatted on the ground washing his underwear in his helmet. "Hell, I thought I was a goner a hundred times, especially when we got caught in that mortar attack in Sassetta."

"You find yourself in a picture-perfect mountain village, and the next minute you're in hell," I said.

Our company had set up camp in an olive grove four miles from Naples, and we spent our days washing clothes, cleaning equipment, sleeping, and loafing around. The Sarge and Tom had gone to get our rations, while Samurai and Hideo were tying lines between olive trees so we could dry our clothes. It was a hot day with a breeze, perfect for laundry.

"We're alive, but the war isn't over yet," said Hideo.

"Hideo, Hideo, we're going to France—you know what that means?" said George.

"Let me guess," I said. "Sitting at a table with a mademoiselle outside a café on the Seine, drinking wine and listening to jazz?"

"Hell yes, Mike, hell yes."

"I haven't seen you have much luck with the ladies in Naples," said Hideo. George was silent for a while.

"In Naples, you can see hunger in their eyes. Lipstick and makeup don't hide it, just make it worse. It's sad."

"I'll be damned, he's got a heart after all," said Hideo.

"George is right," I said. "In the city, you see many people on sidewalks dressed in suits and dresses, shined shoes, but if you look closer, you notice shirts are frayed, jackets and skirts faded and worn, shoes have cardboard soles. And if you step out of the center, there are hordes of barefoot children scrounging around, looking for something to steal or a cat to catch and take home to eat for dinner. Women selling their bodies for rations."

"Why the hell don't we do something, then?" wondered Hideo.

"The war's still going on; there's not enough supplies." It was the Sarge, who appeared with Tom, each carrying a box. "Come get lunch, guys," he said as he put the box down and opened it with a knife. We left the wash for later and went to get our C rations, and sat down next to the trees and ate. Mine had a can of beans and bacon, a small box of crackers, some candy, and four Chelsea cigarettes. Tasteless and boring and not enough to satisfy, but at least it was some food, and while eating I thought of all those hungry people not far from here.

"In a couple of weeks we'll board transport ships for France, and remember: the sooner we kick Hitler's ass, the sooner life will get better for those people in Naples," said the Sarge. After finishing lunch I moved to a secluded spot and sat on the grass, my back against a gnarled, Van Gogh olive tree. I took *Twenty Thousand Leagues Under the Sea* out of my pack and flipped through it. Maybe it could distract me from the faces and the eyes of the women, some almost children, standing against ruins, resigned to do anything to remain alive. I found solace just by looking at its green cover, with the black imprint of a sailing ship and the words "The Winston Bookshelf" around it. The volume had frayed corners, but it was still in good shape; just holding it made me feel better. I wondered what Captain Nemo was up to.

While on certain occasions Captain Nemo dined alone or with top officers in his dining room, he usually took his meals in the galley with the crew. We had eaten with the second shift and the Captain had invited me into the library to talk. Even though the salon, with its windows, artworks, and fountain, was a marvel, I liked the library best. Nemo told me that at one time he had 12,000 volumes. Then, due to the weight, he decided to move most of them onto his base, but at least two thousand books still lined the walls, and with the busts and artifacts in the display cases, it felt like heaven to me. He poured us each a glass of brandy. We sank into the velvet chairs and talked about the formative experiences of our youth.

"Captain, in a display case I noticed a small bronze statuette of Dancing Shiva. Do you subscribe to the Hindu religion?" I asked, after taking a sip of the ambrosia.

"That small sculpture was one of my grandmother's most precious possessions, and when I moved to Europe for my studies she gave it to me. It has sentimental value, but I'm not religious. Yes, if the image is read metaphorically, it can have spiritual value, but I remember as a child seeing how untouchables were treated, and can still feel the deep sense of injustice that surged in me. That was my first reaction to what I later learned was the caste system, which was rationalized by my religion. We must transcend the ego and realize that we are all Atman and ultimately Brahman, yet a profound inequality pervades all of society. What a farce! Even though just a child, I vowed then that I would have nothing to do with religion, yet I hold that object dear to my heart, because it belonged to my dear *nani*.

"When I find myself in a melancholy mood, I don't read the Vedas, I read Plato and Schopenhauer, go to the salon and find healing by basking in the wonder and beauty of art. Or I play the organ. But what about you: are you religious, Mr. Anami?" he inquired as he poured more brandy in our goblets.

"Thank you. I must say that I've grown fond of this liquor. It brightens my mood without causing any negative effects." I thought about the question for a moment; then, just as I was about to answer, there was a knock on the door. It was an ensign, who alerted the Captain of a fast-approaching ship. We rushed to the bridge, where Kanda, who stood behind the helmsman, turned to Nemo.

"English Albacore-class gunboat at two o'clock, Captain, steaming at seven knots, approximate distance, three miles." Nemo studied the ship for a minute with his monocular, then looked at her.

"Excellent. It won't be a long chase, but in daylight we must minimize the chance of detection, dive to thirty feet, and when we're at striking distance, go to ramming depth."

"Yes, Captain," replied Kanda, who began giving orders to the helmsman and the attack control officer. Tore, the tall Swede at the helm, turned the brass-and-mahogany wheel and glanced at the depth gauge. To his sides were the hydroplane valves and the wheels for flooding and blowing. In a few minutes, we reached attack distance.

"Go to ram depth, full speed ahead, prepare for impact," ordered Kanda. We soon sliced through the ship's hull in a booming blast of disparate sounds: smashing, scraping, screeching, but it felt different from previous attacks. Even though I held firmly to a bulkhead, the sudden impact slammed me onto the floor.

"Are you all right, Mr. Anami?" asked Nemo as he rushed toward me.

"Should have held tighter, Captain," I said as I got up when suddenly, the lights went out.

"Emergency lights," ordered Kanda in a steady voice. I heard someone pull a switch, and a dim red light came on as we started to list toward the bow. Behind and above us, a dull explosion marked the dying of the warship.

"I can no longer control our depth—we're sinking," said Tore.

"Are emergency ballast controls operational?"

"Negative."

"Steer toward shore; turn planes so we'll sink in shallower water."

"Yes, Captain." After a few minutes there was a dull

impact, then a scraping noise from below as the submarine came to rest on the sea bottom.

"Our depth?"

"One hundred and ten feet, Captain."

"Optimal. Manage the situation and formulate a solution."

"Yes, Captain," said Kanda as she left to assess the damage. In the dim red light, with her upturned eyes, Nubian nose, high cheekbones, and full lips, she looked like the bronze statue of a goddess. Her long raven hair flowed down on either side of her breasts, and the golden medallion of Isis glowed in the center of her jacket.

Luckily we were in warm, clear water, and even at that depth, through the two large round windows, dim light still reached us. We rested on a sandy reef, with a bank of seaweed undulating lazily to our left.

"Not much we can do on the bridge," said Nemo as he turned and climbed down the ladder. "Let's make sure no one has been hurt."

We passed the galley and the crew's quarters and whenever we encountered crew members, Nemo would ask, "Are you all right? Is anyone hurt?" Everyone appeared to be fine, except for cuts and bruises. Just before reaching the engine compartment, we met Kanda and the engineers.

"The impact severed control cables and their relay switches, Captain," said the chief engineer.

"Solution?"

"We need to reconnect cables and replace switch arrays; it will take a few hours. We also need to go outside and inspect the hull for damage."

"Very well, let's get to work."

"Captain," said Kanda, "there is a bed of Hermes kelp nearby. While the repairs and external inspection are being made, a team can go harvest some; we're running low."

"Very well, let's stock up since we're here." Then he turned toward me and said, "Mr. Anami, this would be a great opportunity for you to go out for a walk on the bottom of the sea. What do you say?" I must have taken a step back in surprise.

"It's always been my dream to do this," I managed to say.

While Nemo and Kanda remained on board to supervise repairs, I went to the dive compartment with four others to suit up for the excursion. A crew member handed me warm clothes to wear, then he helped me suit up and a diving helmet was attached to the metal collar. The breathing apparatus was secured to my back with straps that locked on my chest, and I was guided to the underwater airlock chamber—before I knew it, I was outside. The weighted boots kept me on the sea bottom, and after a few minutes of rapid breathing I calmed down and began to take deep, slow breaths. Two men went to examine the external skin of the *Nautilus*, while two others walked next to me and pointed to an undulating field of purple kelp to our left. One of Nemo's crew members, a chemist, had discovered this kelp had medicinal properties, and after distilling the healing substance into a powder, Nemo distributed it to the natives of many islands. In the distance, a manta ray glided slowly over the sand bank; with its two horns, flapping wings and tail, in the twilight, it truly looked like a devil. The heavy wool undergarments and the thick rubber suit protected me from the cold, and as I followed the two crew members, my attention was aimed at walking steadily since I still found it difficult to keep my balance. Once at the kelp bed I was handed a net and a pair of clippers, and as my companions began to cut the long purple strands and store them in their nets, so did I. When I'd filled my net I noticed a huge flat rock nearby, and as my companions were now some distance away, I walked toward it and sat down. I rested with my arms extended behind me, my palms on the smooth stone, and looked up. Hard to believe that more than a hundred feet of water weighed on me. The light, dim as it is at dusk, made visibility difficult, but as I gazed upward I saw faint sun rays come down like they do from dark cloudy skies at times. I could hear the sound of my breathing and the bubbles of CO_2 rushing from the diving apparatus.

I remembered Nemo's words, that underwater the rule of nations ends and one can find independence and freedom in the sea's bosom. The words rang true, and I felt free and at peace. Then I thought about the men who were dying this very moment not far from here, all those men on that ship that we rammed. Disturbing, yes, but they manned a military vessel sent by an imperialist nation to wreak havoc and misery on other human beings. The men on that ship were not innocents, but willing participants in the defense of a hateful, racist and imperialistic world order.

A school of mullets glided overhead, like a passing cloud, as the weak light seemed to ignite the water's sparkling salts. When naked apes became aware of their existence, when they raised their eyes to the sky and began to wonder, the human story began. They had to have answers, and so they weaved myths and religions, spun arts and sciences, but could not transcend their primate heritage—territoriality, the impulse to fight and dominate, hence slavery, imperialism, racism, and war.

The more I thought of such things the more I admired Captain Nemo, that Nietzschean monk who abandoned the vicissitudes of the world to lead his restless monastery in a watery desert. I closed my eyelids and rested in the darkness, lulled by the mechanical swoosh of the bubbles released by the breathing apparatus. And then I began to think of time.

We are the clock, Heidegger says; we are not in a now that is simply one of a succession of countless discrete instances, we create this moment brought forth by the past and pulled forward by our future. The future: why the hell even think about it? Sometimes I wish I were a dog, living in an eternal present, oblivious to time.

Unfortunately, I'm a human being, so the clock is ticking, but for how long?

The sea floor sloped downward in front of me, and the darker blue water intimated depth and the unknown. What was that? I could have sworn I had seen some moving things undulating in the dark. I got up and walked closer to get a better look. Probably a school of fish or manta rays. They moved fast, maybe thirty of them, and then an icy lightning bolt ran through me—they were men. Men without diving gear, wearing only sailor's clothes—pants, shirts, jackets— they swam swiftly toward me, their expressionless faces white like the bellies of dead fish. I turned around and tried to run back toward the *Nautilus*, but could only walk clumsily, and the brass tips of my heavy boots digging into the ocean's floor raised a cloud of sand. My rapid inhalations taxed the breathing apparatus as it struggled to meet the panicked demand of my lungs, and a crazy stream of CO_2 rushed from the external valve, so that I quickly found myself in a fog of sand and bubbles, and then two of the men grabbed me and as I struggled, blinded by terror, guttural sounds filling the diving helmet, they dragged me deeper and deeper, toward the darkness.

8

———

1944

"Incoming, Mike, Mike!" Samurai yells out as we run through firs and pines. Huge trunks rise up from the underbrush and disappear into low-hanging fog. Branches covered with pine needles jut out from creeping clouds as shrieking artillery shells bite into the earth and spit out dirt, rocks, and pieces of men. We're trying to take the hills around Bruyères, deep in the Vosges Mountains. A vital road passes through the town, and the Germans control it from these damn hills.

"Let's go!" I scream to Tom and Samurai, who had hit the ground as soon as the barrage started. Mist drops in white veils hiding the outlines of hills and trees, the driving rain makes everything shadowy and blurry, washes away my body too; I'm only the tank's roar and bursts of machine guns.

"Come on, we're close now!" yells Samurai. Deep scents of pine and cordite enter my nostrils and move upward, penetrating my brain. We dash across a clearing and crouch behind an oak. "Tom, keep them busy from here; see the ridge up the hill? Mike and I'll take out the tank from there." As Tom begins to squeeze a few rounds at a time from his rifle, Samurai and I run behind the firs, to the right of the hillside. We start to crawl up, but I slide down reddish, gooey slime. "There, look." Samurai points toward the left. "Let's hold onto those clumps of grass and shrubs." I begin to climb, awkwardly, trying to keep the long barrel of the Browning automatic rifle from dragging in the mud. Try to see through the rain, try not to slide back down; the BAR's sling scrapes my shoulder, but I feel no pain; I'm not real, I don't have a body. The tank's roar increases as we reach the top. The tracks' mechanical creaking, so eerie as it comes from the fog, sends a chill through me.

"Six of them behind the tank," whispers Samurai as he crouches down next to a pine tree, balancing the bazooka on his right shoulder.

I grab a rocket from his pack, load it, and move out of the blast area. For a few seconds everything is still. I only hear the tank's approaching and the rain falling on the leaves, then the bazooka's blast passes through me.

"You missed—they've seen us now!" I let out, wiping the rain from my face with my jacket sleeve.

"Reload, reload!" he shouts. The tank stops; the turret begins to rotate toward us. I slide another rocket in and pat him on the helmet. After a few seconds another hot blast rattles me. As the tank, hit, comes to a grinding halt, Samurai throws down the bazooka and unshoulders his M1. Some of the soldiers are still alive. We run down, blasting away as we seek cover behind trees. There are three of them left, and now they crumple to the ground, blood spurting from olive-green uniforms.

"Damn," says Tom, running toward us. His eyes shine as he slaps me on the back. Our men have silenced the machine guns and are approaching. It's midday, but the light is dim, choked by dark clouds, fog, and thick rain.

"Great job!" the Sarge exclaims as he approaches. "Maybe we'll take this fucking hill before sundown." He lights a cigarette and looks at the burning tank. I glance toward the bodies on the ground, things now. Steam escapes from wounds as rain mixes with blood and runs down uniforms on mud and grass. Next to one of the bodies a crow writhes in dark red mud, struggling to take flight.

*Dense black smoke rises angrily, impervious to the rain as the fumes
of gasoline and burning rubber constrict my throat.*

*My legs feel unsteady, rubbery. I sit on a rock and close my eyes.
I've seen this before but still can't get used to it, fight it, keep it
down, avoid thinking about it. Make it empty, void. I must find that
crack between life and death, that space where motion surrenders to
stillness. Drops of water hit my face, but I feel nothing.*

~

October 26, 1944. In a few days it will be my mother's birthday. My being alive would've been the greatest gift I could
have given her, but the odds were not good. The Vosges
Mountains, steep, thick with underbrush and pine trees,
soaked in rain and fog, turned into a thrilling, dreamy hell.
The Germans, entrenched in defensive positions, had stopped
our advance up the Rhône Valley, making us pay for every
inch of ground with blood and flesh. For days (or was it
weeks, or months?) we fought, and many died in rain and
sludge in order to take the little town of Bruyères and the
village of Biffontaine.

The Waffen-SS troops fought fiercely, grinding down our
regiment. Our squad, made up mostly of guys from Hawaii
and California, had been lucky; we lost only three men, Tadao
Tamaka, Mark Ihara, and Jack Umeda. Even though I didn't
know them well, I felt their absence as I felt the icy air that
made every breath visible.

This morning we pitched camp in a clearing, near a
stream. Biffontaine was below us, to the east. Even trees,
ferns, and bushes seemed to rest now that the rain had
stopped. After putting up our pup tents, we huddled around
a fire and rested. Some guys slept, others mended their socks
or smoked. The Sarge had gone to talk to Lieutenant Akers. I
took my poncho and put it over the ground next to a spruce
that reminded me of a giant Christmas tree and sat down

with my back against the trunk. I felt the dampness through my jacket, so I put a rucksack behind me.

"Is the coffee ready yet?" I wondered out loud.

"What's your rush? The longer it boils, the better it'll kick your ass," said George as he cut his toenails with the pearl-handled knife he had taken from a dead German. Samurai lay on a poncho by the fire, his head propped up against an ammo box, lost in *Life* magazine. A pungent smell of smoke brought me out of my head; it was the cigar Hideo had just lit up.

"We're freezing our asses off on these damn mountains and Paris is only 250 miles east of here," said Hideo as he tried to get comfortable near the fire. At the sound of "Paris," George perked up.

"Oh, man! Think about the girls there—I'm getting hard just thinking about it," he said. Hideo laughed.

"George, you don't have to think about it; just hearing the word *Paris* gives you a hard-on," he said. I got up and went to get some coffee.

"You want a cup of joe?" I asked Hideo as I passed by him.

"And a slice of apple pie, please," he replied as he turned to acknowledge me.

"Coming up, and à la mode," I said as I filled two tin mugs with the black liquid, handed one to Hideo, and walked back to my tree. I took a sip, careful not to burn my mouth. Crows landed on the top branches of pines, cawing and preening. I closed my eyes and took more sips of coffee. It was strong, but strangely not bitter, as I expected it to be. I enjoyed the warm vapor rising from the mug, the sun's weak rays, the gold and orange canopies of beech trees, the crisp air, the soothing music of the rushing stream a few yards away. When I finished the coffee, I grabbed the BAR leaning against the tree and began to take it apart. Dried mud covered the barrel and stock. The Browning automatic rifle had been

Mark Ihara's weapon. I picked it up when he got disembow-eled by a mortar blast in Biffontane, and the Sarge let me keep it. Nobody else wanted it because it was forty-eight inches long and weighed twenty pounds. It was a .30-caliber machine gun and very accurate.

As I began to clean it, I thought of home. What a strange word! Could anyone really go home now? Home was the warm living room on Thanksgiving Day when you sat on the sofa and drank a beer as your mother and sisters cooked in the kitchen, your father listened to the game on the radio, and your brother sat next to you talking about cars, and the smell of turkey was all around.

I sat there oiling the BAR as the guys' words and laughter receded in the mist descending from pines and firs, and the melancholy calls of the crows took me back to it again. Steve lying in the casket, dressed in his Sunday suit. His face white, wax-like, his mustache so black. The small chapel full of people, the Buddhist priest in his robes chanting in Japanese, my parents sitting behind and to the right of the casket. The smell of incense heavy in the air, the crying of my sisters subdued but flowing, like the water in the creek behind me. My parents sat, dressed in black, with impassive faces, showing no emotion. My parents did not shed a tear in the presence of others, but I saw again their stony faces, back in the barrack, as they sat by the hibachi, and the way the glowing coals turned their eyes into pools of lava. But that was long ago.

The 442nd landed in Marseille in late September and by truck they took us to northeastern France, where the fighting was heaviest, and now, a month later, I was still alive. A crow swooped across camp and perched on top of a dead pine. As I looked up, I saw the Sarge approach with that harried look he had when there was something important to tell us. "We got orders to move out tomorrow morning," he said. The men groaned. It was going to start all over again.

~

We'd been marching in single file since four in the morning, holding onto each other's packs in pitch darkness. We climbed over narrow ridges and made our way through thick underbrush. The rain fell steadily on pines and ferns, on our helmets and ponchos. I loved to walk around Balboa Park in San Diego when it rained, but I hated to be cold and wet, marching for hours under it to kill and be killed.

Never before the war had I realized how much I wanted to live. The knowledge that at any time I could have been snuffed out of existence filled me with dread, as it had since the first day of combat. Just to sleep on a bed, read, take a shit in a bathroom, to be dry, would have made life luxurious. And yet, even If I could have, I wouldn't have gone back to the relocation camp. What a ridiculous word: *relocation*. Better to die here in the mountains with a weapon in my hands. We marched uphill and downhill, in mud and freezing water. The sun had risen, and a pale light oozed from the fog creeping on treetops. At least we didn't have to hold onto each other anymore. Samurai marched in front of me, bazooka on a sling, M1 in his hands. Just his being near me made me less fearful, calmer.

"How can you be so damn relaxed?" I asked him. A long silence followed, and I thought he didn't want to talk, but then he said, "Back home I used to surf, and on a perfect March day, while riding a monster wave I wiped out and lost the board. I couldn't swim back to shore, a rip current kept dragging me out—I tried all the tricks but the ocean wanted me. I couldn't keep my head above water. I finally let go, resigned myself to death. As I started to sink down—several feet below the surface—indescribable happiness filled me, a peace beyond words. Then someone pulled me up—a friend who had seen me struggling. If to die is like that, it's okay."

Before I could say anything I heard a loud thud to our

right, then another. Hideo, behind me, turned and fired toward the trees. We scattered and moved closer to the area where the sound came from, but saw no one.

"Where are they?" asked the Sarge.

"Up there," said Hideo as he crouched behind the reddish bark of a tree. He'd barely let the words out when a pine cone fell on his helmet. He jumped up and aimed his rifle at the branches.

"What do you want to do, kill the damn tree? You heard pine cones falling on the ground, damn it. Let's go," said the Sarge. We began marching again.

I snapped a twig from a branch and smelled the pine needles; the fresh and deep scent made me think of the Laguna Mountains and the times Steve and I went up there to camp, then a rumbling and crashing filled my ears and the treetops shattered in thousands of jagged projectiles. I fell to the ground and buried my face in the wet grass as I heard screams of pain. The explosions finally passed by us, angry footsteps of a giant that made the earth tremble and my insides shake. The enemy kept pounding us with artillery and we didn't have anywhere to hide. As the Lieutenant called on the radio for artillery support, Tom and Samurai ran toward me.

"Mike, there are two guys back there who look like porcupines. I never would've thought trees could kill!" said Tom. We were almost at the hillside when the treetops exploded again. We dropped to the ground, trying to seek cover.

"God damn it, isn't that our artillery?" the Lieutenant yelled. "Give me the fucking radio!" He took the unlit pipe out of his mouth as someone handed him the walkie-talkie. "They can't pinpoint positions in these hills and mountains," he finally said.

The ground shook and vibrated like a giant animal going into spasms. A faraway voice told us to dig in. It was the Sarge. I got up, took my spade, and started to dig a hole, as the earth continued to shudder, as screams filled the air, as smoke and soil, rocks and pieces of trees rained all over. I dug an indentation in the hillside, big enough for me to fit in, sideways. At least I had some cover, even if the rain drenched me. Thuds and whines, crashing and shattering filled my ears; the smell of gunpowder and soil, my nose; my insides shook as the hill shuddered under the pummeling. Then the rain stopped and a rainbow appeared over the mountain peaks. I glanced at my watch: 1530. *What's that?* A rumbling coming from the hill.

"A tank!" someone shouted. The Sarge, short and stocky, looked like a bulldog running toward us.

"They're advancing; a tank is leading the attack. Company K to our left flank has been cut to pieces—let's stop that tank! Samurai, get your bazooka and move out; George and Mike, go with him."

Rifle fire broke out as the Germans moved closer. We climbed up the hill, seeking cover behind trees, and inched closer to the tank as exploding shells fell around us and machine gun rounds ripped into the underbrush and the trees.

"There!" I shouted as I hid behind a fir. The tank advanced in a southeasterly direction, with several Germans behind it. Samurai and George worked their way toward the tank. I lost sight of them for a few seconds, then I saw them crouched beside a fir. Samurai fired and the tank disappeared in a cloud of fire and smoke.

"Watch out!" I yelled to Samurai as three gunmen trained their submachine guns on him. I pulled the trigger and got one, but the others opened fire; Samurai fell backwards as I ran toward the Germans. I tripped on a root and dropped to the ground, but I kept firing until they crumpled forward. Without the tank to lead the attack, the others pulled back. In a daze, I got up and ran back. Samurai's chest and neck looked like shredded barbecued meat, dark and red. George squatted next to him and searched for his dog tag. "Samurai, god damn it!" he said as he unhooked the chain smeared with gore and put the dog tag in a handkerchief. "Samurai, Samurai . . ." George kept repeating. Thick fog hovered over green mountain peaks as we ran back in silence. I glanced up: heavy, grayish clouds, giant ghosts, swiftly flew across the sky.

～

Another day in hell. They told us to keep advancing in spite of fierce enemy resistance. In mist and rain I'd seen our men cut down and blown apart, their blood shockingly bright in the hazy landscape of whites and grays. The sun had gone down and the forest began to look like a black-and-white film. Pines and hills became two-dimensional cardboard figures. If only I were an extra in a movie, and soon the director would yell, "Okay, it's a take!" and the lights would go back on, and everyone would go home for the night. I had the wool cap over my ears, but they still felt as if I had pins stuck into them. We made camp about two hundred yards from where we were this morning. I sat with my back next to a tree away from the others and ate cold gunk from a can. It was supposed to be ham stew, but I only tasted a vague sweetness. Samurai was dead; why then did my eyes still search for him, hoping to see him sitting under a tree, eating his ration or smoking a cigarette? Someone approached—Tom. He sat next to me and lit a Lucky Strike.

"Why the damn rush? Can't we wait for reinforcements?" I said without looking at him.

"I heard we're supposed to break through to the 1st Battalion from the 141st, the Texans. They got surrounded," he said, looking away toward the mountain peaks, still visible in the dying light. I took a sip of warm coffee from my tin cup.

"Sometimes I think I'm fighting for the wrong side," I said. I remembered that night at Hattiesburg, the face of the black man with a rope around his neck, saw again his desperate resistance through his struggling body. I never gave much thought, as I was growing up in El Centro, to the fact that Negroes only lived east of the tracks.

"There's something rotten in the heart of America," I said.

"Think of the people back home—fight for them." The last hints of light had gone and the wind began to pierce my chest.

"Who would've thought we'd wind up here? Remember our university days?" I asked. He smiled, and his face relaxed.

"I did all the time at Manzanar. I couldn't believe I was in a sprawling prison camp surrounded by barbed-wire fences. The guard towers had searchlights and armed guards with machine guns looked down on us, making sure we didn't escape. There was a demonstration once and the military police shot into the crowd with Thompson submachine guns, killing two young guys, wounding nine. One day I woke up wishing I hadn't. I dressed shivering in the freezing barrack, stood in line at the communal latrine, stood in line at the mess hall, then walking in the rain under the eyes of an armed guard up in his tower, I looked at the Sierras covered with snow and decided I'd rather die in the mountains than spend another year or two in the camp. When I had the chance to enlist, I took it. So here I am, in the mountains. It's a good place to die, don't you think?"

I only had to think about it for an instant.

"Yeah, better here than in Poston." Night had descended and a half-moon shone between clouds. We walked back to camp. I lay under the pup tent, wrapped myself in blankets, and tried to fall asleep. *Yes, this is a good place to die*, I thought, but my body disagreed.

Why am I so full of fear? I'm a rational being. Everything here can be logically analyzed and understood. My mistake is to think about the future; endless days of combat make my survival questionable. That big question mark pulls the ground from under me and everything loses its reality. If only I could tap into Samurai's state of being, throw myself completely into every instant without second-guessing, without thinking. But why would I want to do that? What kind of a philosopher would I be if I didn't think?

A drizzle began to fall on the tent as I thought about Hegel's master–slave dialectic. According to Hegel, only by risking one's life are self-consciousness and freedom actualized. Only by putting my life on the line would I prove my loyalty to my country. I understood that clearly, but wasn't that what every soldier did? Wasn't I more of a slave, divested of my social position and property, of my very rights as a citizen, and forced in a camp surrounded by barbed wire and guarded by armed guards? Now I understood much more the thousands of internees who refused to fight and were thrown in the Tule Lake camp to languish until deported.

I opened my eyes and saw Captain Nemo bent over me, scrutinizing my face.

"Mr. Anami, how do you feel?" His voice had a tone of concern.

"Tired, Captain, and I have a headache. What happened?" I heard an electrical hum and sensed motion. I propped myself up on my elbows and looked around; I was in my cabin on the *Nautilus*.

"You wandered in deeper water and fell prey to nitrogen narcosis. When your companions tried to bring you back, you struggled wildly until you lost consciousness. Thanks to the ministrations of Dr. Torres you have recovered. When you feel up to it, get something to eat. I will meet you this evening in the library." He got up from the chair by the bunk and left. I lay down again, resting my head on the pillow. I remembered sitting on the boulder on the sandy bank more than a hundred feet underwater and looking upward, thinking about Heidegger and time, but nothing after that.

We were sailing on the surface, so the repairs must have been done, I thought as I got up and staggered down the passageway to the washroom. It felt good to take a hot shower. The *Nautilus* had superior technology for its day and a small crew, so it was clean, spacious, and well ventilated, and thanks to its superior evaporators, we had all the fresh water we could use. After having eaten a hearty meal of broiled fish and seaweed bread, I went to thank the two crew members who'd brought me back in the *Nautilus* and Dr. Torres. Then I returned to my room to draw plans for a technical modification. In the evening I went to the library and spread the plans on a table.

"Captain," I said, "the *Nautilus* would benefit from a device that would enable you to see what's on the surface while submerged. It's a long metal tube with mirrors at either end; as you can see, I've drawn the details here. While at shallow depth, you'll be able to see targets without being seen." He looked intently at the plans.

"Wonderful! It is a rather simple instrument; I don't know why I hadn't thought of it. As soon as we get to base I'll have one built and installed. This proves, Mr. Anami, that I need someone to inspire me and help me see things from different angles."

Surrounded by cabinets full of books and the sculptures Nemo had found at the bottom of the seas, I felt at peace.

Soldiers marching silently in the forest. Black boots on wet grass, moss-covered rocks, muddy ground. A silvery light appears behind

dark firs, as invisible birds announce the new day. Music from the second movement of Beethoven's Pastoral Symphony plays in my head. A tinge of pink is born in the white sky. And then, explosions. Everything moves slowly, and all I hear is the music. I run for cover and fall in a shell crater; smoke and dust choke me; I cough, trying to bury myself in the earth as violins and flutes play in my head. I must think only of the music, I must become the music. Music cannot be killed. I can see the stream flowing, feel the sun's warmth. Now clarinets and bassoons play . . . I remember the first time I heard the Pastoral; I was a freshman at UCLA and had gone to a concert with friends. What magic! Someone shakes me. "Mike? Mike! You all right?" It's Hideo. Looking at his face reassures me; I glance at my arms, chest, legs.

"I'm okay."

"Let's go—we got support. Our artillery is fucking them up good. Let's go!" yells the Sarge. I get up slowly, brush off the dirt from the BAR, and follow Hideo up the ridge. Our company is fanning out and moving forward through firs, alders, and ferns. Rifle shots erupt from the left, and as I look up I see men in green uniforms standing up with raised arms.

"Stop your fire!" orders the Sarge. "They're surrendering!"

I can see them now, many of them just boys, wide liquid eyes darting left and right in pale, drawn faces. We have taken seventy prisoners but paid dearly for them.

In late afternoon clouds had broken up in the west, but the light contracted like a white blossom in the cold, leaving more mountain peaks and crests to the mercy of the dark. We made camp and rested. The Lieutenant sat on the stump of a tree and talked on the radio. "Yes, Captain, I understand, but we suffered heavy casualties, couldn't we wait for . . . Yes, Sir, at any cost . . . Right, Sir." He put the phone back in his pack. "They want us to push through at any cost. Tomorrow morning we attack again," he said as he stomped away. I liked the Lieutenant; he cared for us.

I got up and walked toward the trees. Emerald moss covered white rocks, pines and firs rose as high as two hundred feet above me, and up in the darkening sky, hawks glided in circles. I climbed on top of a boulder and sat down on the icy white granite. I watched the sun rapidly sink, a blurry orange shape, like a giant dead goldfish. A cold rain began to rustle the branches as crows cawed above. I saw myself as a child, the evening I won a goldfish at the California Midwinter Fair. That night I put the small bowl on my nightstand, sat on the floor, and watched the fish swim lazily around. I thought about Yoshiko, about my parents and sisters, about Akira and Samurai; then it became darker, and I climbed back down to camp. Tom, Hideo, and the others were eating spaghetti from cans.

"You know how many guys are trapped by the Jerries?" asked Hideo.

"About two hundred," replied George as he chomped on a Baby Ruth.

"Well," continued Hideo, "don't you think we lost almost as many men? And yet they keep pushing us to break through to those guys. You know why? 'Cause they're white and we're just Japs." He threw the half-full can of spaghetti toward some trees and lit a cigarette. I poured some coffee in a cup and sat down with my back propped against a tree.

"Hey Mike, take a look," said George with a wink as he threw some German propaganda flyers at my feet. On one side most of them had pictures of pinups: girls in bathing suits, smiling and showing off their legs and breasts, the word *LIFE* printed in white in the upper left-hand corner against a red background, just like *Life* magazine; while on the other side the word *DEATH* appeared, with a skull wearing a GI helmet.

One of the flyers was different, though. One side had the

picture of a cheerleader flaunting her legs. The writing said: "Have a good look at this! Maybe it's the last good look you'll have in your life!" And on the other side: "What are your prospects for the future? First: you may be killed outright. Second: you may be totally disabled. Third: you may wind up in a German P.O.W. camp. In the last case you have a chance of having another 'good look'!" I put the flyers down. What if I died without making love to a woman again? The thought filled me with fear and a wave of desire rushed over me; I wanted to smell a woman, kiss and taste her skin, make love to her. Beads of sweat formed on my forehead and I felt cold.

I couldn't sleep, so I lay in my sleeping bag, my mind jumping around, until I heard a ghostly moan. I crawled out of the tent and looked around. In the moonlight, someone sat cross-legged on a crate, chanting. As I walked closer, I recognized George.

"What the hell are you doing?" Startled, he turned around.

"It's for Samurai, a bit of scripture I learned at a Buddhist church long ago."

"How does it go?"

"It's very short; we used to chant it with other lines of scripture. It goes something like this:

How great the robe of liberation
Field beyond form and emptiness
Enveloped by the Buddha's teachings
We vow to save all beings.

It sounded soothing, and in the moonlight and the cold, otherworldly. "Samurai would like it," I said, and went back to my pup tent. I closed my eyes and listened to the chanting until I fell asleep.

We attacked at dawn under heavy rain and gained some ground before they stopped us cold. The Germans had dug themselves in and the approaches to them were mined. We had taken cover behind some boulders, and as we waited and smoked cigarettes, the Sarge came striding toward us, holding a map as if it were an astrological forecast, and we gathered around him to find out what it had to say about our future.

"Okay, look," he said, "the only approach to the hill is this ridge, and there's room on it for just two companies to attack. We'll go around the minefield on the right and come back up the slope on the flank of the enemy positions. The 3rd Battalion will push through directly. Any questions?"

"Will we have artillery support?" Hideo asked.

"Yeah, but remember, this area is all hills covered with trees. They may not be able to pinpoint their fire. Watch your asses."

"Damn it, if the Jerries don't kill us our own people will," someone said.

"They'll do the best they can. Let's go," said the Sarge.

We strode through the firs, thick underbrush slashing our legs. I saw myself running on trails on the Laguna Mountains back home, like I used to do when Steve and I went camping there. I loved to run there, especially after it rained, the forest purified, its scents released in the air. The chatter of machine guns startled me, and I dropped to the ground. Someone to my left screamed in pain. "Medic! Medic!" I yelled. Machine guns continued to fire and mortar rounds began to fall closer and closer.

"Let's try moving to the left!" yelled Tom. I got up and followed him, Hideo and George behind me. We ran horizontally, but there was no escaping the machine gun fire. Rounds bit the ground and whizzed by my head. I dove into the underbrush again, behind oaks and pines. The others did the same.

"They have interlocking fire," I said. "Let's wait a while."

Explosions rocked the trees behind us.

"What the hell's our artillery doing?" yelled Hideo. "They're hitting us." I buried my face in the wet grass, inhaled its fresh, green smell, and imagined that my face was pressed between a woman's legs, and I pushed harder. Yells, screams, whines, and thuds pierced the rain until I couldn't stand it anymore. I slowly got up on my knees as Tom stared at me. "You okay?" he asked.

"Let's move, or we'll be hit by the big stuff. Come on," I urged.

We were moving slowly from tree to tree, returning fire with fire, when a scream next to me made me jump—Hideo had fallen backwards. "Hideo!" I yelled as I ran toward him. Dark red blood oozed through his jacket, and his arms trembled. He lay on the rocky ground trying to prop himself up. "Medic! Medic!" I yelled out as he grabbed my arm and looked into my eyes.

"Mike, keep me alive. Come see me in Seattle!"

Before I could speak, he stopped breathing. Rounds whizzed by my right ear; I threw myself down and turned. I spotted a machine gun nest on a ridge to my right and moved toward it under the cover of trees. *Yes, just a little bit closer . . . now!* I ran toward the side and started firing. Caught by surprise, the two Germans crumpled like dolls. Trees shattered and showers of wood and leaves fell to earth; men buckled up and dropped; the air filled with the pungent smell of cordite, the staccato of machine guns, the reports of rifles, the thuds of mortars.

"Let's go for broke!" I heard someone yell out. Our fingers pulling on burning triggers, we kept moving ahead. *Kill. Shoot them down.* And then I saw them. Germans, but I saw the smiling folks who took our furniture, our farm, our land.

The government officials who threw us in a camp, the good Christians who called us dirty Japs, the guard who killed my brother. Something cracked within me, releasing a force that rose from my guts into my shoulders, arms, and fingers, like angry fire.

"They're pulling back!" George yelled out.

"Mike, Mike!" I turned my head and saw Tom, who grabbed me by the shoulder. "They're falling back," he said. We kept on going; then I saw them. The Texans of the lost battalion. They waved and cheered, they shook our hands, some of them had tears in their eyes. We had broken through.

9

1944–1945

Below me, restless gray clouds and snow-covered mountains, nothing else. Crouched on top of my observation post, I scanned the winding roads with field glasses; a heavy jacket and wool gloves and scarf protected me well enough from the cold. I wore a wool cap under my helmet, and it did a great job at keeping my head and ears warm. We received a Distinguished Unit Citation for the lost battalion's rescue, but we'd lost two-thirds of our regiment. They relieved us on November sixth, and on the seventeenth we were ordered to Nice, on the French Riviera. Things happened so fast I had no time to let them sink in. *Hideo will relieve me in an hour. No, no, Hideo is dead. His watch is on my wrist.* I wanted the Sarge to send it to his parents, but he said no, Hideo wanted me to have it. We didn't get much of a Thanksgiving, just took positions on the highest peak in order to protect the right flank of the 6th Army Group, and so we watched from our Olympus, ready to rain flashes of lightning on the German Army.

I received a letter from Yoshiko. I sat on my bunk, opened the envelope, and unfolded the letter. September 12, 1944,

Poston, Arizona. Small, well-formed blue words jumped from the whiteness of the paper.

Dear Mike,

I hope this letter finds you well. Yesterday we had a sandstorm and now everything in the barrack is covered with a layer of sand. I wake up early when my aunt is still asleep, and before going to work at the post office, I practice zazen. I sit down on the floor, cross my legs, keep my back straight, close my eyes and let go. It's been hard, but I found a new peace, and now I see what is truly important is within us and can't be imprisoned in a camp or taken away. It's not easy to explain, but I've found within me a calm spring of refreshing water. Don't laugh. My mother is in the hospital for her bad lungs, so it's just my aunt and I now. Your parents and sisters are in good health. So many families have been told their sons have died in action, I write this without knowing if you'll ever read it, but I feel your presence strongly. I know we have drifted apart, but you're still in my heart. Please write.

Love, Yoshiko.

I used to wait eagerly for these letters, but they were messages from a faraway world I no longer belonged to.

Stars sparkled above. I sat outside the tent, my back leaning against supply crates, and sipped from a bottle of whisky.

Oh, Carmelita! "*Hijo,* come make the stars," she would say, handing me a piece of black cardboard and a nail. I would sit down on the kitchen floor and punch tiny holes in the board and then she would put it behind the nativity scene in the living room, pull the drapes over the window, turn on the light bulb behind the board, and we would stand back and admire the shepherds and the manger underneath the twinkling night sky. "*Hijo,* look what you did! You made the stars," she would tell me, and I truly thought I had a hand in the creation of the universe.

I took another swallow of whisky and as a warm blanket

covered my insides, I glanced up again at the sky. What happened to the child who found magic in a piece of cardboard and a nail?

The cold felt like burning needles, but the liquor flowed down smoothly, and then a warm wave surged and began to melt the sharp edges of thoughts and feelings. *Rise, whisky tide, melt me away until only the dark and the stars remain.* The thought occurred to me that if I fell asleep I'd die, so I struggled to get up. That's all I remembered the following morning, but I must have been successful, because I woke up snuggled in my sleeping bag.

At the end of November we came down the mountains and camped east of Menton. With the German 34th Division right across the border, Lieutenant Akers had told us, we needed to be here in case they decided to roll on through and advance north. The guys were happy to be on the French Riviera, but I missed the isolation, the solitude of the mountain peaks, with their snow and fog. Lieutenant Akers had told us that several instances of drunkenness, pillaging, assaults, and rapes by American soldiers had been reported—none involving our regiment, thankfully. People were furious at the lawless behavior of their "liberators" and he warned us to be on our best behavior.

Snowcapped mountains in the distance, the sea surprisingly calm in the foreground. On the beach, soft sand and rowboats. Boys in white shirts and short pants smiled and shrieked as we gave them chocolate bars, chewing gum, and candy. Soldiers strolled along the beach, as local men and women dressed in their Sunday best helped us with the Christmas party we organized for the orphanage. Some of the townspeople brought us fresh cabbages, rice, eggs, and flowers.

As I unloaded boxes of gifts from a jeep, a little boy, maybe five years old, stood crying next to a blue boat beached on sawhorses. I walked up to him, squatted down, and handed him a Baby Ruth. "Mike," I said as I pointed at myself. "And you?" He stopped crying, his big brown eyes studied me for a few seconds, then he grabbed the candy bar and ran off. The familiar smell of the sea, the cold breeze, the sun above, the laughter of children, these friendly people; all this I will never forget.

Through dense, charcoal-gray smoke, two German soldiers suddenly appear. I'm startled as the BAR becomes alive in my hands—three, four shots ring out, and they buckle over and drop to the ground. Blood oozes from their crumpled bodies and spreads over white rocks polished by time into skull smoothness, over jade moss, naked roots. I move closer. They lie on their sides. I push their shoulders with my boot and the bodies fall on their backs. Their helmets come off, and I see their faces. The smooth features of blond young men. Sitting on a boulder a few feet away I see my brother. His face is pale. He looks at me with a distant, sad expression and says, "Is this what a philosopher does?"

I opened my eyes and tried to swallow, but couldn't. I fumbled in the dark, put on pants and boots, found my canteen, and ran out of my tent. The moonlight bathed tents and firs in steel. I took a long swallow of water and lit a cigarette. I began to shiver in the chilly air, but sweat drenched my tee shirt.

I began to breathe faster and felt a pounding in my chest. I could see the men I killed not too long ago playing with toys under the loving glances of their mothers. They were young, like me, full of life and dreams. A cold wave rushed over me. *They're the enemy, they're shooting at you,* a voice told me, but it wasn't enough to alleviate the sorrow.

Another sleepless night. I sat outside the tent and smoked a cigarette. It was not too chilly but overcast, the silence interrupted now and then by the barking of foxes. I heard again the words of Mitsuo, the Kibei, at Poston. "They think we're inferior, not quiet human, and you want to join the Army and die for them?" I saw again the buses full of the people who had refused allegiance to the country that had taken away their freedom and had made the choice to be shipped to Tule Lake to do hard time and await deportation.

Maybe they were right. Why were the lives of the lost battalion more important than ours? We'd suffered hundreds of casualties to save about 230. I thought of Commodore Perry showing up near Edo in 1853 with his black ships, forcing Japan to trade under threat of military attack. The foreign intrusion contributed to events leading to the Boshin War. Then in the 1880s when the Japanese immigrated to the US to work in the mines, on the railroads, and in farming, they were beaten and forced to live on the outskirts of towns. And here I was now, sent to die to save their own. Where was Captain Nemo?

We are in the library, sitting on comfortable reading chairs, smoking cigars.

"Mr. Anami, I hope you will enjoy a glass of this beverage;

it comes from the sea," said the Captain, as he poured a transparent liquid into two brandy glasses. He handed me the crystal snifter, inscribed with the letter *N*. I took a sip and was surprised.

"It tastes like excellent brandy—thank you, Captain."

"One of my men is a chemist, and has distilled this from sea anemones. It's rather different from what we've had before."

"Captain," I said, "it's not going to be enough to simply ram their ships; it will not work for long. We must think of ways to destroy their vessels by launching bombs at them while submerged. To fight imperialism and oppression, we must keep the nations from developing their industry or they will build their own underwater ships. Once they do, they will give us chase and destroy the *Nautilus*. We must also think of ways to destroy their military installations on land. Would it be possible for the *Nautilus* to launch bombs on land?"

"Mr. Anami," said the Captain, "I am surprised at the eager commitment you express toward my cause, and I must admit that so far I haven't formulated any long-range plans to prevent nations from slaughtering each other. I have a trusted crew and some allies on land, but I have lacked the powerful inspiration you give me." He took a puff from his cigar and leaned toward me. "In you I sense a powerful wellspring of hate for injustice; it overflows, entering into me, giving me inspiration and new creative energy. We will work very well together, my brother. Let us toast to the future of our cause."

Our glasses clinked, but what I raised to my lips was my canteen. I took a long swallow of water as I sat on an ammo box, shivering. I went back in, got into the sleeping bag, closed my eyes, and hoped for unconsciousness.

March 26, 1945. Still cold, but I could detect a change in the weather: nights not as frigid, the days longer. I sat in late afternoon on an old, broken-down chair outside my tent and read Heidegger in twilight.

Yes, I am an ongoing project; I create myself through my actions, but this requires time, which I'm very likely to run out of, in this war. Death is a fundamental possibility of my being. It could become actual at any moment, and if I accepted this, I could live in an impassioned freedom toward death. When we discussed this in class I thought I understood it, but when I see broken bodies of friends on the ground, white bones sticking out of shredded meat, words lose their meaning.

"Here he is, philosophizing." Tom and George, all spruced up in clean uniforms, had shown up.

"Mike, we've been on the French Riviera for months and all you do on your time off is read that damn book," said Tom impatiently.

"Yeah, and drink rot-gut whisky," interjected George as he sat down on the edge of a crate.

"You know Menton is right by the beach. Don't you want to hear waves splash on sand? Smell the sea?" asked Tom.

"We can have a jeep in a couple of hours, but this is the last day," said George. "You know we're moving out soon. Come on, damn it. We won't stay long. Just a couple of drinks away from here."

Waves splashing on sand, the salty, fresh scent of the sea.

"Okay, let's go!"

I sat in the back of the jeep, lost in thoughts, the night serene. The narrow and bumpy road forced me to hold onto the front seat to keep from falling off. The metal frame was cold, so I grabbed the canvas cover. Farmhouses, trees, and hills appeared suddenly in the headlights and quickly reeled past, like a painted canvas set moved on rollers. The rushing air brought scents of pines and flowers. In the horizon, a hazy glow silhouetted a line of hills.

"Do you want to kill us before we even get there?" Tom let out as he held onto George's seat. The jeep, screeching, had reached the edge of a curve.

"You're getting too jittery in your old age. Calm down—I know what I'm doing," replied George, and then he turned his head toward me and winked.

"I'd rather die in battle than in a stupid car accident," Tom retorted.

"Look, the sea," said George, searching for me in the rearview mirror.

Suddenly, I see Steve. He holds the steering wheel with his right hand, his left resting on the edge of the car door. The wind ruffles our hair. His face is tired, his eyes pierce through me. I sit next to him in his black Dodge as a piece by Benny Goodman plays on the radio. La Jolla Cove is up ahead, bathed in moonlight. He looks at me and says, "You know, I've always been jealous of you. Your smarts, your books made me feel small. I was just interested in cars and farming."

"But I was always envious of you! Of how easily you took an engine apart and put it back together; I envied your strength, your love of the earth."

"Can you smell the ocean?" he says and smiles.

"I love that ocean smell," I replied, but before I finished the sentence, I was back in the jeep.

"It's not really an ocean, you know, but a sea," said Tom.

"What the hell's the difference—it's salt water, ain't it?" replied George in an impatient tone.

"There are sharks in the ocean," I said.

"The sea has its sharks too," responded Tom.

"Fucking assholes," said George. "I'll bet you guys have never even seen a shark. I used to surf among them, you chickens."

You're wrong, George, I've been face to face with a big white, I thought, but didn't say. I didn't feel like talking. As we turned around a bend, lighted buildings appeared below us, pushed by dark hills to the edge of the sea. Soon we drove by the beach, stately hotels and restaurants to our left eerily white in the glow of streetlamps. Groups of Army guys in dress uniforms smoking cigarettes and laughing strolled on the boardwalk; couples held hands; an old man dressed in black sat alone on a bench.

We parked in front of a hotel, next to other jeeps, and walked until we saw a neon sign in front of a bar that promised great music and good wines, *La Perle*. The place was dark and full of local people. On a small stage three old guys played a jazzy tune, and a few couples danced. We sat at a corner table and ordered wine. The waiter soon arrived with a one-liter carafe of *vin de la maison*, which was surprisingly light and smooth.

"I didn't drink wine until I came to France," said George, lighting a Pall Mall. He took a sip and tasted it as if he were a connoisseur. "I like beer," he continued. "I grew up in Honolulu, and they have good beer there. I'll never forget the luau my parents gave me on my eighteenth birthday: pig cooked in a pit, platters and bowls of cold turkey, yams, raw salmon, poi, shrimp, abalone, olives, rice, the works. And very good beer; I can still taste it. My dad managed a hotel on Beretania Street; now my family is in Manzanar, and here I am on the French Riviera drinking wine." He shook his head and drained his glass.

"I'd like to have some sashimi and rice right now," I said.

"You guys think about food all the time. I'm going to see if one of those beauties wants to dance," said Tom. He took a sip of wine and got up. George followed him. I refilled my glass and lit another cigarette. A group of men, maybe five—I couldn't see very well through the crowd—stood at the counter and glared at Tom and George, who had found a couple of girls to dance with.

I began to think about Yoshiko. There were moments when I missed her, when I wished I could hold her in my arms, go for a walk with her. I put out the cigarette and ran my fingers over the tabletop; it was made of rough wood, with cigarette burns and scratches. I took another drink of wine when two of the men at the counter walked up to George and Tom and grabbed them by the shoulders. As I got up to see what was going on, one of them pushed George and told him something in an angry tone.

"You Americans, leave our women alone," warned the other man. He was in his forties, with graying hair, tall and stocky. The music had stopped and people stared. "You think you can do whatever you want, just because you are winning the war," he said as the others moved closer. Something glimmered in his hand as he moved under a spotlight, maybe a knife—I couldn't tell.

"You cannot do anything you want," he continued as another man grabbed a bottle from the counter by the neck. The other three surrounded Tom and George. At this point, a well-dressed older man got up from a table and walked toward us.

"Calm down," he said. "These soldiers mean no harm. They were just dancing."

"But Monsieur Cardon, you know what happened in town last week," complained one of the men.

"*Oui*, but they are not all like that. And we've had no trouble with the *Americains d'origine japonaise*," he said. Then turning toward us, he continued: "Please allow me to introduce myself—my name is Pierre Cardon. Will you join me for a drink at my home?" We agreed, and followed him out of the bar.

Lamps lit the street and the palm trees on the other side in ethereal bronze. I could see the outline of the beach in the lights' glow and heard splashing waves. To our left, tall buildings in shades of gold lined the street. Dark wooden shutters hid windows, and barely visible flowerpots on balconies seemed offerings left to appease the night.

"You must excuse my compatriots," said Mr. Cardon, stopping for a moment. "Last week we had an unfortunate incident involving an American soldier and a young girl, and people are angry."

"We deeply apologize for the behavior of that soldier," I replied. "My name is Mike Anami, and my friends' names are Tom Nakama and George Tajima." We shook hands and resumed walking. "This is our last opportunity to be in Menton. All I wanted to do was hear the waves and smell the sea." He looked at me somewhat surprised.

"Well, let's cross the street—we'll be right on the beach. I am happy you agreed to have a glass of wine with me; I don't want you to leave with a bad impression of the French," he said. He wore a gray suit, a white shirt, and a light blue tie.

I lit a Chesterfield and offered him one. He retrieved a small blue pack from his inside jacket pocket, took out a cigarette, and handed it to me.

"Monsieur Anami, you must try a Gauloises," he said as he handed me a short, stubby unfiltered cigarette. "This is a blend of tobaccos from Syria and Turkey, much more flavorful than your American smokes." It did smell fragrant, so I gave my cigarette to George and lit the short, stubby one. An exotic aroma rose from it. I took a puff and felt slightly dizzy.

"It has a kick and a spicy taste," I said.

We walked on sand now, and the sound of waves slowed and deepened my breathing. The stiffness in my muscles dissolved, and I felt reconnected to an earlier self, the one who belonged to the time before Pearl Harbor, Poston, and the war.

"See up there, the church between those two buildings? We go that way, gentlemen." Mr. Cardon pointed to his left, toward the facades across the street. Above them, a pale glow backlit the top part of a church and a cylindrical bell tower crowned by a cross. It was the moon's calling card. We crossed the street again and followed him up a series of steep, zigzagging staircases.

"Where's the Sarge?" asked George jokingly. "I feel like we're back on the march again."

"The reward for this arduous climb is a heavenly sight, Monsieur Tajima," replied Mr. Cardon.

"Please call me George, sir."

"Okay, and please call me Pierre," said the Frenchman as he kept on climbing. Finally we reached the top of the stairs. As we stood on a small square, the facade of a church came out of the dark. "This is the Church of Saint-Michel-Archange, a jewel of baroque architecture. It is one of the main reasons for my evening walks," said Pierre. Yes, this was a heavenly sight. Four pairs of Ionic columns resting on massive bases, three wooden doors topped with life-sized statues in niches. And as I turned to my left I noticed, down the hill, the sea like a dark, sleeping animal.

"My house is not far from here," said Pierre. We followed him and climbed up a road paved in stones. Nestled behind trees and shrubs hid villas, and the sweet scent of lilacs perfumed the air. Only the occasional barking of a dog broke the silence.

"Monsieur Cardon, where did you learn to speak English so well?" asked Tom.

"I studied English and German in school, but after the Great War I lived in London for a year; it really helped." For a man in his sixties he walked vigorously up the hill, and after about twenty minutes we reached a gate.

"Here's my house—please come in," he said. Beyond the gate, past lemon and orange trees, a small villa seemed to be waiting. A terra-cotta pot with a red geranium stood guard by the door. Inside the foyer, Pierre sat on a bench and took his shoes off.

"I think in many respects the Japanese are more civilized than we Europeans," he said. "To take one's shoes off before entering the house is a custom I have adopted."

We sat on the opposite bench, took off our boots, hung our jackets on the clothes stand, and followed Pierre into the living room. A faded Persian rug covered the wooden floor, three easy chairs and a sofa flanked the fireplace, and a large window overlooked the sea.

"Please sit down," he said. After taking his jacket off he went into the kitchen and came back with a bottle and four glasses on a tray. "This is a light wine from Nice, a blend with mostly Tibouren grapes." He laid the tray on the coffee table, filled the glasses, and handed them to us.

"*Chin-chin*, gentlemen," he said as we clinked glasses. I didn't know much about wines, but could tell this was smooth, with nice body and a lingering taste of berries. "Please, relax, make yourselves at home. The bathroom is down the hall, first door on the left; the kitchen is on the right." He asked us if we had heard much French music and when we said no, he walked to a cabinet, picked a record from a stack, and placed it on a gramophone.

"This is an old song by Fréhel, "*La Java Bleue*," he said as he sat down. A woman's singing came alive in the room, accompanied by accordion, piano, and saxophone. He asked us about ourselves and we talked about our lives before the war. Intrigued by our backgrounds, he kept asking us questions. The song long over, he got up and put on "*La Der Des Der*," also by Fréhel. I couldn't understand the lyrics, but the sonorous voice and bright music made us tap our feet. After another glass of wine, he asked us if we were hungry.

"Let's go in the kitchen and see what we can find," he said. We got up and followed him down the hall. He turned the lights on and we entered a large room.

"On the counter there's a bowl of *roquette* I picked in the garden this morning," he said as he looked in a cabinet. He took out half a loaf of bread, then opened the icebox and retrieved something wrapped in paper. "I have some cheese … oh, and a piece of sea bass a fisherman friend gave me this morning at the harbor."

"Do you have any rice, sir?" asked George. Pierre thought for a moment, then looked in one of the cabinets.

"Here's a box of Italian rice."

"It looks like short-grained white rice," George said. "Sir, may I cook it the Japanese way? And if you don't mind, we could eat the sea bass sashimi style. Too bad we don't have wasabi . . . but maybe you have horseradish?"

"Yes, we keep some in the icebox; we use it in some meat dishes," he replied, and George's eyes lit up.

"Oh boy oh boy, we're going to have us a party," he said. Then he looked at Pierre and added, "If it's okay with you, sir —I don't mean to be impertinent."

"Go ahead, please," said Pierre with a wave of the hand. "It is I who should be preparing something for you." He showed George and Tom where everything was, then prepared a plate with slices of bread and cheese.

"Here, something to eat with the wine—please help yourselves. I am going to put another record on," he said. I grabbed a piece of bread, spread some cheese on it, and followed him. A dark wooden bookcase on the right wall of the living room drew my attention. Slender Ionic columns flanked the sides; its lion's paws' feet rested on the floor. Behind glass doors stood thick, hardbound volumes. Light from a floor lamp reflected on the lacquered cherry wood, giving the bookcase an impression of warmth and life.

"This is 'J'Attendrai,' Rina Ketty sings . . ." said Pierre as he sat down on an easy chair.

"You have many books on medicine, psychology, and

philosophy, Monsieur Cardon," I said as I went to sit on the opposite chair.

"I was a doctor, and during the Great War spent two years in field hospitals, mending bodies, sawing off limbs. When peace came I was sick at heart. I sought relief in psychoanalysis, and in 1919 went to Vienna to study with Sigmund Freud. When I returned to France, I practiced psychoanalysis until the German occupation forced me to move to Zurich with my wife. Carl Jung was there at the time, a source of newly found energy and intellectual possibilities, but as I saw the world increasingly engulfed in madness I found refuge in Nietzsche and art. Nietzsche, that radical optimist! He is a middle finger in the face of social conventions, an embrace of life, life as animal impulse transformed through poetry and art in pure spirituality. You mentioned earlier that you studied philosophy; do you find it consoling?"

"Philosophy for me is a way of life dedicated to the pursuit of wisdom, of truth. Lately I've been obsessed with a book I brought with me when I left the university, Martin Heidegger's *Being and Time*. There are days when it speaks to me, days when I just hold it and flip through its pages as if it were a talisman, and there are occasions when I can't even look at it, it seems so meaningless and irrelevant in war."

"I read *Sein und Zeit* ages ago. I found it in its essence remarkably Buddhist. During my stay in Zurich I read some essays by Dogen Zenji, the founder of the Soto Zen School, and his discussion of being and time is very Heideggerian, or we should say, Heidegger's philosophy is very Zenjian. Dogen wrote in the middle of the thirteenth century, after all..." He stopped and glanced at me. "I am sorry, here I am prattling on—you must forgive me, I got carried away," he said as he handed me a cigarette.

"I'm honored to be here, talking to you, Monsieur Cardon," I said. As I took a drag from the Gauloises, I felt again slightly light-headed, the peppery taste in my mouth. "I thought human beings were ultimately rational, and if confronted with evidence, facts, and cogent arguments, they would accept them. But it's not true. People have a perverse ability to believe whatever they want to believe, regardless of the evidence. And if a great part of the self is unconscious, how can we ever know ourselves? How do we know that what we want and believe, our attitudes, reactions, are truly *ours*?" He moved forward to put out the cigarette butt in the ashtray, loosened his tie, and leaning back, crossed his legs as he began to speak.

"I believe we can know what is truly ours by listening to the whisperings of our unconscious. But to hear we must still the noise within, and here I've found Zen meditation most helpful. It's possible, in theory, for most of us to transcend social conventions and live on the ground of our own sense of life, but it's very hard. Maybe that's why Nietzsche called such people the '*Ubermensch*.'" He got up again to attend to the music, and as he sat back down, George came in.

"Sir . . . Pierre, we were wondering if you had some sticks we could use to make chopsticks. It would be strange to eat sashimi with forks."

"Well, let me think," he replied as he put his glass down and scratched his cheek. "Outside the kitchen door there is firewood and a bunch of sticks I use for kindling. You might find what you need there. There are also utility knives in the cabinet drawer by the kitchen door. I'm excited—I've never eaten sashimi."

George returned to the kitchen and Pierre put another record on, sat down, and continued telling me about himself.

"I plan to spend the rest of my days here. I love Menton, even though it can get crowded in summertime. Unfortunately, the rich come here in search of health and relaxation. I tend to my lemon and orange trees, sit on the back terrace, and gaze at the sea as the cool breeze washes over my face. I am here to mourn the millions of people who suffered and died in the wars I've lived through, and all I have lost: my innocence, my youth, my belief in human progress and whatever faith I had in human beings. Besides Nietzsche's writings, I find consolation in art. Take that watercolor by Émile Appay," he said as he pointed at a framed picture on the wall next to the bookcase. "You can see Menton in the distance, framed by cliffs and trees, rosy clouds in the background. I find it healing. Yes, that's the word. I believe in the healing power of images."

"I wish I could do the same. I used to think my whole life was ahead of me, but in combat I could easily die. The world turned out to be drastically different from the way I thought it was. The country we believed was 'ours' threw us in camps surrounded by barbed wire. I feel like the character in Kafka's story who wakes up one morning to find he had turned into a cockroach..."

I wanted to continue, but Tom came in and told us dinner was ready. Pierre jumped up and turned the radio on before we walked into the kitchen.

Tom and George had set the table with plates and glasses. A platter of pink and white slices of fish and a bowl of rice had center stage.

"I thought we could have some of this lettuce with the fish and rice," said Tom as he put the wooden bowl of *roquette* on the table. As we sat down, we discovered a pair of roughly made chopsticks on each of the white cloth napkins. *Hideo would have liked them*, I thought.

"I hope you'll forgive me for all this, Pierre," said George sheepishly, "but I couldn't resist once I saw the fresh fish and the rice. I grated some horseradish and found some Worcestershire we can use as a substitute for soy sauce." A wide smile broke on Pierre's face as he admired the table.

"I'm the one who must thank you gentlemen. Tonight I taste a new dish from a distant land in amiable company. But what shall we drink? I'm afraid I have only some wine bottled in Nice by a relative."

"Wine will be just fine," replied Tom. Pierre went to get a couple of bottles, uncorked one, and as we sat down he filled our glasses. George showed Pierre how to pick up a slice of fish with the chopsticks, lightly brush it against the horseradish, barely dip it in the sauce, then eat it in one bite, to be followed by the rice.

"Excellent, George and Tom!" exclaimed Pierre. "I feel like I am tasting the essence of the sea—it's a clean, elegant flavor. And what an explosion of sensations with the warm rice so aromatic, the intensity of the horseradish, the sauce, *est très bon!*" He took a swig of wine, looked at the chopsticks, and grinned.

"From now on, whenever I look at my kindling, I will see chopsticks," he said, and we laughed. A lively tune from the radio filled the kitchen with guitars and violins, which Pierre identified as a piece by Django Reinhardt and his Quintette du Hot Club.

"I first heard jazz during the Great War, when black American soldiers brought it to France. What a revolution it was, what a shot of new life in the arm of our wilting culture! The Nazis outlawed jazz, but thanks to you Americans, we can hear it again."

We ate and drank as we talked about music, food, California, Hawaii, and France. Then as we cleaned up the kitchen, our host made a pot of strong coffee. Back in the living room, we sat down as Pierre turned the radio off and played another record.

"This is '*Seule ce soir*' by Léo Marjane," he said as a sultry feminine voice came alive. We sat down, drank our coffee, and smoked cigarettes. "Let's have a glass of cognac," said Pierre as he opened a cabinet. "I brought it from Zurich when we returned last year, after you liberated us from the

Germans," he said as he poured the amber liquid in four glasses.

As I settled down in the easy chair with the snifter, facing our host, I suddenly had the impression of being in the *Nautilus*. Pierre looked like an older Captain Nemo, surrounded by his books and art, finding freedom and peace in his villa, a submarine facing the sea. Was I in Nemo's library? And then the bookcase, the floor lamp with its warm yellow glow, Pierre, Tom, and George, Appay's painting, the moon framed by the window, became parts of a luminous, delicate image. Like a soap bubble, it would soon burst, but now it floated in splendor. Joy and tenderness filled me, and if I had died, it would have been all right.

But the time came for us to go.

"I am so happy for your company. This is the best thing that has happened to me in so long; I shall never forget it," said Pierre as he shook our hands and accompanied us to the gate. He gave us his card and asked us to write him if we desired.

"Just follow the road to the church, then go down the steps. You can't get lost as long as you go downhill," he said. "Goodbye, Mike, George, and Tom. Good luck! And if you are ever in Menton, come see me."

It was cold now, and the moon shone through restless clouds as we waved at Pierre.

"I haven't felt this good in a long time," said Tom as we hurried down the road, accompanied by the scents of orange blossoms and lemons.

"What a great guy!" said George. "I hope he wasn't offended—after all, I took over his kitchen."

"He enjoyed it," I replied. "And thank you for suggesting it. It was a treat, and what a fascinating man! He was a doctor in the Great War, studied with Freud and Jung." Soon we reached the church, and the moon, higher in the sky now, shone on the edges of the statues in the niches above the doors. Saint Michael with his sword seemed to follow me with his gaze as we went down the stairs. The waves came to rest leisurely on the beach, and my mind rested in their whispering as we walked toward the hotel where we had left the jeep.

"I'll drive," said Tom. "I had less to drink than you guys." On the way back, under the stars, with trees rolling by, I bounced up and down and leaned left and right as we went around bends and hit potholes. It was cold, but I felt warm and at peace.

10

1945

Cigarette smoke curled up and floated under the canvas top as dust settled in my hair, eyes, and tongue. The roar of trucks filled my head. Under cover of night the regiment moved to Italy, again. How many hours had I been sitting in the back of the truck with twenty other dead-tired grunts? I shifted my weight but couldn't get comfortable; at times I drifted off to sleep only to be jarred into awareness when a tire plunged into a hole or hit a rock on the road. We headed for a place called San Martino, near Lucca, where we were supposed to get new weapons and replacements for the impending campaign. If only I had some hot coffee—not the crap we usually drank, but the stuff Steve brewed at home, rich and strong. It was time to go see Captain Nemo.

As soon as we surfaced inside the spent volcano, workers proceeded to safely secure the vessel to the dock. I was introduced to many of the Captain's lieutenants, and after a good day's rest, I explained to the chief engineers the basic concepts of the modifications I had suggested to the Captain. Within days, work proceeded to retrofit the *Nautilus* with a tube for launching hellsharks (bombs with propellers) and a periscope. Nemo had an impressive operation, with more than a hundred dedicated people. Most of the crater, filled with water that flowed through an underwater channel, looked like a lake, but part of it was several meters above sea level, and on this land a few buildings stood, including a small plant for processing coal. I met geologists, engineers, and biologists who worked on research. It was a self-sustainable world with a library, gymnasium, mess hall, and living quarters. A room in one of the service buildings was assigned to me, small but comfortable. It had a bed, closet, desk, and a small telescope on a tripod. One night I moved the small refractor outside and spent a long time gazing at the moon.

"Mr. Anami, I didn't know you were interested in astronomy," I heard Captain Nemo say. I directed my attention to the tall figure walking toward me.

"I've always loved very dark nights and bright stars. As a child growing up in the desert, I felt intimidated by them; I had the impression they could fall on me at any moment, and yet, mesmerized, I would keep looking at them. And when the full moon appeared, I'd wonder what the dark regions were. I thought they may have been huge fields of lettuce." The Captain smiled.

"I used to imagine the dark areas were seas, with ships crossing them. But come, let me show you the telescope we have here." We walked behind the supply depot and stepped on a small lift built into the rock wall. Nemo pushed a lever and we began to move upward, accompanied by the high-pitched whine of the motor. "Since we're surrounded by steep walls, to have a better view of the sky I had to build our observatory almost on the lip of the volcano," he said. Just before the very top, on an outcrop of rock, the lift stopped and we stepped in front of a dome-like structure. The Captain opened a door, pressed a button, and a faint, reddish light began to glow from a tube. A motor began to part the top of the dome, and the sky became visible. In the center of the round room, a strange contraption stood on a heavy metal pedestal.

"This," said Nemo, "is a thirty-six-inch reflector. I studied with Lord Rosse, who built several telescopes, including one with a mirror twice the diameter of this one. I traveled to Ireland to meet him and we passed many days together. What he taught me has been indispensable to my study of astronomy. It wasn't easy to build this, especially here, but when you have all the riches of the oceans at your disposal, even greater feats are possible." The Captain looked at his watch, moved to a table, and studied several charts. After making some calculations, he operated a motor that increased the telescope's elevation, then stood on a small ladder and peeked into the eyepiece.

"Have you ever seen a galaxy?" He stepped down and invited me to climb up. I did, and peered into the tube.

"I see a glowing round eye with arms coming out of it, and there are stars in the faint veil-like arms," I said.

"That is galaxy M51, which I studied in detail with Lord Rosse. What you're looking at are billions of stars, solar systems, and dust held together by gravitation."

As I gazed into the tube, I suddenly felt as if instead of upward I were looking down at a strange jellyfish floating in a black ocean.

"Do you think there are other worlds out there, Captain, other planets where sentient beings don't torture, kill, and enslave one another?" I asked as I turned to look into his dark brown eyes.

"In your question I detect a hope, a desire to believe in a better world. We will probably never know if somewhere out there sentient life forms have reached a higher spiritual plane, but we can wonder, Mr. Anami, we can wonder, imagine, and dream." The Captain showed me other galaxies and planets, until the time came for us to go back. I helped to close the dome and put charts and instruments away, and we went back down.

"Get some sleep; there is much to be done tomorrow, my friend," said Nemo. As I walked back to my quarters, I turned to glance at his back. He walked slightly bent, as if under a heavy burden, and I wondered what may have been in his mind and heart.

The truck ground to a halt in a squealing of brakes as the driver banged on the back of the cab to let us know we had arrived. We scrambled out into the pale dawn light. Swallows darted about and screeched overhead, and the sun began to lace the sky with violet and orange hues. The air carried the scent of lush grass, and white daisies and scarlet poppies dotted it like a Monet landscape. I came back to life; weariness left me, and everything appeared new. I arched my back, trying to straighten out as the Sarge shuffled toward us, rubbing his red eyes. With his scraggly mustache and stubbled chin, he looked like a Russian revolutionary.

"All right, guys," he said in a raspy voice, "we'll be here for a few days. Set up the tents and get some sleep; we'll build ranges in the afternoon." I set up my pup tent, took my boots off, and stretched out, glad to be on firm ground again. I closed my eyes, and caressed by the cool, early morning air blowing in from the open flaps, serenaded by the swallows, I fell asleep.

The following day, most of the guys received new weapons and spent hours adjusting sights on the makeshift ranges we had set up. I kept the BAR. I had grown attached to it and trusted it. Our squad received six replacements. Two of them stood out: Toshio, a chubby guy from Hawaii, and Wayne, a pimply-faced teenager from Fresno, California. As I sat on a crate next to the guys and thought about the dream I had the previous night, I saw the Sarge walk toward us. "Show them the ropes," he had growled to Tom, George, and me, and so we gave them tips that might have increased their chances to survive at least the first firefight.

On April third, a cool, overcast day, General Clark, the tall and imposing commanding general of the 15th Army Group, inspected us and found us ready to go. Early the next day, in our trucks and jeeps we rumbled toward the jagged hills south of Montignoso. The enemy had built an elaborate system of fortifications on bare, precipitous mountains running from north of Pisa to Genoa. Hundreds of bunkers provided an unlimited view of the Ligurian coast and Highway 1, thus making our advance to Genoa impossible. Five crack infantry battalions had reinforced the enemy, veterans of the 281st Regiment, 148th Division.

April 4, 1945. We woke up at four o'clock to prepare for the advance. I hadn't slept well and felt tired and anxious. Toshio managed to heat some water in a canteen, and so we had a cup of Nescafé "soluble coffee product." Better than nothing. The Sarge strode toward us, but this time he didn't have a map. He greeted us and then pointed way in the distance, at a steep, rocky hill.

"That's the 'Georgia' peak, our first objective. At least fifteen enemy emplacements are up there—machine gun nests, mortars, all dug into solid rock. Other battalions have been trying to take this hill for the past five months, but they can't do it, so they sent us. You can hear our artillery trying to soften them up, but you know what I say? Fuck the artillery. We don't need it. Besides, sometimes they fuck up and kill our own men. At oh-five-hundred hours we attack; let's give them hell." He unwrapped a stick of gum as he gazed in the misty dawn light. He reminded me of a football coach, so full of confidence and energy, and yet, he wasn't going to stand on the side and yell out instructions—he was going with us. The ground shook and the air vibrated with the thunder of our artillery. In spite of the Sarge's boast, I was glad to hear that thunder. Tom, George, Wayne, and Toshio crouched outside their tents and smoked cigarettes in silence.

"All right, let's go!" yelled the Sarge. We'd plodded up the rocky hillside for about three hundred yards when suddenly a bright flash and a squeal pierced the stillness. Someone had stepped on a mine. As we scrambled for cover, more explosions shook the ground. "We're tripping mines!" the Sarge yelled out. Machines guns opened up and grenades went off. We were pinned down.

"We got to knock off those machine guns—follow me," said the Sarge. We obeyed, crawling on the stony soil. A flash of hot white light and a cloud of smoke blinded me. My ears rang and dirt rained on me. I opened my eyes again and saw a bloody torso on a patch of grass just a few yards from me, a bloody blackened thing. Behind me someone cried in pain.

"Move, let's go!" yelled the Sarge. He was about twenty yards in front of me, crawling up toward a bunker. Tom, Wayne, and I covered him until he tossed in a grenade and charged with his tommy gun, wiping out the gunner and the assistant.

All right, let's go for broke—we don't give a damn. Dig with boots in the hillside, hold on to gnarled tree roots sticking out of the ground like rotting arms and fingers, pull the trigger, feel the heat, smell the gunpowder.

"Wayne, George!" the Sarge called out as he pointed at a bunker in the right side of the hill. "Mike, cover them," he said. I took the tripod from my pack, placed it on the ground, and attached the BAR to it. George turned toward Wayne. "Let's approach from the side," he told him. Wayne's face was pale, but his eyes showed firmness. He nodded and started to crawl ahead, swiftly, behind scraggly bushes as I began to fire. *Yeah, like that, a bit more so they can throw the grenades.* There was a scream more of surprise than pain, then silence. *No, No, Wayne!* George pulled the pin, threw his grenade, and dove for cover. After the blast I jumped up and rushed forward, the BAR still attached to the tripod, shooting, but there was no one left alive in the bunker. We ran to check on Wayne. He was lying on his stomach, blood oozing from a gaping hole in his chest. George put a finger on his carotid artery. No pulse. "Wayne, Wayne. . ." whispered Toshio, who had appeared with Tom and the others. "Wayne … Wayne …" he repeated as he stood, frozen, a few feet away from his friend's body.

We gained the peak's crest in half an hour, but as we moved out enemy guns pinned us down again. The staccato of machine guns reverberated in my head; the acrid scent of cordite made me drunk. The pines turned vividly green; the sky pulsated above me.

"Sarge, we need support!" I cried out.

"They're too close; we got to filter through and destroy the bunkers one by one. Tell the others." I crawled thirty yards to my left and passed the word to George, who in turn passed it down. The warm sun in the clear sky, the smell of gunpowder, the *ta-ta-ta-ta-ta-ta-tat* of machine guns, sudden reports of rifles like angry exclamation marks, the fury of hand grenades, screams of pain; bits and pieces of a moment in which I lived on the highest peak, I couldn't be more fully alive. My crotch swelled and a warm wave of pleasure ran over me.

∽

We sit behind a boulder, resting with our backs against the smooth stone, smoke cigarettes and eat chocolate bars. I close my eyes and enjoy the cool air against my face. I'm at peace. I see that "my life" isn't necessarily a span of time full of plans that I project into the future, but this moment, here and now; this moment contains all of my life, whether I die in a minute or live to be a hundred. I remember that night in Pierre's living room, when everything became a holy picture, the joy I felt and how the thought of its transience made it even more radiant. What if other moments could be like that? I open my eyes and glance at Toshio, who sits next to me.

"What're you thinking about?" I ask him. He slowly looks up at me, as if it hurts him to move, and says, "This is not like I pictured it." He takes a deep drag and turns his head toward the trees. "Not like I pictured it."

"Don't think too much about it," I say, and Tom looks askance at me. I take a last drag and snuff the cigarette butt in the dirt. "If you keep thinking about it," I go on, "you'll become distracted, and you'll be dead. Be fully present here and now. Concentrate on your cigarette, the taste of the candy bar, those pine trees and how they look like dark jade in the twilight. And don't forget that you have friends here; you're not alone."

"The philosopher has spoken," says Tom as he slaps Toshio on the shoulder. Toshio grins.

"Screw you, Tom," I say playfully.

Day turns into night, and it still goes on. At midnight the Germans mount a counteroffensive, but after an hourlong fight they retreat. I lie down under a tree, cover myself up with a blanket, and close my eyes. A breeze rustles branches and leaves overhead.

A faint smell of smoke reminds me of cabins in the Laguna Mountains. What fragrant smoke came out of their chimneys, when Steve and I went camping in the fall! We'd pass by them on our hikes and I'd fantasize about cozy sofas in front of glowing fireplaces, glasses of warm brandy, a beautiful woman, and good books in fancy bookcases.

My mind starts to spin, and an icy shiver flashes down my back.

I want to think, read, study, travel, love, but I stand on the edge of an abyss called "he died valiantly on the field of battle." I gaze into the future and see nothing, but what else ought I to see? The future doesn't exist; it's the projections of my wishes and plans that I see. I need to calm down, stop the film playing in my head. I'm going to die, that's for sure, but now a cold breeze ruffles my hair and speaks softly in my ears; the faint scent of smoke is still in the air. I close my eyes and after a while fall asleep.

The Sarge woke us up after four hours. He lit up a cigarette as he stood in the middle of camp and carefully unfolded the map.

"Okay, guys, the enemy is still holding the three 'Ohio' peaks and Mount Cerreta. The 3rd Battalion will attack from the north; we'll attack from the south. Expect heavy mortar and artillery fire. Let's go to work." For two hours we tried to advance on the first of the "Ohio" peaks, but the enemy fire proved too heavy. We huddled behind a ridge while the Sarge went to talk to Lieutenant Akers. Toshio crouched next to me and sipped water from his canteen.

"Where the hell are we, anyway?" he asked. "I know we're in the middle of Tuscany somewhere, but it's all damn mountains and hills."

"We're on the top part of Italy's spine, what they call the northern Apennines. Florence is about seventy miles to the southeast, and La Spezia is just twenty-five miles northwest of here," I replied, "at least according to the Sarge's maps."

"Hang in there, Toshio, and soon you'll be on the Riviera frolicking in the cool waves with a gorgeous Italian beauty," George said, and gave him a pat on the shoulder.

"Yeah, and they'll feed you grapes as you lie on the beach under an umbrella, am I right, George?" said Tom.

"Now you're learning," replied George with a smile.

General Clark finally called for an air strike on the enemy positions, and after our planes bombed and strafed the hell out of them, a ten-minute artillery barrage squashed them into the ground. It was up to us to finish the job. We encountered stiff resistance from small groups, but we finally took Mount Ceretta.

The bloated sun dropped behind mutilated pine trees to bring the ghosts of exhausted sleep. I sat outside my pup tent, took *Sein und Zeit* out of my pack, and flipped through it. Still a solid and elegant book. The smell of paper, ink, and cloth reassured me. A hawk swooped down from a silvery sky streaked with magenta into a world rapidly turning into black silhouettes and dark blues and greens. The cool breeze brought the smell of coffee. It was going to be ready soon.

In trucks and jeeps, we rode across the Frigido River over a makeshift bridge under a white sky. To the right and above us, I spotted the outskirts of a town. We passed by a stone wall that looked like a castle fortification, more than one hundred feet high, with a white marble balustrade on top. Women dressed in black stood with their elbows on the railing and stared down at us. They looked so small from way down there. I waved; some waved back. We drove on by rolling hills covered with grapevines and farmhouses; it was cold, and birds weaved patterns above us. Way ahead, the white marble mountains of Carrara seemed covered with snow.

The Sarge's maps were so clean and neat, everything looked ordered and planned, but when he told us our next objective was to occupy Antona, the map said nothing about our four men shredded by mortars; when he showed us the way to Colonnata, the map said nothing about the grueling eight-hour march to get there; and when he told us we'd have to take Gragnana, the map said nothing about the enemy barrage that forced us to hide for three hours in a stable, crouched in dung.

"Here you are again with your fucking map! You're the angel of doom, Urada!" said Tom with a grimace, as he unwrapped a K ration fruit bar. The Sarge didn't even glance at him.

"If you want my job you can have it," he said, as he squatted near us and unfolded his map. "Look, guys, we're almost at the end of this thing. Try hard not to fuck up and you might still get to taste some pussy."

"Pussy? What's that?" replied George with a smirk.

"Who knows?" said the Sarge with a surprised look on his face as if the words just escaped from his mouth. He laughed as he unfolded the map on the ground. "Look, here's the town of Aulla. We got to take it if we want to cut off the Germans at La Spezia and keep them from retreating toward the Po Valley. We'll attack on the right; the 2nd will attack the center. They're already withdrawing, so it'll be a piece of cake. We go tomorrow morning at oh-eight-hundred; get some rest."

We attack in the morning, but it doesn't turn out to be a piece of cake. The Germans are entrenched in machine gun nests and fight fiercely for five days. Minutes and hours, nights and days pass in a sort of hallucination. No longer afraid or hopeful, I feel nothing; I move and go through the motions mechanically, flowing with the tide.

We walk into the bombed-out town seeking cover behind fountains and walls as we nervously scan windows and doors for snipers. Abruptly, machine gun and rifle fire forces us into a palazzo. One of the apartments' doors is open, so I run in and crouch down by the kitchen wall with the Sarge, Tom, George, Toshio, and the rest of the squad. An old man and a little girl huddle under a table in the center of the room. Explosions rock the building and pieces of plaster and dust rain from the ceiling. The little girl, her long black hair full of white powder, stares at me with wide dark eyes. I wink at her and smile, then get a chocolate bar from my pocket, break it in two, and give her a piece. She takes it hesitantly, looks at it for a moment, then takes a bite and chews avidly. I give the other half to the old man, who takes it and says, "Grazie, grazie."

"You gotta take out those mortars and machine guns—we're pinned down!" yells the Sarge in the field phone receiver. A calendar on the wall informs me that today is April twenty-fifth. That white piece of paper with the black date appears odd, out of place, a meaningless artifact. Suddenly, stillness shakes us. "They must've taken out the mortars; let's move out!" barks the Sarge. "Ciao," I say to the girl as I jump up and walk to the door.

The sun traveling westward, the watch-hand pointing at different numbers, hunger pangs squeezing my guts: signs that what we call time is passing. Get that sniper. Hold your breath, pull the trigger, crawl on cobblestone alleys, crouch against walls, pull the pins, throw the grenades, wipe out the machine gun nests. With the 2nd Battalion advancing from the east and other companies from the northwest, we finally take Aulla.

Thick black smoke escapes from burning enemy tanks and bombed-out buildings; dense clouds snake upward swiftly, angrily. The rushing sound of a torrent floods my head as dirt and dust rain down over ghostly figures firing rifles at other ghosts. I crouch behind a smoldering jeep and search windows for snipers when the stench of shit dives down my nostrils and pulls my stomach up; I turn my head to the right and see a partly burned body. I can't make out whether it's a German or one of our men; it was a human being, but now it's only a carcass with its abdomen split open, the intestines pink and black trailing across the street and sticking on a palazzo's gray wall. As I get up to get the hell out of there, I spot the unmistakable silhouette of a German helmet in a window. I hide again behind the front of the jeep, get down on one knee, and steady the BAR against the jeep's side. I take aim, hold my breath, and pull the trigger; a jerk, a blast, and the figure falls backward. Just like at the fair—yeah, that's where I am, the carnival at the California Midwinter Fair, and I'm trying to win a stuffed blue lion.

"What a piece of work is man! In action how like an angel! In apprehension how like a God!" Is this what gods do? "Run to the right, let's move!" Deafening explosions. Where the hell am I? Is this Biffontaine? Aulla? No, it's Busalla. The sky is azure, the air cool, the smell of dust and gunpowder reassuring, the weapon in my hand an old friend.

The setting sun ignites a dirty sky, turning it into a dying, red sea. Stars witness as always, unmoved. What do they care if maggots recently risen from the mud are killing each other on a ball of dirt lost in the dark? I see my mother's smiling face as she sings a lullaby. Yoshiko, naked on the wet grass at Sunbeam Lake. The feeling of infinite joy as I suck her breasts. Blood. Dark, thick, oozing from broken bodies. Green uniformed men with arms raised walking toward us: Serravalle. And then, finally, there are no more men to kill, and exhausted, feverish, I lie on the ground and close my eyes.

Days became longer, and poplars and oaks grew new leaves. I tried to sleep but couldn't. I stared at the olive-green roof of the "hospital" tent and listened to the swallows screeching. Vivaldi's spring burst outside, but Mahler's Ninth Symphony played inside me. I was almost over the bronchitis that had landed me here, but my chest still felt tight and my throat scratchy. I heard guys yell and scream as Tom, George, and Toshio rushed into the tent yelling, "They surrendered, the Germans surrendered! The goddamn war is over!" "It's over and we're alive. Alive. We made it, Mike!" I jumped up and hugged them. "We beat them, we're alive," is all I could say, and then I slumped back on the bed as they rushed out again. Yes, I was alive, but couldn't get very excited over it; a great fatigue made me heavy, and I just lay there and listened to the screeching swallows.

11

1945

"Victory in Europe is ours. After more than five and a half years of the bitterest and bloodiest fighting that this continent has ever known, the armed might of Germany, the Wehrmacht and the Nazi party has been defeated—finally and utterly." So read the first paragraph of the *Stars and Stripes* on May 8, 1945, a paragraph under a headline that covered half a page and proclaimed, "It's All Over Over Here."

I sat at a table in the mess tent, drank coffee, and leafed through the paper until I came to the page with the Dick Tracy cartoon and the sports news. The New York Giants had defeated the Boston Braves yesterday, and Joe Louis was twenty pounds overweight. The Sarge sat in front of me, put a steaming mug of coffee down, and lit a cigarette. He took a copy of the paper from his back pocket and glanced at the front page.

"The war may be over, Mike, but we aren't going home. Germans are surrendering by battalions and companies all over Italy, and we're going to be the guys who'll process and guard them."

"Sounds good to me, Sarge," I said, putting the paper down. "It'll be just like a vacation. Where're we going?"

"We'll leave in a few days for Brescia, after we get our medals. It's about 120 miles northeast of here, not too far from Lake Garda."

"Sarge, what'll you do when we get home?"

"Finish college and teach geography. I like maps and what they tell. They structure reality, give a sense of order and purpose; I can see myself spending the rest of my life in a classroom, surrounded by maps and kids. And you?"

"I'm not sure anymore," I said, contemplating the oily membrane floating on my coffee. "Whenever I think of the future, a fog rushes in my mind."

"You gotta get your head out of the ass of the war. It'll take a while, but that fog will clear out. We're the lucky ones; we gotta make our lives count." He went back to reading the paper, and I to my coffee. I kept rereading the giant headline and the first paragraph. Was the war over just because it had been so declared? No, it was still going on. I wasn't getting shot at, but it was still going on.

As I stood at attention with the rest of the regiment at the airfield near Novi Ligure and General Truscott pinned a Bronze Star on my chest, a wave of pride took hold of me. A warm sun peeked through clouds as the 206th AGF Band broke into a Sousa march. As the general kept pinning medals and affixing Distinguished Unit Citation streamers, the pride and jubilation rising within me collapsed at the realization that I stood there in the warmth of victory only because of pure chance; so many of us were at this very moment rotting under French and Italian soil, and existence revealed itself once again as capricious, arbitrary, and irrational, a constant game of Russian roulette. The regiment, the general and other officers, the sky—everything held together in this moment with no guarantee it would do so the next. How ephemeral everything is! Beads of sweat formed on my forehead, and I bent my knees slightly, to make sure not to pass out. *Maybe in the next moment everything will disappear, but now I live and breathe, I stand in the pride of victory.* I took a deep breath and lived that moment to the fullest.

On May sixteenth the regiment moved to Ghedi, near Brescia, where surrendering German soldiers reported. The 125 miles through the rich farmland of northern Italy had been a spiritual balm. We rode by fields of wheat and rice, vineyards interspersed with stone farmhouses and vegetable gardens, men and women working the land. In the distance, castles rose from mountaintops. As we crossed the Po River, a flock of black birds flew in formation against the setting sun. The reddish sky and poplars reflected on the darkening river as its surface trembled in the breeze. We finally arrived in a large, flat grassy area with rocky hills in the background, and rapidly set up camp.

The following day, a continuous stream of German soldiers began to show up in trucks, on bicycles, on horses, and on foot, ragged and hungry. We ordered them to get in line as they arrived, sprayed them with DDT, confiscated their money, knives, and guns, and detained them in a barbed-wire field, where they slept in tents. One morning Tom took a photograph of me wearing an Iron Cross and posing with some of the things we'd taken from the prisoners. It was the same morning a tall, skinny soldier in a ragged uniform showed up at the gate. Unlike most of the others, he had shaved, and looked very young, maybe eighteen. He held what looked like a small wooden suitcase.

"Halt! What is that?" I asked him.

"*Musik, mein Leben,*" he answered as he looked at me with concerned hazel eyes, holding it tight against his chest with both hands.

"Leave it here; maybe later you can have it," I said. He wouldn't let it go, so I tried to pry it out of his hands. "Later you can have it back," I repeated. His hands slowly relaxed their grip, and with an anxious expression on his face, he finally let go.

"Karl, Karl Mayer," he said, pointing to himself, "please do not forget, tomorrow, *bitte*." He didn't have any weapons, just four discs in his pack. Rachmaninoff records. That evening, when I opened the box I saw that it was a gramophone with a wind-up crank. I sat on an ammo crate outside my tent and played the discs. Piano Concerto No. 2, which I had never heard before, filled me with longing, and I felt alone and incomplete. I desired softness, understanding, flowers, an embrace. I thought about Yoshiko, but my feelings passed through her and searched still, in the night. A cool breeze carried the fragrance of black locusts and ailanthuses in bloom, and the moon shone through cloudy veils. And so I rode on the music, up ecstatic heights where I communed with the moon and the stars, and suddenly plunged down forsaken seas where I swam in the dark until, paralyzed by exhaustion, I abandoned myself to death, only to be lifted up again, up, higher and higher in the night's cold embrace and the beckoning stars.

The next morning I returned the gramophone and the discs to the prisoner. His eyes lit up when he saw me.

"Last night, I heard *musik*. I walk to fence and listen. *Es war gut!*" he said, and he clutched the gramophone and the discs to his chest. "For you," he said as he handed me the green cloth insignia of the German Army that he must have taken from his uniform the night before. "For remember."

"*Danke*," I replied. As I walked out of the prisoner's area, I opened my hand and looked at the green eagle holding the swastika in its claws, sensing the coarseness of the cloth with my fingers. I wondered how many young men who had so recently been children died with this symbol on their chests.

How many had I killed? I imagined myself a young German inspired by the hope for renewal, new glory for one's country, dreams about the future, the stirring songs, the parades. And even if I hadn't volunteered, they would have drafted me, and I would have fought for my country. And if I had survived, I may very well have been a prisoner of war.

I received a letter from my sister Umeko. My family had finally returned to the Imperial Valley in late April. They rented a small house in El Centro. My father found a job as a foreman and Umeko began working as a secretary for an insurance company. Myoko was still convalescing from her bout of pneumonia and my mother busied herself in the kitchen and the backyard. Only a few of the Japanese-American families returned to Imperial Valley, and the ones who did faced angry people who called them dirty Japs and wanted them to go away. Much of the Japanese Americans' land and crops had been seized or bought for practically nothing by the white farmers, and now they didn't want us back. Some Japanese Americans had their barns burned down; others were beaten. Thousands of people gathered on the football field of Brawley Union High School to demand we not be allowed to return because we were "yellow-bellied sneaks" not to be trusted. Even so, there were some people who had remained friendly to us and tried to help us get back on our feet.

As the weeks passed and summer arrived, nightmares made me afraid of falling asleep. I relived the deaths of Akira, Samurai, Hideo, Wayne, and others every night. Since whisky seemed to be the only cure, I began to drink it almost every evening, usually by myself, outside my pup tent. Lieutenant Akers and the Sarge, both history buffs, began to write journals about the war. They'd talk for hours, trying to agree on what happened in certain battles. We spent most of our free time in the camp. At times we had softball games; at times some of the guys played football.

~

I had been up since five processing prisoners and it was time for a break. I went to the mess tent, poured myself a mug of coffee, grabbed a copy of *The Stars and Stripes*, and went to sit at an empty table. Only mid-morning, but it was already warm. I took a sip of coffee, careful not to burn my tongue as I unfolded the paper. The banner headline read, "Atomic Bomb Hits Japs," and below it, "Yanks drop new super missile: Equals 20,000 Dynamite Tons." I reread this line.

The story mentioned that "Allied scientists had succeeded in harnessing the action of the atom, basic power of the universe, to serve the ends of war . . ." and that 125,000 workers had been involved in making the bomb.

I gazed at the long wooden surface, the guys who sat at other tables smoking cigarettes and drinking coffee, the green canvas tent walls, and felt distanced from them; they had become parts of a reality I was no longer a part of. I couldn't breathe, couldn't make sense of it. I got up and walked out, and once outside I forced my boots down on the ground to prove to myself I was real. I punched my left open hand with my right fist, realized I was breathing again. I went to tell the Sarge I wasn't feeling well and received permission to go to my tent to rest for a while. "Many of us aren't feeling well this morning," he said. He told me his grandparents lived near Hiroshima, and how before Pearl Harbor, his mother and father had dreamed of going to visit them. Now he didn't know if his relatives were still alive.

It was crowded in the camp, with soldiers escorting prisoners, carrying supplies, and standing guard, and afraid someone was going to notice something wrong with me, I hurried to my tent, looking down.

I lay on my cot and closed my eyes, taking deep, slow breaths. "Get a hold of yourself, damn it!" An icy bolt ran through me—what if I wasn't going to be able to get back to the world I knew? How could my country have dropped such a weapon of mass destruction on a city? According to the article, Hiroshima had a "major quartermaster depot and large ordnance, machine tool, and aircraft plants," but why couldn't they have been targeted with conventional bombs? Thousands of children lived in Hiroshima. Were they just expendable, unfortunate side effects of war?

According to the official justification, dropping the atomic bomb hastened Japan's surrender, thereby saving more lives in the long run. But was it true? Did it really have to be dropped?

I had good reasons to distrust my country. It told me I had God-given rights under the Constitution, but it threw me in a concentration camp. It told me all men were created equal, but it forced the surviving Native Americans into "reservations." It enslaved African Americans and treated Asians with contempt.

Wasn't even the effort to defend dropping an atomic bomb on a city obscene? How naive I had been! I had bought completely the propaganda about America being the home of the free, a welcoming land grounded in moral standards and higher ideals. I had felt so proud of being an American when I was in high school. But how to explain Poston and the Indian reservation it was built on? How to explain the separate drinking fountains and the lynching of the black man?

I took the mirror from my shaving kit and looked at my reflection. A Japanese face stared back at me, and as I moved the mirror lower I saw my US Army shirt. I wore the uniform of the perpetrator but had the face of the victim.

What kind of abomination was I? Some kind of Frankenstein monster? Then I began to think about all the cities in Japan the Americans had firebombed. Hundreds of thousands of civilians killed. How many children? My parents' city—Fukuoka—among them. Were my grandparents, uncles and aunts, nieces and nephews still alive or had they burned to death?

I needed to calm down; I couldn't fall apart now. If I couldn't get back, I could always end it later. It was time to escape, to go see Captain Nemo.

~

As the *Nautilus* approached the Midway Atoll, the Captain and I stood on the deck platform enjoying the fresh air and the sun. Nemo, tall, dressed in a white turtleneck, gazed quietly into the distance. "It's a beautiful world—the ocean, the sun, cool air cleansing our lungs."I thought he was going to say more, but he stopped suddenly and his face darkened.

"Is something wrong, Captain?"

"Even after so many years there are times when my wife and children come alive in my mind, not as faint memories, but as powerful presences. They're no more, tortured and killed, but in those rare moments when I find peace in the beauty of the world, they come to remind me that they have been robbed of life."

"Is that smoke to starboard?" I asked, as I pointed toward a faint line rising from the sea.

He peered through his spyglass. "It looks like a sloop of war—let's get below," he said.

I scrambled down followed by Nemo, who closed and sealed the hatch as he said, "This is our chance to test the improvements you suggested, Mr. Anami."

Instructions were given to the officers on deck to dive to scope depth and turn toward the sloop. My heart raced as we picked up speed and glided toward our prey. Kanda stood behind the helmsman, the navigator, and the hellshark officer.

Nemo looked again in the scope. "It's the USS *Lackawanna*, three masts and a smokestack, armed with howitzers. We're too close; reverse engine." After a few minutes of what to me seemed a complicated maneuver, the Captain ordered, "Fire hellshark!" A shudder passed through the hull, and the sound of a propeller faintly whined in the water. "Brace for impact!" After several seconds a blast shook the boat and I almost fell forward.

He looked away from the scope and said, "Right on target! Take a look, Mr. Anami. I must congratulate you on your ideas. I have to agree with you, this is more effective than ramming." I looked through the scope and gazed at the burning ship. Almost cut in two, it started to sink. Thick, black smoke rose from the flames.

"An American sloop of war near the Brook Islands. I am not surprised to find them here; the Americans are planning to extend their imperial reach to Japan," he said.

He gave new coordinates to Kanda and turned to me. "Come, Mr. Anami, follow me to the library; it's time for a drink." As we entered the salon a serene, orderly, and cultured world greeted us: paintings on bulkheads, hundreds of books secured on shelves, display cases protecting precious fragments of rare corals and ancient artifacts. Nemo poured brandy in two glasses as I admired the paintings.

"You have works by Caravaggio, Titian, and Bernini; I've only seen their paintings in books."

"Actually, they're copies; the originals are at my base. I've tried to control the temperature and humidity in this room, but there could always be a malfunction, so I decided not to risk damage to what does not make me completely ashamed of being a member of the human species. The books are safe enough, even though the ones I most prize are also in my library on terra firma. Have a seat, Mr. Anami, and let's have a libation." He handed me a glass as we sat down. "Let's drink to the memory of the men who perished today on the American ship of war. I do not rejoice in their demise: they're unlucky tools of higher powers, be they the currents of history or politics and economics, but they were intent on the subjugation of other nations, and they had to be stopped."

~

"Mike, you okay?" Tom's voice brought me back inside my tent. It was hot, and beads of sweat dripped down my cheeks. I got up and crawled out.

"I'm okay." I stood up and dried my face with a handkerchief. "Did you hear about Hiroshima?"

"I know we're at war with Japan," he said, "but did they really have to drop an atomic bomb on a city? And I heard hundreds of thousands of civilians have been burned to death in dozens of cities. Our parents are barely out of concentration camps, and they're killing our grandparents who live in Japan."

"God damn it!" I yanked the cap off my head and threw it on the ground.

"Calm down," he said as he handed me a cigarette and lit it. "We can't think about it now; we're still in the Army." He lit a cigarette for himself and took a drag. "Our people back home are counting on us." I became aware of olive-green tents of all sizes everywhere I looked, the sun almost overhead, English and German voices, the sounds of trucks and jeeps, the smells of gasoline, machine oil, and smoke. "Come on, Mike, let's go—prisoners are still coming by the thousands. We have a job to do." Tom started walking toward the processing area. I didn't want to move, but I picked up my cap and followed him in silence.

~

"*Dieci lire per le ciliege,*" said the old man. "*Un dollaro per una cassa, va bene?*" I answered and showed him a dollar. He nodded. Italians had started to come on bicycles to sell us cherries, and even the prisoners bought them, even though they weren't supposed to have any money. It was a hot July afternoon, and the cherries were ripe and sweet. Tom walked to the gate and said to the old man, "Rice, how you say . . . *riso*. You bring *riso*; we give you meat, *carne*, okay?"

"*Va bene*, okay," replied the Italian. He wore a sleeveless white tee shirt and an olive-green fedora.

"And eggs, tell him to bring eggs, and you guys better give me some of those cherries," said the Sarge as he walked toward us. "Guess what, guys? Most of the regiment is going home, but our squad is going to guard prisoners in Ardenza, near Livorno." He grinned as he popped a cherry in his mouth.

"Livorno? Where the hell's that?" Tom wondered.

"In Tuscany, on the coast, not far from Pisa. It's a beautiful city, or at least, it was, before we bombed it to hell. It's the second most important port city in Italy. It'll be different there: we'll stay in rooms, we'll be able to go into town, sight-see," replied the Sarge.

"When do we leave?" asked Tom.

"Next week. You guys need to start getting ready."

The following week the squad left in jeeps and trucks and moved into Tuscany, in a fraction of Livorno called Ardenza, by the sea. The prisoners were housed in tents behind a hospital, an old palazzo that somehow had survived the bombings. Tall stone pines gave it shade, and the sea I loved so much was about two hundred yards away. It seemed a luxurious resort.

One morning, during my rounds of the prisoners' area, as I walked through the rows of tents I heard classical music. Intrigued, I followed it until I saw the prisoner I had met before, the one with the record player. He sat on a piece of canvas on the ground and was cranking the gramophone, which rested on an empty crate. Clean shaven, wearing a newly washed shirt and pants, with his soldier's cap on, he seemed a technician operating a vital piece of machinery.

"Karl!" I called out, and he raised his head toward me.

"American soldier, hallo," he said with a smile.

"What are you playing?"

"'*Der Wanderer*,' Franz Schubert song. You like?"

"Very much, *sehr viel*." His face brightened, and I sat down next to him and offered him a cigarette.

"*Danke!* I remember, Rachmaninoff, you like."

"My name is Mike," I said as I pointed to myself.

"Mike? *Gut* to see you again." We sat in silence and listened to the song, and as it ended, he turned the record over.

"This is very *gut* song, Mike, "*Du bist die Ruh*," Schubert, Elisabeth Schumann sings, I like very much," he said as he sat down again. A piano started playing and as the soprano began singing, I closed my eyes and felt lifted up by angels, away from this world into Plato's realm of pure forms, all the way to the Form of the Good, and my heart opened and radiance entered, acceptance of all things, forgiveness, love, and when the song ended, Karl and I had tears in our eyes.

I don't know how he did it, but Karl managed to find new recordings, and I began to look around in Livorno for records to give to him. We often sat outside his tent listening to music, in silence.

Karl was born and grew up in Braunschweig, an ancient city in Lower Saxony. An important center of commerce in the Middle Ages, it had been his whole world until he was drafted into the Wehrmacht. In October of 1944, more than two hundred English heavy bombers dropped 12,000 block-busters and 200,000 phosphorus and incendiary bombs, which lit up the city like a roaring bonfire. The medieval center destroyed, the city burned for days, but luckily more than 23,000 people took refuge in bunkers and managed to survive, including Karl's family.

He remembered how on Monday mornings he went with his mother and sister to the Altstadtmarkt to buy freshly baked bread, sausages, cheese, fruits, and vegetables. The main city's square, full of stalls and tables, surrounded by the Church of Saint Martin, with its two Gothic towers, the Old Customs House, and the city hall buildings, sparked his interest in architecture. On Sundays, weather permitting, he would jump on his bike and pedal all the way to Goslar to see Emma Weber, his girlfriend. It was a long bike ride, which he liked, because he could think, revel, and wonder, all alone on country roads. Emma, a tall girl with long red hair, had lived across the street from his house, but she moved with her family when her father, an engineer, found a job at the Rummelsburg copper mine. The Webers lived in a house with a charcoal-gray slate rock exterior, which reminded him of the scales of a giant fish.

Karl's city was gone in smoke and ashes, but he considered himself blessed; he and his family had survived, as had Emma and her family as well—now he ached to go back to see his family again, marry Emma, and start rebuilding the city he loved.

I stood guard outside the hospital gate on a perfect August morning, enjoying the scents of pine and sea that wafted on a cool breeze. The irritating spiderwebs of my thoughts left my mind, and I listened to the surf and the birds' chirping. The war was over and we'd soon go home, our guard duty was practically a vacation, but I could not get rid of the nightmares. Steve dead on his cot, Akira's mangled body under the moonlight, Samurai getting blown up, Hideo's eyes when he asked me to keep him alive, corpses with maggots oozing out their eyes and broken skulls. I even woke up with the stench of rotting flesh in my nostrils. I glanced at my watch: almost twelve thirty, time to go to lunch.

I washed up and hurried into the mess hall. Aldo, a tall Livornese in his thirties, stood behind the food trays, a serious air about him as he cooked steaks on the grill.

"*Ciao*, Aldo. *Una bistecca, rara.*"

"Mike, I give you big steak!" he said, and he broke into a wide smile as he worked. "*Tutto bene*, Mike?" he asked as he threw a piece of meat on the sizzling grill.

"Everything okay," I replied. As I sat at the table chomping down the steak, potatoes, and salad, Tom sat next to me, put his tray down, and proceeded to cover his food with pepper. I glanced at the mound of mashed potatoes that towered over his steak and spinach. Tom loved mashed potatoes, and he would talk Aldo—who didn't care much about such a dish—into making them often.

"There's going to be a USO dance Saturday night," he said, without looking at me.

"Tom, you know I don't dance—why even ask me?"

"You can just have a couple of drinks, listen to the music. Besides, who knows? You might meet somebody."

I didn't say anything for a while as I gave my attention to the tender meat in front of me, then I said, "You didn't do so bad; that girl you met a couple of weeks ago is a beauty. I've never seen a girl with such long black hair and large eyes."

"Her name's Giulia, and she's smart, too—don't forget that," he said and filled his mouth with mashed potatoes.

As I sat in the mess hall in Ardenza, dressed in a clean, pressed uniform, eating good food, I wondered what my parents and sisters were eating in El Centro.

Twilight gave way to night as I lay on my cot. My room, even though small, had a high ceiling, white walls, and a huge window that overlooked a courtyard. As I lay there in my underwear, drenched in sweat, I longed for a cool breeze, but only moths and the prisoners' talk entered the open window. I picked up *Sein und Zeit* from the chair and felt its rough cloth cover, opened the book, ran my fingers over the heavy paper leaves, then laid it back on the chair and got up. I needed fresh air. I got dressed and left the building.

Weariness weighted me down as I crossed the street and walked on the beach.

All strength leaves me, and I become an abandoned shell full of sand. The moon shines above billowing clouds like a bright lamp on top of dark marble mountains. A shimmering road descends from it and crosses the tremulous back of the dreaming sea. If only I could step on that trembling path and walk all the way to the brightness, the dark peace! I put one foot in front of the other, my boots sinking lightly in wet sand. To my right, in the distance, yellow light escapes from windows. The salty, fresh smell of the sea lingers in the still air. I look at my hand, my fingers. Nothing. I can do nothing with this hand, not in this world. Am I dead? Did I die in one of the countless battles and refuse to accept it? Am I a ghost walking on the beach? Why is my heart pounding? Why is sweat running down my face? I need to put my foot forward, but where is forward? Those are stars in the black sand; aren't they supposed to be in the sky? Where is up, where is down? I fall on my knees, inhale deeply. I must slow my breathing. "I'm alive, I'm alive," I repeat aloud, over and over. What's my problem? After all, I made it. That's what my mind tells me, but my body tells me something else. I find it painful to look at myself in a mirror because my reflection reminds me that my country had made me a living contradiction: the face of a Japanese man, the uniform of an American soldier.

I finally decided to go to the party; after all, I didn't have to socialize with anyone, I could just drink. I killed my fifth whisky and water. I took a drag from a cigarette as I sat at a table in the corner and looked around. We all dressed the same: khaki pants and shirts, shiny black shoes, ties and caps. Couples danced the boogie-woogie in low light, and even though the windows were open and a couple of electric fans lazily stirred, it was hot. *How can I dance and laugh*, I thought, *when my brother is dead? When Samurai, Akira, Hideo, and so many others are rotting in the ground? When I killed so many men?* I got up and tried to walk straight in the general direction of the table with the goodies so I could refill my glass, when I heard my name. I turned around and saw Tom with Giulia.

"Where've you guys been?" I asked.

"Wouldn't you like to know," replied Tom with a grin on his face.

"Mike, I want you to meet my best friend," said Giulia as she turned to the girl at her side. "This is Ornella."

I couldn't see her well in the dim light, but as I stepped forward to shake her hand, she appeared like a vision: a delicate oval face, a perfect Roman nose, full lips, light brown eyes.

"You . . . you are . . . the most beautiful girl in this place," I blurted out as I swept the hall with my right arm.

"You must have looked carefully at all of them," she said with a smile. We sat at the corner table. Whisky and water, cigarettes, stuffy warm air, couples dancing. Words entered my head and popped like soap bubbles.

The following morning when I walked into the mess hall, my head throbbed and my stomach burned. Aldo glanced at me from behind the counter and shook his head.

"You need much *caffè*, Mike. And food. You want some eggs?"

"Only two this morning," I said. Aldo had three kids, and after his shift, when I was on duty, I let him take some food home: eggs, meat, canned goods. After all, now we had stuff coming out of our ears. Giving me as many portions as I wanted was his way of thanking me. As I sat at a table and devoured the eggs and bread chased by strong black coffee, Tom sat down next to me. He shook pepper on his eggs.

"So you're still alive?"

"Did I dance with her?"

"In a manner of speaking. You could hardly stand up."

"Who was she, anyway?"

"She works as a typist in some office near Piazza Grande; her last name is D'Amato. Ornella D'Amato."

I didn't remember much about last night, but I still saw her delicate face, her mouth, her long brown hair. I wanted to see her again, but a whisper in my head said, "You fool. You're a Jap; she's white. You may think you're a hero, but you're different. Haven't you noticed how people turn and stare at you when you walk around?"

Tom looked at me for a while as he ate, then put his fork down.

"What's happened to you? What kind of philosopher are you? All you do in your time off is drink and mope."

His words felt like a slap. What kind of a philosopher was I, indeed? I did drink cheap whisky and mope, but I also thought about things a great deal. Did I think human life had a meaning? No, none whatsoever, except for the meaning people give to it. What meaning did I give to my life? By pure luck I'd survived the war unscathed; now what? The war, the relocation camps, Hiroshima and Nagasaki had changed the world forever.

"I've got a horrible headache—see you later," I said. I took a long sip of water and left.

The following day Giulia gave me Ornella's work phone number. I struggled for three days to gather enough courage to call her and ask her out for a cup of coffee, and when I finally did, she said she could have a drink with me at the bar near Piazza Micheli.

I managed to get a jeep and drove downtown, under a cloudless sky and with the sea to my left. Livorno had been heavily damaged by bombings, but it was still a charming city. It began as a fishing village, probably a thousand years ago, then in the 1500s the Medici made it a major harbor, and a canal was built that allowed navigation to Pisa. I parked the jeep near Piazza Micheli, walked to the bar, and sat at one of the outside tables. I drank a coffee and watched people on the sidewalk. A cool breeze came from the sea; a horn blew from the harbor. I had finished my coffee when Ornella arrived and sat down. She wore a white blouse and a flowery skirt. Her long brown hair cascaded down her shoulders and big gold loops hung from her earlobes. She sat in front of me with her right elbow resting on the back of a chair and smiled with closed lips. She tilted her head lightly to the side and looked in my eyes.

"You were very drunk at the dance. You do that often?"

"Where did you learn English so well?" I asked her, trying to change the subject.

"At the University of Siena, where I studied Italian literature and English. I met a girl there who had lived in America for many years; she helped me with the pronunciation. Then the war came, and I couldn't finish my studies. You speak Italian?"

"*Sì. Tu sei molta bella.*" I carefully enunciated the words Aldo had taught me. She laughed as she lit a cigarette. We ordered two Camparis and continued talking. Soon after the waiter returned with the drinks, I found the courage to ask her if she wanted to go to dinner that night.

"Tonight I have to go to the Teatro Goldoni—I'm an extra in *La Bohème*. Have you been to the Goldoni? You Americans have shows there at times."

"I've never been there, but I could come tonight, and we could have some pizza after the performance."

"Do you like opera?" she asked after she studied me for a few seconds.

"*Certo*," I said. "Life is opera."

"Tragedy or comedy?"

"That depends on you."

"I'll say yes, then, to not make your life a tragedy," she said and smiled. She got up and left, as I'd told her I'd see her later that night. I sat down again and watched people walk back and forth in the hot August afternoon. Couples held hands; old men stood at the corner and talked, gesticulating.

Ships' horns sounded off in the distance and seagulls flew low over the water. I sank deeper in the wicker seat of the wooden chair and felt as if I belonged; the chair, the stone floor, were the particular ways in which being itself supported me. The air smelled of the sea, of coffee, of hot focaccia. I ordered another Campari and sat there for a long time.

12

1945

As I sat in the darkened theater, surrounded by music and singing, I began to live in the story unfolding onstage—a self-contained world like the village in the glass ball Carmelita had on her cabinet. How often as a child did I hold it in my hand, shake it, and watch the snow whirl around the church campanile and fall on the red roofs?

Rodolfo opened the door and a woman, pale and graceful, appeared with a candle in one hand and a key in the other; she opened her mouth and her voice lifted me above the chair. "*Mi chiamano Mimi,*" she sang, "*vivo solo soletta in una bianca cameretta.*" I had been transported into a different world, an alternate reality. The setting changed, and now in a busy square bustling with activity, in the background, appeared Ornella dressed as one of the flower girls. Her gold loop earrings sparkled in the light.

I had never been to an opera before. What a strange world, and yet so familiar! Instead of speaking, people sang; the scenes took place on a bright stage, in front of painted backdrops; and the music was the manifestation of the gods weaving the destiny of those creatures who believe themselves free but are determined by their fate.

I didn't understand most of the words, but I felt what was going on: the dignified poverty of the artists, the desperate attempts to find redemption and meaning in love, the ever-present shadow of death, the pain of regret. As the scenes unfolded and the orchestra ebbed and flowed, in my mind the cold attic in Montmartre became a wooden barrack in a relocation camp in the Arizona desert, and the characters looked more and more Japanese.

During the last scene, when Mimi died on a bed in the artists' attic with Rodolfo crying by her side, I saw Kay in her bed in Poston, holding onto Yoshiko's paper rose, and her husband, Jimmie, his face buried in the blanket at her bedside. I quickly got up and walked out. Cold sweat made me shiver, and my hand trembled as I held the cigarette I had started smoking.

I stood in front of the theater, a golden palazzo with a facade bathed in yellow light. It had seven semicircular arches supporting a white balustrade, with corresponding windows on the second level. Men dressed in black suits and women sparkling in flowing gowns poured out, laughing and talking. They walked down streets flanked by bombed-out ruins, faraway ghostlike figures. Or maybe I was the ghost haunting this place with my delusions and longings. And then through ghosts in black suits and white gowns she appeared, radiant in a crimson blouse and a blue skirt.

"*Ciao*," she said with a smile. "Did you like it?"

"*Molto*, and you sparkled onstage."

She laughed. "It's a way to make some extra money, but I really do it because it's fun and I love opera."

We began to walk down Via Goldoni. The broken stone and cement rib cages of what had once been ancient palazzi lay at our sides.

"I could only understand a few words, but I've never had such an experience. In opera, scenes are contrived and over-dramatized, and yet, you lose yourself in what's going on."

"The emotions are real. They enter you and connect with what is deep inside. At least, I think so. Oh, let's turn here, let's go to Vito's," she said, and took me by the arm. We turned on Via dei Mulini as I tried to deal with her touch. A current passed from her hand through my arm, short-circuiting my brain. As we walked down the narrow cobblestone street transmuted by light blazing from tenements' open windows, talk and laughter, children's voices, and infants' crying floated down with the smells of sautéing garlic and onions.

"Here we are," said Ornella. We stopped in front of an open door leading down a steep stairway to a well-lit basement. Above the door a wooden sign with flaking green paint announced: "Trattoria di Vito." We climbed down carefully and turned left into a large, crowded room. We sat down at a small round table by a wall and ordered two pizzas and a liter of local red. The bare whitewashed walls amplified the mouthwatering aromas of fresh basil, tomato sauce, and mysterious dishes at nearby tables. An old man with a white beard wandered from table to table, playing an accordion. He swayed to and fro as he played with sprightliness, a big smile on his moon face.

"What did you do before you became a soldier?" Ornella asked me as she lit a cigarette.

"I studied philosophy at a university in California."

"A philosopher soldier! Unusual. And how did you acquire such an interest?"

"When I was ten, Carmelita, an old woman who lived near us, often talked to me about the stars, life, and God. I began to wonder about such things, and when I got older, in the school library I found a collection of Plato's dialogues. I didn't understand much of what I read, but I realized he talked about what is most important in life, and so I decided I wanted to find the answers to all the big questions."

"And did you find them?"

I laughed. "The war . . ."

"Ah yes, *la guerra*. I was in my second year studying literature at the University of Siena when I had to quit. But war can also be a great teacher, don't you think?"

I nodded. "But a cruel one. You grew up here in Livorno?"

"No, I spent my childhood on a small farm on the hills overlooking Porto Santo Stefano. It's a small seaside town near Orbetello; it's not very far from here. There I learned to love the sea. I would go for walks along the small harbor and watch the fishermen come back with their boats full. I would stand there, as if hypnotized, staring at all the strange living things: octopus, squid, perch, still alive in the boxes. I felt sad for them. Ah, here are the pizzas."

We ate the thin-crusted pizzas and drank the smooth, dry local wine as she told me about her father, a tall and imposing man with a handlebar mustache who was employed by the state railroads; her mother, who owned a small piece of land in Porto Santo Stefano; and her two brothers.

"When we were kids we would steal sausages from the pantry, run and hide in the fields, and then eat them with freshly baked bread. When we got home our father would spank us with his belt, but it was worth it," she said, laughing.

We talked for a long time, and then I walked her home. We strolled along the Fosso Reale, toward the harbor. Just like the Venice I had seen in pictures, this section of Livorno had a canal right in the middle of buildings and palazzi, with bridges connecting the streets. Cool air brought the scent of the sea from the canal, and stars shone in a clear sky. Streetlamps, skeletal philosophers that could not think but only illuminate, painted the streets with orange light. A skinny calico cat sat near a lamppost and looked at us. Ornella held onto my arm as we turned onto Via Cialdini, on the harbor, and strolled by disemboweled palazzi and hacked apartment buildings, their carcasses white under the moon, until she stopped in front of a gaping dark crater, a pile of ruins rising from the center.

"My apartment used to be here," she said, matter-of-factly. "One afternoon the air raid alarm sounded, we all scrambled to the bomb shelter, and when we came out, the building was gone. They had to drag me away. I lost everything I had, but I have my life—that's the important thing." A bittersweet smile formed on her face as we moved on in silence, then she stopped again in front of a building's heavy wooden door.

"I live here."

"I would like to learn Italian. Could you teach it to me when you're not busy?"

"Okay, if you teach me philosophy."

"It's a deal." I wanted to put my arms around her and kiss her gently on the lips, but I felt paralyzed.

"*Buona notte,*" she said, gave me a kiss on the cheek, and went in.

"*Buona notte,*" I repeated. As I walked toward Piazza Micheli where I had parked the jeep, I took deep breaths of sea air. The chorus of the waves splashing on the shore exulted in my mood, and I became aware of a clearing within me, a quiet, sunny meadow where I could lie down and feel at peace.

13

1945

S oon after we met, Ornella invited me to dinner. As I walked down Via Cialdini on the way to her apartment, a red rose in one hand and a bottle of wine in the other, I passed by the rubble where her former apartment once stood. The ruins appeared otherworldly in the twilight as contorted iron bars and slabs of cement reflected a reddish glow. The water, just a few yards off to my right, smelled briny as it lapped against the harbor wall. After another block or so, I entered the building, climbed up the four flights of stairs, and knocked on the door.

"Mike, *come stai?*" she said as she hugged me.

"*Bene, cara,*" I replied, and kissed her. I handed her the rose and the bottle, and she thanked me as she walked into the kitchen to pour the wine. I sat down on the sofa and looked around. I really liked her place, especially the living room: spacious, with high ceilings and large windows that now, after the bombs razed most of the buildings in front, overlooked the harbor. From the windows I could see the fishing vessels come into port, the sun dive into the sea. The sparse furnishings gave the apartment an austere, simple atmosphere I found appealing. The bare white walls, the reddish cherry color of the small table and the four chairs, and the green plant on a wooden chest imparted a simple elegance. The yellowish glow of a bronze floor lamp bathed the sofa in warm light, leaving the rest of the room in penumbra. "Mmmm, what's that smell?" I asked.

"Cioppino, a Livornese specialty, a fish soup," she said as she put a record on the phonograph. A Mozart piano concerto began to play as she handed me a glass of wine and sat next to me.

"What am I kissing?" she asked as she kissed my nose.

"*Un naso,*" I replied.

She kissed my forehead. "And this?"

"*Fronte.*"

She kissed me again on the lips. "*Labbre,*" I said.

"Bravo! You get a ten," she replied.

"Ah, the cioppino is ready—let's eat." She got up, put a white cloth on the table, followed by two white china dishes with cloth napkins and spoons and a wicker basket full of sliced bread, and then brought the bowl with the steaming soup. We sat at the table and ate. Shrimp, mussels, clams, crab, fish; I had never eaten them in such a savory sauce. She ran to turn the record over and was back in a few seconds. Mozart went on, and the dry, white wine, smooth and fruity, added a warm glow to the soup's flavors.

"*Delizioso!*" I exclaimed after a sip of wine. I'd never eaten a fish soup like this. I couldn't help dipping slices of bread in the cioppino and stuffing my mouth.

"I'm glad you like it," she said, "Fish is an important part of Japanese cuisine, yes?"

"*Sì,* even though I lived most of my life far away from the sea. Only once a year, for two weeks of vacation, I would go with my family to San Diego, which is right by the ocean, and my brother and I fished for abalone."

She didn't know what abalone was, but after some explanation she said in Italy they are called *orecchie di mare,* literally, "ears of the sea." We kept on eating and talking until I helped her clean up, and then we sat on the sofa and drank coffee. She put her open hand over her mouth as she yawned. "I'm sorry," she said, "I didn't sleep well last night; I had nightmares."

"About the war?"

She nodded and remained quiet for a while, then she said, "I had a government job as a typist, and when the Americans landed in Italy, we went to Luino, on the Swiss border, in a truck convoy escorted by the Germans. The typist pool was part of what was left of the fascist administration. Along the way, American and English planes strafed us with machine guns. I jumped out of the truck I was in, ran in the wheat fields, and buried my face in the earth as bullets whizzed by my ears. Last night I dreamed about it again."

I didn't know what to say. She looked at me and went on, "My father was *una camicia nera*, a black shirt, a proud member of the party. As a child I was a Balilla, part of the youth movement. There were exciting songs, music, the uniforms and symbols; it was the way the world was made. Then as time passed, I began to have doubts. The exciting feelings of pride and hope disappeared, and when Mussolini joined Hitler I knew we were lost."

"But why did you remain a party member then?"

"I had to work, I had to live. It's hard to go against your family, your friends, your upbringing." She sat, stooped, partly lit by the yellow glow of the lamp; she grasped the coffee saucer with thumbs and forefingers and stared at the empty cup with a blank expression in her eyes, as muffled talking and laughter floated from the street below. Mozart had stopped playing a long time before. Her fingers tightened on the saucer as if it were a diminutive lifesaver that could keep her from sinking. We sat in silence, and it seemed as if time stopped; and even though only a few inches separated us, I suddenly felt as if the sofa had telescoped and we were so far apart we could barely see each other.

I wasn't surprised that she had been a fascist; I assumed most Italians had been, I just didn't know how to reach her. I took slow deep breaths and drank the last sip of cold coffee. I glanced to my left and she was next to me again. I turned toward her and with my left hand caressed her hair.

"Look," I said, "that world is gone. The war is over, life begins anew; for Italy, for you, for us. We need to forgive ourselves and each other, or we won't be free." I continued to caress her hair, then I got up and stood in front of the window. Bordered by mangled pale ruins, the moon appeared close to the sea, spreading a golden carpet on the glimmering water. "Come see the moon—it has made a path for us." She got up and stood close to me.

"It looks like we could walk to it. It makes me think of Beethoven's 'Moonlight Sonata.' Let's listen to the first movement. I have it by Paderewski, my favorite pianist. It's one of the few records I have left; most of them I lost with the apartment, but luckily I had left some at my parents' house." She got up, put it on the phonograph, and as the music started, we sat down on the sofa again. A cool breeze caressed my neck, and the hiss accompanying the music sounded like the splashing of waves. I looked at her slender hands, at her flowing brown hair, and then gazed into her eyes. I put my hand over hers, felt the warmth of her smooth skin, and kissed her forehead, nose, and lips. I moved my left arm over her shoulders and drew her close to me.

"*Ti amo*," I said, and kissed her cheek and neck.

"I love you too," she whispered as she hugged me. I kissed her ear, ran my lips gently over her neck, tasted the sweetness of her skin, as the breeze, the briny scent from the harbor, and the voices coming from the street washed over us.

～

In the following days I kept thinking about what Ornella went through. I pictured her riding on a truck from Livorno to Luino, the long hours of discomfort punctuated by the sudden terror of Allied strafings and bombardments. Fifty-six bombardments during the course of the war, she said, then the disintegration of the fascists in the north. In the chaos surrounding her, she paid a truck driver for passage from Luino to Pisa. She rode all night hidden under blankets in the back of a truck loaded with wooden barrels full of wine. The driver dropped her off in the morning, in a square teeming with American soldiers, jeeps, and trucks. At first she was terrified, because she had been brought up to believe Americans were torturers, but then she mustered enough courage to ask for a ride to Livorno, which they gave her. Her fear of Americans abated, but she would still wake up in the middle of the night covered in sweat, gasping for air, and the bombardments continued, so many more than the fifty-six she survived during the war. The bombs would catch her vulnerable, helpless, in her sleep, and she would turn on the light, get up to drink a glass of water, and put on an aria by Puccini.

When I stayed at her apartment and she broke the night with sudden screams or strange animal squeals, I held her in my arms to quiet her down. And then there were nights when I was the one haunted by the past, and Ornella would hold me, and in her warmth I'd find solace.

One day Aldo asked me if I could give him a ride home, since his bike was being repaired. "I'll give you a box of tomatoes," he said. "I grow the best *pomodori* in Toscana!" I told him my father grew the best tomatoes in California, so I couldn't wait to compare them. He lived in a small house on the outskirts of the city, an ancient-looking farmhouse that his grandfather passed on to his father. After work I picked him up in a jeep and drove with the sea on our left and ruins on the other side, until we found ourselves in fields covered with round bales of hay. Strange how peaceful this part of the countryside seemed, compared to bombed-out Livorno.

"I make my own wine—come inside, you drink!" Aldo said as I pulled in front of the house. I turned the engine off and as soon as we stepped down, his wife and kids came to greet us. "*Babbo, babbo!*" two boys and a girl said, as Aldo introduced me to Laura, his wife. She was a slender woman with long black hair who told me in Italian that Aldo had said a lot of good things about me. She excused herself and went with the boys to water plants. Even though it was a hot August day, it was cool and dark in the living room. An old Beretta shotgun hung on the wall above the fireplace, and a wooden sideboard flanked a credenza.

"Sit down, please," Aldo said as he pointed to the round table and chairs in the middle of the room. I sat down as he brought a bottle of red wine with two glasses. "Mike," he said as he poured, "this is *vino leggero*, how do you say, light, but good. *Salute!*" He hit my glass with his and took a sip. "Mike, listen to some of the songs that gave me courage when I was in the mountains, fighting *i tedeschi*."

He got up and put a record on the player. "This one is called 'Bandiera Rossa.'" A deep male voice and stirring martial music came out of the player.

"Avanti o popolo, alla riscossa
Bandiera rossa, Bandiera rossa.
Avanti o popolo, all riscossa,
Bandiera rossa trionferà.
Bandiera rossa la trionferà
Bandiera rossa la trionferà
Evviva il comunismo e la libertà."

I could understand the simple lyrics: "Forward oh people, to the rescue, red flag, red flag. The red flag will triumph, the red flag will triumph, long live communism and liberty." I could see courageous men and women willing to fight and die for freedom and a better world, a world of golden wheat fields and busy factories where industrious workers forged a better tomorrow. "Mike, the music, do you like?" Aldo asked me as he filled my glass again.

"*Sì*," I replied. "It stirs the blood." He smiled.

"We listen to some more, okay?" he said, as he took a few more records out of a cabinet. We sat at the kitchen table and drank the whole bottle, listening to songs the partisans sang: "*Bella Ciao*" ("Bye Beautiful"), "*Fischia il Vento*" ("The Wind Whistles"), and others whose titles I can't remember. He sat at the table facing me and at times seemed to stare through me as if enthralled by a vision. He looked at me and said, "What do you think, Mike, you think one day, we all live as brothers?"

I took a long swig of wine and said, "*Forse*. Maybe, *ma* Aldo, *guardami*, look at me. My eyes, my face. Different. People hate, are afraid of, what is different, and then people are selfish, greedy, want power, to control. You think we'll live as brothers soon?"

He poured some more wine and said, "People that way because society make them, but *se educati*, how do you say, education, Mike; if people different education, people can change. I believe! In *società comunista*, all people free."

I took a Chesterfield from my pack and handed it to him. "*Grazie*," he said as I took out another one and with my Zippo lit his, then mine. I took a drag and said, "I would like all people free, equal, but how is it going to happen? What do you mean by 'different education'?"

He looked at me and replied, "Did you know Communist Party founded here in Livorno in 1921? I only eight years old but my father went there, he told me he talked to Antonio Gramsci, one of Communist Party leaders. Gramsci talk about education, different values, new way to look at world. If you, me, and others teach people, then society can change!"

"Maybe you are right, Aldo. Maybe society can be changed; maybe this is the right time, after the war."

He smiled, and then we just sat there and listened to the playing record:

"Fischia il vento ed infuria la bufera,

Scarpe rotte e pur bisogna andar

A conquistare la rossa primavera

Dove sorge il sol dell'avvenir . . ."

The wind whistles, the storm rages, our shoes are broken but we must go on, to conquer the red spring where rises the sun of the future.

When I left, I could not get the stirring music out of my head. Aldo had surprised me; I hadn't known this side of him. Could all men live as brothers? I didn't think so, but if enough people's way of looking at things could be changed, then just maybe, someday, we could all meet where the sun of the future rises.

After my visit at Aldo's house, I started to wonder about the fascists' songs. I had heard a few of their melodies on the radio, and they sounded stirring. I told Ornella I wanted to hear some of them and she told me to ask Stefano, who may have had some recordings. She said Stefano had been a high school teacher who had lived in New Jersey for a few years, where he worked at his uncle's restaurant. He had earned much more there, but Stefano didn't like life in America, missed Tuscany too much, so he returned and taught school again in Florence. He had been a minor official in the Fascist Party, and when the government collapsed, he moved to Livorno and opened a trattoria with money sent by his uncle. So I talked to Stefano. "Meet me Sunday morning at eight, when I'm closed. I'll be waiting for you," he had said, an interested look on his face.

On Sunday I knocked on the trattoria's door. Stefano let me in and took me in the back, to a storage room full of crates and sacks. I sat down on a chair as he went to an old desk, unlocked a drawer, and pulled out some records.

"I've had these for a long time; it's all I was able to save." He turned on the player and we listened to songs like "Youth, Youth, Spring of Beauty," "Little Black Face of Abyssinia," "Ciao Little Blonde," and *"Vincere."* The music stirred, the lyrics hypnotized. Stefano sat on a sack full of flour, staring into his cappuccino. On a wall hung an old poster of Il Duce, in profile, powerful jaw pushing forward, burning eye imprinting its gaze over Italy, a world full of weakness and moral degeneration to be purified, cleansed, educated, and, as the helmet showed, to be defended and fought for.

"Vincere. Great Britain, France, and other European nations invaded other countries and colonized them, and when Italy demanded its right to expand into Abyssinia and Libya, those same murderous, land-thirsty countries whined and accused Italy of unlawful attacks. *Me ne frego.* I don't give a damn! And what about the United States? Its whole history a nightmare of genocide and slavery, America had the gall to accuse Italy of aggression. Didn't Il Duce transform a bunch of peasants and shopkeepers who couldn't even understand each other's dialects into one people, one nation, didn't he fill them with pride and honor? Didn't he give them an identity, hopes and dreams? Who made the trains run on time? Who turned malaria-infested swamps into fertile, valuable land? Who built highways, buildings, and monuments, who improved the schools? Socialists and communists just talked, but it was Il Duce who raised the poor, the marginalized, and the hopeless into proud Italians. Yes, he had his eccentricities, his faults, and his mistakes finally destroyed not just himself, but the dream of a prosperous, proud greater Italy, with its own great reserves of petroleum, of conquered land her new generations could colonize. Hitler, anti-Semitism, poisoned fascism. But don't ask me to deny my whole life, to renounce the dream, to

regret having once loved Il Duce. I was, am, and always will be proud of having worn a black shirt with the silver insignias, of having marched in parades singing fascist songs; those were the best days of my life, and I will never renounce them. We lost the war, and it was a good thing, since by the end, it was Hitler who ruled, and Il Duce became just a sick man on the run. Italy will be very different now, but life goes on. I'll try to have the best trattoria in Livorno, and one of these days I'll get married and have children. I am glad the war is over, Mike."

I thanked Stefano, then I left confused by my liking both the partisans' and the fascists' songs. I supported the partisans, of course, but the music of both sides had an uncanny emotional power. What was the relationship between music and ideology? Between aesthetics and ethics? These were questions I needed to investigate.

In the middle of August, Ornella and I went for a long walk to Antignano, a small town south of Livorno. We left Ardenza around nine in the morning under an overcast sky and, for a change, a cool breeze. An unexpected respite from the heat of late summer. The Ligurian Sea to our right, in a brooding mood, lapped at the rocky cliffs; stone pines lined the street on the other side. Ornella in a flowery summer dress and straw hat reminded me of the Goddess of the Seasons in Botticelli's *Birth of Venus*. I wore a pair of khaki pants with a white short-sleeved shirt and the pair of brown shoes I'd bought the day before. Without my boots I felt light, as if a gust of wind or a push might lift me off the ground. I kept touching my head to feel the cap and its absence annoyed me. My shirt looked like a surrender flag. The narrow road had no shoulder, so whenever we could we walked through the trees. Surrounded by pines and brush, nothing reminded me of history; with no human artifacts of any kind, it could have been another century.

"Heidegger is right," I said. "Time is not something out there like water flowing down a river, we *are* time."

"That reminds me, I was going to teach you Italian if you were going to tell me about philosophy, and you have, but you haven't told me what your views are."

What *were* my philosophical views? I liked the history of philosophy, reading about the ideas of the great thinkers, Plato, Kant, Hegel, Nietzsche, and Heidegger. When I started reading philosophy, I enjoyed the essays of Bertrand Russell and A. J. Ayer; I liked the clear analytical way in which they approached problems. That was before I met Professor Kesselman, of course, before my reading of Heidegger's *Being and Time*, before the relocation camps and the war.

"You were right when you said war is a great teacher. It taught me life is absurd, there is no overarching meaning, no cosmic, ultimate purpose. We exist in the world with others, and our ways of existing uncover things and they show themselves to us in their mystery and beauty. Confronted by death we become aware of choices, we are spurred to take risks, to dig deep, to unpeel ourselves, to create our lives."

She looked at me attentively, and then with a flash of recognition said, "What you say reminds me of a book I heard of at the university. It was a novel by a French writer, Sartre was his name, I think. Anyway, it was supposed to be about a man who realizes existence is devoid of meaning, and we must make our choices to live or die in the face of that stark fact. At the time it seemed appalling to me, but now, I think I understand what he meant."

"I never heard of him; I'd like to read it. Maybe there's an English translation."

"Or maybe an Italian one; after all, you're learning it fast."

"Yesterday I bought a copy of *Il Corriere della Sera*, and

actually understood some of the articles. You're a great teacher," I said, and she laughed.

A flock of seagulls flew overhead, heading toward the sea. They reminded me of the fields in the Imperial Valley, often visited by seagulls flying from the Sea of Cortez in Baja to the Salton Sea. The sky, still ivory, showed patches of blue toward the east, and the air smelled of pines and grass. We had started our walk on a paved road, but wandered on the edges of cliffs and at times on the other side, among the trees.

Villas nestled on hills overlooking the coast reminded me of La Jolla, and as I looked at the blue-green expanse, at the cliffs, and inhaled the briny air, I saw myself and my brother between the Cove and La Jolla Shores, bobbing up and the down on the waves, fishing for abalone. Aleppo pines and Phoenician junipers jutted out the edges of crags. Cliffs transmuted the crashing waves into diaphanous veils desiring to enfold us. Ornella motioned to me; we needed to go to the other side, toward the small town beyond the curve. We waited for a truck to go by, then we crossed the road.

The clouds had dissipated, and the sun showed itself overhead. We had arrived at the outskirts of Antignano: narrow streets paved with rocks, beige and sienna-colored houses, green wooden shutters, clotheslines aflutter with white sheets and underwear. Some women walked by, and an old man pulling a cart full of rags smiled at us as he passed. We entered a *salumeria*, a small shop with strings of dried sausages hanging from the ceiling like stalactites. We walked through rows of shelves displaying tins of biscuits and olive oil, cans of Simmenthal beef, green olives and red peppers in jars. A mix of scents hung in the air: freshly baked bread, cured meats, tobacco. Behind a counter at the end stood a tall man in his forties with a mustache and a short, hideous-smelling cigar between his teeth. He stood in front of shelves stacked with bread loaves and I thought of my bookcase in Los Angeles. On a small shelf below the bread a wooden

Pinocchio sat with arms extended, smiling at me. With a red pointed hat and shirt, green shorts and big black shoes he seemed to say, "Hey, look at me!" We bought some salami sandwiches, cheese, and a bottle of wine, then we walked back toward the seashore.

"I really liked that Pinocchio," I said. Ornella smiled.

"He's the one who got me interested in literature."

"The movie?"

"No, the book. In elementary school one day the teacher began to read to us from Collodi's *The Adventures of Pinocchio*, and I sat at my desk enthralled. I couldn't wait to go to school to hear what happened next, and my mother began to worry about me, because usually I didn't like school. Then *al liceo*— how do you say it? —in high school, I fell in love with the poems of Giacomo Leopardi, and that's when I decided I wanted to study and teach literature."

"I'd like to read some of Leopardi's poems," I said, intrigued.

"I'll have to help you. His language is difficult even for Italians." We sat on the grass underneath a pine. Ornella searched in her bag for something and took out two small glasses.

"Do you always walk around with wineglasses in your purse?" I asked, surprised.

She laughed. "I had a feeling we might need them."

The man behind the counter had told us he made the wine from his grapes, and the bottle had no label, just a cork I easily twisted off. I poured, then Ornella and I clinked glasses and drank. Light and smooth, the wine went well with the salami sandwiches. The clouds retreated toward the horizon, and the sun surrounded by blue advanced overhead. The breeze played with two orange dragonflies as they tried to land on the tip of a branch. Scents of hay met the manic chanting of the cicadas, and resting my head against the trunk of a pine, I drank my wine.

"I'm surprised there are no ants on this tree," I said.

Ornella, who sat next to me, took a sip from her glass and said, "Strange, they're usually everywhere. Oh well, maybe they decided to leave us alone." She smiled and looked off in the distance, toward the sea. She remained quiet for a while. I poured some more wine into our glasses and admired the scenery.

"What are you thinking?"

"Oh, almost every year in summer my family and I went to San Diego on vacation for a couple of weeks. We rented a small bungalow near La Jolla and often went to a small cove to lie on the sand under a big white umbrella. We'd swim and read, and my brother and I fished for abalone. The sea in front of us and those houses on the hillsides to our right remind me of it."

"What was the cove like?"

"Just a patch of sand flanked by cliffs extending from the bluffs like protecting arms," I said, raising my arms in front of me as if about to hug someone. "I often thought the cove seemed to call to the ocean. She whispered, 'Come, come to me. Rest your head on my sandy breast, listen to my heart.' And I always thought the ocean, restless, lost in its vast loneliness, found peace in her arms." The dragonflies had landed on the tip of a low-hanging branch, facing each other, and didn't move. The branch danced in the breeze, and they danced with it, as if they had now become part of it, a strange blossom.

"I will be your cove if you are my ocean," she said. I turned to look at my goddess of the seasons; her golden loop earrings sparkled in the sun as I caressed her long brown hair. A tide of joy washed over me. I put the glass down on the grass and drew her close to me. She smelled of the sea, the sun, and the pines, and as she extended her arms in an embrace I rested my head on her breast.

14

1945

Livorno, a proud harbor city more than nine hundred years old, had been pounded by thousands of bombing runs, its churches and buildings turned into rubble, the local economy destroyed, and yet the people—the ones who stayed and the ones who returned right after the end of the war—threw themselves into rebuilding the city. Groups of men, women, and children could be seen everywhere, with picks, shovels, and old rusted wheelbarrows, digging into the ruins.

Under the leadership of Mayor Furio Diaz, amid the bombed-out city blocks, like new green buds, one could see signs of rebirth: shops, cafés, and cinemas opened, new buildings went up, operas were performed.

I sat with Tom at a table outside the café near Piazza Micheli with a copy *of Il Messaggero* as we waited for Giulia and Ornella. In a corner of the piazza, a balding man in a sleeveless tee shirt sold watermelon slices to passersby. The thick slices rested on chunks of ice, and people gathered under the tent for refreshment. We sat under an umbrella, but the sun made me squint, so I put on my sunglasses and tried to read an essay in the cultural page.

"How did you learn Italian so fast?" asked Tom as he looked at girls walking by.

"I have a really good teacher, in case you haven't noticed," I replied, without telling him I had learned Spanish as a child from Carmelita, which made it easier to master Italian. With Ornella's help I began to read Giacomo Leopardi. At first his poems were impenetrable, but her explanations enabled me to enter the poet's world, painful and beautiful, ruled by amore e morte, love and death. Leopardi said death is the queen of time, so if I am time, then death is my queen. I liked that image.

"You've sure changed since you met Ornella; you're not drinking shitty booze and moping anymore."

"I'm madly in love, in case you haven't noticed," I said without taking my eyes off the page. I knew he was going to have something to say about that.

He snickered. "I thought you didn't believe in love."

"I'm a philosopher, remember? I examine new evidence and information objectively and revise my views accordingly." I glanced at him with a straight face.

He shook his head and grinned. I took a sip of the dense, steaming coffee. Almost four in the afternoon, the place was filling up with people. A short, middle-aged man with a guitar came out of the bar and began to sing in a melodious cadence, "*Uscite dalle finestre, fanciulle care . . .*" A blond girl dressed in a white blouse and a red skirt followed him and sang parts of the song with him. "*Vola, stornello vola . . .*" she harmonized as she gracefully walked behind the man. I laid the paper down and listened to the melody, to the story that they sang in turn, about fervent declarations of love and their skeptical rebuttals.

"Here comes Giulia," said Tom as he drained his coffee and got up. In a light green dress, with her long, flowing black hair, she looked gorgeous.

"*Ciao*, Giulia, where's Ornella?" I asked her, as I, too, stood up to greet her. She kissed Tom on the lips, gave me a peck on the cheek, and then we sat down.

"Ornella is not feeling well; she won't come," she said, as she looked down at the table.

"Giulia, is something wrong?" I asked, as I gently touched her on the shoulder. She shook her head.

"Many people here are ignorant; there is much prejudice." She wouldn't say more, but I kept asking her questions until reluctantly she said, "Some of Ornella's friends don't talk to her anymore because she's with you. Mike, do not worry—many people *sono stronzi*, they can go to hell."

With trembling hands I folded the paper and got up, dropped some money on the table for the coffee, and left. I headed for Ornella's place but at the last moment turned on Via Grande instead. I walked aimlessly, not paying attention to passersby. Where was Captain Nemo?

I lay in my bunk enjoying the fresh air blowing from the vent. We had sailed back to the base in the volcano to load more hellsharks. The night before, the Captain had taken me up to his telescope and we spent hours peering into the dark sky.

He had invited me to attend a special dinner and it was time for me to get ready. I got up and dressed in a crew member's summer uniform: blue trousers, light blue shirt, and black work boots. When I entered the hall, most of Nemo's crew already sat at tables covered with platters of shrimp, scallops, crabs, octopus, slices of fish, and dishes prepared with seaweed, anemones, and who knows what else. I found an empty spot and sat down. I knew three of the men at the table: Tore the helmsman, William the chief engineer, and Dr. Torres, who had treated me when I suffered the bends on my underwater excursion. "What a feast!" I said as I looked at the platters of food.

"We have this special dinner every year to commemorate our life together," said Tore. I scanned the hall: there must have been more than a hundred men sitting at the tables.

"There are no women in your community except for Kanda. She seems very special," I commented.

"Indeed," replied the doctor. "She is the daughter of a Nubian queen, grew up in Egypt, and was sent to Istanbul Technical University to study ship building and cartography. Captain Nemo was a student there at the time. Her kingdom was crushed by the Egyptians a long time ago, but surviving Nubians still maintained the royal line. When the Captain asked her to join him on his mission, she accepted. She helped him design the *Nautilus* and supervised its construction."

"We engineers look after the daily running of the ship, but she has a much deeper knowledge of it and its capabilities," said the chief engineer.

"We are not monks, Mr. Anami. We have not taken a vow of celibacy. We periodically spend time on land, researching or conducting business. If we find women willing to join our cause, they will be welcomed," said Dr. Torres.

We faced a platform and above it, a large painting of the sun hanging low on the ocean. Captain Nemo and Kanda walked in and stood in front of us, in the center of the platform. He scanned the room slowly with a warm gaze, then began to speak.

"Sister, brothers! Today we celebrate another year of our community. We did not abandon the world, only the web of nationalistic prejudices, racist ideology, and shallow social conventions that entangle it. We escaped from the spider of capitalism, an act that freed us from its paralyzing poison, the sticky threads of its lying promises, and from having life sucked out of us until only our hollow husks remained. In this spent volcano we have dedicated ourselves to the life of the mind and the spirit. We work, think, wonder, research, create, and rest, truly rest undisturbed by the demands, distractions, and hatreds that roil humankind. We did not abandon the world, for we have brought with us languages, music, philosophy, the sciences, art, and literature.

"I am often away from you, roaming the seas, but know that in spirit I am with you. Let us eat, drink, and rejoice in the unity of our minds and hearts. But first, let us give thanks to the sun and the sea, for they are the givers of life." He looked at Kanda and moved to the side, as she took center stage. Tall, dressed in black, with her gold chain around her neck and the medallion of Isis on her chest, she looked regal. She raised her hands above her head and spoke.

"Great Helios and great Ocean, from you we came, to you we shall return. We thank you for our lives and for all your gifts." Everyone got up and repeated her words.

"Now let us enjoy this food and drink," said Captain Nemo, and we all sat down and enjoyed the feast.

After the commemoration I took a walk around most of the crater's perimeter. I had stuffed myself and had partaken of a few pints of seaweed beer. It must have been almost midnight, according to the constellations I could see in the circle of stars above me. No breeze cooled the crater and the air was balmy. I forced my eyes open, but after a few seconds they would close again, so I turned around to go back to my cabin. A faint red light on a pole in front of every structure guided my steps, and as I walked by the library, an imposing figure stepped out the door.

"Mr. Anami, I hope you enjoyed the dinner," Kanda said.

"Perhaps a bit too much, I'm afraid. I hoped to feel better by getting some air, but it's time to rest."

"I'll walk with you then; the engineering building is that way."

"I heard you are a queen's daughter, and went to Istanbul Technical University. Did your parents send you there?"

"My parents expected me to marry someone chosen for me and immerse myself in the role of the princess. But since childhood I was interested in how things worked, and I would take clocks and machines apart and try to put them back together again. I nagged my father and mother to exasperation until they relented and allowed me to go to the university."

"Please forgive my curiosity, but what made you decide to join the Captain's mission?"

"I share with the Captain a deep aversion for conquerors and oppressors. We are grateful to you, Mr. Anami. With the periscope and hellsharks, we are much more effective against them. Well, here you are—better get some rest. Good night." She smiled and left me at the door of the residence area. I could no longer see her in the darkness. I was elated by the encounter, but could hardly keep my eyes open. It was time for me to go to sleep.

The snarl of a Vespa passing by took me away from the *Nautilus*. I found myself in a small park, just a patch of green grass, a few benches, and a water spigot surrounded mostly by ruins. I sat down on one of the wooden benches and stared at the poplars, tall and deep green. Pigeons flew down at my feet as two old ladies dressed in black sat on a bench to my right and talked.

I closed my eyes and stopped my fantasizing. *I need to calm down*, I told myself. I could hear birds fluttering and chirping, women's voices rising and lowering, the occasional whine of a Vespa or Lambretta, the monotonous singsong of the cicadas, the gurgling of water from a drinking fountain; smell the bread and focaccia from a nearby bakery; feel the sun on my skin, so warm and soothing. I remembered the times when back in my Los Angeles room I'd lose myself in Beethoven's music, the beauty of Mrs. McClurg's roses and the jacaranda tree. I remembered Samurai, how he filled every moment with his being in the world. I sat there for an hour, then got up and headed back toward the harbor.

My reflection glided along shop windows, a ghostly Nisei soldier with hands in pockets, khaki pants tucked in black boots, shirt, tie, and cap. *Where are you coming from?* I asked it. *Where are you going? After years of reading and studying all those books, did you find any answers?* No, the most important answers are not found in books. War is a great teacher, it's true; it shows how trivial and meaningless most things are. My red, white, and blue "Go for Broke" pin ignited for a moment as it caught the sun, and I began to think of Samurai, Akira, and Hideo.

I turned on Via Cialdini, lined by craters, some half full of black water, and bombed-out palazzi, like missing or broken teeth in an old man's mouth.

When I arrived at Ornella's door, a haunting voice seemed to come from far away. It was *"E lucevan le stelle"* by Puccini. I listened for a while as I rested my head on the door, running my fingers on the smooth, lacquered surface, then knocked. She turned the volume of the player down and opened the door a little. "I don't want to see you right now," she said in an irritated tone.

"Giulia told me what happened."

"I don't want to talk about it now. Please, Mike, go away. We'll talk later." My breath caught in my throat. I couldn't just walk away.

"No, we need to talk now. What the hell is going on? Yesterday you were all lovey-dovey, and today you tell me to go away?" She opened the door wider and let me in. I had never seen her eyes so puffy before, her face so pale.

"Ornella, have I done something wrong?"

"It's nothing you have done. I have known some women for a long time, thought of them as sisters. Now they avoid me, laugh, and say terrible things behind my back."

"What things?"

"They say I'm a whore; they say I'm going with you only because of what I can get from an American, that I am a traitor to my race. I believed they were good friends, but they betrayed me." She turned her focus to the window, unable to meet my eyes.

"I can't change the way I look. Last week on the sidewalk, three or four boys walked in front of me, and when they noticed me, they kept looking back, staring and laughing, as if they had seen a funny animal at the zoo. One of them made his eyes into slits with his index fingers. I brush these incidents off, but somewhere deep they wear me down, like water wearing down rocks. Even the kisses of the devout eat away the feet of bronze saints."

She turned back to look at me and placed her hand on my arm. "It's not easy for me either. I am not angry at you, only at those people. But my family, they will accept you. They know you are a Japanese American. Most people in Italy have never even seen a Japanese man. There is much ignorance here, but basically most people are generous and accepting. They'll have to get used to you. What would your family say if they knew about me?" She paused for a moment. "You haven't even told them about us, have you?"

Taken off guard, I sat on the sofa, leaned back, and ran my hands through my hair. I felt exhausted, as if I had marched for hours. What would my parents say? Would they accept a non-Japanese daughter-in-law? Steve and Rosa came to my mind, and their impossible love.

"I will tell them," I replied.

"Why didn't you?"

I got up again and walked toward the window. "Maybe because I don't feel like they need to know everything about my life."

"Or because this is a just a fling for you, and in a few months when you go back home, you'll forget about me, so why bother?"

"How can you say such a thing? I love you!" We stood facing each other.

"Are you sure?"

"Yes!"

"Even more than Heidegger?"

"Even more than Heidegger," I replied with a smile as I hugged her.

"I love you, too, can't you get that through your philosopher's head? We love each other; that's all that matters."

"That's all that matters," I repeated.

15

1945

On September 2, 1945, the Japanese formally surrendered in Tokyo Bay, and four years of war came to an end. We of the 442nd Regiment marched that day in a parade through the streets of Livorno, at the head of 15,000 Allied troops. It had been a long road from the desert prison of Poston to this day in Italy, and as I marched with Tom, the Sarge, Lieutenant Akers, and the others, images passed through my head like swift-moving clouds in the wind. Treading water off La Jolla Cove, watching houses on the hills sparkle in the sun; my mother and sisters sitting on their suitcases waiting for the bus to take them to the camp; ; the faces of Samurai, Hideo, Akira, and George; Ornella as a flower girl on the stage of the Goldoni. Thousands of people on sidewalks clapped and threw flowers as martial music stirred my blood. I had survived the war, but I might just as easily have been a corpse rotting in a grave. *I'm alive. These drums and trombones filling the air with oomphs and ta-ta-taaas, these smiling girls, the yells of "Bravi! Bravi!" and the warm bright air, suddenly shift and become unreal, a delicate burst of visible matter, a dandelion's scattered fluff in the wind, a rainbow after the rain. It didn't have to be but it is, and after this day it will disappear. And all of life is like this. By millions of chance occurrences I was born; at any time I could die.* The sheer contingency of it all, the utter impermanence and fluidity of all things—they were not mere thoughts in my head but my very being. I relaxed and threw myself into that fluidity and impermanence, and as we approached Piazza Grande I saw Ornella on the sidewalk, in front of the crowd lining the street. She waved, threw a kiss and a red rose toward me, and as I lost sight of her, everything became radiant and achingly tender.

The following day, Tom and Giulia married in a small wood-paneled chapel in the hospital. It was the most convenient location, and Tom knew the chaplain. It was a brief civil ceremony attended by just Ornella and me. The slow-moving ceiling fan blew humid air in our faces as Tom, in his uniform, stood next to Giulia, in a white dress, a bouquet of pink carnations in her hands.

"Do you, Tom Nakama, take Giulia Miglio as your wife, to have and to hold until death do you part?" asked chaplain Frank Jogima, a short, stocky man in wire-rimmed glasses.

"I do," replied Tom.

"And do you, Giulia Miglio, take Tom Nakama as your husband, to have and to hold, until death do you part?"

"I do," said Giulia. Ornella and I stood behind the bride and groom. I turned my head slightly toward Ornella and our gazes met. We smiled, and then we heard the chaplain exclaim, "I now pronounce you husband and wife!"

"*Viva gli sposi! Viva gli sposi!*" said Ornella as she hugged Giulia.

"You really did it!" I said as I shook Tom's hand. "Giulia, *tante congratulazioni!*" I hugged and kissed the bride, and then we left in the jeep.

As soon as we walked into Vito's trattoria we were assaulted by shouts of "*Viva gli sposi! Tanta felicita!*" Vito was there, dressed in black pants, a white shirt, and a black tie, along with Aldo and his wife and kids, some friends of Giulia and Ornella, George, the Sarge and a few guys from the base. They hugged and kissed the married couple, shook hands, and then we all proceeded *a fare festa*, to party. The same middle-aged guy with a guitar that I saw one day was singing *stornelli toscani*, and we ate macaroni *al ragù, cacciucco, fusilli al salmone*, bread, and cheese, and drank lots of wine. Aldo's two boys, ages nine and twelve, came to ask me questions about my "Go for Broke" pin while his five-year-old daughter sat on a chair and stuffed a piece of cake in her mouth. Lieutenant Akers talked to a young Italian woman in a corner, a slender brunette with hair down to her waist. I didn't know it then, but she was his girlfriend, and they later married. In addition to the singer with the guitar, someone had a fancy accordion, and he sure knew how to play it. People sang along and danced until toward evening Tom and Giulia left in the jeep for three days in Siena, and after some more coffee, everyone, stuffed and tipsy, went home.

Ornella had told me that Giulia had run away from home on her seventeenth birthday with a German soldier, a blond, delicate youth who belonged to a garrison camped not far from her parents' house. She saw him one morning as she stood by the side of the road in Orbetello as he marched with his platoon. He had smiled at her and had given her a chocolate bar, then in the evening he met her as she walked to the store, and that's how it started. He spoke some Italian, and on the days when he was off duty they went for long walks in the pine groves of Ansedonia, and they made love near Caravaggio's tomb. He had studied art before he was drafted in the Wehrmacht, and the day she took him to Caravaggio's grave his blue eyes sparkled and he had lifted her up and told her he loved her. She fell madly for him, and when time came for the garrison to move north, she ran away with him. When he died in a firefight, somehow she found herself in the Mauthausen concentration camp. "Ich bin kein Jude" she had said over and over, but no one listened and when the Americans arrived and she was freed, she weighed 90 pounds and had lost half of her teeth. When she showed up at home, her mother didn't recognize her at first, and her dowry had to be sold to fix her teeth. Seeing her radiant, cuddling next to Tom as the jeep left for Siena, made us happy.

As September ended, the days turned colder and shorter, plane trees dropped their leaves, and rain began to pour. Ornella and I spent more and more time together; we went to concerts, operas, and films. The Goldoni Theater became one of my favorite places; I loved to sit surrounded by its golden boxes, the glass roof overhead, overwhelmed by music, singing, colorful costumes, and the scenes unfolding on the stage. At times Ornella would be an extra, and when I saw her, in a way I felt like part of the performance. We walked all around the city, sat in cafés, talked, laughed, and drank dark beer, wine, and coffee. I also became a fan of Italian films; I especially liked Vittorio De Sica, Roberto Rossellini, and Mario Mattoli. One night we saw a film that resonated deeply with us, Mattoli's *La Vita Ricomincia*, the story of an Italian prisoner of war's struggle, upon his return home, to rebuild a life with his family. Ornella and I, along with many others in the theater, were in tears when the lights came on. How strange that the title of the film was what we had been telling each other: that life begins anew. With summer's end, our units began to return to the States. Tom and I volunteered to remain another six months, but at the end of that time we would have to leave. Only six months had passed since the end of the war in Europe; it seemed so far away and yet as close as the occasional cold sweats and nightmares that still visited me at night, and the ruins all around Livorno. I wrote a letter to Yoshiko and told her about Ornella; by that time, there wasn't anything romantic anymore between us. We had drifted away, fond memories the only connection.

∾

I opened my eyes in the darkness, uncertain of place and time. Was the Sarge going to barge in and yell at us to get up? Was the eerie whistling of mortar rounds going to fill my ears? I turned my head and saw Ornella sleeping next to me and it came back. I was in her apartment; the war was over. I sat up and put my feet on the rug, felt the solid marble floor underneath. I took a deep breath and glanced toward the window; through the wooden shutters dim light announced the dawn. The radiator did its best to warm the room, but it was still cold. I put my socks on, got up and walked into the living room, where I rummaged through the records until I found the one that Karl had loaned me, a Columbia recording of Adagietto, Part 1 of Mahler's Symphony No. 5, and put it on the player. Then I went in the kitchen, washed the Bialetti moka pot, ground some coffee beans, filled the bottom part with water, put it on the stove, and turned the fire on. My hands shook and a pounding in my chest took my breath away. I was here, but somehow also there, in the forest, cordite in my nostrils and bullets screaming by my ears. I sat on a chair and took deep, slow breaths. The music, dreamy, full of longing and acceptance, calmed me down, and my hands stopped shaking; the violins, cellos, basses, and violas caught the disparate feelings, thoughts, sensations, and perceptions that swirled around the room and structured them into a coherent self in a stable reality. I moved the play-er's needle back so the disc could start again from the beginning. The gurgling of the pot told me it was ready, so I poured coffee in two small cups, added sugar, and took them into the bedroom. As I put a cup on her nightstand, Ornella turned and smiled.

"Mmmmm, *grazie, amore.*" She sat up and took a sip as I got back into bed. "Merry Christmas!" she added.

"*Buon Natale,*" I replied, and kissed her as I gave her the present I had hidden under the bed.

"Oh, are you Santa Claus?" A look of surprise and delight

on her face, she unwrapped it slowly. I had gotten her a red wool scarf.

"Thank you, it's really going to keep me warm." She wrapped it around her neck, jumped out of bed, ran into the living room, and came back with a present. With the red scarf around her neck and her short nighty she looked comical and sexy at the same time.

"Look at what Babbo Natale left for you!" She jumped back in bed and gave me a box wrapped in plain brown paper with a red ribbon. It was a beautifully bound volume of Giacomo Leopardi's poems.

"I remembered how much you liked those poems we read; there's many more there!" she said as she went in the kitchen to get the coffeepot. She refilled our cups, then restarted the record from the beginning.

I ran my fingers along the blue cloth binding, opened the book, and smelled the pages—they smelled like literature, libraries, quivering feelings and twitching thoughts eager to be released, waiting for reading to unlock the words and let them out, for a consciousness to give them awareness, for a human being with a history to make them real.

"*Grazie*, Ornella," I said. "It's a wonderful book; I can't wait to read it!" She moved closer and her leg brushed against mine. I put the book on the nightstand, turned and caressed her smooth, warm thigh. I kissed her, tasted the coffee on the tip of her tongue, and as she embraced me, the room dropped like a discarded robe, leaving naked the haunting beauty of the Adagietto.

After a quick breakfast of chunks of bread in a bowl of coffee and hot milk, we left for Orbetello. We were going to have Christmas dinner with Ornella's family. They were finally going to meet me. I felt nervous but tried not to show it. I had the day off and had borrowed a jeep. It was a clear, cold day and we were bundled up in coats and gloves. We took the Aurelia, the Tuscan road built by the Romans but modernized by Mussolini, and snaked around smooth, green and brown rolling hills, domestic pines, farmhouses built of stones, vegetable gardens full of artichokes and cabbages, persimmon trees with black contorted limbs heavy with bright fruit. We passed through places with names like Cecina, San Guido, and Follonica. Ornella said that the cypress trees at San Guido inspired a famous poem by Giosuè Carducci. *What will her parents and brothers think of me?* An uneasiness began to eat at me, and I lit up a Chesterfield. "Don't worry," Ornella said, "they want to meet you. They'll like you!" We passed Grosseto, to our left, the provincial seat of the Maremma region, passed a strange-looking tall building in the distance to our left, which Ornella identified as a storehouse for grain, and headed for Orbetello, the blue Tyrrhenian Sea glistening to our right, between groves of stone pines. The cold air carried the scent of sea and pines and the timid sun tried to warm us.

"Turn right at the next street," said Ornella, and a few minutes later I crossed two railway lines and parked in front of an ocher house with green wooden shutters. As we got out of the jeep, a tall man in his forties with thick black hair and a handlebar mustache came out the front door, followed by a shorter, chubby woman dressed in black. Ornella ran toward them, and hugged and kissed them. *"Mamma! Papà! Come state?"* she asked.

"Figlia mia! Figlia mia!" cried her mother.

"Mamma, Papà, this is Mike," said Ornella as I stepped forward to shake their hands. "Mike, this is my father, Giovanni, and my mother, Luisa."

"Piacere di fare la tua conoscenza," said her father as he almost crushed my hand in his.

"Benvenuto, benvenuto," said Ornella's mother in a loud voice as she hugged me and kissed me on the cheeks.

"And these are my brothers," said Ornella as she hugged and kissed the two young men who had come from behind the house. "This is Pietro, and the little one is Salvatore." We shook hands, and then we all went inside.

It was warm in the living room and it smelled of food and coffee. We sat on chairs in front of the fireplace, Luisa served steaming coffees, and Ornella and I took the canned food, panettoni, meat, and other things from the bags we had brought in and laid them on the coffee table. "*Buon Natale*," everyone said, "*Buon Natale*." We talked with Ornella's translating efforts until dinner was ready.

"*È pronto, venite a mangiare*," announced Ornella's mother, and we all sat down around the rectangular table. We began with a first plate of *tagliatelle al ragù*, and as we ate and talked I found out that Pietro, who short and stocky, reminded me of Cagney, worked as a machinist in Grosseto, while Salvatore, fourteen years old, delivered bread with his bicycle. When we finished the pasta, Ornella helped her mom take our empty plates back to the kitchen, and then they returned with plates covered with vegetables and chicken. Ornella's mother walked to my right side, smiled proudly, and put a plate in front of me.

"Especially for you," she said. I looked at the plate and almost jumped from the chair. A boiled chicken's head stared at me with indifferent eyes.

"Excuse me," I said as I got up and quickly walked outside. I inhaled the fresh air as I leaned with my left hand on the wall.

"Mike! What's wrong?" asked Ornella, who had run after me.

"Nothing, the chicken's head . . ." I could only say as I fought the nausea.

"My mother thought she was doing you an honor—chicken heads are considered a delicacy by many people around here," explained Ornella. "*Mamma, dacci un altro pezzo di pollo, la testa non li piace*," she told her mom, who had come out the door in alarm. As I returned to my place and sat down, the head was replaced by a breast.

"*Bevi, bevi,* this is wine from my grapes," said Ornella's father proudly as he poured some red wine in my glass. Salvatore giggled, as he watched his mom eat the chicken's head.

"I no like head," said Pietro as he shook his head.

After dinner and coffee, Giovanni set a bottle of clear liquid on the table and said, "You know what this is? Grappa. Here, you drink," and poured some in my empty glass. He filled his glass, hit my glass with his, said, "To you and my Ornella, happiness!" and downed the grappa in one swig.

"*Salute!*" I said, and swallowed. My stomach felt as if it had exploded, and the flames rose up to my eyes.

"Good?" asked Giovanni. I finally caught my breath, and whispered, "*Buona, buona.*"

Ornella came in from the kitchen and said, "Papa! Do you want to kill him?" Then, turning to me, she said, "Come, I'll show you around the place."

She took me by the hand and led me out. "Here, on the left side of the house, is my father's vineyard." She looked at me and kissed me. "My poor Mike! Are you okay? Are my parents torturing you?"

"I'm having a good time, except for the chicken's head," I replied.

"And this is where they keep the chickens." We walked behind the house and went inside a small shack where maybe twenty chickens were kept. They ran toward us expecting food. In the right-hand corner, I noticed three eggs on a mound of hay. The eggs moved and I crouched down to see better, and Ornella did the same. "Oh, they're hatching!" she said. The eggs, one by one, cracked, and chicks struggled out of the shells, the hen helping them by pecking gently at the shells. I had never seen chicks hatch, even though I was raised on a farm, and I couldn't take my eyes off the little yellow things as they forced their way out of the hard shells and then tried to stand up on their legs. I turned my head toward Ornella and looked into her eyes.

"I love you," I said. We stood up, I put my arms around her, drew her tight to me, and kissed her.

We walked around for a while holding hands, and then we went back into the house, sat next to the Christmas tree, and talked some more with her family. I gave Salvatore my army compass and a dynamo-powered flashlight to Pietro. After another shot of grappa and long, affectionate goodbyes, we left with two bags full of fresh bread, smoked eels, cheese, salami, olive oil, eggs, and wine.

On the way back it was even colder, but I didn't mind. Bundled up in the red scarf I gave her, Ornella snuggled next to me.

The sun almost touched the horizon, and the sky turned red and purple. In the distance, on our left, near the sea, playing hide-and-seek with the jagged coast and umbrella pines, a train passed, trailing smoke, and flocks of birds flew southward.

16

1946

I walked on the beach under an overcast sky with hands in my pockets, detached from the mechanical movement of placing one foot in front of the other. I listened to the waves as they splashed on the shore and retreated, seeming to whisper over and over: "You have to leave, you have to leave, you have to leave," reminding me that my time here was short.

My heart jumped. In the distance, a white shark seemed to wait for me on the sand; I stopped in confusion, then moved closer and realized I had seen a tree trunk. I sat on the bleached wood, took a sheet of paper from my shirt pocket, and unfolded it. "Dear Mike," the letter from my sister Umeko began, "I hope you're well and we'll get to see you soon. Why did you volunteer to stay an extra six months? You must have hit your head! They finally let us go home now that it's all over, and we rented a small house north of El Centro. Mom and Dad are okay, and Myoko is doing better. She had pneumonia and was sick for a long time. I guess you'll be here in a month, so we'll talk more then." Umeko's short letter, with its "El Centro, California" postmark, might as well have come from another planet, a world far away not only in space but in time; three years had passed since I saw my family and Yoshiko. She lived in fleeting memories: Yoshiko and I playing hide-and-seek on her eighth birthday behind my father's farm, Yoshiko wearing a pink dress at the prom, the Saturday nights at the drive-in when we paid more attention to each other than to the screen—memory shards from long ago. I put the letter back in my jacket's pocket and got up.

"Hey, Mike! What the hell are you doing? I've been looking everywhere for you!" yelled Tom from the street. I trotted across the sand and jumped in the jeep as Tom sped off. "We're late, they're waiting for us!"

"I've been thinking," I replied.

"That's always been the damn problem with you!"

"Tom, in a month or two we'll have to leave. What are you going to do?"

"Visit relatives and friends, get some money together, and come back! And you?"

I missed my family at times, but felt at home here; I enjoyed the sea and the umbrella-shaped pines, cappuccinos in the mornings, coffees at the corner bar in the evenings, the way people enjoyed life here, even in hard times, all the history and art everywhere, and most important of all, I loved Ornella.

"I can't stand the thought of leaving!" I replied.

"It's settled, then: we'll come back together." It was a cold February day. Ornella and Giulia had just arrived at the bar near Piazza Cialdini; we weren't late after all. Ornella wore a gray overcoat, black woolen gloves, and the red scarf I had given her; Giulia looked adventurous in a light brown suede jacket, brown boots, and mauve mittens. They climbed in the back of the jeep, and then we drove toward Pisa.

Poplars thrust their naked branches upward and a pale sun forced itself through thunderheads. We drove by smooth rolling hills that reminded me of Northern California, green fields of wheat and corn, naked grapevines and farmhouses. As we approached Pisa, in the flat countryside ahead, the gray tower looked like an exclamation mark written by someone in a hurry. I remembered how magnificent the tower looked in the calendar Mr. Fasso gave me the night at his restaurant, but in the distance, it looked incongruous and precarious. I wondered why I hadn't seen it as we fought our way north. The Arno flowed green and calm under bridges and old fortresses as beige and ocher palazzi reflected on the rippling water. Tremulous golden cornices, dreamy ivory windows, and restless green shutters seemed to float on the river's sides. Along the *lungarno*, ornate black lampposts stood guard; their octagonal pillars, slender posts, and glass lanterns for some reason reminded me of Edgar Allan Poe.

I wouldn't have minded living the rest of my life in a place like this; everywhere I turned I was face to face with beauty, with history. Pisa wasn't far from Livorno; why hadn't we come here before? I turned to Ornella, who sat next to Giulia in the narrow, primitive backseat of the jeep, and smiled. And to think that soon I'd have to leave!

Tom turned on Via Pisano and parked near Il Campo dei Miracoli. It felt good to get out and stretch our legs. We wandered along a side street and discovered a small trattoria, where we ate *mostaccioli* and *bistecchine alla marsala*. After lunch we walked through the Porta Nuova into the Square of Miracles. The Baptistery, a cylindrical building with Gothic decorations, loomed in front of us.

"The dome looks like a giant red helmet," said Giulia as we walked inside. Under the great dome, two hundred feet high, enclosed by marble and light, my heart leapt toward the heights. I stood in front of Pisano's pulpit, where Greek, Roman, Jewish, and Christian ideas are embodied in pink and gray marble (dug up not far from here, and who knows, maybe from the mountains where we fought the Germans) shaped by medieval workmen. We sat outside on the grass in front of the cathedral to watch the moving clouds and the sun change the facade's colors; delicate pink and yellow hues, like fleeting thoughts, passed over the three great doors, the arches, and the five layers of columns. If I was so shaken by the beauty of this cathedral, what must medieval peasants have felt, faced by such grandeur and wonder?

"*Andiamo alla torre,*" said Giulia, so we climbed all the way to the top of the leaning tower. I held Ornella's hand and pulled her as we climbed higher and higher on the steep and worn marble steps. I stopped a couple of times to glance downward but pulled back. At the top we sat next to the huge green bells and admired the campaniles rising from a sea of red roofs. As my gaze moved across Pisa, I saw myself lying down in my El Centro room gazing back at myself here, in the calendar picture of the Tower that had hung on the wall. So much art and history, under my feet and around, as far as I could see.

"Last time I was here I was so scared of Americans, and now I love one!" said Ornella, as she looked down at the piazza. I put my arms around her and hugged her tight. We were trying to put it out of our minds, but it was there nevertheless, palpable, painful: the thought that soon we would be apart. What awaited me back "home"? After the government forced us out of our homes, destroyed our livelihoods, took our possessions, and locked us up in camps, we were supposed to go "home"?

I found myself walking into the *Nautilus*'s salon with Nemo. Ancient Egyptian, Greek, and Roman faces watched us come in. We sat on a red velvet divan, and as Nemo poured brandy in two glasses from a crystal decanter, I turned toward him.

"Captain, we must make sure we never allow the nations of the world to develop beyond steam capability; they must never be allowed to use the power of reason to create technology that can burn to death one hundred thousand people in one night, to annihilate two hundred thousand civilians with two bombs, to use the most advanced scientific knowledge to build a machinery of death to murder millions of people. We must build more ships like the *Nautilus*; we must dedicate ourselves to the selfless duty of policing the world, to keep people from destroying themselves and the planet." The Captain handed me a glass but before he could reply, I was yanked back to another time.

~

"What are you thinking?" Ornella asked me.

"I wish we could live here. We could open a restaurant, 'Basta Pasta' we could call it. We would serve sushi, sashimi, hot dogs and hamburgers, tacos and burritos. What do you think?"

"I think you're crazy. Italians are not very adventurous when it comes to food. We would have to close after a few weeks. I like the name of our restaurant, though." She laughed, and I felt better. Giulia and Tom, who had been talking on the other side of the bells, came toward us. We went for a long walk on the *lungarno*, had coffee at a bar, and then we drove back to Livorno.

~

When I told Karl that Mozart's *The Magic Flute* was going to be performed at the Goldoni, his eyes brightened; he couldn't stand still.

"Mike, before I go home, I must see *Die Zauberflöte* with you, in Italy!"

"I'll see what can be done," I replied. The prisoners had started to be sent back to Germany. Security was not tight; still, it would have been against regulations for a POW to leave the camp to go see an opera.

I talked to Ornella, who managed to get another ticket. Stefano borrowed a suit for Karl, and Tom convinced the guard on duty to let us through without asking questions, and so one night Ornella, Karl, and I sat in the Goldoni and experienced Mozart's renowned work. In the navy-blue suit and tie, Karl looked debonair, and he sat bent forward, his jaw relaxed, mouth slightly open, eyes glued to the stage. Through a friend who worked there, Ornella had managed to get good seats for us, in the center of the orchestra section. When the performance ended we all jumped to our feet to applaud, and Karl must have clapped his hands raw. Afterward we went to Trattoria di Vito, sat at a table in the back where it was quieter, and ordered wine and *cacciucco*. The restaurant was crowded as usual, but our table was separated by a screen, since it was Stefano's private space, where he liked to read *Il Giornale* and do paperwork. The four-panel screen, white with plum blossoms, was the latest addition to the place, and Stefano never tired of reminding me that it had been handmade in Japan. That night he was out of town, so we didn't see him. He had managed to get scraps of salvaged marine material and used it for decorations. He'd nailed a fishing boat's steering wheel on a wall; an anchor, nets, gauges, and other instruments adorned other walls, and on the counter by the door stood a brass-and-copper sea diver's helmet. The place was well lit with several white-globed lamps that hung from the ceiling, and the wooden tables had no cloths, just white paper place mats. The waiter had brought us a basket of bread and a liter of the local white wine, and now the steaming *cacciucco* arrived.

"The music, the singing, and now here with you, eating good food, I'm in heaven," said Karl, who attacked the fish stew with gusto.

"I liked the sets and costumes very much," said Ornella, "but what really struck me was how in the beginning I thought the Queen of the Night was on the side of good and

Sarastro the evil one, but it was the other way around! It reminds me of how they told us that Mussolini and the *fascisti* were on the side of the good, the Americans evil and cruel people!"

"Teachers, newspapers, told us Hitler and Nazi Party on the side of good, English and Americans bad, but not true!" Karl had wanted to learn English, and he had made much progress.

"Strange, how opera brings forth the truth," said Ornella.

"How can we believe what society tell us? What is truth? It started with Mama *und* Papa telling me Santa Claus real, then minister in church say Hitler savior for Germany. We must find out, wonder, ask questions," said Karl. The waiter brought some more bread, hot from the oven, and we dipped chunks of it in our fish stew and washed them down with the wine. Yes, I, too, had believed in the Queen of the Night and had to change my belief, a reversal that increased my philosophical skepticism. But what had captivated me was Sarastro and the brotherhood he led: contemplatives, scholars, and philosophers who worked tirelessly to preserve truth, beauty, and love. I wanted to join Sarastro and dedicate my life to the pursuit of wisdom.

Spring marched forward. Days became longer and warmer, wheat fields greener and taller; leaves began to grow on black locusts and plane trees. A year had passed since I came to Livorno; it had become my home, but now I had to go back. We had a little get-together at Vito's yesterday for the Sarge and Lieutenant Akers, who were leaving today. I had finished the morning duty, and now that almost all the prisoners had gone home, there wasn't much for me to do, just walk around the compound periodically. I entered the large room that we used as a lounge area and greeted Tom, two soldiers, the

Sarge, and the Lieutenant. The Sarge and the Lieutenant had their duffel bags and were ready to leave. All they had to do was jump in the back of a jeep and ride a short distance to the pier where the ship that would take them to the States was moored.

"Well, this is it, guys! We're finally going home!" said the Sarge as he shook our hands. "I thought I'd never say this, Sarge, but I'm sad to see you go," said Tom. The Sarge laughed.

"Have a great life, Tom. You too, Mike! Write me when you find the answers to the meaning of life, eh?" he said as he turned to me.

"Have fun teaching geography to those brats!" I replied. Lieutenant Akers had tears in his eyes.

"It's been an honor serving with you, guys," he said. Deep down he didn't want to leave; he loved the woman he'd met here, Margherita, and had fallen in love with Italy, just as I had. He shook our hands, and then we walked outside, where Tom and I watched the officers take off in the jeep. In about three weeks it would be my turn. Tom and George were scheduled to leave on another ship. How easy it is: you get on a ship and after ten days you're in New York, but like Lieutenant Akers, deep down I didn't want to go back. I kept thinking about Ornella. I didn't want to leave her, nor did I want to leave Italy. One could spend years just studying the history and art of Livorno alone, from the Etruscan era to the Roman, Medieval, Renaissance, Baroque, and so on. Everywhere you turned there was an old fortress, a cathedral, a church or monument with its history and art, and I found myself more and more drawn not just to know more about all this, but to experience the synthesis, the cocktail of all these layers of history, art, literature, and architecture, and how, illumined by today's light, allowed into the open space of my life, all this can *be*. I finally began to understand what Heidegger meant by "being." And then I started to think about Pisa, and Siena, Florence, Perugia, Genoa, Rome, Venice, Trieste, Naples, Palermo, and my head started to spin. Even the smallest town had its treasures, its connections to important works of literature and art, to historical events. Garibaldi slept in this house, Nietzsche rented this room, Cosimo de' Medici built this fortress, Carducci was inspired by these trees. I ached to bathe myself in all this, but I had to leave.

The last of the German prisoners left last week, among them Karl. It was early morning and we stood behind the truck that would take him to the railway station. He wore civilian clothes and carried his canvas bag, his gramophone by his feet.

"Mike, thank you for everything. Friendship and music. You and Ornella come visit me in Braunschweig, okay?"

"Thank you, Karl, for friendship and music. Go rebuild your city—we'll come see you! Maybe by that time you'll have many children!" His hazel eyes shone with a hint of sadness and great excitement. We shook hands, then he gave me a hug and Mahler's "Adagietto." I gave him a Columbia disc of Beethoven's *The Ruins of Athens*, conducted by Mengelberg, and a disc of "Stornelli Toscani." Then he threw the canvas bag in the truck, picked up the gramophone, and climbed in. As the truck sped off he waved, and I waved back.

The *Nautilus* floated gently offshore one of the small islands in the Suwarrow Atoll. Nemo and I, wearing only shorts, sat on towels on a stretch of white beach. We punched holes in coconuts and with short silver tubes drank the refreshing milk as we soaked in the sun. Farther inland, crew members collected breadfruits, yams, coconuts, and other vegetables. Nemo drained a coconut and lay down on the beach towel.

"Ah, I've forgotten how good it feels to do nothing. My *nani* would take me to the beach when I was a boy, and I would spend hours with my head stuck underwater, looking at pebbles, seashells, hoping to see a fish or who knows what? I was given a pair of goggles for my birthday, among other things, and they turned out to be my favorite gift."

"You sound very fond of your grandmother."

"My parents were usually occupied with affairs of state; it was my grandmother who told me stories, read books to me, took me on outings."

"My father worked all the time and my mother was too busy taking care of us to give me much attention, so I spent a lot of time in the company of an old woman who lived nearby. She, too, told me stories and took me places." As I said this I felt a pang of loneliness; I missed Carmelita, and hoped that she was doing okay.

"Strange: images of my wife and children just entered my mind, and I only felt warmth and affection. In the past, sadness and rage would have accompanied them. Why do I have this feeling of peace?" Nemo wondered.

"Maybe we cannot live our whole lives filled with rage and hate, Captain. Maybe there are moments when we have to let go of them, find some enjoyment in being alive."

"I do find pleasure in reading, music, art, and in many social interactions, in nature and good meals. And let's not forget cigars and brandy." In the distance, seagulls circled the *Nautilus* as crew members fished from the platform. To our left a thick line of palm trees extended almost to the water, and with trunks and branches leaning forward they appeared eager to leave the island. I wanted to tell Nemo that very soon every square meter of this planet would be mapped, explored, colonized, and exploited, but he must have known that already. "We are the scourge of the earth, a plague that might destroy the planet. Do not forget your mission, Captain," I wanted to tell him, but I had never seen him so at ease with himself and the world, so I said nothing and just handed him another coconut.

I was going to leave the next day. Ornella and I went for a last stroll by the sea. "The island of Elba," said Ornella, pointing toward the horizon. "Can you see it? Napoleon stayed there a while." I squinted and shaded my eyes with my hand.

"Yes," I said, and in my mind I could see him pacing back and forth on the beach, bent over by rheumatism and rage, planning his comeback. One hundred and thirty years separated his world from mine, but of late, time had become transparent, and I lived with the ancient Romans and Michelangelo, Giotto, Saint Francis, and Garibaldi; here history no longer consisted of books to be read but became a living world to be explored. We walked on the beach near Orbetello; the sky met the sea cleanly on this clear day, and the calm waves rolled lazily to our bare feet. Monte Argentario rose to our left, and we could see Porto Santo Stefano, Ornella's birthplace, huddled on the promontory like a dove resting on the grass. I inhaled sea-scented air and took Ornella's hand in mine.

"Look over there," she said, and pointed to the right, "there, on the tip of that promontory. Can you see the castle? That's Talamone. Dante mentions it in the *Divina Commedia*. The people of Siena bought the harbor there in thirteen hundred because they wanted to compete with Genova . . . I read Dante in school, and whenever I see that castle by the sea I think about him."

"It reminds me of Ballast Point, in San Diego. There isn't a castle there, but a lighthouse. Portuguese explorers landed there in the fifteen hundreds." She turned her head toward me and squeezed my hand.

"I'll come here when I visit my parents. I'll walk on this

beach, look at Talamone, and think about San Diego, and you!"

"And Dante?

"I'll think about him, too!" she said with a smile. But the expression on her face changed, the muscles underneath the skin tensed, and tears appeared in her eyes.

"What's wrong?" I asked her.

"Before I met you I felt lost in a gray world, then you came into my life and everything changed. I could laugh again, hope. I may never see you again. My brother Pietro doesn't believe you'll come back. He said he'll eat his hat if you do!"

"Tell him to tenderize it, because he'll have to eat it soon," I replied. "I love you, I care about you, and I'll come back." I hugged her tight and kissed her, an army of tall pines on one side and the sea on the other, Porto Santo Stefano to the south and Talamone, aloof and gray, to the north.

17

1946

As the taxi bumped up and down the dirt road toward the farmhouse my parents had rented, I stared at the fields of alfalfa and lettuce passing by the window. Those vast green fields, crowned by a brilliant blue dome, so familiar and yet strangely alien, caused dormant memories to bubble up in my consciousness like nitrogen seeping into the blood of a diver with the bends.

The dirt rose in a cloud trailing the cab, and even though beads of sweat had begun to drip down my face, I rolled up the window. It was only May, but it must have been 90 degrees in the car. I tried to sit up straight and rubbed my lower back with my hand, but after a couple of minutes I began to sink down again. The driver, a fat young man with a crew cut, a thin mustache, and small eyes smoked a cigarette and drove with his left hand, elbow resting on the window edge, slouching on the grimy seat.

"I had forgotten how hot it gets here," I said, but he didn't say anything.

It had been an exhausting trip: ten days on the ship from Livorno to New York, a grueling flight to Los Angeles, and then the long bus ride to the Valley.

"This must be it," said the driver without taking his eyes off the road. He slowed down and stopped in front of a small farmhouse shaded by a huge tamarisk tree. I paid the driver and jumped out of the cab, grabbed my duffel bag and a box from the trunk, and strode toward the house. The door opened and my father came out, lifting his right hand in a greeting that reminded me of a pledge.

"Otosan," I whispered as I bowed.

Short and frail in an oversized shirt and baggy khaki pants, with a gaunt and lined face, he looked much older.

"Had a good trip?" he asked.

"I made it back," I replied as I turned toward my mother and bowed.

"Mike, Mike!" Myoko rushed out the door, jumped down the wooden steps, bowed for a second, and hugged me.

Umeko came out and said in a quivering voice, "It's good to have you back." We stepped inside and I dropped my duffel bag and the box on the cracked linoleum floor. Two sofas faced a coffee table, and an old water cooler blew humid air around. A framed photo of Steve propped on a shelf made my heart contract.

"You must be bushed," said Umeko.

"I am a little tired," I replied, as Myoko brought iced tea and we all sat down. *What am I doing here in this strange place with these people who look familiar and yet foreign? Maybe I'll wake up soon in my room at the prisoner compound in Ardenza, go to the mess hall and see Aldo. Or maybe I'll walk to the bar in Piazza Micheli and have a cappuccino. Where is Ornella?*

"Well, tell us about your trip." Umeko's words brought me back and I began to tell them about my long journey.

In the evening we sat around the kitchen table and ate steamed rice with fried catfish. A light bulb in a yellowish shade hanging from the ceiling lit the table but left our faces in shadow. My father sat facing me, eating without taking his eyes off the plate. My mother picked up *tsukemono* from a small bowl with her chopsticks. How strange to eat like this after so long!

The open window framed a flock of geese crossing the darkening red sky and crickets began their song. Myoko stooped over her plate and picked at the food. Her face pale, cheeks sunk in, she seemed a ghost of the carefree girl that loved root beer and milk shakes. She looked at me, smiled, and said, "So, you really like Italy?" I nodded in agreement.

"What do you like about it?" she asked, with a little girl's eager curiosity.

"The sea, the pine trees that look like giant umbrellas, castles and towns perched on steep mountains, the coffee, the food, buildings thousands of years old. Everything is so different from here."

Her face lit up. "I wish I could go!" she exclaimed.

"Maybe we can go together, huh?" I answered with a smile.

"He's got rocks in his head; he just got here and wants to go back!" blurted out Umeko, and everyone stared at their plates in silence.

"It'd be nice to go, that's all I meant," I replied as I helped myself to more rice. The angry tone in Umeko's voice had caught me off guard. I chewed, swallowed, took a sip of tea, then asked, "Any news about Yoshiko?"

"After her mother died in the camp, she had a hard time, but now she's better; she's living with her aunt in Los Angeles," Umeko replied.

"It'll be good to see her after so long," I said in a low voice and then finished the rest of the rice. I felt as if I had been on a forced march in the mountains; I ached all over and had to fight to keep my eyes open.

After dinner, my father and I went to sit in the living room. He lit a cigarette and offered me one.

"Jackie Robinson signed up with the Dodgers but he won't play for them until next year," he said.

"He'll stir things up," I answered, trying to look excited.

When my mother and sisters joined us, I got up and went to get the box. "I hope you like this," I said. I opened the package and pulled out a Silvertone record player with some Duke Ellington records. Myoko almost jumped up and down with glee.

"Oh Mike! It's beautiful—now we can listen to records. I've always dreamed of one," she said. I set it up on a stool, plugged it in, put a record on, and moved the arm in place. The Duke's music began to play in the room. After a while I turned it down so it'd play in the background as we talked. I found out that Umeko worked as a clerk for Roberto Garcia, an accountant who had been a friend of the family for a long time, and that Myoko cut hair at a beauty parlor.

"Mike, you'd better go to bed," said Myoko.

Startled, I opened my eyes. "You're right, sis, it's been quite a day."

"You'll sleep in my room," said Myoko. "We set up a cot for me in Umeko's room."

I apologized for the inconvenience, but Umeko and Myoko brushed off my concerns. I said good night to everyone and went to bed. On the chest of drawers I noticed my old book bag. I ran my fingers across the smooth brown leather, sat on the bed, and opened it. Inside I found the schedule of classes for the spring of 1942 and the pen Natalie had given me. Artifacts from a different epoch, they awakened my desire to be in classrooms, to read philosophy books and take notes. As I turned the bedside lamp off and lay under the sheet in the dark, I could hear frogs in the canal behind the house. It had cooled down a little, and it felt good to stretch out and close my eyes.

In sleep, Captain Nemo came to see me.

"Mr. Anami," I heard a voice call me, "Mr. Anami, please forgive me for this intrusion. I stood for hours on the platform above, looking at the stars and listening to the waves, thinking about what you told me that day in the library. What you said forced me to seriously think about the essence of my mission. I began it with a strong desire to leave the world of men and to avenge the deaths of my loved ones, but you are right: eventually, and probably soon, the world will develop the ability to find and destroy me. The only way to prevent it would be to somehow keep the nations from developing their technology. However, it would involve the creation of a massive organization and a high level of violence that would result—if we ever succeeded—in the injury and death of many civilians."

I sat up in bed, and in the faint, reddish glow of the cabin's lamp, I saw Nemo sitting on a chair beside me.

"To keep the nations of the world from developing beyond steam technology we would have to establish a complicated network of agents, spies, informers, operatives; we would have to assassinate inventors and bomb research centers. We could not keep such an operation secret, and I'm afraid many innocent people would perish. Do you think that our desire for a better world excuses the suffering and annihilation of innocents?"

I began to think of Dostoevsky's *The Brothers Karamazov*, the part when Ivan asks his brother if he could accept a world if its existence necessitated the suffering and death of one innocent child.

"No, Captain," I said. "I see now I spoke in anger; it would not be worth it."

"When you proposed your plans to me a while back, I began to seriously ponder my mission. I realize they will eventually find me; I can't sink all their warships. Damn it, Mr. Anami, your crazy plan has caused me to question my whole life. My wife and children were brutally murdered; I don't want to find myself in a position where I will be guilty of the same acts."

"Captain, you can still travel under the seas, research and study. They will not discover your base for some years; meanwhile you can search for a refuge that will be even harder to discover. Eventually they will explore every square centimeter of this planet, so you'll need to find ever remoter hiding places."

"I will be safe in the volcano for a few years—if a ship approaches, I can sink it—but you are correct: eventually I will be found out—but I think I'll be dead by then." His face relaxed, and I saw something change in his brown eyes. "I plan to stop sinking warships and devote the rest of my life to exploration of the seas and my studies. I have ancient texts that were considered lost, plays by Euripides and writings by Aristotle, to name a few. It's time I devoted myself to them. Someday I may share such treasures with the world. Now I must be going. Sleep well, Mr. Anami, and thank you." He slowly got up and turned toward the door.

"No, thank *you*, Captain," I replied, "thank you."

Still dark, even though a pale light appeared in the eastern sky. In the Chevrolet's light beams, cottontails darted across the dirt road and Johnny owls opened their wings and sprung up from fence posts. I drove my father to work so I could use the truck. It wasn't a Ford, but my father was lucky to have found someone willing to sell it to him on credit. In spite of the lines in his face, his stoic determination still showed through.

"Was it hard to find work when you came back?" I asked as I glanced at him.

"People here know I'm a good farmer; Richardson offered me a foreman job right away. If I save enough money, I might be able to lease some land and start farming again. They hit us hard and we fell on our knees, but we're up now. Turn right and stop in front of the shed," he said, as the pickup truck bounced over the graveled road. I stopped in front of the outbuilding, and just before opening the door my father turned toward me.

"I'm proud of you. You made us all proud," he said, and got out of the truck.

I turned around and drove back home. I felt taller and lighter. A faint band of red lined the horizon ahead, and I glanced at Mount Signal, visible now on my right. I had been back three days already, mainly sleeping, but still didn't feel right. At times I felt as if I had somehow lost myself in the past, when I used to live here, and couldn't get back to the present of Ornella and Italy; at times it seemed as if I had never left this place, the war, Ornella, and Italy dreams soon to be forgotten.

When I arrived back home, Umeko and Myoko were getting ready to go to work. I offered to drive them, but a girl-friend was going to pick them up. As I poured some coffee in a mug, Umeko came in and fixed herself a cup of tea.

"It's good to have you back. Now that Steve's gone, it'll really help to have you here," she said. Before I could think of something to say, she wished me a good day and left. I went back to the room Myoko had kindly allowed me to use.

I quickly made the bed, then plopped down on it and started reading some of the notes I had written in the margins of *Being and Time*. I especially liked the section on our being in the world as basically made up of idle talk and an unexam-ined acceptance of social conventions, since it opened up the possibility of trying to forge for oneself an authentic path. I found it hard to believe I still had the book after so many years. It had survived Poston and the war. I had read it twice in its entirety and some sections several times, but did I understand it? At times I thought I did; at other times I wasn't so sure. There was a knock at the door. It was Myoko, who had come in to get her scissors, brushes, and combs from her room.

"Don't tell me you're reading a philosophy book," she said as she picked up a small leather bag from a drawer.

"No, I'm actually reading a romance by Faith Baldwin," I said with a straight face. "Really?" she blurted out, and I started laughing.

"You were right, it's a philosophy book. Oh, I picked up a book for you, too." I got up and searched in my duffel. "Here it is, Steinbeck's new novel, *Cannery Row*." Her eyes lit up.

"Oh, thank you, Mike. I really liked *Of Mice and Men*; I can't wait to read this one." She dropped the leather bag on the bed, took the book and drew it to her chest, then opened it and smelled the pages. "Mmm, I love the smell of books," she said as she closed her eyes.

"You too? I thought I was the only one. I hope you like his new book." I looked at her and felt an ache inside. "How have you been, Myoko?" She sat at the foot of the bed and stared at the book in silence for a while.

"There were times in the camp when I wished I'd die, and when I got sick I thought, this is it, my way out, but I got better, so here I am. The war is over and we're back, but everything has changed. I used to have my own shop; now I rent a chair in somebody else's place. Otosan had his own farm; now he works for Richardson. Steve is dead."

"Steve is gone, things will never be as they were, but you've been back just a few months. It'll take some time, but things will get better. Here's a plan: let's take good care of ourselves and not think so much about the past. Let's throw ourselves into today; let's open ourselves to the future. Myoko, what do you think, is it a good plan?" She looked at me and smiled.

"It's a good plan."

A car pulled in front of the house and a horn sounded.

"That's Hisako—she's picking Umeko and me up. Thank you, Mike," she said as she gave me a kiss on the cheek. She picked up her leather bag and walked out the room, still holding the book close to her chest.

I followed them outside and waved goodbye as they got into the car. I began to realize how lucky Myoko was to be alive. So many people died in the camp of pneumonia, tuberculosis, or depression. Maybe I fought the easier war, where the enemy wore a different uniform and spoke a different language. Would I have survived another two years at Poston? I went back inside but couldn't read anymore. I laid the book on the nightstand and went into the kitchen.

My mother sat at the table slicing daikon radishes on a board. I thought of the morning I left for the Army; I saw again my parents and sisters in front of the barrack door watching me walk toward the bus that would take me to Camp Shelby. I sat by a window and as the bus left, I had turned my head to watch her wave at me. I had wondered if I would ever see her again. My mother's hair was whiter now, the lines in her face deeper. I sat next to her and she asked me if I had been sleeping well. I nodded, and then I asked her how she was. Apart from a few aches and pains, fine, she said. She looked at me through her thick eyeglasses and said, "I prayed for you all this time, and you are here." *It seems like a dream to be all together again,* I wanted to say, but then I remembered that Steve was dead.

She told me she had buried something under a tree and wanted to know if it was still there, so I gave her a ride in the pickup. We drove on Ross until we came to Bowker Road. Surrounded by fields, a tall eucalyptus stood on the left corner. "Park here," she said, and when I stopped she walked to the tree, looked carefully around it, then knelt on the ground and started digging with the hoe she had brought with her. What could she have been looking for? After a few minutes she retrieved a shoe box wrapped in waterproof canvas. She wiped off the dirt and opened it. She took out another bundle of canvas, unwrapped it, and showed me her doll. Fourteen inches tall, the "beautiful lady" was made of unglazed clay, with white skin, black hair with golden *kanzashi* (hairpins), and red lips. She wore a purple-and-white silk kimono and stood elegantly on a black wooden stand. My mother beamed as she brushed some dirt off the doll with her hand.

"After Pearl Harbor, everything Japanese became bad, so I buried her here. Then when you left for the Army, I told myself I would only come for her if you came back."

"Okasan," I whispered as I hugged her. When was the last time I had hugged my mother? Maybe as a toddler, because in our family we didn't hug, we bowed. But I was tired of bowing. As I held her in my arms I felt her heartbeat and remembered how she'd tell me stories of her youth when as a child I couldn't go to sleep.

She'd describe the white seabirds she'd see flying over the Naka River as she walked to the harbor in the morning, how in the fall the road to the temple would be covered with golden leaves falling from the ginkgo trees, how she'd see foxes sleeping on the laps of buddha statues in the forest when she went looking for mushrooms. I saw her in my mind's eye on the train as she waved goodbye to her family, a girl leaving home forever, holding the doll they had given her as a going-away gift, and my eyes filled with tears.

Before going home I drove down Main Street, past the Bank of America Building, the Waffle Shop, and the Hotel Barbara Worth, with its arched arcade and imposing signs on the roof. Very posh inside, it had murals painted by Vysekal, a renowned Czech immigrant painter. I wondered if I could have gotten a room there, not being white. On the other side of the street not much had changed. The Elks Club, Thrifty Drugs, Sears, and the gas station were still there. We stopped at Mel's and had a hamburger with an icy root beer. Sitting at the counter next to me munching on her burger, my mother turned to look at me and smiled, and for a moment I saw the young woman she had been.

~

I pushed down on the gas as I passed by Mount Signal, the fields hazy under the bright sun. I turned onto a dirt road and drove up to a small wooden house as the sun made the car an oven, drenching my shirt in sweat. I parked in front and knocked on the door.

"*Hijo! Dios mio!*" Carmelita said as she hugged me. "So much time I didn't see you, come in, come in!" I sat at the kitchen table as she gave me a glass of sun tea. She sat in front of me and looked at me with her dark eyes; her face was more wrinkled than ever. "I prayed for you and your family, *hijo*; I lit a candle for you in the church."

"Whatever you did worked, Carmelita—I'm alive. Here, Carmelita, I brought something for you." I handed her a small box wrapped in colored paper.

"What is it, *hijo*?" she wondered. I knew she was going to like it. It was a mahogany cross about six inches tall with an ivory Christ on it. A surprised expression appeared on her face. "It's beautiful! *Muchas gracias,* oh, thank you Mike!" Her eyes filled with tears. "I am so happy," she said as she put the crucifix on the running board behind the kitchen table.

"Are you hungry?" She got up and limped to the stove. "I cooked this morning," she said, and came back with a bowl of hot beans and tortillas.

"Mmm. Carmelita, *que bueno!*" I ate spoonfuls of the buttery pinto beans and the warm and spicy liquid with bites of the thick corn tortillas, sometimes with my eyes closed. I had forgotten how good they tasted. When I finished the bowl, I had another one with two more tortillas, then I said, "No, thank you, Carmelita, but I'm full now—just a little more tea, please." She sat in front of me sipping iced tea, her shoulders hunched forward more than I remembered, her head white like the marble mountains in Carrara. "Carmelita, how have you been all these years?"

"*Bien, hijo*. I have some stiffness but still work in my field, cook, and pray. And Ramón, he lives in my heart, so I am not lonely," she said.

"Is Father Velasquez still alive?

"Ah *sí*, that priest will live longer than any of us," she said and laughed. "I see him every Sunday in church; he has talked about how wrong it was for the government to put you in camps, and has prayed for you during mass."

"That's good to hear." I picked up the glass ball from the credenza, shook it, and watched the snow swirl around the church campanile and fall on the red roofs. I thought of Pisa and peeked inside the ball, trying to see the Leaning Tower and maybe Ornella and me gazing from the top. "Carmelita, in Italy I met a woman and fell in love. I want to go back to her, but my family would not approve."

"*Hijo*, I'm just a poor old woman. I never went to school, but I am happy because I always followed my heart. Follow your heart. It is not easy; *el demonio* confuses us. You must pray; God will show you your true heart."

I couldn't pray. I didn't believe there was an all-good, all-loving Supreme Being. It wasn't just a conclusion I had arrived at on philosophical grounds, but a deep, existential response to my life and to the world. But I couldn't bring myself to say this to Carmelita. She was also silent for a while, then she said, "Mike, if you can't pray, then listen. That's praying, too. Maybe you'll hear a voice."

"I'll try," I said. She sat on the chair with her leathery hands on the table and looked at me with moist eyes. On a running board behind her, in a silver frame, was the photo of Ramón and her on their wedding day, and a picture of Our Lady of Guadalupe.

I told her I had to go and got up. She got up too and said, *"Vaya con Dios.* I will pray for you."

I hugged her, and then walked to the pickup. Carmelita stood in front of the door and waved as I left.

I turned on Ross Road, drove by the small town of Seeley —don't blink or you'll miss it was the running joke—and headed toward El Centro. Eucalyptus and palm trees lined the road, and as far as the eye could see extended fields, the flatness broken up only by Mount Signal, a few miles on the right. From here it didn't look like a sleeping dragon; compared to the mountains I'd seen in Italy, it seemed more like a napping cat.

I drove home remembering how often I went to see Carmelita as a child, how she'd feed me, tell me stories, take me for walks. I suddenly stomped on the brake, and in a cloud of dust and a screeching of tires, I turned around and drove back. I stopped in front of the house, ran out of the car, knocked on the door, and when she came out, I said in a trembling voice, "Carmelita, thank you for showing me how to make the stars." I hugged her thin, bent frame.

"Está bien, está bien," she whispered.

After three weeks in El Centro, I decided to take the bus to Los Angeles and go see Dr. Walter Kesselman and Tom. I had called my old professor earlier, and in his jovial voice he had boomed, "Come right away!" He lived in a one-story house not far from the university. The bus dropped me off a few blocks away, thus giving me an opportunity to decompress, to psychically adjust to an encounter with someone who belonged to an atmosphere I had left a long time ago. I didn't have to go very far.

Four years had passed since I saw my favorite professor; it was with trepidation that I walked to his home. It was a quiet block, a wide street lined with tall fan palms and jacarandas in bloom. "You can't miss my house; it's the one with the Greek columns," Kesselman had said on the phone, and here it was, the charcoal-gray front door flanked by white Ionic columns supporting a lintel decorated with fighting Greek warriors. "Be right there!" I heard him bellow as I knocked.

"Mike, my dear Mike! What a pleasure to see you after so long. Come in, come in, what a surprise when you called, sit down," he said as he motioned toward one of two well-worn burgundy leather chairs in the living room. Four years had made him thinner and almost bald, but time didn't extinguish the contagious enthusiasm that had fired me up as a student. He still dressed like a blue-collar worker: jeans and a denim shirt with folded sleeves, brown workers' shoes. He went in the kitchen and came back with two scotches, handed me one, eased himself in a corner of the art deco sofa that faced the chairs, looked at me with a grin, and said as he raised his glass, "Here's to you, Mike." We took a swig and looked at each other, smiling. "You're a hero, Mike. A hero. And now you're back. You look good, healthy, in great shape."

"Well, the last year was really an Italian vacation. The fresh sea air and the food worked wonders."

"Maggie and I went to Italy on our honeymoon, Venice, Trieste in winter. Ah, how the fog and the rain made those ancient cities dreamy, ephemeral! If heaven existed I would want it to be like that: rain and fog, brooding lagoons and seas, art, so much art and music and the aromas of mysterious coffees . . ." He paused for a while as if suddenly lost, then said, "Are you ready to come back?"

"Professor, in Italy I fell in love. I want to go back . . ."

He stared at the ice cubes in his glass, then took another swig.

"What would you do in Italy? You'd be a foreigner there. You need to finish your BA and go on to graduate school. You already lost four years. You were lonely; the pain and horrors of war, so much time away from home, you met a pretty girl, fell in love. All that is understandable, and important—I don't mean to trivialize your feelings for her, but what about your future? You can be a professor, have a brilliant career; if you go back to Italy, what kind of work could you get?" He lit up a Camel and inhaled deeply, and the exhaled smoke swirled above him like clouds on a mountaintop. "I was in France during the Great War, and fell in love with a girl; many of us did. And of course, when it came time to leave, we swore we'd come back, and we meant it, too. We were sincere. But when we returned we realized we belonged home; everything was here—our past, our families, our life's work. And those girls we left behind, they forgot about us. They went on with life and married men from their towns. Mike, I can't tell you what to do, but think about it carefully, think about your future."

"I will, Professor. But you, how have you been?" The muscles in his face tightened and he pursed his lips. He glanced at a large framed photo of his wife that hung on the wall.

"I'm getting along. I miss Maggie, who died last year. . ." He was going to continue, but I interrupted by offering my condolences.

"Thank you, Mike. The university and my studies keep me busy, and I still have philosophy and all my books." He pointed at the floor-to-ceiling bookcases bulging with volumes that lined the room. He got up and walked to the shelves, contemplating the books, then picked one out. "Remember this one? I gave you a copy in 'forty-one," he said as he sat back down and handed me *Being and Time*.

I took the heavily used book in my hands, opened it and flipped through the leaves; the professor had turned every page into a battlefield of underlines, notes, and marks.

"How can I forget this book? I've been reading and thinking about it for the past four years."

"You took the book to Poston and to war?"

"Yes, even though for long periods of time I didn't even open it."

'What do you think of the book now?"

I pondered the question for a while, my mind a blank. "It's the most important book I've read in my life," I finally said. "It gets to the bottom of things in a radical way. I find it true, that the most fundamental question is the question of being. We're usually so preoccupied with satisfying our physical and emotional needs that we seldom if ever take a step back and ask ourselves that question. And the analysis of what it means to be a human being is as elegant and breathtaking as a cathedral. I create myself and the world through my projects and actions; I am time and freedom. Fundamentally, I am nothing."

"Nothing?"

"I'm no-thing, not an entity, but an event, a happening, a manifestation of being in its becoming; Heidegger's view of existence makes sense to me, Professor, as far as I understand it, and I agree with his discussion of authenticity, his claim that our being is to care for ourselves and the world. I didn't find it very helpful in war, however, when time, the future, could've been withdrawn at any moment. The book made me more aware of the awesome finality of death, and for a long time the dread that followed was very difficult to work through. I didn't know if I was going to be alive by the end of the day."

The professor slowly swirled the ice cubes in his glass, then took a sip of scotch.

"War confronts us directly with death, and when it's so near we can feel its breath we tremble and want to recoil. Everyday mundane concerns dissolve; we're left with the naked fact of our being and its impending annihilation. But do you remember what Heidegger says about an impassioned freedom toward death? To stare it in the face and go forward makes possible our authentic existence. What do you think?" He went in the kitchen to get the bottle, poured some more scotch in our glasses, and sat down again.

"For a long time, before or after combat, I thought about all the projects and plans I had, and how I was probably never going to live to achieve them. But later I began to live more fully in each moment, and not to think about the future in a conventional sense, as a very long time."

"The future is a field of possibilities; how extensive the field is depends on situations we often have no control over—hell, we are time, and we're dying as we speak, so let's enjoy this good scotch!" He raised his glass and took a drink. He rested the right foot over the thigh of his left leg and looked at the photo of his wife. "I still feel Maggie's presence, like an echo of a voice now silent, but there's no denying the absence and the pain." Then his gaze moved to the bookcases. "See all those books? To me they're not just dusty stacks of paper bound in cloth and cardboard, but thinkers of long ago that come alive and speak to me the moment I read them. I've been engaged in conversation with them since my student days, and I introduce them to others in the classroom. Something magical and noble can happen in a classroom, as it can happen when you sit alone in your study and read a book. Mike, come back to the university. I'd love to have you as my assistant—you'll make a great philosophy professor. You could begin in the fall; the GI Bill would take care of it. By next year you could be working on your PhD."

"I'll seriously think about it, Professor," I said.

We talked some more, until the time came for me to leave. I told Kesselman I was going to see Yoshiko and got up.

"Give Yoshiko my regards, and think about registering for classes." We shook hands vigorously, then he looked in my eyes and squeezed my shoulder.

"What has happened in these four years has changed

everything, I know, but come back—I'll be behind you all the way. Take care."

"You've been my mentor, my model, Professor. Once I even bought a pack of Camels and smoked them just like you do. I'll give you a call soon." As I walked back to the bus stop, I imagined a possible future.

I stand in front of a class and lecture. It's a spring day and the open windows let in warmth and birds' chirping. I wear comfortable black oxfords, cotton pants, a tweed jacket, white shirt, and tie. Heraclitus and Parmenides. Two sides of the same coin; reality is a flux, reality never changes. You can't step into the same river twice; you have always stepped into the same river. How can things change and still remain the same? This was the problem Plato tried to solve. There is an eternal aspect to reality that never changes and imparts whatever reality our changing world has. I turn around and draw Plato's divided line on the board: the sensible world on one side, with its shadows, opinions, and things, and the world of eternal forms on the other, with its shining reality and knowledge. I am a living bridge between Plato now reduced to a dusty book and these young minds in front of me, and the magic involves making present and plausible ideas thought two thousand years ago and now encased in black marks on sheets of paper. I raise my hand toward the blackboard, open my mouth, and the words in the old book tremble, become alive and fly off the yellowing paper, butter-flies dancing around the room. And the bell rings, and as the students walk out, a woman comes in. She wears a light blue cotton skirt, a blouse, and a white sweater. We're going to lunch today. I give her a peck on the lips, put my books in the leather briefcase, and we leave.

～

I couldn't bring myself to see Yoshiko. I wanted to see her and talk to her, but instead I called Tom. "Drop by," he said. "I'd come pick you up, but I don't have a car yet."

As I sat in the bus, I took Ornella's picture out of my billfold and stared at it for a long time. I missed her, I missed Livorno, I wanted to go back, but now that I was here it didn't seem so simple. I could go to UCLA and pursue my academic career, I would be close to my family who needed me, and within a few years I could be teaching.

I arrived in Anaheim in the early evening. Once off the bus I hailed a cab, but it didn't stop. I walked to one parked in front of the depot, but the driver looked at me and said he didn't give rides to Japs. Eventually I found one who agreed to take me. Talking to Professor Kesselman brought out of me a desire to take courses again, to study, to be with people who were passionate about philosophy, and this filled me with confusion and dread. As the cab approached the house, I saw Tom sitting on the steps of the porch. "Mike! Damn, it's great to see you." We shook hands and hugged.

"You look good," I replied. We stood in front of a two-story country house with a grove of sycamores in front and grassy rolling hills all around. "So this is your parents' place?"

"They're renting it. They're visiting relatives in Oakland now, so I have it all to myself. Come and have a beer—you look thirsty and tired."

We sat at the kitchen table as he took a couple of bottles from the icebox.

"What the hell have you been doing?" I asked.

"Just taking it easy, visiting relatives and friends, resting."

"Have you heard from Giulia?"

"Got a letter a week ago. She's working in a store in Orbetello. She said Aldo and Vito are waiting for us so we can have a big dinner." He took a long swig from the bottle.

"When are you going back?" I asked. There was a pause, then he looked at me and said, "I'm going back to the university in the fall. I've always wanted to be an engineer, and here's my chance—the GI Bill will pay for it."

"But what about Giulia? Our plans to go back?"

"God damn it, Mike, in Livorno we didn't have to worry about how to make a living. What the hell are we going to do if we go back? You have to be an Italian citizen to work there. We made it back alive; we can make something of ourselves. Don't look at me that way. I miss her, and think about her, but you know what? It seems like a dream, a faraway dream." He got up, took a bottle of whisky and two glasses out of the cabinet, and said, "Let's go sit on the porch; it's cooler there." We sat on two chairs by the door.

"The first week home I couldn't stop thinking about going back," I said, "but now . . ." I took a sip of the Johnnie Walker and a warm wave passed over me. "Now I'm not so sure." Tom was right: in Italy we hadn't had to worry about finding a job, and as part of the victorious army we'd had privileges, but if I went back it would be drastically different. What would we do in Italy? I had buried that question in the back of my mind for a long time, but now it began to surface. "What could I do there?" I wondered.

Tom looked at me and said, "You might be able to work in the kitchen at Vito's place, wash dishes, clean floors." He laughed. "Let's face it, we don't have a future there. Here we can finish our education, have solid careers." He took a swig from his glass, offered me a cigarette, and we lit up.

"I wish I had one of those Gauloises Pierre smoked," I said. The sun had gone down, and only the crowns of trees were bathed in a muted yellow light. Once in a while a cottontail darted from the side of the house toward the grassy field in front.

"We could find rooms in the same boardinghouse, go out in the evening, like old times," he said, but how could we go back to pre–Pearl Harbor, pre-internment and pre-war times?

"We're not the same persons we were four years ago, and you know it. On top of that, we promised Giulia and Ornella that we'd come back!"

"My parents don't even know about Giulia." Tom poured some more liquor in our glasses. "We're six thousand miles from Italy, Mike. We were born here, our families are here, we'll go back to the university, make something of ourselves. We won the fucking war, we're alive and young." Then he opened his arms and said, "The world is ours!"

"Calm down, you're getting drunk already," I said. The more I sat there and listened to Tom, the more Ornella and Italy receded as realities and the more they took on the characteristics of faraway memories. It's funny how when I was in Italy, my family, Yoshiko, and California had the same distant, unreal quality. What was the relationship between immediacy and reality?

It was dark now, I couldn't see the moon, but the stars reminded me of Carmelita, and of all the nights when Ornella and I walked in Livorno and looked up at the sky. An owl hooted, and there must have been a pond or stream nearby, because frogs began their chant. A cool breeze caressed me and the whisky began to make me feel light and carefree.

"Tom, I can't believe we survived the war. All those firefights, the mines, the mortars, the bombardments, and we didn't even get wounded!"

"Lady Luck smiled over us," said Tom. "I don't even want to think about it. If I do, then I become scared. Isn't it strange? No, I want to forget as soon as I can."

"I've noticed it too, that if I start to think about what I went through, I become afraid."

"Let's forget about it. Let's make plans for next semester and the courses we'll be taking," he said, and took another swig.

"I could take a course on Hegel, one on Nietzsche, and two seminars in eighteenth-century philosophy. I'd also like to study ancient Greek."

"That's the spirit. By the way, have you heard from Yoshiko?"

"She's in Santa Monica. I haven't written to her in months. To tell you the truth, I'm afraid to go see her."

"Maybe you could marry her. She was your girlfriend for so long, she looks good, and she's smart. Remember what you used to tell me? She'd have made a warm womb for your scholarly life."

"It's something to think about," I replied as I lit another cigarette.

"It's settled, then. We'll register next semester and start our new lives!" he said as he raised his glass.

"I'll drink to that," I said, as I raised mine. I felt euphoric, full of confidence. Ornella and Italy were on the other side of the world; I was home, near my family, Professor Kesselman, and Tom, my best friend, and why not? Maybe I could get together with Yoshiko again; maybe I could pick up the life I had to drop in 1942 and live it to the fullest. Maybe Heraclitus was wrong, and I could step into the same river twice.

18

1946

Bright gold awakens me, early morning light reflected from the brass lamp on the end table. I'm lying on the sofa in Tom's living room, rubbing my aching forehead. My mouth and throat are parched. I sit up, rub my eyes, put my shoes on, stumble in the kitchen and gulp down a glass of water. Through the window in front of the sink, trees and a shed come into focus. I put the empty glass on the counter, walk to the door, turn the knob, and walk out into the crisp air. A calico cat sits on an empty steel drum, turns her head toward me, closes her eyes, and begins to lick a paw. A scent of dried grass is in the cool air. The sun breaks through a bank of lead-silver clouds above the hills as hidden birds chirp in the sycamores' branches. I pass the rusty drum and peek inside the shed—on the dirt floor next to a tool bench a white duck is squatting on a bunch of hay. As she moves, three trembling eggs become visible. I walk softly inside and kneel down to get a better view. Cracks appear on the shells as ducklings struggle to come out. Wet and white, they push through, and it is as if the whole world struggles to come forth; the slanted sunlight warms the living things fighting to break their prison walls.

The universe comes out of the eggs, itself an egg hatching an infinity of births: butterflies struggling to come out of cocoons, trees struggling to come out of seeds, animals struggling to come out of wombs, peace struggling to come out of war, love struggling to come out of selfishness, spirit struggling to come out of matter. Each human being struggling to come out of weakness and fear. I feel weightless; I hover above the floor; I hear a voice. It repeats one word: Ornella. Ornella. Ornella. *I get up and run into the house.*

"Tom, Tom! I'm going back!"

He lay, sprawled, still dressed, on the floor.

"What the hell are you talking about?"

"I'm going to go back to Italy and marry Ornella."

"You cracked up."

"Yeah, that's it—I cracked up."

"Wait, I'll make some coffee," he said as he got up. I flopped down on the sofa and a few minutes later he came out of the bathroom, his face washed and hair neatly combed. He motioned me to follow him into the kitchen, where he filled two glasses at the faucet and gave me one. "Better drink lots of water, considering all the whisky we had."

I sat on a chair at the table while he made coffee, fried eggs, and toast. I rubbed my head and my eyes wanted to close.

"Have some coffee—you look like you need it," he said as he put a steaming mug in front of me. We ate in silence, then he drained his water glass and looked at me.

"I fell in love with Giulia and wanted to live in Italy, but when I came back it was almost like I woke up from a dream. At times I wonder if I was ever there. What the hell did we think we were going to do as civilians in Italy? It was easy to fantasize about it, but wasn't it just bravado? I thought I had an analytical mind, and you're thinking all the time—what happened?"

"Maybe after what we went through we didn't want to think logically about the future. And making a living in Italy didn't seem as hard to me as Poston or the war."

"It sounded romantic, but are you willing to do anything

to live there? Ever since I was in high school I dreamed of being an engineer, and I thought you wanted to become a professor."

"Haven't you seen the 'Japs not welcome' signs in Los Angeles? Yesterday I had trouble finding a cab driver willing to give me a ride. I'd rather be a stranger in a foreign country than in my own. But I don't know what I'd do in Italy, damn it. I just can't forget Ornella."

"What about your parents? What are they going to say?"

"They'll be opposed, but I'm going to marry who I want to. I respect them, but I have to make my own decisions. I've heard of other soldiers bringing their foreign wives back. I know she'd be willing to marry me and move to California."

"I can't have Giulia come here. If my family knew I married an Italian they would disown me. It's too much for me to think about now—my head is too crowded with stuff. I need to forget about the past or I won't make it. I won't make it." He took another gulp of coffee and lit a cigarette. The sparks of confidence and playfulness he usually had in his eyes were gone.

"It's okay. You write, and I'll talk to her. She survived Mauthausen; she'll survive this. Who knows? Maybe she already forgot about you."

He seemed relieved by my words as he nodded in agreement.

In late morning I called a cab. I had to get back to the Valley as soon as possible. I was going to go to Italy, marry Ornella, and bring her here. That's all there was to it. Everything else would have to follow from that. As the taxi sped off, I turned to say goodbye to Tom. He stood in front of the house and waved. I raised my hand and forced a smile. We were already very far apart.

∾

Before I went back to El Centro there was someone else I had to see. Yoshiko lived with her aunt in a Spanish-style stucco house near Santa Monica. In the front yard stood a king palm heavy with bunches of vermillion seeds hanging from the trunk, and as I walked by, the intensity of the color and the exuberance of the round, fleshy berries made me dizzy. I took a deep breath and knocked—the door opened almost instantly, and her aunt Etsuko appeared. Her hair had turned whiter, and deeper furrows etched her face. She greeted me warmly, led the way toward the kitchen, and opened the back door. She motioned for me to go on and closed the door behind me.

Yoshiko sat, back straight, eyes closed, and hands on her lap, on a white garden chair under an elm. As I walked toward her, a wave of expectation unsettled me. She opened her eyes and turned her head. She jumped up when she saw me, called my name, and put her arms around me. We hugged under the gnarled branches of the tree; only her heartbeat, the warmth of her body, the fragrance of her hair existed. Then she took a step back.

"Let me look at you . . ." She studied me with her eyes, brown like the mountainsides near Julian, when splits made by the rain exposed the deeper flesh of the earth. She motioned me to sit down on one of the chairs. Her face had become thinner, more sculpted. She had always been slim, but as I held her in my arms her frame felt tougher, willowy.

"Yoshiko . . ." is all I could say as we sat down.

"You went to war and here you are, healthier than when you left."

"Sheer luck, believe me."

"Maybe it wasn't luck, who knows?"

"Either way, I'm grateful. But when I think of all the guys who didn't come back, I feel like I betrayed them, like I don't belong in the world of the living."

"You're here now, that's what matters. What do you plan to do?"

"I've written to you about Ornella. I want to bring her here. I'd like to live in Italy, but I can't live there and finish my studies. I'm not at home anywhere."

She looked me in the eyes. "When I was a child my father would come home from work in late afternoon. I'd hear his truck and I'd run to the front door, open it, push the screen door with my little hands, and yell, 'Otosan, Otosan!' He'd call my name, pick me up, and swing me over his head as I giggled and squealed. One day I waited for a long time at the screen door, but he didn't come home. At the funeral, I didn't understand what was going on. What did it have to do with my father? And without him, the house didn't feel like home anymore. I didn't feel at home at my aunt's, when my mother and I moved in with her, and I certainly didn't feel at home in Poston. Remember when I started to meditate in the camp? It's a practice I've embraced. Meditation has helped me realize 'home' is inside me, so anywhere can be home."

"I love you, as a good friend. After Pearl Harbor, something changed, and in the camp I lost part of myself."

"You weren't the only one who suffered after Pearl Harbor. So many nights in Poston, my tears mixed with the sand on my pillow. When I needed your warmth the most, you turned into ice. My love for you became a painful wound. I was so angry with you, and the loneliness felt like invisible quicksand always ready to swallow me. Then Kay showed me how to meditate, and I grabbed that rope and pulled myself up." Her words shook me to my very foundation. I closed my eyes and felt again the terrible pain of regret. The inexorable determinism of deeds: once done they cannot be undone. How could I have been so selfish? And the suffering I caused her could not be taken away.

"I'm sorry, Yoshiko," I said as I turned and touched her shoulder. "I didn't mean to hurt you. I'm really sorry." I cradled her hands in mine and raised them to my bowed forehead. "Please, forgive me, I beg you."

"I forgave you long ago. I'm at peace with myself and hope you can be, too."

Etsuko called from the back door to tell us dinner was ready.

It was a simple but delicious meal of broiled yellowfin tuna, sautéed kale, and steamed rice. "I am so happy to see you again," said Etsuko as she sat down. "You look young and strong. I still remember how kind you were to bring us abalone. It was the summer of 1941. A lifetime ago." After we ate, she shooed us into the living room and washed the dishes. Yoshiko and I sat on the sofa and talked about our experiences and plans over tea.

"I'm going to Japan by the end of the year to study Zen and deepen my knowledge of the language," she said, as excited as she had been that day in Poston when she told me she was going to start meditating. Etsuko joined us and we talked until it grew dark outside. It was time to leave. I gave Yoshiko a hug and once inside the taxi, unrolled the window and waved. The cab sped off as they waved back. I had grown up with Yoshiko; now we were on different paths.

As the taxi sped off to the bus depot for my trip back to El Centro, I realized Yoshiko had been more successful at being than I. She radiated peace, acceptance, and strength. I had underestimated her, dismissed her interest in Zen as unworthy of a philosopher's attention, but I had been wrong. I held the D. T. Suzuki book she gave me on my lap as I took a deep breath, gazed out the cab's window, and acknowledged the sea of stars above me. I wanted to lose myself in that brightness. I wanted to become the night and all those stars.

My mother had fried pork chops with soy sauce and sliced

green onions, and we ate them with rice, steamed broccoli, and a salad. It was seven in the evening and the sun sank slowly toward the edge of the sky, a deep blue dome like the glass globe on Carmelita's credenza. I had thrown out the trash and walked alongside the canal ditch. It wasn't too hot, but humidity rose from the water flowing in the narrow canal. I had to tell my family about my plans. How were they going to react? My heart beat faster and my hands began to shake like the first time I aimed a rifle at an enemy soldier. They probably expected me to go back to the university, but they knew nothing about Ornella. I gazed westward at the Coyote Mountains, barely visible. I knew behind them stood the Lagunas, and beyond them lay San Diego and the ocean.

Back in the house, I sat on the sofa next to my mother. Her eyesight had worsened, and even with glasses she needed to be close to a bright lamp to knit. The water cooler droned on, doing its best to keep us cool. My father relaxed on the easy chair he had recently bought second hand. He smoked a cigarette and read a copy of the Japanese-language newspaper. My sisters worked on a jigsaw puzzle they had set up on the kitchen table.

"I'm going back to the university in September," I blurted out. "Professor Kesselman is going to make me his assistant, and with the GI Bill, I'll manage." I had the impression no one heard my words.

"We could really use your help around here," said Umeko, breaking the silence.

"I can't stay here. Before they threw us in Poston I was in my fourth year at the university. I want to go back and finish. Besides, what could I do in El Centro? Otosan is working, as are you and Myoko. You're managing okay." She was shaking her head.

"Once you finish you will be a professor?" asked my father, looking at me from above his reading glasses.

"After I get the PhD, yes."

"You never liked farming. You could get a job someplace, maybe the post office, I don't know," he said.

"The post office, Otosan? I want to go to the university and work on my degree—and there is also something else. When I was in Italy, I met a woman. I want to go back, marry her, and bring her to Los Angeles." There, I had finally said it. More silence.

"What's her name?" asked Myoko.

"Ornella."

"Or-nell-a! What a pretty name," she replied. Not a word had escaped from Umeko. She just sat there staring at the puzzle, but then she got up and confronted me.

"Have you known her long?"

"Almost a year."

"Why didn't you say anything about her in your letters? You said nothing for a year, then you drop this bombshell on us—you're a coward!"

My father sat up straight and the newspaper fell to the floor. "How could you say such a thing? Your brother enlisted in the Army and fought in many battles. He has brought honor to our family!" Umeko looked down, then glared at me.

"You were supposed to marry Yoshiko when you came back. You betrayed us, and you betrayed Yoshiko!" With a swipe of her hand, she threw the multicolored pieces of the puzzle on the floor and stormed out.

"It had been arranged through Etsuko with Yoshiko's mother; you two were going to be married," said my mother.

"I care for Yoshiko, but things have changed between us. Poston, the war, time pulled us apart. I love Ornella."

"Love is not the most important part of a marriage. It matters that you are compatible, can live together, share the same customs and traditions," my mother said. "Love comes later, like a lotus flower slowly appearing in the pond."

"We are not in Japan! This is America!"

"You have known this woman for only a year; she belongs to a different culture. You and Yoshiko grew up together, have known each other most of your lives, loved each other. Now you want to forget about her and marry a stranger? I do not understand you," replied my mother.

My father leaned back in his chair, took his reading glasses off, and looked at me. "You were born in this new world, you fought for it, and it's yours now. Your mother and I were very young when we left Japan and worked hard to make a good life here. Then the FBI came in the middle of the night and took me away like a traitor. They took everything from us and forced us to live in a prison camp for three years. They killed your brother. All he wanted to do was be a good farmer. We have heard nothing from our relatives in Japan. Maybe they're all dead. I don't understand the world anymore. All we had left was our heritage and our customs. We hoped we could keep them alive through you, but you belong to America now. I am tired. I just live day by day."

"Now, let's not forget the old saying, 'Fall down seven times, stand up eight,'" said my mother. "We must live as well as we can to bring honor to the ancestors and to those who will come after us. I don't understand this new world, but the land I came from and my family live inside me. If I close my eyes I can see the white cranes flying low on the river, feel the cherry blossoms fall on my head as I walk to the temple, hear the bright red and yellow maple leaves under my feet as I wander over the mountain trails in the fall. The faces of my parents, sister, and brothers are fuzzy now, but I still feel them inside me. And who knows what is good or bad?" She turned toward me. "You are right: we are not in Japan and as Otosan said, this is your world. But always stand up straight and never forget your family name." I was moved by their generosity of spirit and in gratitude, bowed deeply to my parents.

~

Steve. Remember the day when we went camping in the Laguna Mountains, and we hiked up Garnet Peak in the early morning in the dark so we could see the sun rise? The wind rolled through Jeffrey pines and black oaks, like the surf on a winter's day. The moon rained on the trail, turning manzanita berries into copper pearls. We caught scents of pine as we climbed, the sky so clear the stars seemed within reach, if only we had a ladder. When we gained the peak we sat by the boulders, a few feet from the edge, Storm Canyon six thousand feet below us, and the desert extending all the way to Yuma, a sea of solitude. "We're standing at the edge of the world," you said. And then purple streaks opened up in the sky like cracks on the shell of a giant egg, and the sun came out in an incandescent explosion of orange, yellow, and purple. The red disk rose and we stood up, as the fiery light reached pines and oaks, turning them into a burning sea. The mountainsides, showing their ribs, dropped vertiginously to the desert below, a desert as white as a wedding dress. We didn't speak a word. We witnessed the birth of the world.

EPILOGUE

1990

I continue my walk on the beach. The sun is shining in the clearing sky, and I unbutton my jacket. Almost fifty years have passed since the summer of 1941, when Steve and I dove for abalone off La Jolla Cove. If Martin Heidegger is right and we are time, then I am time that has telescoped, zoomed out. I look back at myself as a young man, at people and events now distant memories. My son had asked me to write about my war years, so today I peered into the past. Tomorrow I'll begin giving form to remembrance.

During the two weeks on the ship on the way back to Italy I read the book Yoshiko had given me, *Zen Essays* by D. T. Suzuki. I found Buddhism in its essence not far from Heidegger's philosophy, and began to meditate, a practice I continued to follow.

Back in Livorno, with a bouquet of roses in my hand, I knocked on Ornella's door, and when she opened it, she nearly crushed me in her embrace. Her brother had said he was going to eat his hat if I returned, and even now, when I see him, I ask him, "Pietro, when are you going to eat your hat?" We married, and after a brief honeymoon in Rome, I began the paperwork required for Ornella to come to the United States. I returned to Los Angeles in time to register for courses, and Professor Kesselman, happy at my return, made me his assistant and later served as the chairman of my PhD.

A few months later, Ornella arrived and a new phase of our lives began. With the GI Bill and my assistantship, Ornella and I managed to get by, and when she found a job at the Italian Consulate, our financial situation improved. A few years after she arrived, Ornella became a naturalized American citizen. I can still see her at the ceremony, dressed in a new outfit, holding a little American flag.

It took a while for Giulia to recover from Tom's betrayal, but with the passage of time she remarried and still lives in Orbetello. Tom and I drifted apart, and after graduation he found an engineering job out of state. I still have fond memories of our pre–Pearl Harbor university days, but our friendship could not survive his abandonment of Giulia.

After I received my doctorate I began teaching. I had finally achieved my dream of becoming a philosophy professor. Ornella worked on a degree in Italian and taught Italian literature at a state college until retirement.

Ornella and I had two children, Hisao and Carla, and the decades passed full of teaching, writing, reading, raising children, and vacations. But I never lost my love for Italy, and when after thirty years Ornella and I retired, we moved back to the land of Dante, Leopardi, and Michelangelo.

My parents warmed to Ornella and looked forward to seeing their grandchildren. My mother made sure Hisao and Carla grew up liking rice and sashimi, miso soup and mochi cakes. At home they ate lots of pasta, chicken cacciatore, cioppino, and tiramisù, so I used to call them my "little gourmets." Umeko and Myoko married, and had children and grandchildren. Umeko worked as a secretary, and when she retired she devoted herself to deep-sea fishing. When we lived in Los Angeles, she used to send us cases of tuna she caught and canned. Myoko fulfilled her dream of having her own hair salon. They're old ladies now, spoiling their grandkids.

Yoshiko spent six years at a monastery in Tokyo, meditating and studying. She eventually became a professor of Japanese Studies at UC Santa Barbara, and when she retired she moved to Kyoto, Japan. We keep in touch with letters and post cards.

George opened a restaurant in Honolulu and is still working. In a letter, he said he was already in paradise so he didn't need to retire. But he spends more time going fishing with his grandkids.

"Keep me alive," Hideo had told me as he lay on the ground, dying. I try to do my best. I still wear his watch, and sometimes, just before going to sleep, I close my eyes and go see him in his shop. After we talk for a while we go to his house and have dinner with his family. There are nights when he visits me in dreams, as do Steve, Samurai, Akira, and others.

Karl married his sweetheart, became the proud father of three children, and worked as an architect for more than thirty years. Since we moved to Italy, every summer he and Emma stay at a campsite in a pine grove near Orbetello. Last December, Ornella and I went to Braunschweig to see Karl and Emma. We drank lots of beer and brandy, laughed and talked in front of a roaring fireplace, and walked down snowy streets illuminated by Christmas lights. The city had been largely rebuilt, and the restoration of historical buildings still went on.

After *Being and Time*, a stream of books by Heidegger was published. Books I still read and think about. In my youth I approached philosophy books with deference; now they're old friends who tell me the same stories over and over, but I enjoy them and still find something new in them. Professor Kesselman was right; philosophy is not just an academic discipline, but a way of life, and I'm still living it.

Often, in the early morning, I take the local train to Siena or Florence and spend hours basking in art and architecture, and in early afternoon when I take the train back home I feel fulfilled and at peace. Pierre, our host in Menton, had been right: images can heal, and now I can see almost any moment as an image overflowing with beauty. And its impermanence makes it even more poignant and precious.

Captain Nemo still roams the oceans in the *Nautilus*, but for research and study. He contributed much of his wealth to progressive and scientific organizations worldwide and once in a while an ancient manuscript, a painting, or a statue was "discovered" and found its way into a museum or art gallery. He and Kanda had two children, who were sent to European universities for their education. When I go visit him we smoke cigars, drink brandy, and talk about philosophy, history, and politics.

Look at that sand dollar. They're not easy to find here. I bend down to pick it up and hear a voice calling me. It's Ornella. She's coming toward me, dressed in a blue windbreaker, her brown hair streaked with white. I give her a kiss on the lips.

"I wanted to tell you Hisao and Carla called and said they will be here on Christmas Eve," she says. I look at her. Her face is more beautiful to me now than fifty years ago.

"That's good," I say. I hold her hand as we walk on the soft, pale sand. Our backs are slightly bent, our hair whiter. I remember walking here with Ornella the day before my departure to the States, in 1946. It's a fading image of the past, like the light from a star no longer there, but it still resonates and enriches the present. Our children are grown now and have families of their own. Hisao is a biologist, Carla a translator. They live in California, so it'll be special to have them here for Christmas.

Ornella and I live in a small house by the sea, near Orbetello.

The pine groves to our right are vividly green, and in front of us, way in the distance, the castle of Talamone rises from the promontory. The fishing village of Porto Santo Stefano looks like a white dove on the grass, and Monte Argentario, steep and aloof, is behind us. I take a deep breath of sea-scented air, look at Ornella, and tell her I love her. She looks at me and smiles. "I love you too," she says.

ACKNOWLEDGMENTS

Lloyd Farrar, Bill Blake, Chris Edwards and Richard Hann read early drafts of this novel and offered helpful comments. Thanks to Cornelia Feye's constructive criticism, encouragement and suggestions, and to Lisa Wolff's copy editing, this novel is much better than it would have been. A longtime resident of Imperial Valley with extensive knowledge of its history, Carol Hann has graciously offered much research material. The cover photo of my parents was provided by my sister Sandrina Shigematsu. Thank you Lily Mihalik for the front cover design. The author's photo was taken by my son, Joseph. Finally, I would like to thank my wife Stephanie for her love, encouragement and support.

REFERENCES:

Bailey, Paul. *City in The Sun.* Los Angeles: Westernlore Press, 1971.

Heidegger, Martin. *Being and Time.* Translated by John Macquarrie & Edward Robinson. New York: Harper & Row, 1962.

Shirey, Orville C. *Americans: The Story of the 442d Combat Team.* Washington: Infantry Journal Press, 1946.

Verne, Jules. *Twenty Thousand Leagues Under the Sea.* Chicago: The John C. Winston Company, 1932.

http://www.newspapers.com/ The Los Angeles Times Archives.

www.ingramcontent.com/pod-product-compliance
Lightning Source LLC
Chambersburg PA
CBHW021812110726

47902CB00006B/1753